PRAISE FOR

The Trouble with Mary

"A charming, humorous, and just plain fun novel."
—*Romantic Times*

"A hilarious romance chock-full of delightful
characters . . . Delicious and lively, Criswell's clever
romance will leave readers hungry for more."
—*Booklist*

"Criswell makes a delightful contemporary
debut with a funny and sexy romance. . . .
A worthwhile read."
—*Publishers Weekly*

What to Do About Annie?
Chosen by *Booklist* as One of the Top
Ten Romances of the Year

"Fast-paced, hilarious, and thoroughly
delightful . . . A winner that will have fans
waiting to see what she will come up with next."
—*Library Journal*

"A tantalizing tale . . . The eccentric Russo
clan . . . delights readers once again with their
insatiable wit and boundless spirit. . . . Criswell's
dialogue is sharp and humorous."
—*Publishers Weekly*

"This book is a gem. Very entertaining, lots of
laughs, and some tears."
—*Philadelphia Inquirer*

By Millie Criswell
Published by Ivy Books

THE TROUBLE WITH MARY
WHAT TO DO ABOUT ANNIE?
THE TRIALS OF ANGELA
MAD ABOUT MIA*

Forthcoming

THE TRIALS OF ANGELA

Millie Criswell

IVY BOOKS • NEW YORK

This book contains an excerpt from the forthcoming paperback edition of *Mad About Mia* by Millie Criswell. This excerpt has been set for this edition only and may not reflect the final content of the forthcoming edition.

An Ivy Book
Published by The Ballantine Publishing Group
Copyright © 2002 by Millie Criswell
Excerpt from *Mad About Mia* by Millie Criswell © 2002 by Millie Criswell.

Ivy Books and colophon are trademarks of Random House, Inc.

www.ballantinebooks.com

ISBN 0-8041-1993-7

Manufactured in the United States of America

First Edition: May 2002

10 9 8 7 6 5 4 3 2 1

My mother always told me that there were many fish in the sea. Of course, I didn't believe her, not until I landed mine thirty-three years ago. His name is Larry. I love him like crazy, and this book is dedicated to him. Which just goes to prove that mothers are usually correct.

ONE

*What's the difference between a female attorney
and a pit bull?*
Lipstick.

Angela DeNero was having a bad day.

Actually she was having a bad life.

As lives went, hers ranked right up there with having chocolate-induced cellulite, a refrigerator stocked with nothing but health food, and jeans that refused to zip up.

There was nothing worse than that.

Except her life.

It sucked.

She suspected she'd feel better in time. She was resilient, after all, and would bounce back.

Just not today.

The dragon she called landlady, Mrs. Foragi, was leaving daily Post-it note reminders on her door about her overzealous bulldog, Winston—threats, someone less generous would call them. The law firm she had struggled so valiantly to open was experiencing more than its share of growing pains, like clients who conveniently forgot to pay her. And to top it all off, she'd been feeling awful all week with flulike symptoms. Not to mention that her hair had gone from sleek to curly as soon as she'd stepped out in the rain this morning. Harpo Marx had nothing on her do.

Add bad hair day to list.

So when she entered the police station, Angela's mood was as foul as the weather. Actually, her mood had soured the moment she'd picked up the phone this morning to find Sophia Russo on the other end.

Sophia was the busybody of Little Italy, and the most disagreeable woman Angela had ever met. She was opinionated and domineering, and made Angela's mother look saintly by comparison; no easy feat, considering Rosalie DeNero was no shrinking violet when it came to dispensing opinions or rendering advice that no one wanted. She just did it with more subtlety.

"My crazy mother-in-law has been picked up for shoplifting. Dio mio! We are disgraced. You must go to the police station and get her out of jail. I don't care if she rots there, but my husband is upset and told me to call you. He'll pay whatever you want."

Ah, the magic word: *money.*

Visions of dollar signs danced in her head, as did the knowledge that Flora Russo had sticky fingers and was probably guilty. This wasn't the first time the old lady had been picked up for "borrowing" other people's merchandise, though she'd never been booked before. The police, who were quite familiar with Flora's antics, had always released her to her son's custody. Not this time, however.

Grandma Flora had a larcenous heart, even though she rarely stole things for herself. But she was Joe's grandmother, and since Joe Russo had been generous about giving her extra legal work at the Crisis Center, where she worked part-time, she couldn't very well let him down.

How would it look for an ex-priest's grandmother to be convicted of stealing? Not good, she was thinking.

Angela spotted Grandma Flora as soon as she approached the front desk area. The old woman, dressed in unrelenting black like a professional mourner, was seated on a folding chair, a pocketbook the size of Minnesota on her lap, cane resting between her knees, looking more formidable than fragile, and none too pleased. Next to her stood the arresting officer.

"*Vaffunculo! Bastardo!* How dare you treat an old woman like a criminal! I will call the President of the United States. I voted for him. He owesa me."

"Calm down, ma'am," the officer said very patiently. "And it would go better for you if you'd quit cursing me in Italian. I speak the language, and I don't like being flipped off, even if it is verbally."

"Grandma Flora," Angela warned when the woman opened her mouth to say something else, nasty, no doubt.

Grandma turned to look at Angela. "I'va been busted. These pigs are trying to tossa me in the slammer." It seemed obvious that Grandma Flora had been watching *The Sopranos* a little too diligently. "I didn't do anyting wrong. I wanna go home now. You fix it, Angela, so they let me go home. *Capisce?*"

Angela heaved a sigh. She understood, all right, but that didn't mean she could make all of Grandma Flora's troubles disappear, though she'd give it her best shot. She turned to Bobby Malcuso, the "pig" that had brought Joe's grandmother in. "I think there's been a misunderstanding, Officer Malcuso. I'm sure we can get it straightened out." *Misunderstanding* was lawyer talk for "My client screwed up, so how do we make it go away?"

With a look of apology, he shook his head. "No, ma'am. Mrs. Russo was caught red-handed stealing merchandise from Geppetto's Toy Store. The owner swore out a complaint and is bringing charges against her. I had no choice but to arrest her. I feel badly about it, Miss DeNero. I've got a grandmother. But Mrs. Russo broke the law, so I had to bring her in."

Aware of the man's responsibility in the matter, Angela nodded in understanding, then went on to explain, "According to her daughter-in-law, Mrs. Russo is in the habit of taking toys from Geppetto's. The former owner used to keep track of what she took, and then Mrs. Russo's son would come in and pay for it. They had an arrangement. Obviously she was not aware that the store had been sold." She wished the old lady's relatives had been here to corroborate her story, but Flora's daughter-in-law had explained on the phone that Frank was sick and she, Sophia, didn't drive.

The young officer brushed back his thinning, sandy-colored hair. "Mr. Patel's lawyer intends to speak to the district attorney; he's on his way here now. If they still want to file charges . . ." He shrugged, indicating it was out of his hands.

Sitting down next to the old woman, Angela tried to re-assure her, though Joe's grandmother looked more pissed off than scared. "I think we're in a pickle, Grandma Flora. We're going to have to wait here a while longer to see what the store owner's attorney has to say."

"Nazis! They're all Nazis. Don't they have better tings to do than bother an old woman? You, Hitler," she said to the officer, "I needa some water to takea my pills. Maybe I'll drop dead, and then my son will sue you. God should make it so."

Clearly relieved to have a chore that would remove him from the old woman's sharp tongue, he hurried off to do her bidding, though Angela doubted he'd be back any time soon. She fetched Grandma Flora a cold soda from the vending machine.

A few minutes later, a tall, dark-haired man walked in. He was wearing a brown leather bomber jacket over a navy T-shirt, faded jeans, and a day's growth of beard. Angela recognized him instantly, and a rush of pleasure swept through her.

John Franco was not a man a woman could easily forget; even if that woman had been eighteen the last time she'd laid eyes on him. She and John had attended high school together, and Angela had dated his best friend, Tony Stefano, for a brief time.

Tony had been a really nice guy, and a much safer choice for a sheltered girl with no experience. And though Angela had secretly harbored a fascination for John Franco, conjuring up wildly erotic thoughts no decent girl would ever admit having, she would have never had the courage to act on them.

John Franco was forbidden fruit.

He'd been the quintessential bad boy of Bridgemont High—a reckless troublemaker with a terrible attitude. And he had never given her the time of day. In fact, he had always been rather hostile toward her, and she had absolutely no idea why.

He was still very handsome, in a Russell Crowe kind of way—not pretty handsome, but rugged, virile. The man oozed masculinity.

"Ah, here comes Johnny. Soon he will help you fix tings. A good boy, my grandson Johnny."

Grandson! Angela snapped her mouth shut, raised her eyes from the man's . . . ah, *masculinity,* and hoped she wasn't drooling all over herself.

Damn! Why hadn't she remembered that John Franco was connected to the Russo family?

He walked over and bussed his grandmother on the cheek; there was love shining in his eyes, and maybe a hint of admiration, as well. "You've been a naughty girl again, haven't you, Grandma Flora?"

Flora winked at him, and he grinned, obviously used to her outrageous behavior. "Talk to my lawyer, Johnny. Angela's going to fix tings. Isn't she *bellisima*? And smart, too. She goes to college, like you."

John studied Angela for a moment, and she could tell the moment recognition dawned. He smiled a hundred-watt smile that sent her pulses racing. Angela revised her earlier opinion. Flora's Johnny wasn't handsome. He was chocolate, whipped cream, and all things yummy rolled into one fabulous package.

"Very," he replied to his grandmother's question, then said to Angela, "Nice to see you again, Angela." He held out his hand and clasped hers and three hundred volts of electricity raced up her arm. "John Franco. Do you remember me from high school?" When she nodded mutely, he went on to explain, "I'm here on my client's behalf. Mr. Patel owns the store that my grandmother robbed."

Yummy turned crummy. Angela's jaw unhinged, and she finally found her voice. "You're *his* attorney? But how can that be? The woman your client's filing charges against is your grandmother. And I think *robbed* is too strong a word, don't you?" Good Lord! This whole situation just kept getting better by the minute.

Where was a good coma when you needed one?

Those comatose people didn't know how good they had it. They didn't have to worry about zipping up jeans, frizzy hair, wacky old ladies who shoplifted just for the hell of it, or high school bad boys who'd turned into respectable lawyers. They just slept peacefully in blessed oblivion, unaware of life's many trials and tribulations.

Angela sighed. No doubt she'd be the only comatose patient in history who suffered from insomnia.

Looking uncomfortable, John rubbed the back of his neck. "I'm well aware of that, Angela. But a crime has been committed, and it's my duty as Mr. Patel's lawyer to—"

"She's your grandmother, for godsake! Where's your loyalty? Your compassion? She's an old woman."

"That'sa righta, Johnny," Grandma Flora interjected, thrusting out her chin. "How come you go against your family? What will your mama say when she findsa out? Adele is a good daughter. She's gotta big mouth, but still she'sa good to her mama. She won'ta be happy. Family is everything."

She shook her head of gray curls, which were so tightly wound her pink scalp peeked through. "Young people are *stupido*. There isa no respect given to the old anymore. I don'ta know how mucha longer I'll be on thisa earth, and you do thisa terrible ting to me? *Bah!*"

"Now, Grandma, be reasonable," John said, kneeling down before her and drawing her wrinkled hands into his; the gesture did not go unnoticed by Angela, who found it very appealing, despite her annoyance with the man. "I've talked to my client. Mr. Patel's upset, and he's adamant about bringing you up on charges. I'm hoping to talk to the district attorney, and—"

"And what? Have her put in the electric chair? What kind of man are you?" Angela was growing more incensed by the minute. John Franco was a persecutor of old women. She told him so.

His blue eyes turned glacial. "I'm behaving rationally, which is more than I can say for you, Angela DeNero. Or didn't you learn anything at that fancy law school you attended?"

Her cheeks flooded with color. "How dare you! I am not irrational. I'm—" Angela felt nausea rise to her throat and clamped a hand over her mouth. Shaking her head at his questioning gaze, she made a beeline for the women's rest room, avoiding the stares of the people she passed, where she promptly tossed up her breakfast.

Oh, God! I'm going to hurl again.

John Franco had literally turned her stomach. Not a propitious beginning to a professional working relationship. But par for the course for this miserable day.

A few minutes later, somewhat recovered from her ordeal, and a whole lot humiliated, she splashed cold water on her face, rinsed out her mouth with the minty-fresh mouthwash she always kept in her purse for emergencies, and returned to find the aggravating man—*traitor!*—with his arm around her client. He was taller than she remembered, massively built, and he made Grandma Flora look even more shriveled than usual.

"I'm very sorry," she said, grinding to a halt before them. "I think I might be coming down with the flu. I haven't been feeling well these past few days."

Looking concerned, Grandma Flora tsked several times. "You gotta eat more, Angela. You're too thin. A thin woman isa prone to sickness. Your blood isa not rich enough. You gotta eat more meat."

In an Italian family food was the panacea for everything. If you were sick, you ate to get well. If you felt happy, you ate to celebrate. If you were despondent . . . well, food always made a body feel better, especially if there were sweets involved.

By all rights, Angela should have weighed three hundred pounds, not the hundred and ten the scale admitted to this morning.

Flora turned to her grandson. "Johnny, why don't you take Angela out for a nicea steak dinner? I like her. She's a lawyer, you're a lawyer. And you already know each other. What coulda be better?"

Angela's face crimsoned at his amused smile, and bile rose to her throat once again, but she fought it down, pretending to ignore the woman's matchmaking efforts. Assuming a professional demeanor, she said, "If your client persists in this course of action, Mr. Franco, then I guess we'll see you in court."

He towered over both women, like some mountain of granite, forcing her to look up. "I look forward to it, Miss DeNero," he said, smiling at her formality. "But I doubt things will go that far. I'll be in touch." He bent down and kissed the top of his grandmother's head. "I'll see you soon, Grandma. Say hi to Uncle Frank and Aunt Sophia for me."

"*Bah!*" The old lady shook her head. "Sophia Graziano has poison in her heart. I don'ta speak to her unless I have to. She wantsa to have me committed. Says I'ma *pazzesco nella testa*. Tell me, who coulda be more crazy than my daughter-in-law?"

Though John didn't respond, he seemed to agree with his grandmother's opinion.

Eyes wide, Angela shook her head disapprovingly. Grandma Flora seemed a lot saner than most of the people she knew, including her own father, but she wouldn't go there. That would require entering the realm of the unbelievable—*The Twilight Zone*, without a good script.

"I'm sure Mrs. Russo's just upset by all that's happened. I'll speak to her."

"My daughter-in-law is a heartless *puttana*. I curse the day she married my Frank. He's too good for her. The man is a saint to have stayed with her all these years."

John disappeared for a moment, had a conversation with Officer Malcuso, and then returned, indicating with a nod of his head that his grandmother was free to go.

Clasping the woman's hand gently, and noting how small and parchmentlike it felt, as if one squeeze would break the frail bones, she said, "Come on, Grandma Flora. I'll drive you home. You look worn out." Thanks to John's assistance with the district attorney, Flora Russo would be released on her own recognizance.

The old lady's eyes twinkled; it was obvious she had enjoyed her escapade, despite being tired. "Are you springing me, like in the movies? Good ting, because I gotta connections back in Italy. You seen *Goodfellas*? You seen *The Godfather*? Luca Brasi swims with the fishes." She drew a cutting finger across her throat. "That means he'sa dead."

Definitely too much of The Sopranos.

Angela and John exchanged indulgent smiles, and Angela forgot for a moment that he irritated her. Her pulse rate quickened and then began a John Philip Sousa march to her head. "Uh . . . yes, you'll be released to go home."

"No more shopping for you, Grandma. *Capisce?*" John cautioned from the doorway, winking rakishly at Angela, who blushed in response.

The old lady smiled enigmatically, which didn't bode well for the remaining merchants of Little Italy.

"See you around, Angela," he said.

"I hope not," she couldn't keep herself from replying.

John was having a difficult time concentrating on what Tony was telling him. Images of Angela DeNero kept filling his head. The dark-eyed beauty intrigued him, and always had, he guessed. And he found her indignation regarding his grandmother's arrest mildly amusing, when he wasn't being irritated by her presumption and preconceived opinions, that was.

Opinionated women tended to leave a bad taste in his mouth. He had enough to contend with in his own family.

And did she really think I would have my own grandmother tossed in jail?

Patel would drop the charges. John would see to it. He didn't need any comments from snotty Harvard graduates to remind him of his familial duties.

"Are you listening, John? I said, we need to discuss the Rothburg versus Gallagher custody case. Rothburg is insisting that we handle the matter for him. He's our biggest, most lucrative client. I've already told him we'd proceed."

Turning his attention fully to the matter at hand, and his business partner, Tony Stefano, who was seated behind his desk, smoking a cigarette, John shook his head, trying to ignore the enticing scent of tobacco. "I told you before, Tony, I want nothing to do with it. For chrissake,

Mary's my cousin! I can't take sides against my own family. Are you crazy? My aunt Sophia would probably take out a contract on me, or sic that crazy brother of hers on me. Uncle Alfredo claims to be connected, you know." John didn't believe a word of the old guy's claim that he was affiliated with the Gotti crime family, but still. . . .

"Be reasonable, John. Sharon Gallagher Rothburg wants her child back. You know Charles can't represent himself in this matter. It would be a conflict of interest for his firm to take on the case." He stubbed out his cigarette and then promptly lit another, which he left burning in the ashtray, lettered FRANCO'S DRY CLEANING.

"Well, it's a conflict for me, as well, personally and otherwise. I refuse to have anything to do with it. You're on your own with this one."

His face turning an unbecoming beet color, his forehead beaded with sweat, Tony rubbed his chest with circular motions, as if stressed by the entire discussion. "I need your help. And we're hardly in a position to refuse the handsome retainer Rothburg's paid us. We're barely making ends meet now, and I've got a family to consider. Rothburg puts food on the table for my two kids." He slapped the top of his desk. "We're trying this goddamn case, and that's final!"

Noting the man's agitated state, John tried reasoning with him. "Sharon Rothburg abandoned custody of her child to her former husband months ago. Just dumped him like so much garbage on Dan Gallagher's doorstep and ran off with her studmuffin aerobics instructor. What kind of mother does that?"

Leaning back in his swivel chair, Tony loosened the knot of his green silk tie, along with the top button of his shirt before replying. "You know how it is. She got bored, wanted a little excitement in her life. The aerobics guy fed her a good line, and off she went. She claims she always intended to come back for her son. She never meant for the custody to remain permanent."

"That's bullshit, and you know it! Dan Gallagher is a responsible individual, a good provider, who's given his son a stable home. And Mary has been a kind and caring stepmother. Opposing counsel will crush you if you go into court and try to claim otherwise. And I'll be in the gallery cheering him on."

Tony's face contorted in anger, and he rubbed his chest again, making John's frown deepen. Tony's cholesterol was off the charts, he smoked like a fiend, and had flunked his last stress test. The doctor told him in no uncertain terms to lose weight and monitor his blood pressure. But, of course, Tony hadn't listened. His friend had a bad habit of ignoring what he didn't want to hear, like John's argument in not taking the case.

"Hey, are you all right, man? You look a little peaked."

Tony disregarded John's question. "Winning this case is not going to be a walk in the park. I realize that. But our firm is building a reputation. We are, thank God, perceived as winners. If we prevail with Rothburg versus Gallagher, it would go a long way to building the kind of client base we need to survive. Rothburg will toss all kinds of referrals our way."

John's expression conveyed contempt. "Rothburg's got a dubious reputation for underhanded dealings. He's a bloodsucking parasite, and you know it. We should never have taken him on in the first place."

"Yes, but he's our bloodsucking parasite, and we need him. Have you taken a look at the books lately? We're up to our asses in debt."

Knowing the truth of his partner's words, John tried a different tack. "Do you know who opposing counsel is?"

"Rumor has it, it's Angela DeNero. She's moved back here from Boston. Do you remember Angela? I dated her in high school. Man, she was one hot . . ." Tony smiled at the memory, which annoyed the hell out of John.

"Anyway, she's Harvard Law, graduated in the top one percent of her class, and she's had experience with these kinds of cases before."

So Miss Harvard Law was going to be opposing counsel on Rothburg vs. Gallagher? *Now, that was interesting.*

Unlike John, who'd had to work and scrape his way through University of Maryland Law, Angela had been given a scholarship to law school after graduation from high school. It had galled him at the time. Not because she didn't deserve the free ride—Angela had always been at the top of the class. But because after she and Tony had broken up he'd harbored hope that she would start dating him. But she left town before that had ever happened, much to his regret.

He'd had a crush on her all through high school, but had never acted on it, figuring Angela was Little Miss Perfect—too smart, too pretty, too virginal, and too damn intimidating with her straight A's and big vocabulary.

John hadn't graduated at the top of his class. Far from it. If he had, he would have been able to write his own ticket. But school and studying had never come easy for him. In fact, if it hadn't been for Tony's persistent prodding and never-ending help, he may never have graduated. He owed him big for that.

His brother, Michael, the big-shot heart surgeon, had received all the brains and glory, but it was John who'd inherited the Franco grit and determination, along with a large dose of stubbornness.

"I remember her," he said. "In fact, I ran into Angela at the police station this morning. She seems to be the emotional type. She'll probably get nervous and puke in front of the judge and courtroom, like she did today at the police station." Everyone had weaknesses. Angela's was a nervous stomach. It was obvious she didn't handle stress very well.

Easing into a confident smile, Tony stood and began to pace. "Well, there you go. It'll be an easy win for us."

John swore beneath his breath, grabbed his jacket off the back of his chair, and shrugged it on. "Haven't you been listening to a word I've said, Stefano? There is no *us*. I'm not assisting you with this case. And that's final!" He moved toward the door.

"Goddammit, John!"

"You're Italian, Tony. You know perfectly well that Italians are not forgiving when it comes to disloyalty. And I would definitely be disloyal if I took sides against my cousin and her husband."

"The hell with you, then. I'll do it myself, and—" Suddenly Tony clutched his chest, his face contorting into a mask of pain as he turned as white as his shirt. "I—"

Alarmed, John rushed forward, yelling, "Tony!" just as his friend hit the floor with a thud, narrowly missing slamming his head on the corner of the oak desk. Squatting down beside him, he felt for a pulse. Finding a weak one, he breathed a sigh of relief. "Hang in there, Stefano."

Removing the cell phone from his jacket pocket, John called 911, cradling Tony's head in his lap. "Don't die, you dumb bastard! Don't you dare die!"

TWO

What's the difference between God and a lawyer?
God doesn't think She's a lawyer.

"Good Lord! What happened to you, girl? You look like death's gone and slapped you silly alongside the head. Did somebody run over you with a semi, or what?"

Smiling wanly at the nattily dressed woman seated behind the black-lacquered desk, Angela felt as crappy as she looked. "Thanks a lot! It's always nice for a woman to hear that she looks like shit so early in the day." She wondered if John Franco had thought the same thing, then chastised herself for even thinking about the insensitive man.

"I had a call from our cheapskate landlord, Levins. He's going to replace the carpeting next week."

"Hallelujah!" Angela looked down at the stained, threadbare olive-green carpeting beneath her feet and made a face of disgust. It had taken them more than a dozen phone calls to get their landlord to agree to replace the outdated, smelly floor covering.

Since her move back to Baltimore Angela shared office space with Wanda Washington, in a dilapidated brick building on Eastern Avenue that had seen its glory days back in the '50s. The rooms were large, the Palladian windows abundant, allowing plenty of natural sunlight to drift in. And though their offices smelled musty and the carpeting needed replacing, they had lovely walnut-paneled walls and lots of built-in bookcases, so they couldn't complain overly much. She suspected the unpleasant odor would go away once the carpeting did.

The two attorneys shared rent, expenses, and a budding friendship. Though their law practices were separate, they assisted each other on difficult cases, from time to time.

Wanda, who graduated law school the same year as Angela, and was about the same age—Angela abhorred the fact she'd be thirty-three this year—was an excellent attorney, specializing in discrimination cases. She was never shy about expressing opinions, holding to the belief that what she had to say was usually worth hearing.

Angela had grown fond of the outspoken woman in the short time they'd been working together. And Angela didn't doubt for a second that she looked like death warmed over, especially after the recent barfing incident at the police station. Not one of her finer moments, to be sure. And quite a humiliating one, to say the least!

And why did I have to lose my cookies in the presence of John Franco? Angela shuddered to think of the impression she'd made. Not that she cared, mind you. Since Bill's defection she had sworn off men.

"I think I've got the flu. My stomach's been upset all morning."

A look of horror on her face, Wanda pushed away from her desk, gliding back toward the tall window behind her, as if the reincarnation of Typhoid Mary stood before her, ready to spew forth infestation. "Don't you dare give it to me! I can't afford to get sick right now. Bunny the Blimp's coming up for trial."

Wanda was in the habit of giving colorful nicknames to all of her clients, and some of her friends, too. In addition to Bunny, there was Larry "Sugar Lips" Goldstein, who bestowed sloppy, wet kisses on everyone he came in contact with; Marty "the Dangler" Verrazano, who had in his younger days starred in over thirty-three porno films; and Bertha "Major Mounds" Washington, a well-endowed, distant cousin of the attorney's.

So far Angela had been spared a nickname. Of course, no one had ever accused her of having major mounds. She wasn't flat-chested by any stretch of the imagination, but she doubted anyone would mistake her for Pamela Anderson, either. But then, the all-boobs, no-substance television star wasn't likely to be mistaken for a lawyer.

Wanda didn't assign nicknames out of meanness; the black woman didn't have a mean bone in her body. She did so because it was fun. And Wanda firmly believed that the law should be fun, not so staid and serious. She also prided herself on being a conforming nonconformist, the perfect example being her rather unorthodox behavior in the courtroom. Though she wore smart, dignified business suits to trial, she usually wore thigh-high panty hose, no panties, and a tiny scrap of lace that could hardly qualify as a bra, beneath them, believing it gave her a powerful edge, knowing something her opponent did not.

Angela didn't have the guts to try such a stunt. "Bunny? You mean the guy who weighs four hundred pounds and was fired from his job at Clyde's Auto Wreckers a few weeks back?"

"The very same. Bunny Beccacio's actually closer to three hundred fifty, but why split *hares*? Hares. Bunny. Get it?" Angela made an exasperated face, and Wanda grinned, going on to say, "Clyde claims Bunny can't fit into the tow truck."

"Can he?"

"Well, not exactly. Not behind the steering wheel, anyway. Bunny's addicted to Krispy Kremes—lives on them from morning till night—but that isn't the only reason he's so overweight. He has a medical condition and shouldn't have been fired. I intend to prove that in court."

If anyone could turn a blimp into a stealth bomber, it was Wanda. "Bunny's got good taste, I'll give him that."

Though the thought of eating the tasty donuts didn't sound at all appealing at the moment, which was an oddity in itself.

Angela adored junk food. If it was loaded with fat, sugar, and cholesterol—the three major DeNero food groups—it went into her mouth, and then straight to her hips. She jogged to keep ahead of the calories.

"So are you going home? Maybe take a nap? You should, you know. You've been working too hard, and it's starting to show. You've got bags the size of a Bloomies big brown under your eyes, girl." Wanda's wide grin displayed an impressive set of evenly spaced, perfectly matched, pearly whites. The woman had been blessed with a dynamite smile.

"All work and no *foreplay* makes for an unhappy, not to mention unfulfilled, lawyer," she added.

John Franco's wicked, sexy smile suddenly materialized, and Angela blinked several times to dispel it, wondering why the man continued to plague her.

Maybe she was overworked, as her friend suggested.

There was no disputing she was unfulfilled.

The only thing warming her bed at night since Bill's departure and change of heart was her bulldog, Winston.

Well, at least Winston didn't lie to her, didn't say he loved her and wanted to marry her. And he would never break her heart, the way Bill McElroy had. Bill "the Bastard" McElroy, she amended. No explanation necessary.

Glancing at her Minnie Mouse wristwatch—last year's Christmas gift from her sister—she heaved a sigh and pushed aside the unpleasant memories.

A nap sounded heavenly. Lately she'd been feeling tired and dragged out. *"You've got iron-poor blood, like in that old Geritol commercial,"* her mother insisted whenever Angela complained of feeling sluggish or spent. *"You're going to end up in the hospital with mono, like my friend Phyllis's kid."*

Angela thought her tiredness had nothing to do with mono and everything to do with the fourteen-hour days she was putting in. Not to mention that her mother was the world's most accomplished worrier. According to Rosalie DeNero—the Duchess of Doom, as Angela and Mia had nicknamed their worrywart mother— Armageddon was about to descend.

Well, bring it on. What else can go wrong that hasn't already?

"Earth to Angela. Are you going home early or not?"

Angela smiled apologetically at Wanda, knowing her mind had wandered off again. "Can't. The Gallaghers will be here in a few minutes to go over the details of their custody case. I'm sure they have a million questions. It could take a while." And she didn't want to rush Mary and Dan, knowing what a trying time this was for them, no matter how tired she felt.

She was very fond of the couple. Mary Gallagher, who owned Mama Sophia's Restaurant, located on the ground floor of Angela's apartment building, was Joe's younger sister, and the nicest person you'd ever want to meet.

Mary was always trudging up the stairs and bringing Angela food from the restaurant, leaving it on her doorstep if she wasn't at home. On a couple of those occasions Angela had discovered some of the food had gone missing, and she suspected the culprit was her overweight, always hungry landlady.

Mrs. Foragi had earned every one of her two hundred plus pounds the old-fashioned way: by stuffing her face. Angela had seen the woman devour an entire mushroom, sausage, and pepperoni pizza in the time it took to walk from Mama Sophia's and up the stairs to her apartment.

Five minutes, tops!

It was an amazing feat of *mandible* dexterity.

Like Angela, Mary Gallagher was also a chocolate

freak, which gave her extra likeability points. Though instead of the chocolate cannoli the pregnant woman adored, Angela was addicted to Milk Duds, and she kept a glass jar filled with the candies on her desk, for frequent cravings, which she succumbed to more often than not.

Mary's husband, Dan, was the Sports editor for the *Baltimore Sun*, and part owner of Danny Boy's, a sports bar/restaurant that was about to open in Little Italy. It was Dan's former wife, Sharon, who was suing for custody of their child, though she'd abandoned Matthew to Dan's care last winter.

"I had dinner at Mama Sophia's last night," Wanda stated, drawing Angela's attention back. "Mary's restaurant is top-notch. I'd kill to be able to cook like that. Actually, I'd kill to be able to cook at all. I'm a big disappointment to my mother. Mama thinks the microwave was invented by Satan; she says all of us thirty-somethings are culinarily challenged."

Angela arched a dark brow. "I thought you weren't partial to Italian food."

"When in Rome, honey." Wanda patted her flat tummy. "Gotta watch it, though. Italian food can really pack on the pounds in a hurry."

Coming from a large Italian family, Angela knew that all too well. Her mother was an excellent cook, as was her father, though she suspected Sam's love of the kitchen had more to do with wearing his wife's frilly aprons.

"Food is like religion to an Italian. You must worship at the altar of lasagna and manicotti, the holiest of dishes." Angela genuflected to make her point, then laughed when her friend rolled her eyes.

"Man, you *paisans* are weird. Give me fried chicken and mashed potatoes any day. At least it's good old-fashioned American food, even if it is fattening."

"Now what kind of biased talk is that, coming from a

lawyer who deals in discrimination cases. Shame on you, Miss Washington."

"Honey, you can keep your tiramisu. When it comes to dessert, I'll take my mama's apple pie any day of the week."

The cardiology waiting room of Mercy Hospital was depressingly full. Anxious families seeking word on their loved ones looked as haggard and scared as John felt while he waited to hear if his best friend was going to live or die.

He paced the confines of the somber green room, his heels soundless on the grayish-green industrial-strength carpeting, and ignored the other inhabitants, who were lost in worlds of their own. It was times like these when he wished he hadn't quit smoking. It had been a long, agonizing month, made worse by inhaling Tony's second-hand tobacco smoke.

John wouldn't kid himself. He missed smoking, missed holding a cigarette, drawing the smoke into his lungs, and feeling that temporary nicotine euphoria. But he knew damn well that if he hadn't given up his two-pack-a-day habit, he'd be occupying the bed next to Tony's.

He had gotten to the point where he could hardly walk up two flights of stairs without huffing and puffing and his lungs hurting so bad they felt as if they would burst. His morning jogs had become endurance tests, then finally impossible. Deciding that he liked running more than smoking, and living more than dying, he'd quit.

Unfortunately, Tony hadn't.

His friend had looked pale as death and much older than his thirty-four years when they'd wheeled him into the cardiology care unit. His wife, Marie, was with him now, their two children left at home with a neighbor. John couldn't help but wonder what Marie and the kids would do if the worst happened and Tony didn't make it.

Who would love and nurture them? Provide the emotional and financial support they would need? John would do what he could, but he knew it would never be enough.

He felt responsible. If he hadn't been arguing with Tony . . .

"Mr. Franco?"

Grinding to a halt, he turned to find one of the duty nurses motioning him forward. She looked efficient, dour, and in command. The whiteness of her uniform dazzled, matching the color of her hair. "Mr. Stefano has been stabilized. You may see him, but only for a moment. He's been sedated, so his heart doesn't have to work as hard."

John made his way to Tony's room, kissing Marie's pale cheek when he entered. Tony had tubes running into his nose, EKG leads taped to his chest, and an IV inserted into his left arm. The sight made the seriousness of his condition seem all too real and hideous.

His friend didn't look a whole lot better than when he'd first had the attack, except that the oxygen pumping into his bloodstream had added a bit more color to his cheeks, making them appear more gray than white. The heart monitor beeped steadily, reassuring in its rhythm.

"Thank God you were with him, John," Marie said softly, clutching his hand for support and squeezing it, her dark eyes moist with tears. "If you hadn't been there, I don't know what we would have done. Tony might not be alive right now. Dr. Winters, the cardiologist on call, said that in thirty-three percent of heart attack cases chest pains are entirely absent. I—" She began to cry, then wiped her eyes with the handkerchief he handed her. "I'm sorry. I'm just so worried."

"I know you're frightened, Marie." He wrapped his arm about her slender shoulders and tried to offer what comfort he could. "I'm concerned, too. But I'm sure

Tony will be fine. You know what a tough guy he is." He had to believe that, to get through the next few hours.

She sniffed several times. "His brain is tough, I'll give you that. I told him to quit smoking, to eat right, but he wouldn't listen. Tony never listens to anyone."

John couldn't argue with that. His friend was a hard-headed son of a bitch, but he had no intention of getting into the middle of Marie and Tony's marital disagreements. He loved them both too much to take sides.

Opting for safer ground, he asked, "What else did the doctor say?"

"Three of Tony's arteries are blocked, and they're going to operate on him tomorrow morning. Your brother is doing the surgery, and for that I'm relieved."

Michael was a gifted surgeon, and for once John was grateful for his expertise in the operating room. If anyone could pull Tony through, it would be his big brother.

But it was damn galling to admit such a thing, even to himself.

The shadow his brother cast was large, and John had been swallowed up by it for most of his life, never allowed to shine with his own accomplishments. To his parents' way of thinking, Michael could do no wrong. The sun rose and set on the straight-A student, the star quarterback of the football team, and the man voted "Most Likely to Succeed" by his classmates. His becoming a doctor had been the frosting on the cake.

John was the screwup, the troublemaker and black sheep of the family. And he had embellished and relished that role, in order to gain their attention. It had worked for a time—he'd caused his parents plenty of grief during his adolescence. But in the end it hadn't been the kind of attention he'd craved. He'd wanted praise, adoration, and love, like Michael received, not the ridicule and punishment that always followed his rebellious behavior.

Of course, he'd been too young to understand that respect and love had to be earned. But even after he'd straightened himself out, he'd still been treated like a second-class citizen by family members, never quite measuring up to Saint Michael.

A JD wasn't quite as impressive as an MD, in Robert and Adele Franco's opinion. His parents believed that lawyers preyed on other's misfortunes, while doctors saved lives.

John tried not to feel resentful, but it was damn difficult. Even now, at thirty-four, he had unresolved issues with his family, and he doubted they even knew it.

"So is Michael going to perform a triple bypass?" He moved to the side of the bed and gazed down at the sleeping man. Marie nodded, and a lump of fear caught in his throat.

John and Tony had grown up together, played on the same football team, and double-dated in high school, although never when Tony was with Angela. So much of their lives had been shared, the good times and the bad. Stefano knew all of John's faults and loved him anyway. Tony was his best friend, his law partner, and his fishing buddy. John had stood up for him at his wedding, and was godfather to Katy and Anthony Jr. He couldn't bear the thought of losing him.

"What's the prognosis?" he asked, clearing his throat in an effort to hide his emotions. John was good at doing that; he'd had a lot of practice.

"Good, providing he survives the surgery."

"I need to talk to Tony, reassure him that everything's going to be okay." *And tell him how sorry I am that we argued.*

But he knew he wouldn't.

It wouldn't be fair to unload his guilty conscience on a sick man. He would call his brother instead and find out exactly what his friend's chances were for surviving the operation, knowing Mike wouldn't bullshit him about something so important.

"Tony wanted to talk to you, too." Marie wore a puzzled expression. "He kept mumbling incoherently. Something about Rosenburg, Rothstein." She shook her head. "I can't remember now, but it sounded important, at least to him."

"Rothburg."

"*There is no us. I'm not assisting you with this case. And that's final!*"

John added, "It's a case he's working on."

She clasped his hand again and squeezed. "I'm so glad he has you. Tony won't worry, knowing you're taking care of everything. The doctor says he's not to get stressed about work during his recovery period, and you know how obsessive he can be. It's very important that his heart has time to heal."

"I wasn't working the Rothburg case, Marie. It's Tony's baby. But I'll try to find out if it's been scheduled and motion the court for a continuance."

She looked up at him with large, trusting eyes, certain that he'd do the right thing where her husband was concerned. "Whatever you think is best."

Her words stabbed at his conscience. "I'll be back tomorrow. Call me if anything happens in the meantime, or if you and the kids need anything. Anything at all, you understand?"

Marie smiled wanly and nodded. "You're a good friend, Johnny. Thank you."

He kissed her cheek, took one last look at Tony, as if it might be his last, and then disappeared out the door.

"I brought you some tiramisu." Mary walked into Angela's office and handed the foil-wrapped package to the attorney, who was seated behind the massive mahogany desk that had been a gift from her parents upon graduation from law school.

Mia had received an adorable red Mustang convertible after graduating from Boston College with a liberal arts degree. Angela drove a Saturn. Being the practical, conservative daughter definitely had its drawbacks.

"Marco made it fresh this morning, so don't wait too long to eat it," Mary said. "I can truthfully testify that it's delicious. I've got the pounds to prove it." The pregnant woman plopped down on the chair fronting the desk.

Fighting the urge to gag—the thought of the rich, wine-flavored dessert sent her tummy tumbling—Angela plastered on a grateful smile, setting the tiramisu to the far side of the desk so she wouldn't have to smell it. "Thanks. It was kind of you to think of me. Again. You know, you really shouldn't feel like you have to feed me, Mary, though I appreciate your kindness."

Seated next to his wife, Dan smiled at her indulgently. "Mary's not happy unless she's pawning food off on everyone, Angela. I suspect she wants to make all the women in Little Italy as pleasingly plump as she is." He patted his wife's slightly swollen abdomen, and she stuck her tongue out at him, making his grin widen.

"Guess I'll pay for that one, won't I?" he said.

"You'd better believe it, Irishman."

"When's the baby due?" Angela asked, envious of the loving look that passed between the couple. Bill hadn't been the demonstrative type. He usually sent a memo.

"Angela, you look lovely this morning. But I noted a spot on the collar of your blouse. You might want to take care of that before one of the clients sees it."

With Bill you always got *buts*. He'd been a perfectionist and ambitious, and noting a kindred spirit when she saw one, that had appealed to her.

Now she wondered why.

"Early spring, but it can come right now, as far as I'm concerned. I'm still having occasional bouts of nausea. Not to mention I'm starting to feel like an elephant. Of course, that might have something to do with the number of chocolate cannoli I've been scarfing down." Her dark eyes sparkled. "Cravings, you know. I'm tired, too, that's the worst part. I used to have tons of energy, but now I feel sleepy all the time."

Mary's symptoms, so similar to Angela's, struck a chord with the attorney. "Really? I've been feeling kind of queasy and tired myself. I think I've got some kind of virus."

"Do you have a fever? That's usually the first sign of the flu."

"No, I—" Angela's forehead wrinkled at the perfectly sensible question; then she shook her head, unwilling to delve any deeper at the moment, the conclusion she'd be forced to draw unthinkable.

"Never mind. We aren't here to talk about my health problems; we're here to discuss your upcoming custody hearing. I'm sure you have lots of questions. But before we get to them I thought I'd give you a brief idea of what Maryland law dictates, as far as these types of cases go."

The couple appeared nervous, and Angela smiled reassuringly. "The question the judge is going to ask is, what is in the best interest of the child?"

"But Matt is happy and thriving where he is," Mary insisted.

"And I'm sure that will be taken into consideration."

"Sharon had legal custody when we divorced," Dan pointed out, shooting his wife an uneasy look. "My job as a sports reporter kept me on the road a great deal of the time. And I thought because of Matt's age—he was four when we split—it would be best if Sharon made all the important decisions regarding his health, education, that sort of thing. So I waived custody in her favor, while retaining visitation rights. I can see now that I made a big mistake." He withdrew a roll of antacids from his pocket and popped a few into his mouth.

Angela tapped her pencil on the desktop while she thought. "That might prove to be a problem, and then again, it might not. Your former wife abandoned her child to run off with . . ." She glanced down at the hastily scribbled notes on her yellow legal pad and tried to keep her face impassive, though she was feeling anything but toward Sharon Gallagher Rothburg. The woman wasn't fit to be a mother. Of course, that wasn't her decision to make, but the court's. "Her aerobics instructor," she finished.

"Mrs. Rothburg's fitness as a mother will be taken into consideration, as will her character and reputation. We'll be petitioning the court for permanent legal and physical custody."

"But she's married to an upstanding member of the legal community," Mary interjected, her brows drawing together. "We're worried that will go in her favor."

"You and Dan have a lot going for you. You've provided a stable, loving home for Matt. And he seems perfectly content where he is. And as you pointed out when we last spoke, Mrs. Rothburg neglected to get in contact with her son the entire time she was gone, which was detrimental to his emotional state."

Mary nodded. "That's true. Matt was one sad little boy when I first met him. Some of the questions he asked about his mother's absence were heartbreaking."

His anguish apparent, Dan sighed. "I'm hoping we won't have to drag my son into court over this matter. He's been through a lot already, and I don't want Matt forced into having to choose between Sharon and myself. That wouldn't be fair to him. He's just a kid. And he loves his mother."

It was clear that Dan Gallagher put the welfare of his son above all else. Angela doubted Sharon Rothburg could claim the same. "It's possible that the judge will want to interview Matthew, Dan, but that will likely be done in the privacy of his chambers, so I wouldn't worry about that just yet.

"For now, I'd like you and Mary to prepare a list of people, professional and otherwise, who can testify to Matt's emotional state immediately after his mother left, and during the time he's been living with you.

"I think his teacher and pediatrician can probably give the court a good assessment of Matt's condition right after his mother abandoned him to your care. I'll want to depose them, and anyone else you can think of that might be helpful to our case.

"I intend to ask a qualified therapist to evaluate your son's behavior and present emotional state, and then give her conclusions to the judge. Expert testimony can be very compelling in these situations. That process will probably take four to six weeks, prior to the court date, once it's set."

"What do you think our chances are of winning, Angela? We can't bear the thought of losing Matt." Mary grasped her husband's hand and squeezed, fear clouding her eyes.

"I play to win. I wouldn't have taken this case if I didn't think our chances were good. But I won't mislead you or paint a rosy picture.

"In most instances custody is awarded to the mother. But the good news is that in the State of Maryland there is no maternal preference. We're dealing with extenuating circumstances, and I think the judge will take those into consideration." Mary's eyes filled with tears, and Angela's heart went out to her. These types of situations were always so difficult for the parties involved.

"You're not to worry, Mary, especially in your condition. Leave the work and the worry to me. That's what you're paying me for."

"But I feel so helpless. I want to help."

"If you really want to help, then pray. I've found that it never hurts."

Mary smiled tremulously. "I used to have a direct link to God. My brother, as you know, was a priest. But now that Joe's married to Annie, I'm on my own."

"Not quite," Dan said, brushing tears from his wife's cheeks and smiling confidently, despite his own worries. "Are you forgetting your mother and grandmother? I've never seen two Catholics who could recite the rosary faster and with more emotion. Those women could put the fear of God in anyone."

And had, apparently. Mary's husband sounded like he spoke from experience. Some things were universal when it came to Italian Catholic women, and instilling the fear of God was your basic standard operating procedure from the Italian mother's manual, which usually included

1. The third degree: How to interrogate prospective sons- or daughters-in-law. All dates were eyed as likely candidates.

2. Extolling virtues of daughter or son, ad nauseum, and to the point of embarrassment.

3. Instilling the fear of God prior to every date: i.e., no hanky panky. Reciting of Bible scripture, if necessary.

4. Invoking names of highly placed church officials— priest, rabbi, etc.—and/or mob connections, real or fictional.

Of course, there were others, too numerous to mention.

"Sophia's not taking any chances," Mary said, easing into a smile. "Besides reciting the rosary on a daily basis, she's been bringing curses down on Sharon Rothburg's head. The woman is doomed till Kingdom Come. No one can level a curse like my mother."

Ah, the curse. Angela knew that one all too well. Sophia had tried her hardest to push Angela and Joe together and had been quite unhappy when her machinations didn't work. At the time, Joe's overbearing mother hadn't approved of Joe's choice of Annie Goldman, and had decided that Angela, not Annie, would make the perfect wife for her son. Fortunately Joe had ideas of his own, and now he and Annie were happily married.

Annie was a lucky woman. Joe Russo was a kind and caring man. And it seemed Mary, too, had lucked out in the husband department. Dan doted on her every word, and it was clear that he was crazy in love with her.

What would it be like to find a love such as theirs? she wondered, sighing deeply.

Get over it!

You're a career woman with a batting average of zip, nada, nothing, in the love and marriage department. Not everyone can find happily-ever-after. Be happy you've got a career, a loving family, and a dog that worships the ground you walk on.

But the words felt hollow, even to Angela.

THREE

How can you tell when a lawyer is lying?
His lips are moving.

John walked into Tony's hospital room the day after the surgery, carrying a large split-leaf philodendron and sporting a relieved smile.

Reclining against the bed pillows, the recovering patient was watching the Ravens vs. Tampa game, and John could see by his friend's annoyed expression that he was growing more agitated by the minute.

Tony and football were a bad combination, as were Tony and baseball, Tony and wrestling . . .

"You shouldn't be watching that game, Stefano. You know how pissed off you get when you watch football. It's hardly a stress-relieving activity, even when the Ravens are up by two touchdowns."

At the sound of John's voice, Tony turned his head, his face lighting in relief, as if the cavalry had just arrived to save the day. "Hey, Johnny! Am I ever glad to see you. I'm bored to death, and it's only been a day since the surgery. Thank God you're here to keep me company. I've found that my own stinks."

His friend looked utterly miserable, and John bit back a smile. "I've been telling you that for years, Stefano."

"Yeah, but who knew?"

"You scared the hell outta me, you know that? I should beat the crap out of you for taking ten years off my life."

Tony tried to return John's smile, but it was a poor effort at best and came out looking more like a grimace. "Thanks for the offer, Franco, but I think someone's already beat you to it. I've got an incision running down my chest that looks like something Dr. Frankenstein or Jack the Ripper created. I think those medical miracle workers used the Jaws of Life to open me up. It hurts like hell."

Wincing in pain, his hand went to the bandage covering his chest. "That brother of yours is a butcher. Whoever said the guy was brilliant must have been nuts. Lou Santini could have done a better job cutting me open, and he would have probably thrown in a pound of salami and provolone while he was at it."

"Mike had to cut your ribs," John explained, the graphic image making him cringe. "I'm sure it'll be uncomfortable for a while." He wouldn't bother telling him what Mike said about the itching once the incision began to heal.

"You look a helluva lot better than the last time I saw you. Thought for sure I was gonna lose you, buddy." A look of love and gratitude passed between them, but neither alluded to it. Men didn't say "I love you" to other men. But it wasn't necessary, anyway; John and Tony knew how the other felt.

"Marie told me you were here for the surgery and also in the recovery room. I didn't know. Guess I was out of it."

"Michael had you doped up on morphine. You were flying pretty high, as I recall. But the good news is that, according to my brother, you're going to live, providing you mind your diet, exercise regularly, quit smoking, and stop allowing things—sports, in particular—to provoke you."

Remote in hand, Tony clicked off the TV and snorted in disgust. "Marie's already been on my case about quitting smoking, along with a million other things she's found

to bitch at me about. And the damn nurses have been in
here dragging me out of bed every hour on the hour and
making me walk around. That white-haired one is the
worst. She keeps trying to help me piss. Figures that a
woman only wants to grab your dick when you're not in
a position to use it."

John grinned but didn't interrupt the tirade.

"A man can't get a decent night's sleep around here. I
can't wait to get the hell outta here, so I can get some
rest."

Spying the plant John had set on the table next to the
bed, Tony didn't bother to hide his displeasure. "This
room's turning into a goddamn flower shop. I might as
well be dead, since I'm living in a funeral home. Whoever
said 'Say it with flowers' was a sadist." The cloying scent
of gardenias and roses permeated the room, giving cre-
dence to the man's complaint.

Tony had never been a very good patient. Even at age
ten when he'd had his tonsils removed, he'd been every
doctor's and nurse's worst nightmare, tossing things, refusing to eat; he'd even thrown up on the candy striper.
Old Doc Colombo had released him two days earlier
than normal to prevent the nurses on the pediatric floor
from going out on strike.

"John," Tony said, his tone suddenly serious, "Marie
told me you were handling the Rothburg case. I just want
you to know how grateful I am. I know you didn't want
to do it, and . . . well, I'm grateful, that's all."

Tony wasn't the effusive type, nor did he admit to
being wrong that often. And rarely did he share the vulnerable side of himself by offering gratitude. It just
wasn't his way. So John knew his friend's words were
heartfelt, which made him feel even guiltier. "Tony—"

"I didn't want to tell you—pride, I guess—but we've
been having a few financial problems since Marie lost
her job at the library," Tony continued, not giving John

the chance to unburden himself. "Nothing serious. We're managing, but . . ."

Taken completely by surprise, John's eyes widened. "Why didn't you say something? I could have helped." No wonder Tony had been so adamant about taking the custody case. It all made sense now.

"Not necessary. We're learning to live within our means. And your taking on Rothburg versus Gallagher has really taken a load off. I feel better already."

Heat crept up John's neck. He'd just come from the courthouse, where he'd made a motion for a continuance, but he had no intention of telling his friend that. Tony wasn't supposed to get upset, or even think about work-related matters. "I'm handling everything. You're not to worry about Rothburg, or anything else. Just get well. That's the only thing you need to concentrate on right now."

"I appreciate your saying that, John, but . . ." Tony's dark brows drew together and he hesitated a moment before continuing. "It's going to be some time before I can go back to work. Marie is insisting that I take some extra time off after I'm released from the hospital. Are you sure you can handle everything until then? I feel lousy putting the burden on your shoulders."

"They're big shoulders, so don't worry about it. And Marie is absolutely right. You've been working too hard and need to slow down. That heart attack was a wake-up call. Use this time to reassess things. You only get one life, Tony, so make the most of it." Leaning over the bed, John gave his friend an awkward hug. "Gotta go. Get well, you stupid son of a bitch, you hear?"

Tony smiled affectionately. "Yeah, I hear you, Franco. And Johnny . . ." Pausing by the door, John looked back, his brow raised in question. "Thanks for saving my life."

Shutting the door behind him, John felt like the biggest piece of shit on the planet. Tony thought he was going forward with the Rothburg case. He didn't want to mislead his partner, but he couldn't very well tell Tony the truth and cause him to have another heart attack.

"I'm damned if I do, and damned if I don't," he muttered, walking down the long hospital corridor toward the exit and wishing like hell he had as easy a way out of the Rothburg case.

It was a lose-lose situation any way you looked at it.

And John hated to lose.

Seated in the hospital coffee shop, the dull gray walls closing in around her, Angela's thoughts were centered on her client, Mrs. Thomas, an elderly woman who'd been involved in a terrible car accident that morning.

Having just come from the surgical floor, Angela was not certain Mrs. Thomas was going to make it through the night. Apparently, neither was Mrs. Thomas, who had directed Angela to get her affairs in order—a most unpleasant task for any lawyer to handle.

Angela had just formed that thought when a shadow fell across her table. She looked up to find John Franco standing beside it. He was smiling down at her with his sexy grin and big blue eyes, and her heart gave a funny little lurch. It seemed time hadn't lessened the attraction she'd felt for him all those years ago.

"Mind if I join you?" He didn't wait for an answer but pulled out the chair and sat down next to her, as if he had every right in the world to intrude on her space.

"I wasn't expecting to see you again so soon," she replied.

"Yeah, well, I was upstairs on the Cardiology floor visiting Tony Stefano. He had a heart attack the other day."

Angela's eyes widened, her voice filling with dismay. "Oh, how awful! Is he okay? Was there any permanent damage done, Mr. Franco?"

John grinned. "No. And I think we can dispense with the formalities, don't you, Angela? After all, we have known each other for quite a while."

"Yes, but not all that well. You never gave me the time of day in high school."

His brow shot up. "Would you have wanted me to? You ran with a different crowd than I did, except for Tony. Couldn't figure out why you two hit it off. You never seemed like Stefano's type." Tony, of course, had thought Angela was the perfect specimen of womanhood. He'd go on for hours extolling her many virtues, while John had sat back and listened, gritting his teeth. He'd been jealous of their relationship, but had never really admitted that until now.

She stiffened in her chair. "Oh? And what type of girl do you think Tony belonged with?" She and Tony hadn't had much in common, except for the fact that they both wanted to be lawyers, but she had no intention of revealing that.

"The kind he ended up marrying. Marie's content to be a housewife; she allows Tony to be the center of her world. He's rather old-fashioned in that respect. He would have never settled for a career-oriented woman. He's too much of a family man."

"Unlike you, I suppose?"

He shrugged. "I was married for a time, but it didn't work out. Two lawyers in the family was one too many. I didn't enjoy competing with my own wife. Grace was a bit of an overachiever." Actually she was a selfish, self-centered bitch, but he didn't want to open up old wounds in front of a woman he hadn't seen in years. And yes, he was a family man, or would have been, if Grace hadn't taken it upon herself to— He pushed the painful thought aside.

"Nothing wrong with that," Angela replied, feeling somewhat put out by his archaic attitude. After all, she was an overachiever and career-minded and didn't see a problem with it.

"Guess it depends on where you're sitting."

Could her dedication to her work have been the reason for her failed relationship with Bill? No, she thought, he'd been as obsessed as she. Bill's failure to keep his pants zipped was the real reason things hadn't worked out between them.

"So what made you decide to move back to Baltimore? As I recall, you couldn't wait to blow this place. Everyone in school knew how anxious you were to move to Boston."

"A scholarship to Harvard wasn't something I could pass up. Plus, my dad had a job offer from the Boston Police Department, so everything just sort of fell into place at once."

"Too bad."

Her eyes widened before she replied, "Well, actually I was rather pleased about the way everything turned out."

"Yeah, I guess you would be."

"What's that supposed to mean?"

He shook his head, wondering why he was trying so hard to antagonize her. After all, she hadn't even known that he'd been attracted to her. Was still attracted to her, even after all these years. "Nothing. It's just that . . . well, this is going to sound stupid, but I used to have a crush on you back in high school. I was going to ask you out after you split with Tony, but you moved away and I never got the chance."

Her mouth fell open. "You're kidding! I certainly never got that impression." Why was her heart racing so fast? High school was a lifetime ago. A lot had happened to both of them since then, but still, the thought that he'd found her interesting enough to date, had a crush on her . . .

"Yeah, I figured you were out of my league back then.

And I had to protect my image as the town bad boy. Rumor had it that you were untouchable."

She stiffened. "I suppose you heard that from Tony."

"What can I say? Men talk. And you can't really blame Tony for trying. It was kind of expected of us guys to put the moves on all the virgins." A grin split his face.

Angela gasped, and her cheeks filled with color. "Are you saying that Tony only dated me to see if I would put out?"

"I can't speak for Tony, but guys look at things differently than women, especially teenagers with raging hormones."

Not quite sure how to respond, she glanced at her wristwatch. "Well, this has been an enlightening conversation, Mr. Franco, but I've got to get back to work." She pushed back her chair and stood.

"It's John."

She smiled sweetly. "Yes, I know, Mr. Franco." When he opened his mouth to object, she added, "And, Mr. Franco, the only thing I've got to say about high school is that you should have tried harder. Good-bye."

It was nearly five o'clock when Angela entered Moressi's Pharmacy on Albemarle Street.

The old sandstone brick pharmacy, like most of the buildings in Little Italy, had been part of the landscape forever. A few short blocks away Baltimore's Inner Harbor bustled, sporting chic clothing boutiques, trendy restaurants, and towering modern hotels. But in Little Italy things tended to stay the same as they had for decades. Change was slow to come, though a bit of modernization—Goldman's Department Store, for one—had taken place. It was still a close-knit Italian neighborhood, oozing with Old World charm, and boasting the best Italian food in the mid-Atlantic region.

Angela had come to Moressi's in the hope that she could find something that might ease the nausea and fatigue she'd been battling for days. She seemed to be getting worse instead of better.

The store looked deserted of customers, for which she was thankful. She wasn't feeling up to making neighborly chitchat. Angela spotted Mr. Moressi standing behind the cash register, reading a magazine, and looking as tired as she felt. She waved in greeting, but he didn't see her.

Moving down the aisles, she passed the hair dye, nail polish and lipstick, face creams, and a gazillion other enticing products she normally would have taken the time to investigate. Angela loved to shop. When she came to the aisle with the cold and flu remedies she slowed, breathing a sigh of relief; help was close at hand. Before she could make her selection, Angela heard a familiar voice that stopped her dead in her tracks.

John Franco stood on the other side of the cough syrups, and she prayed he couldn't see her through the merchandise that was stacked fairly high on the shelves. She had no desire to talk to him, especially as awful as she felt and looked. And after their last embarrassing conversation—the stroll down memory lane—she wasn't quite sure what she would say to him.

The past was in the past. It was best to leave it that way.

Unfortunately John looked as enticing as chocolate.

Okay, so even knowing he was somewhat arrogant, too handsome for a mere mortal, and obviously not the man for her didn't mean she couldn't appreciate the packaging. Milk Duds weren't good for her, either, but they were yummy, just the same.

Unable to resist taking a peek to see what he was up to, Angela pushed aside packaged bottles of Dimetapp Elixir and Triaminic and peered through the narrow opening to get a better view.

And then wished she hadn't.

"How's Tony? I hear he's not doing too good," Mr. Moressi said to John. "He's a young man to have such a bad thing happen."

"Tony's doing much better, thanks. My brother performed a triple bypass on him, and he's on the road to recovery."

A triple bypass! He hadn't mentioned that. Suddenly she felt sorry for Tony Stefano and his family, even if the man's motives for dating her had been cadlike.

Do people still use words like cad?

"God bless Michael Franco!" The white-haired pharmacist crossed himself. "He operated on my Estelle a year ago and saved her life. He's a wonderful doctor, your brother. Your mama and papa are very proud, no?"

In a voice mixed with equal amounts of irritation and resignation, John replied, "Yeah, they're proud as hell."

Apparently he wasn't too happy with the adoration heaped on his—older? younger?—brother.

Angela had never felt in competition with her younger sister. Mia wasn't driven to succeed, to overachieve, to be the best, like Angela. She was laid-back, a bit flighty, but very sweet and loving.

Mia was a woman who definitely marched to the beat of her own drum—kettledrum, to be more precise. She never did anything halfway. She charged at life, like a bull, without a clear idea of where she was going.

Her latest stab at gainful employment was operating a bulldozer on a highway construction crew. How she'd gotten the job was a mystery. Mia's driving left a lot to be desired—her bulldozing, anybody's guess. Not to mention that she was probably a hundred pounds soaking wet, and hardly cut out for construction work. But Mia was nothing if not determined, once she set her mind to something. The good news was that her attention span was short and she didn't stay focused on any one thing for too long.

"What you got there, Johnny?" Mr. Moressi asked, and then started laughing, as if they were sharing one of those "men only" moments. Angela, unable to see what was so amusing, boiled over with curiosity.

"You got a hot date or something?"

John Franco's chuckle skittered down her spine like a feather on bare skin, tickling her interest even further.

Restraint not being one of her strong suits, she was determined to know what Franco had come into the drugstore to purchase. Maybe he suffered from hemorrhoids or jock itch. Or maybe he dyed his hair; it looked too black to be natural.

Standing on tiptoe and leaning into the shelf, she lost her footing and accidentally knocked several bottles of liquid cough medicine onto the other side, where they crashed to the floor, the sound of breaking glass making her wince. Fortunately the pharmacist had left to answer the phone.

Realizing that she'd been rendered quite visible to the man standing there, who was, she could finally see, holding several packets of condoms, Angela held her breath and stared wide-eyed, like a deer who'd been caught in the headlights.

Condoms!

Some of the packets were marked with four Xs. Did that indicate their size? And why oh why did he have to catch her spying on him? God's punishment for the hemorrhoid thought, no doubt.

Finally coming to her senses, Angela ducked, just as John Franco peered over the counter to see what had caused the items to fall. But she wasn't fast enough, and he smiled when he saw her.

"Well, well, we meet again, Angela."

"I dropped my purse," she explained, rather lamely, if his smug expression meant anything. "I was just picking it up when you spotted me."

"I think Grandma Flora's used that excuse a time or two, Counselor."

Red-faced, she gasped. "I was not taking anything, if that's what you're implying, Mr. Franco. How dare you insinuate such a thing? I was merely shopping for . . . for some personal items."

He held up his hands in surrender, and she could see those damn condoms again. *Why is he buying so many? Does he really have need of two dozen?* Her body grew warm just thinking about it.

Get over it!

Mr. Moressi started to walk toward them, but the phone rang again, and he was forced to retreat, thank goodness. The entire episode was embarrassing enough without the pharmacist witnessing her humiliation.

"How's your stomach ailment?" he asked, his gaze traveling over her in such a fashion that she was tempted to cover herself, even though she was fully clothed. Those searing blue eyes made her feel absolutely naked.

"It's better," she lied. "Now, if you'll excuse me, I must find what I was looking for and be on my way."

"And what is it you're looking for? You seem awfully interested in condoms. Would you like to look over the selection? Old man Moressi carries quite an extensive variety: lambskins, ribbed, flavored, colored, and—"

"You know very well that I didn't come in here for prophylactics. I have no need of them, and—"

Shut up! Shut up! Shut up!

"Now, how would I know that? You're young. I assume you're sexually active and smart about taking precautions."

Angela felt her face growing redder by the minute. How come if she was supposedly so sexually active, she didn't know condoms came in flavors? "Please leave me alone. You're making my head hurt."

John finally let loose the grin he'd been holding back, and all the air left her lungs. He was actually better-looking than Russell Crowe! How was that possible? She'd had the biggest crush on the movie actor since seeing him in *L.A. Confidential.*

It had irritated Bill to no end when she made a big deal over Crowe's considerable attributes. Of course, at the time she had no idea that Bill had his own infatuation going on, with someone who wasn't on the silver screen.

Angela thought it unfair that while she had fantasized about a man she could never have, Bill had gone out and screwed his fantasy woman, up one side and down the other, as the saying went.

Had he used colored condoms, or worse, flavored?

"Sorry," John said, not looking at all apologetic. "I've been known to give people headaches, from time to time. I'd be happy to make it up to you. Would you like to go somewhere and have a drink?"

She was rendered mute by the offer. Franco had to have an ulterior motive in asking her out, especially after the conversation they'd had at the hospital. Maybe he thought she was easy and had taken her comment about trying harder as a challenge. *"I assume you're sexually active."* Or maybe he thought— Oh, hell, she didn't know what he thought, and she didn't really care.

Liar! that little voice of conscience blurted.

"Oh, shut up!"

His eyes widened. "Pardon?"

She blushed, shaking her head. "Nothing." She was tempted to accept his offer—she enjoyed his company, for the most part, when he wasn't aggravating her—but she had too much to deal with at the moment, like finding out if she was pregnant. "I'm sorry, but I can't have a drink with you. I have other plans. Thanks anyway."

"Guess you think it might be a conflict of interest, huh?"

She searched his face for signs of disappointment at her refusal, but found none, which, if she was truthful, bothered her. "I thought the situation with your grandmother had been resolved. I received a call from the prosecutor's office; they said the charges against Mrs. Russo had been dropped."

"I wasn't talking about Grandma Flora's case. I was referring to the fact that you'll be representing the Gallaghers in the custody trial against Charles and Sharon Rothburg."

"I don't see how that's any of your—" Eyes widening, she felt ten pounds of lead settle in her already touchy stomach. "Please, tell me you're not representing the Rothburgs." She couldn't imagine what it would be like to face Clarence *"Drop-Dead Gorgeous"* Darrow in court every day. How would she be able to concentrate on the proceedings when his cute . . .

Get over it!

"My law firm represents Charles Rothburg. Tony has been handling the custody case."

"So now that Tony's in the hospital you'll be representing the Rothburgs?" she asked, dreading the answer. He had a reputation as a winner, but then, she reminded herself, so did she.

John shrugged. "That remains to be seen."

Angela had been around long enough to know that evasive answers usually hid a kernel of truth. The wily attorney probably had a whole cob up his sleeve. "I'm sorry about Tony, but I hope you aren't planning to ask for a continuance, because let me assure you, I will fight such a motion aggressively. The Gallaghers deserve to get on with their lives, and delaying this proceeding is out of the question."

The woman's Harvard law degree was showing, John reflected. It would almost be fun to meet her in court and beat the pants off her. Suddenly an image of Angela DeNero standing in front of the jury in only her bra and panties came into focus, making his mouth go dry.

What kind of panties did she wear? Not thongs. She wasn't the thong type. But definitely sheer. And tiny, probably with lots of lace, in bold vibrant colors to match her dark hair and offset her olive complexion.

Giving her the once-over, he noted that she had nice legs, long and shapely. Actually her whole body was nice—firm breasts, not huge, but not small, either. Yep, Angela DeNero had the whole package: brains and beauty. But then, he'd always known that.

Realizing that he'd been staring intently—her face was turning the color of a good cabernet—he cleared his throat. "Is that a fact?"

"Yes, Mr. Franco, it is."

"Johnny," Mr. Moressi called out, "I found the rubbers you were looking for."

Angela's face crimsoned, and John smiled before answering. "Be right there."

"Please don't let me keep you from such an important purchase, Mr. Franco." The world would be a better place without any more John Francos in it, she decided, but refrained from saying so. She'd said quite enough already.

Angela had a terrible habit of running off at the mouth when she was nervous, and that was especially true on dates. When things heated up, she began babbling about the most inconsequential things. It was really most embarrassing, not to mention the sounding of the second-date death knell.

"Take care of that flu, Angela. You look a bit feverish to me."

Angela did feel hot, but she didn't think it had a thing to do with influenza. She watched him walk up to the counter, pay for his purchases, and then disappear from sight; she breathed a sigh of relief.

"I go in the back now to eat my dinner," Mr. Moressi informed her. "You ring the bell on the counter when you are ready to pay, Angela."

"Thanks, Mr. Moressi. I'll do that."

"You need help before I go?"

She waved him off. "No, no. I'm fine. Enjoy your dinner."

When she was finally alone, Angela grabbed a package of Tylenol Flu, then added a box of Theraflu, just to be on the safe side. To quell the nagging doubt that had been plaguing her, though she'd done her best to ignore it up till now, she strolled the aisle that contained the feminine hygiene products and paused before the pregnancy kits, staring, wondering, and thinking back to her conversation with Mary Russo.

Her heart began to race; a feeling of dread consumed her as she looked at the ordinary package. It seemed innocent enough, but it felt like a time bomb in her hand.

God has to be playing a joke on me. I can't be pregnant. I just can't.

But Angela knew very well that she could.

Damn you, Bill! And damn her own stupidity! Her one night of make-up sex may have had devastating consequences.

Well, it was better to know than not, she decided, trying to be pragmatic about the whole thing. And being pregnant wasn't the worst thing that could happen to her. It wasn't like having cancer or Alzheimer's. In less than nine months she would be cured.

Why wasn't that a comforting thought?

Angela wondered if she could use that argument with Sam and Rosalie. She doubted it. Bearing a child out of wedlock was a very un-Italian, un-Catholic, unladylike thing to do. Nice girls didn't put out, even if they were almost thirty-three.

If Sam DeNero had his way, both of his daughters would be locked up in chastity belts. Cops were suspicious by nature, not to mention overprotective, and her father was strict, even by Italian standards.

She could distinctly remember one occasion in high school when she'd arrived home late from a date; midnight had been her curfew, as embarrassing as that was to admit. All her friends had been allowed to stay out until two. Her father had been waiting for her in the front hall, clad in a pair of blue silk boxers—to which her mother had sewn an edging of white lace—beefy arms crossed over his chest, and looking as intimidating as hell . . . well, as intimidating as a man could look in lace-edged underwear, anyway.

He'd drilled her with a probing look, as if by doing so he could see if her virginity was still intact, then calmly pronounced, "We'll talk in the morning, young lady," before going back to bed. Fifteen minutes later she could hear him snoring through the thin walls, while she remained wide awake for the remainder of the night, worrying about what he would say when morning finally came.

Arguing with her father was always an exercise in futility. And as good a lawyer as Angela was, she'd never won an argument with him.

Removing a twenty-dollar bill from her wallet, Angela plopped it and the flu remedies down on the counter, then placed the pregnancy kit in her purse. It wasn't really stealing, she told herself, ringing the bell, because she was going to leave the extra money to pay for it on the counter before she left. She just couldn't take the chance that Mr. Moressi would tell someone about her purchase . . . like Sophia Russo, whose reputation for gossip was legendary.

She refused to think about her parents' reaction if the test proved positive. It was too hideous to even consider. Not to mention nauseating.

Exiting the pharmacy, she felt not only sick to her stomach, but light-headed, as well.

Angela would have felt a whole lot worse if she had noticed the tall man watching her.

John Franco replaced the *Sports Illustrated* on the magazine rack and stared after Angela in disbelief, unable to stem his surprise at her purchase of a pregnancy kit.

Of course, the kit could have been for someone else, a friend, maybe, but he didn't think so, not with all of her flulike symptoms.

Damn! She was involved with someone, seriously involved, from the looks of it.

Just as well, he told himself. He had enough on his plate at the moment.

So why, then, did he feel so disappointed?

FOUR

Why won't sharks attack lawyers?
Professional courtesy.

Mama Sophia's was crowded and noisy when John entered the restaurant a short time later. Outside, darkness had descended, and the tiny white lights entwined in the fake grape arbor overhead twinkled prettily. The restaurant was warm and welcoming compared to the chilled autumn air.

John was still reeling over the possibility that Angela might be pregnant. For Angela to be unmarried and pregnant seemed so out of character. At least, out of character for the woman he'd remembered as being so perfect, who didn't make mistakes, and who seemed to have everything under control.

Why did he care? It wasn't any of his business. For all he knew she was madly in love with the father of her child and planning to marry him. But the furtive way she had put that pregnancy kit into her purse, like she feared someone might see and discover her secret, just didn't bear that out. And quite frankly, he was worried about her.

"Johnny!"

Pushing the disturbing thoughts of Angela to the back of his mind, he turned at the sound of his name to find his cousin rushing up to greet him. Mary looked even lovelier than the last time he'd seen her. She appeared healthy, radiant, glowing—all those clichés that were associated with pregnant women.

Wrapping her arms about his waist, as she'd done so

many times when they were kids, she hugged him tightly. "It's been ages, Johnny. How have you been?"

He kissed her cheek. "Busy. But not as busy as you, I see, *cara*." He gazed down at her swollen tummy and winked. "I heard you were pregnant. It looks good on you. Congratulations!" Her smile exuded happiness and contentment, and it was clear she and Dan had made a good match.

"Are you here for dinner?" Mary asked, then without waiting for a reply grabbed his hand and dragged him forward. "Come on. My parents are here. I know they'd love to see you."

Groaning inwardly, John was tempted to dig in his heels and protest. The last person he wanted to see was his aunt Sophia. Uncle Frank was a good guy, and he enjoyed talking to him about his inventions—he'd actually bought a Bun Warmer heated toiled seat for his bathroom, which came in mighty handy on cold mornings. But Sophia could try the patience of a saint. And he was no saint.

"Look who's here," Mary announced, pulling out a chair for John at her parents' table. "Sit. I'll be right back with some wine. We just got in a new Chianti Classico. I want you to try it and give me your opinion." She hurried off, leaving him to face his aunt's scrutiny alone.

Sophia wasted no time. "You're looking a little thin, Johnny. Haven't you been eating? I'm surprised your mother isn't after you about how thin you've gotten." She tsked several times, drumming her fingers on the colorful tiled tabletop. "A woman wants a man with a little meat on his bones."

"That's why Sophia's so crazy about me," Frank quipped, patting his protruding stomach and grinning. "Who needs diets? *Forgetaboutit*. I'm calling myself full-figured these days."

His wife didn't find his remarks the least bit amusing,

and sneered. "You've got a pot, Frank. Too much *vino* and not enough exercise." He opened his mouth to protest. "And playing bocci while drinking wine with your *goombahs* doesn't count." Frank shut his mouth again.

"Mom quit monitoring what I ate after I turned twelve, Aunt Sophia." John smiled as politely as he could, but his aunt made a rude noise anyway, obviously not liking his answer, and looking like she had more to say on the subject.

"How's Bobby doing?" Frank interjected, not giving Sophia the chance. His uncle had an uncanny knack for knowing when someone needed rescuing from his wife. And for that, John was grateful.

"Last time I spoke to your father he told me his back was bothering him," his uncle said. "Is he better? I meant to give him a call this morning, but time gets away from me when I'm working on a new invention."

"What's the latest bit of genius to emerge from the Russo basement, Uncle Frank?"

"I'm putting the finishing touches on a remote control toilet bowl flusher. Great idea, no? I'm calling it Frank's Flush O'Matic. It should sell like hotcakes. Bathroom accessories are big these days. Must be because of all the time we senior citizens spend in them." He winked.

Though John nodded and smiled enthusiastically, he wasn't sure why anyone would need to flush a toilet bowl remotely. "Dad went to a chiropractor. The guy fixed him right up. Now he thinks he's a miracle worker."

"*Hmph!* Those quacks are no good." Sophia, who was never without an opinion, and not the least bit shy about expressing it, grunted her disapproval. "They practice medicine without a license. Your father should go see his regular doctor, not some stranger. You tell him I said so. He could end up paralyzed, like those men you see in wheelchairs. Then who will run the dry cleaners? Not your mother. She's not capable."

Adele Franco had been assisting her husband in the dry cleaning business for over thirty years, and could run the place with one hand tied behind her back. The only thing she ran more capably was her husband.

Spared from commenting when his cousin arrived with the wine, John, out of habit, and because his aunt made him nuts, searched his pockets for a cigarette, then sighed deeply, remembering he'd quit. "Thanks, Mary," he said, filling his glass with the deep red wine and taking a sip. "*Mmmm.* Very good. Full-bodied. I like it."

"So where's that husband of yours? Is Dan working late at the newspaper?"

Nodding, Mary slid onto the seat next to him. "Dan's been really busy at work. Football season, you know. With the Ravens winning the Super Bowl last year, the whole town's been in the throes of purple mania. He's also trying to get our new eatery ready. It's a cross between an Irish pub and a sports theme restaurant. We're hoping to have the grand opening in just a few weeks. You'll love it. It's very male oriented. But bring a date, because women will like it, too."

Like radar, Sophia homed in on their conversation. "Who are you dating, Johnny? Is it serious? Is she Italian? Does she come from the neighborhood? It's about time you started keeping company. You're not getting any younger, you know. A man's equipment quits working when he gets older." At the outrageous remark, John gulped the remainder of his wine. "And if you had a wife cooking for you, you wouldn't be so undernourished."

"Enough already!" Frank admonished, sending his wife a disgusted look. "Leave the boy alone. He's trying to enjoy his wine and bread. And there's nothing wrong with older equipment," he hastened to add. "Mine still works good. I ain't had no complaints."

Blushing to the roots of her red hair, Sophia clamped her mouth shut.

Dipping a piece of the warm Italian bread into the bowl of flavored olive oil, John took a bite and tried not to grimace. Aunt Sophia in the bedroom was not an image he cared to entertain, now or ever. "I hate to disappoint you, but I'm not seeing anyone in particular right now. I'm very busy at work. Getting a law practice off the ground is no easy feat." Not that he would ever confide details about his personal life to his aunt. The woman had the biggest mouth in all of Little Italy. As far as gossips went, his aunt Sophia was a largemouth bass in a pond of goldfish.

Gossip was a living entity in the neighborhood. Like air, it was necessary to the survival of those who lived there. And no one was excluded. You couldn't gain weight, have an argument, or buy a new suit without everyone knowing and commenting on it. And you could forget about keeping your private life private.

A calculating gleam entered Mary's eyes. "You should meet Angela DeNero, Johnny. She's a lawyer, too. And very pretty."

"We've met. In fact, we went to high school together."

Her brow shot up. "Really? What did you think?"

He shrugged nonchalantly, unwilling to be lured into his cousin's matchmaking web. "She's pretty enough, I guess. Not really my type." Mary wouldn't be content until everyone she knew was married—she had learned well at her mother's hand—and John had no intention of getting hitched. Not again.

His marriage to Grace had left a bitter taste in his mouth, not to mention a gaping wound in his heart. With one selfish act, his wife had destroyed his love, his ability to trust, and his unborn child. The pain of her betrayal still burned deep in his chest.

"What are you talking about?" Sophia slapped her forehead. "Are you crazy? Are you gay? Angela is a beautiful woman. And smart, too." She stared at her nephew, as if he'd lost his mind. "I wanted Joe to marry her. They would have made beautiful children. But he was in love with Annie Goldman. They're married now. It looks like it's working out." She pretended to lock her lips. "I can say no more."

And wouldn't that be a relief? "I know Annie and Joe are married, Aunt Sophia. I was one of their groomsmen, remember? The tall guy in the black tux." And it had been nothing short of miraculous that the wedding had taken place. Sophia had been dead-set against her son marrying Annie Goldman, whom she felt had lured Joe away from the church and wasn't good enough for her precious son.

John had always considered the unconventional woman a good friend. He and Annie had dated briefly several years back, but nothing came of it, except an enduring friendship.

"Oh, that's right." Sophia thumped herself on the head. "I don't know where my mind is sometimes."

John was tempted to tell her, but said instead, "And to answer your earlier question, I'm not gay. But if I were, I wouldn't be ashamed of it."

"Don't go getting on your high horse with me, Johnny Franco. I forgot about your brother coming out of the closet." It had been the chief topic of conversation at Sophia and Frank's forty-third anniversary party several months ago. "*Dio mio!* It's such a shame. He's a nice-looking boy, your brother. And I love him. But what Peter's doing goes against God's law. It's unnatural. It says so right in the Bible." She made a face of distaste. "Not to mention, it's making your mother and father nuts."

"Ma!" Mary interrupted, noting how red John's face had flushed. "I don't think we need to hear your opinion on gays and lesbians. I'm sure it's similar to what you think of the Irish."

Frank chuckled at that. Sophia's dislike of the Irish was well documented, though she tolerated her son-in-law Dan pretty well. Of course, there'd been a time not long ago when she hadn't.

"What Peter does is his business," Mary continued. "Just because he's a homosexual doesn't make him any less a man, or any less a part of our family." Sophia opened her mouth to disagree, but Mary turned away to center her attention on John.

"Did you hear Angela's representing me and Dan in the custody case against his ex-wife and her new husband? We would have asked you, Johnny, but . . . well, Angela has had experience in these types of cases, and she came highly recommended. I hope you don't feel slighted. That wasn't our intention. We know you're a good lawyer."

John didn't feel slighted, not in the least. What he felt was uncomfortable. "Not at all," he replied.

Tell her, John. Tell Mary that there's a chance you may be brought in as opposing counsel on the case. Tell her before it's too late, before she hears it from Angela DeNero or someone else.

He opened his mouth to admit the possibility, to warn her that he might have no choice in the matter, but then snapped it shut again. He couldn't bring himself to do it.

His aunt would go off like a rocket. And he couldn't bear to see his cousin's anguished face, couldn't bear to have Mary think of him as a traitor, which is pretty much how he felt at the moment.

There'd be plenty of time to face the music, once the judge rendered his decision on the continuance. Until then, he would keep his own counsel and pray like hell that everyone else kept theirs.

Angela's hand was shaking as she held the plastic dipstick up to the bright light of the white globes surrounding the bathroom mirror. She gasped in stunned horror when she noted the results—blue! The pale pink color had turned bright blue—Angela dropped the stick as if it were a burning match, watching it float to the floor.

"Oh, my God! I'm pregnant!" She plopped down on the edge of the bathtub, put her head between her knees, and tried to catch her breath. The porcelain felt cold beneath her red silk panties, as did the rest of her body, and she began shaking uncontrollably.

At any moment she would start hyperventilating. She could feel the pressure mounting inside her chest, like steam about to spurt from a teakettle or that *Alien* creature ready to burst from Ripley's chest.

Grabbing a washcloth, she ran cold water over it, wrung it out, and pressed it to her forehead. The tap water poured down the drain, an appropriate metaphor for the direction her life was taking. "Calm down, Angela," she told herself, taking slow, deliberate breaths to decrease her heart rate. "All this stress isn't good for the baby. It—

"Baby!" Her heart began pounding loud in her ears. "I'm going to have a baby!"

Winston, who was at that moment drinking water from the toilet bowl, turned to acknowledge her announcement, then went back to slurping noisily. Fortunately the Tidy Bowl man did not sail the waters of her bathroom, so the water was untreated.

Pressing her hand to her abdomen, Angela started to count backward. The last time she'd been with Bill, in the biblical sense, for the now disastrous make-up session, had been several weeks ago.

Why oh why had she made that stupid trip back to Boston? If only she had resisted the urge to try to work things out between them.

Ha! What a joke. And the joke was on her.

"Damn you, Bill McElroy, you condom-hating, sex-hungry, conniving pig of a man! I hope you rot in hell or, at the very least, drown in the English Channel." Bill had moved to London shortly after their last encounter, to be with the love of his life—the woman with whom he had cheated on Angela—and she knew he had no intention of ever coming back. He had told her as much.

"I'm sorry, Angela. Glynnis lives in London, which is where I want to be. I'm moving there. We're getting married. Be happy for me."

For all the emotion he had expressed, he may as well have sent her another one of his stupid memos:

"Angela, I've been fucking another woman. I don't love you anymore. Best, Bill."

"Good riddance, you deceitful sperm donor!"

Angela had suspected that Bill had been having an affair during the last six months of their relationship. The obvious signs were all there: lipstick and the scent of strange perfume on his shirts—Glynnis wore Eternity; how fitting!—long nights spent at the office, and last-minute weekend trips.

But, of course, he'd vehemently denied the accusations she'd tossed at him, had given her plausible explanations for everything. To put it bluntly, he had outlawyered her, which was why she had stupidly decided to give their relationship one more chance.

They'd been together for almost two years, had been engaged to be married. She thought she owed it to him, to both of them, to try to work things out.

Trusting fool!

"I hope you both drown," she whispered before bursting into tears. Then she began to cry in earnest, heart-wrenching sobs that reached down to the very depths of her soul.

Winston whined, licked her hand, then barked loudly,

offering his support. Angela tried not to think about where his tongue had just been.

How can I have a baby? I have no husband. I have a law practice.

And establishing that practice was taking up every bit of her time and what was left of her energy. At least she now knew the reason for her tiredness. Iron-poor blood would have been far more palatable.

Angela could only imagine what her life would be like once she merged the demands of her practice with the care of a totally dependent human being. She wouldn't even get into the fact that she knew nothing about caring for a child. The thought of such responsibility terrified her.

How could I have been so stupid, so gullible?

This is what you get for leading with your heart, not your head, Angela.

"Oh, shut up! Who asked you?"

The phone rang just then, but Angela had no intention of answering it. It was probably one of those stupid telemarketers, who were always trying to sell her something she didn't need, like lawn service. Even though she'd told the people at Miracle Green a hundred times that she lived in an apartment and didn't have a lawn, they continued to call, which put them into the moron category, as far as she was concerned.

Grabbing her comfortable, but admittedly ugly, white terry cloth robe off the back of the bathroom door, Angela shoved her feet into pink fuzzy slippers, then gazed at Winston, who was staring up at her in drooling confusion. "Come on, Win. Let's go see who's calling." She made her way into the living room, the dog trotting—plodding? Winston at forty pounds was a definite plodder—faithfully behind her, and stood before the answering machine that rested on the painted-pine coffee table.

All the furniture in the apartment—the cranberry leather sofa and loveseat, the hunter-green pine bookcases and tables—belonged to Mary Gallagher, who was allowing Angela to use it.

"Angela, it's your mother. Where are you? I've got such good news."

"Oh . . . my . . . God!" She couldn't talk to Rosalie right now. That would be cruel and unusual punishment. Her mother was intuitive and would know immediately that something was wrong. She'd be able to hear it in Angela's voice, sense it somehow through the phone line.

Italian mothers had built-in sonar and X-ray vision. They were not of this world.

"Your sister is making everyone nuts with that job of hers. Why would a woman want to drive a bulldozing machine? Answer me that. Your father told her to quit, but she refuses. It's so dangerous. I'm beside myself worrying about her. I . . ."

Rosalie was worried? That was hardly a revelation.

Angela plopped down on the leather sofa, and Winston jumped up next to her, placing his head on her lap. She patted him absently, listening as her mother went on about the mundane things that had happened to her and Sam this past week.

"You should see the lovely dress your father bought. It's orange. Not my color. But on him it looks good. The man has such fabulous taste. He bought matching pumps, too."

Angela rolled her eyes. It was bad enough having a father who cross-dressed, but to have a mother who abetted his unorthodox behavior was just too much to deal with. Rosalie thought her daughter's behavior was strange because Mia drove a bulldozer, but didn't think anything of her husband's penchant for wearing panty hose and lipstick.

Go figure. She loved them dearly, but they drove her nuts.

They *were* nuts!

"I wanted it to be a surprise, but I can't wait to tell you our exciting news."

Angela sucked in her breath, then expelled it in one big whoosh. *Exciting news!* What did her mother mean by that? It sounded ominous, not exciting. She leaned toward the machine, listening more intently.

"Your father and I have decided to move. . . ."

"Holy shit! No, please! Anything but that." Time stood still for Angela while she waited for the next bomb to drop.

"You know how much we miss you, so we've sold the house on Oliver Street—got a good price, too—and are moving to Baltimore to be near you, hopefully in a couple of weeks, if we can get our business in order.

"You're probably so excited that you're jumping up and down as you're listening to this. We're excited, too. Mia hasn't decided yet if she will come—she likes that damn job—but I think we'll be able to convince her."

They were moving back to Baltimore. Her parents were moving to Baltimore. In a couple of weeks! Dear God!

You're probably so excited that you're jumping up and down.

"Yeah, Ma! I'm so excited that I'm jumping out the damn window," Angela remarked, glancing toward the double-hung windows. She sighed, remembering that Joe had told her they'd been painted shut years ago.

Gazing up at the ceiling, Angela shook her head. "What have I done to deserve this? Tell me. So I had sex outside of marriage. Okay, I committed a few sins. So sue me. I'm already paying a penalty for that. I pay my taxes. I work hard. I'm good to my dog." She patted Winston's head, and he whimpered in support. "How could you be so cruel?"

"Then we'll be one big happy family again," Rosalie finished, before the message ended and the machine clicked off.

Angela stared at the machine for a moment, feeling utterly helpless, out of control, and totally despondent. For a woman who liked things neat and compartmentalized, who relished peace and order, this recent turn of events was unconscionable.

Unbelievable.

Unacceptable!

Unable to hold back the nausea rising to her throat like Mount Vesuvius at full throttle, she erupted all over Winston, and Mary's cranberry leather sofa.

An hour later, Angela had just settled herself on the newly cleaned sofa with a hot cup of tea and the TV remote control when a knock sounded at the door. Winston was in the other room asleep on the bed and didn't bark, as was his usual habit.

As horrible as she felt and looked, she was tempted to ignore it. But knowing it could be her landlady, Mrs. Foragi, and also knowing that the persistent woman was not likely to give up until she said her piece, Angela tied the belt of her robe more tightly around her and went to answer the summons.

And was stunned to find John Franco standing there.

He smiled softly. "May I come in? I won't stay long. I—I just need to speak to you about something."

Glancing down at the tattered robe she wore, Angela was absolutely horrified that this man would see her at her absolute worst, with no makeup, no decent clothing, smelling of God knew what. She swallowed, then said, "Come in," opening the door and ushering him into the living room. "Is something wrong?"

John seated himself on the sofa, and she took the seat opposite him on the overstuffed chair, trying to keep a safe distance between them, just in case that high school crush he once harbored flashed to life.

Ha! Ha! Ha! Have you looked in the mirror lately, Angela?

"Uh," John rubbed the back of his neck, looking extremely uncomfortable. "I was in the pharmacy today, and—"

"Yes, Mr. Franco, I remember that quite clearly."

"I saw you pick up the pregnancy kit and put it into your purse, Angela."

Her face paled, and he hoped he hadn't upset her.

"Are you intending to turn me in for shoplifting, because you should know that I left the money for the kit."

Angela's fear was almost laughable. For some strange inexplicable reason he felt protective toward her, didn't want to see her get hurt. "Hell, no! I know this sounds crazy, but I couldn't stop thinking about how distraught you looked. And well, I just wanted you to know that if you need a friend, someone to talk to, I'm volunteering. I know we don't know each other all that well, but sometimes that's better."

John's kindness touched Angela, but she didn't know what to do or say. Should she admit her condition and accept his offer of friendship? Or deny what he saw, and make up some ridiculous lie, try to brazen it out? Unfortunately, Angela had never been very good at lying or deception, so she opted for honesty.

"I guess I should thank you, though to be perfectly honest, I'm not exactly thrilled that you were spying on me at Moressi's." He opened his mouth to protest, but she didn't give him the chance. "But since you saw what you did, you may as well know that I am pregnant—pregnant and unmarried, with no husband on the horizon. Pretty stupid, huh, for a woman my age to get caught like this?"

He took a moment to digest her words. "It happens. You shouldn't be too hard on yourself."

No, she should be hard on Bill McElroy, but he was

thousands of miles away, whiling away the days and nights in the arms of Glynnis. And in the end, the fault lay with her. Angela should have been the one to demand that precautions be taken; it was her body, after all.

"I haven't told a soul about this, Mr. . . . John. And I'd appreciate it if you would respect my wishes and not divulge my condition to anyone. I have to come to terms with it in my own way and figure out what I'm going to do. I haven't made any decision as yet."

A pained expression crossed his face, but he said nothing, only nodded.

Angela smiled warmly. "Thank you for coming over. I'm touched by your concern. I'm sure this must be as awkward for you as it is for me."

"Well, actually I think it might be a little more awkward for you." He winked, and then stood. "I'd better get going. I'm sure you have plenty to sort out. Take care of yourself, okay? And call me if you need anything." He pulled a business card out of his wallet and handed it to her. "My home number's listed."

She followed him to the door. "You know, John, if you don't stop being so nice to ladies in distress, you're going to ruin that bad-boy image that it took you so long to develop in high school."

His blue eyes twinkled. "Oh, I'm still bad to the bone, Angela. I just hide it better now."

Leaning against the door, Angela heaved a sigh. Who would have ever guessed that John Franco, the baddest dude at Bridgemont High, would turn out to be so nice, so kind and considerate? She'd been touched by his offer of friendship.

Of course, that didn't mean she was interested in him as anything other than a friend. And that didn't mean that if she faced him in court she wasn't going to try her hardest to win.

FIVE

Why are lawyers like enemas?
You hate them until you need one,
then you still hate them.

"Tell me the truth, Johnny. And be brutally honest. Does my ass look big in these pants? I just bought them yesterday, and I'm absolutely over the moon about the way they feel—worsted wool, you know, but . . ."

Peter, two years younger than John and bearing a marked resemblance to his older brother, save for the shorter, slighter build and brownish hair color, paraded around the living room of his trendy Inner Harbor condo, posing this way and that, like some out-of-control runway model.

Shaking his head in disbelief, John shot his brother a quelling look. "Oh, for chrissake, Pete! How the hell should I know? Your ass looks the same as it always does: skinny and unattractive. So quit waltzing around in front of me like some goddamn prom queen on the make."

Ignoring his brother's harsh comment, Peter stretched his neck and tried to glance behind his back. "Wool is so difficult to wear when you have a large ass. Don't you find that to be true?"

"Are you insinuating that I have a large ass?" John wondered what the hell had come over his usually reserved little brother. He'd always been the quiet, polite child of the family—a man who preferred computers to fast cars. In a word, Pete was a geek. He even had a geek job as head of human resources at a large computer software firm.

Maybe coming out of the closet had had some kind of freeing effect on his personality. John loved his brother, tried hard to be supportive of his lifestyle, but he felt uncomfortable when things got too . . . well, too gay.

"I need a beer. Got any?"

"No, but I have a lovely chilled Chablis. Will that do?" Pete looked hopeful.

John screwed up his face in disgust at the thought of drinking such a sissy drink. He studied his brother for a moment, then noting the mischievous twinkle in his eye, threw back his head and let loose a laugh. "Jesus, Pete, you dumb bastard! You really had me going there for a minute."

Unable to hold back his grin any longer, Peter began laughing, too. "Gotcha." Then he quit the room, returning a moment later with two ice-cold Bud Lights, one of which he handed to John. "I live to exceed expectations, bro."

"I take it you've been to see our parents again? What did they do this time?" Robert and Adele Franco had a knack for turning Peter into an emotional mess whenever they got the chance.

John had been the biggest disappointment in the family, up until the moment his brother had decided to out himself. His parents were having a difficult time dealing with their son's lifestyle, and they didn't mince words when it came to letting him know how they felt.

Adele was of the mind that Pete could be cured of his terrible affliction through prayer, psychiatry, or voodoo incantations, while Robert wore his disappointment like a hair shirt. No son of his could possibly be gay, because that might open up speculation regarding his own masculinity.

Peter had always been rather sensitive, and he wasn't capable of allowing their parents' rude comments and behavior to roll off his back—as John *tried* to do, and not always successfully.

"I was over there this morning helping Dad put away the barbecue and lawn furniture, like I do every fall." Looking miserable, Pete fell onto the gold suede sofa and sipped thoughtfully on his beer. "They didn't do or say anything specific. It's just seeing that disappointed look in their eyes, hearing that succession of heart-wrenching sighs that I know damn well are designed to make me feel guilty."

"So just ignore them. They're old-fashioned and narrow-minded. You should know that by now. Why do you let them get to you? Mom and Dad aren't exactly Ward and June Cleaver, and you're not exactly the Beav."

"Mom and Dad act like I've changed, like I'm different than I was before, but you know that's not true, John. I'm the same person I've always been. I just happen to be in love with a man."

The hurt in Pete's voice saddened John, and he wished there was something he could do to ease his pain. He'd tried talking to his parents, explaining the harm they were doing to their youngest son, but they wouldn't listen.

But then, when had they ever listened?

They'd always been too busy arguing with each other to pay attention to what their kids needed emotionally. Robert and Adele weren't bad parents, just misguided and somewhat selfish. They reveled in their unhappiness and enjoyed making themselves and everyone around them miserable.

The road Pete had chosen for himself, or, more aptly, that had chosen him, was a difficult one. John hoped his brother was strong enough to handle the bumps, prejudice, and cruelty he would encounter along the way and was certain he would need a thicker hide than the one he had now.

"Speaking of men, how's Eric? I thought he was cooking dinner for us tonight." John's eyes suddenly widened in horror at the thought that might not be the case. "Jesus! I hope you're not. Your cooking sucks a big one, Pete."

Eric Loudon was head chef at one of the premier Inner Harbor restaurants. Having eaten there many times, John wasn't ashamed to admit that he intended to finagle as many dinner invitations as he could.

"Don't be bitchy, John. Eric's gone shopping for fresh fish and produce. He'll be back soon. Besides, it's not fashionable to eat before 8:00 P.M. You'd never catch a European, Italians included, dining before then. What's your hurry, anyway? It's Saturday night and you don't have a date."

"I'm starving. And I don't give a shit what people in other parts of the world do. I let my stomach dictate when it's time to eat. And for your information, I did have a date with the voluptuous Danielle, but I opted to come over here instead. I'm starting to regret my decision."

"You mean that pea-brained receptionist with the big boobs?"

Grinning, John replied, "The very same," then gazed around the living room, surprised by how nice it looked. The furniture was different than the last time he'd visited. A colorful red-and-gold oriental rug graced the two-inch oak planks beneath his feet and wooden blinds covered the large picture window.

Peter and Eric had been living together for almost two months, but this was the first time John had been invited for dinner. They'd wanted to fix up the condo before entertaining guests. "Did you just get this place professionally decorated? It looks really nice." He smoothed his hand over the soft fabric of the sofa cushion. "I like the feel of this material."

Smiling proudly, Pete nodded. "Eric and I are doing the decorating ourselves. The natural pine coffee and end tables were his idea. He has really good taste. I picked out the couch and the brown leather recliners. We're going to paint the walls a shade lighter than the couch and accent in deep red and green."

"I should have you come over and fix up my place. It looks like a dump." John had never been one to fuss with furnishings and knickknacks. His apartment was large, functional, sometimes clean, and that was about it. On those occasions when he entertained female guests he just gathered up all the accumulating newspapers and magazines, heaps of dirty clothes, and shoved them into a closet.

Peter smiled fondly at his brother. "Your place looks like you do, John. Lived in. You wouldn't be happy if your apartment didn't look like a disaster had just befallen it. I doubt *InStyle* magazine will come calling any time soon, but I'll be happy to help you decorate. Notice I didn't say *redecorate*, because that would imply you had actually done something to begin with."

Trying his best not to look insulted, but failing miserably, especially after the large-ass comment, John said, "Are you trying to say I'm a slob? Man, the insults are flying free today, little brother."

Peter pulled on his beer. "Not a slob, exactly. You're just not the *GQ* man come to life. I'd say you looked more like the poster boy for the Hell's Angels."

"I dress up when I go to court."

"Yeah, but you always look rumpled, thrown together. That leather jacket you wear has seen better days. And it's rather passé."

Horrified, John could only stare at his brother as if

he'd grown two heads. "I love my jacket! What's wrong with it?"

"Nothing, I guess, if you're Indiana Jones. Why don't you go down to Goldman's and have Annie help you pick out a couple of new suits. She's got great taste."

John mulled over Pete's suggestion. It definitely had merit. He owned two decent suits, and they were getting a bit tattered, but he had no intention of giving up his bomber jacket. "I'll think about it. I haven't seen Annie since her wedding."

Always the romantic, Peter sighed in remembrance. "She made a beautiful bride, didn't she? And it was so worth it to see Aunt Sophia's reaction when Annie walked down the aisle wearing that next-to-nothing dress. I thought she was going to stroke out. Annie's got bigger balls than most of the men I know."

"Yeah, but that's not saying much." John arched a brow. "Most of the men you know are testosterone challenged."

"Well, your testosterone hasn't done you much good. You're still single and not dating all that much, if what Mom says is true. And I'm not counting Miss Dim Wit, just in case you were wondering."

John made a face. "Jesus! First Sophia, then Mary, and now you. I'm surrounded by do-gooders who are determined to sacrifice me on the matrimonial altar. Is there something in the air I don't know about?"

"Having someone special in your life to share things with is rather nice, Johnny. Mine feels so much more complete now that I have Eric. We're soul mates. That's what you need, not some big-breasted bimbo who can't carry on a decent conversation."

"I don't need another wife, and I'm not ready to enter into a serious relationship with anyone. I'm not sure I'll ever be ready." John shook his head. "Are you forgetting my disastrous marriage to Grace?"

"You and Grace weren't right for each other. You were just too in lust to see it. Hell, she wasn't even Italian."

"If I ever do get involved again, and that's a big *if*, it won't be to some competitive, overbearing woman who has no qualms about sacrificing everything to get to the top."

"You shouldn't judge all women by Grace Wilkinson. I know what she did to you was beyond rotten, John, and I know you've suffered for it, but you can't close yourself off to love for fear of getting hurt."

John heaved a sigh. "Okay, so if all women aren't like my conniving ex-wife, then how come God created Mom and Aunt Sophia? Tell me that. Those women were put on this earth to make any male's existence miserable, including mine."

"You condemn the whole gender for the sins of a few, bro. I'm pretty sure God broke the mold when he created Aunt Sophia and Mom. Just because they're strong-willed and opinionated doesn't mean they're bad people. Both have their good points." John's brow shot up, and Pete grinned. "Just don't ask me to elaborate."

"Don't get me wrong, Pete. I love Mom. But I sure as hell don't want to be married to someone like her. Look at what she's done to Dad. She's always harping on him, telling him what to do, what to think, how to dress, how much to eat. He has to fight back or she'll swallow him whole. Lately he hasn't even bothered."

"Dad argues with Mom, but when push comes to shove, he backs down. He's just not strong enough to stand up to her," his brother argued.

"Who is? Conan the Barbarian?"

"You are, which is why she's always ragging on you, why you two butt heads so much of the time. Michael's the smart one. He gives in to Mom's nagging, lets her have her way, or allows her to think so, at any rate."

"Mike's always been a suck-up and a kiss-ass."

Pete grinned naughtily. "He's not the only one, bro, but I guess we're not talking about the same thing."

"Jesus, Pete!" John threw a pillow at his brother's head, and they began to laugh. "You're a sick little shit, you know that?"

"Yeah, that's what everyone tells me."

Sipping hot coffee from the mug she held with one hand, while holding the phone receiver in the other, Angela listened as one of her new clients, Mrs. Mattuci, explained about the injustices that had been perpetrated against the love of her life, who happened, as it turned out, not to be Mr. Mattuci.

"I want to sue those bastards, Miss DeNero. You should see how my Hector looks. They balded him something terrible. How will he hold up his head in the neighborhood? He's humiliated every time we walk down the street. French poodles are very sensitive about their appearance. And the neighbors stare at me as if I'm a child abuser. I can't take much more of this. I'm telling you, I want to sue Doggie Delight, make them pay for what they've done to my Hector."

"Did they give you a reason for shaving off all of Hector's hair without first notifying you? Maybe they found he had a skin condition." Angela made a mental note to never take Winston to Doggie Delight, not that Win had much hair, but still. . . .

"I took him in to be groomed, just like I always do. Hector is a standard poodle, so he needs grooming at least once a month. But when I went to pick him up, he was bald, his pink skin showing plain as day. I burst into tears. He looked so . . . so humiliated.

"The Doggie Delight people claimed his fur was matted and that they couldn't get the kinks out. But I'm telling you that's just not true. My Hector is . . . was—"

she sniffed loudly into the receiver several times "—a beautiful dog. He has apricot fur, you know."

Wanda walked into their suite of offices just then, stood at the doorway outside Angela's office, and whispered loudly, "I thought I was the only one working on Saturday." Angela smiled, shrugged, then turned her attention back to her distraught client.

"Why don't you bring Hector down to the office so I can take a look at him, Mrs. Mattuci. I want to see for myself how bad he looks, and then I'll be able to determine whether or not we have a case."

"Of course we have a case. Animal cruelty. They have dog psychiatrists now. We can get one to testify that my Hector's been mentally and physically abused. He doesn't hold up his head anymore, doesn't prance proudly. It breaks my heart, I'm telling you. Those people should be ashamed to call themselves groomers."

Angela heard the poodle whining pathetically in the background and Mrs. Mattuci trying to soothe his feelings. As a dog lover, she empathized with the woman. If anyone tried to hurt Winston, she'd do them physical harm.

Dogs were loyal, unlike a certain attorney she could think of. They didn't judge; they accepted, unconditionally.

She knew a lot of men who could take lessons from Winston Aloysius DeNero.

"Can you bring your dog in right now, Mrs. Mattuci?" she asked. "I'll only be here another hour or so."

"We'll be right over. I'm five minutes away, ten tops. Don't leave. I want you to see this for yourself."

After assuring the woman that she would wait, Angela replaced the receiver and leaned back in her black leather swivel chair, staring absently out the window. Dark clouds gathered in the gunmetal gray sky, threatening rain. It was gloomy and depressing, just like her mood.

Angela had done a great deal of thinking since last night's shocking discovery, and the only real decision she had made was that she was going to keep the baby. That was a no-brainer.

Angela wanted children, had always planned to have them, just not so soon. And not without a husband. But somehow, someway she would make it all work.

She just wasn't sure how at the moment.

But she was used to meeting and exceeding expectations, first in college, then in law school. So why not in the university of life, aka, the school of hard knocks? Her father had taught her early on that hard work fixed everything, that she could succeed at whatever she wanted to do, as long as she worked hard. Nothing could stand in the way of a determined woman, Sam DeNero had told his daughter.

It was how she lived her life.

So Angela had no intention of allowing this current situation to derail her plans. She'd just have to apply herself even harder. She was self-sufficient, capable, and had a promising career. She didn't need a man in her life, especially an unfaithful one. She and the baby would be fine by themselves.

Besides, she had no more room in her life for any more complications. John Franco's image suddenly surfaced, but she pushed it away. He had offered friendship; she needed a friend, nothing more. Life had a depressing way of intruding on high school fantasies.

And her parents' impending arrival would be complication enough. She needed to call Sam and Rosalie, to find out when they'd be coming. But not yet. Her plate was full at the moment.

"Knock, knock," Wanda said, standing in the open doorway and smiling a hundred-watt smile. "Can I come in, or are you working on something important? You look preoccupied. Is everything all right? Anything I can do to help?"

Angela motioned her friend forward, noting that Wanda was dressed as casually as she was today, in blue jeans and a sweater. She had every intention of confiding in the woman, but not now. In an effort to be helpful and practical, Wanda would offer advice, and Angela wasn't ready to hear it as yet. She was still coming to terms with impending motherhood and needed more time to think.

"Mrs. Mattuci's coming by with her bald dog," she explained, and Wanda flashed a grin.

"Well, I can certainly see why you needed to drop everything and come in today."

"I'm also trying to get some preliminary work done on the Gallaghers' custody case."

"Charles Rothburg is a sleaze," the black woman stated, her smile melting into a disturbed expression. "You be careful around him, Angela. I've heard things about the way he operates. Rothburg doesn't like to lose, and his methods are not always aboveboard. He'll stop at nothing to win."

"Thanks for the heads-up, but I doubt there's anything to worry about. Rothburg's being represented by Tony Stefano and John Franco; they've got a reputation for honesty and integrity. I doubt he'll be able to get away with anything. As a lawyer, he's bound by the same ethics and rules we are."

At the mention of John Franco, Wanda's eyes lit with appreciation. "*Oooh,* but that John Franco is one fine specimen of a man. I wouldn't mind taking a tumble between the sheets with him. We are talking Grade A, number one prime, girlfriend."

"I hadn't noticed."

"You lie! You'd have to be dead not to have noticed his blue eyes and wide shoulders. The man could pass for a lineman. I won't even mention his massive chest. Be still my heart." Wanda fanned herself. "I'm getting hot just thinking about him."

Angela swallowed her smile. "Okay, so I noticed. But I'm determined not to. The truth is, we went to high school together, but he never noticed me." At least, that's what she'd thought. Now, when it was too late, he admitted to having a crush on her.

Timing was indeed everything, and hers sucked.

"John Franco is probably going to be my opposing counsel—Tony Stefano's in the hospital, recuperating from a heart attack—so it's more important than ever that I keep my wits about me. I heard he was good . . . in court," she added at Wanda's sly grin.

"I hear he's good in bed, too. That receptionist, Danielle Johnson, who works for McKinley/Peters, said he was incredible, the best she'd ever had. And, honey, Danielle has humped more men than a rabbit on Viagra."

No wonder he needed two dozen condoms, Angela thought, feeling her own heartbeat quicken.

"What about Kyle?" Angela asked. "I thought you were head over heels in love with the handsome doctor. Any man who looks like Denzel Washington has got to be a keeper, in my book."

"I'm still seeing Kyle. I'm just not sure how involved I want to get. He's so serious about everything."

Puzzled, Angela's brows drew together. "But I thought you were sleeping with him."

"I am. I meant romantically involved. Sex is just . . . well, sex. And though he's good in bed, I'm just not sure I want to take our relationship to the next level."

They were having sex. How many more levels were there?

Angela was saved from asking by a knock at the door, followed by, "*Yooo-hooo,* Miss DeNero, it's me . . . Carmela Mattuci. I've brought Hector to see you." True to her word, the woman had arrived in less than ten minutes.

"Come on in." Angela waved the pink-polyester-clad

woman forward, swallowing her gasp when she took in the appearance of the dog. The poor thing had indeed been balded. His flesh was clearly visible, and there were cuts and abrasions on his skin. Even the rhinestone collar he wore couldn't help him to look attractive.

Anger heated her cheeks. "Mrs. Mattuci . . . Hector." The dog looked away, as if in shame, breaking her heart.

Wanda, who was terrified of most animals, beat a hasty retreat when she spotted the dog, while Angela instructed her distraught client to be seated in front of her desk.

"See," Mrs. Mattuci said, observing Wanda's departure. "That woman is afraid of my Hector. She thinks he looks like a monster."

"Wanda's afraid of all dogs. I'm sure her leaving isn't personal. Now tell me everything again, Mrs. Mattuci, and don't leave anything out." If there was one thing Angela couldn't countenance, it was cruelty to animals, and Hector had obviously been mistreated, there was no doubt about that. She just had to determine if that mistreatment was intentional or accidental.

"I don't have to tell you how important this custody hearing is to us," Charles Rothburg told John, patting his wife's hand consolingly, then straightening his red silk tie, which was slightly askew, rather like his values.

"It's true, Sharon made a mistake by leaving Matthew with her former husband. But as I told Tony, she always intended to come back for him. Leaving the kid with Dan Gallagher was never meant to be permanent."

Leaning on his desktop while listening to Charles Rothburg make excuses for his wife's uncaring behavior toward her only child, John fought the urge to roll his eyes. He wasn't buying Rothburg's account of what had transpired. These two people deserved each other; that much was clear.

Charles Rothburg wore his money well. His charcoal-gray Armani suit had probably cost more than the national debt of most third-world nations. His wife was dressed conservatively in a navy wool suit with shiny gold buttons, her blond hair coiffed just so, the diamond on her left hand large and sparkling. Sharon Rothburg was an attractive woman, though she appeared cold and rather detached, as if she was just going through the motions to please her new husband. She was certainly nothing like his cousin Mary, who was warm, funny, and very loving.

So why am I doing this? John asked himself for the hundredth time.

Tony needs you, was always the answer.

It didn't take a genius to figure out why Charles had married Sharon Gallagher. She was at least twenty-five years his junior and fit all the qualifications of a trophy wife. Nor was there any question in John's mind about why she had married him. Rothburg was one of the wealthiest attorneys in Baltimore . . . correction, in the entire state of Maryland.

"I won't kid either one of you, Mr. and Mrs. Rothburg. I'm not comfortable handling this case. I feel I have a conflict of interest because Mary Gallagher is my cousin. But Judge Baldridge has refused to grant a continuance, and with my partner in the hospital recovering from heart surgery, I have no choice. However, if you'd like to seek other counsel, I'll understand."

Rothburg shook his head. "You've got a reputation as a winner, Mr. Franco. And I like to win. We don't want anyone else representing us in this matter, and I know you won't allow personal feelings to interfere. My wife and I have full confidence in your ability, though we appreciate your candor."

Not the answer he'd been hoping for. John sighed. "Is

that true, Mrs. Rothburg? Do you feel the same as your husband?"

Rothburg's wife smiled, somewhat vapidly. "Whatever Charles thinks is fine with me. He's the expert on these matters. I trust him to make the right decision. And if he's chosen you, Mr. Franco, then so be it. I have nothing against Mary Gallagher. I'm grateful she's given my son a good home. I just want Matthew back. A child belongs with his mother."

"I should warn you, Mrs. Rothburg, that the Gallaghers' attorney will do everything in her power to make you look bad. You abandoned your son to run off with a man ten years your junior. And you never attempted, not even once, to get in contact with him. That will not go in your favor."

"I wasn't myself during that time, Mr. Franco. I felt as if I was having a nervous breakdown, that my life was spiraling out of control. My job as a lobbyist was stressful, and the failure of my marriage hit me very hard."

Not hard enough to prevent her from screwing some boy-toy, he thought, glancing down at his notes. "According to what I was told, you and Mr. Gallagher had been divorced about four years when you abandoned your son."

"*Abandon*'s a rather harsh word, isn't it, Franco?" The older man glared at the younger attorney seated before him.

John didn't flinch. "You've been involved in enough cases to know the kind of condemnation and accusations your wife will have to face. If you want to proceed with this case, you had better get used to hearing the unsympathetic realities.

"I didn't make up the circumstances, Mr. Rothburg, but you can be sure that Miss DeNero is going to embellish them in front of the judge. Your wife will be painted in a very unflattering light, make no mistake about it."

"What do you know about Angela DeNero?" the older attorney asked, his eyes hard and glowing with contempt.

John shrugged. "I've never gone up against her in court, if that's what you're asking. But I believe Miss DeNero's going to be a very tough competitor. There doesn't seem to be much that gets by her. Frankly, I'm impressed." And by more than just her brain.

For all her intelligence, legal acumen, and sharp wit, there was a soft side to Angela, a vulnerability that he hadn't been able to ignore, which is why he'd felt compelled to offer friendship. No doubt she'd be able to handle this twist of fate that life had thrown at her, but he just didn't think it was fair that she had to do it alone.

"The same could be said about you, Franco." Rothburg leaned back in his chair, entwining his hands over his chest. "Your reputation precedes you."

John returned his attention to the matter at hand. "I'll do my best. That's all I can promise. But I expect Mrs. Rothburg to be totally honest with me. If we're going to win this case, then I need to know everything." He turned his attention to the woman.

"I need to know the details of your marriage, your divorce, how your son was treated by his father."

"Dan was a good father, albeit an absent one, most of the time."

"Which is why you were granted full custody, is that correct?"

Sharon nodded. "Because he was on the road so much of the time, Dan thought it would be better for Matthew to remain with me, and so he agreed to relinquish custody."

"So he put his son's welfare before his own?"

"I see where you're heading with this. Dan's a paragon of virtue, while I'm a bitch."

"Sharon, you mustn't talk like that. I'm sure Mr. Franco thinks nothing of the kind." Rothburg stared intently at John, willing him to deny it, but the younger man ignored him.

"It doesn't matter what I think, Rothburg. Anyone who hears what happened is going to think that your wife is a heartless, selfish woman, not to mention a bad mother. It's going to take a lot of explanation to overcome those opinions.

"Judge Baldridge has eight children. Need I say more?"

"I expect you to do whatever it takes to win this custody battle, Franco. I don't care how much money it costs, or what you have to do to win. Do I make myself clear?"

John smiled through thin lips. He really despised Charles Rothburg. The man was pond scum. Successful and rich pond scum, but scum just the same. "Crystal. But I should tell you up front that I won't go outside the law."

The older attorney seemed shocked. "No one's asking you to, Mr. Franco. But I want your heart and soul in this matter. I want two hundred percent of your effort. Anything less will not be acceptable."

Placing a placating hand on her husband's arm, Sharon smiled apologetically. "I'm sure Mr. Franco is on our side in this, Charles. You don't need to beat him over the head with what you expect."

She stood, holding out her hand, which John took. "I have every confidence in your abilities to win, Mr. Franco ... John. Charles and I are at your disposal. Aren't we, darling?"

Bile rose up John's throat as he watched the newly wedded couple walk out the door.

"Jesus, Tony! What the hell have you gotten me into?"

Nothing good. That was for damn certain!

SIX

*What's the difference between a tick
and a lawyer?*
The tick drops off after you're dead.

The stiff autumn breeze felt good against Angela's
cheeks as she jogged down High Street toward Stiles. It
was still very early in the morning, barely six o'clock, the
sun just starting to rise, but she needed to release the
pent-up energy and nervousness she'd been feeling these
past two weeks.

Jogging helped to clear her mind, get her thoughts together, and she was going to need every one of her facul-
ties intact, all of her emotions in good working order;
today was the first day of depositions in the Rothburg vs.
Gallagher custody hearing.

John Franco would be there, and she was nervous at
the thought of seeing him again. She hoped it wouldn't
be too awkward, now that he knew about her condition.
Even though the depositions would be routine, and
nothing she hadn't done many times before, she didn't
like the idea of mixing business with pleas—personal
matters.

Matthew's teacher, guidance counselor, and pediatrician would be the first to be deposed, and they would be
required to answer questions asked by opposing counsel.

Angela would be there to make certain the questions
John solicited were fair, though he'd have license to ask
pretty much what he pleased, unlike the custody hearing,
where she would be free to object and make motions to
strike from the record.

So why, then, did she feel so on edge?

There was still the matter of making an appointment with an obstetrician to make sure everything was fine with her pregnancy, but she didn't want to deal with that just yet. It would make her condition seem all too real.

Not that barfing every morning wasn't as real as it gets.

And her parents' arrival in town a few days ago hadn't helped matters in the least. Although she was happy to see them again, there was still a part of her that wished they had remained in Boston. As lonely as she sometimes was living alone, she liked her independence and having no one to answer to but herself.

Her mistakes were her own, and she wanted to deal with them that way.

Sam and Rosalie were settling into their newly purchased brick house, located only three blocks from where Angela was now. Mia had remained in Boston, but planned to join them soon. And then, as her mother had pointed out numerous times, they would be one big happy family again.

That unwelcome, acid-producing thought made her suddenly ravenous, and Angela headed toward Fiorelli's Bakery/Cafe, her Nikes slapping the sidewalk rhythmically as she ate up the distance.

Andrea Fiorelli made the best coffee, donuts, and bagels around, not to mention a gazillion other pastries, and Angela was in a mood to stuff her face a bit. She'd worry about the calories tomorrow.

Tomorrow. Later. Not yet. All were becoming catchwords. And for a woman who didn't normally procrastinate, it was totally out of character.

Nearing the bakery, she noticed a man in front of the building. He was bent over at the waist, hands on knees, sucking in huge gulps of air. He was obviously out of shape and in a great deal of pain. She could empathize. Beginning any exercise program was no fun. His head was covered with a dark baseball cap, and his sweats appeared to be as old and ragged as hers. He turned, angling away from her, so she couldn't see his face, but Angela noticed that his body was very muscular.

He was probably a body builder, like Lou Santini, the butcher and resident hunk of the neighborhood, who lived with his mother above the meat shop. Angela had gone out with Lou a time or two, but only as friends. They didn't have enough in common to warrant more than that.

Stopping next to the stranger, Angela tapped him on the shoulder. "Excuse me, but are you okay?"

"My lungs are about to burst," he replied, straightening and turning slowly.

Recognizing him instantly, Angela's heart sank to her knees. *Why oh why did it have to be John Franco?* Without her makeup, and with her hair pulled back in a ponytail, Angela knew that she looked about twelve years old. Not that she cared what he thought, she reminded herself. *Friends* didn't care how bad *friends* looked.

Liar!

Shut up! Shut up! Shut up!

John Franco grinned that damn sexy grin of his, and Angela was reminded of the comments Wanda had made about his lovemaking abilities. She felt her face flame and her toes tingle.

Friendship is so overrated!

"Hey, Angela! Nice to see you again." He gave her a quick once-over, his smile melting into concern. "Are you sure you should be jogging in your condition? It might not be good for the baby."

His presumption annoyed her. "I'm in excellent health. And though I appreciate your concern, I'm quite capable of taking care of myself. I've been doing it for years." She knew she sounded a bit huffy, but his question had nagged at her conscience.

"Have you seen a doctor yet?"

Her face flamed again. "Well, no. But I plan to. I've decided to keep the baby."

John smiled with genuine pleasure, not bothering to ask himself why he was so happy about her decision. "That's great!"

"I had no idea you lived around here. Isn't your office located in Fell's Point?" Which was only a few blocks away, but still, it wasn't Little Italy.

"Yep. So is my apartment. I thought I could increase my running distance without killing myself, but apparently I was wrong. My chest feels like it's going to explode."

"If you've just started running, you shouldn't be pushing yourself so hard. Ease into it slowly. Let your body adjust." She allowed herself another lust-filled appraisal. The man was built like Rocky Balboa, and *she* was giving *him* exercise tips? Ha! That was rich!

"I've been running for a number of years, it's my ten-year addiction to cigarettes, which I've recently given up." He pulled up the sleeve of his sweatshirt to reveal the nicotine patch on his left arm, rather proudly, she thought. If she had arms that muscular, she'd be proud, too.

"Good for you."

John looked entirely too appealing in his rumpled state. The Orioles cap he wore made him seem boyish, his cheeks sported a day's growth of beard, and he looked as if he'd just rolled out of the sack.

He looked adorably rumpled, while Angela looked disastrously crumpled.

Figures.

It was the old problem of men aging gracefully, their hair distinguished-looking, not dry and brittle as it grayed, like a used S.O.S. pad. Women, on the other hand, were doomed to enter the world of the wrinkled, shriveled, and, alas, crumpled.

"Well, I'm starving, so—"

"Can I buy you a cup of coffee and a donut?" he asked.

She paused a moment to consider, then shook her head. Tempting though his offer was, she knew it wouldn't be wise. Friendship was all well and good, but they were still adversaries when it came to the courtroom. "I don't think that's a good idea, under the present circumstances, but thanks. In a few hours we'll be seated across the conference table from each other, a court reporter taking down everything we say. It's best that we keep a professional distance."

"Why? Are you worried I'm going to figure out your legal strategy?" He flashed that devastating grin again, and Angela decided there should be a law against men having dimples. The only dimples she had were the ones in her butt cheeks, and there was nothing remotely adorable about them.

"Hardly. I just don't want any conflict of interest. We are on opposite sides of the same case, after all. And I don't think it's a good idea for opposing counsel to fraternize."

"I doubt one cup of coffee is going to corrupt either one of us. Besides, I like living on the edge, don't you?" But he could tell by her appearance that Angela DeNero liked living a well-ordered, placid existence.

Though she wore sweats, it was clear they'd been ironed. Who in their right mind ironed sweats? He barely had time to take his shirts to the laundry.

Her dark hair was pulled back from her face in a restrained ponytail, not a hair out of place. He had the sudden urge to muss it. Even without a shred of makeup, Angela looked adorable, and sexy. And she smelled good, too; clean and fresh, liked she'd just stepped out of the shower, in spite of the fact she was sweating.

"I'll see you this afternoon."

"You really should try letting yourself go once in a while, Angela. I was going to spring for a latte today. And I would have even tossed in two powdered jelly donuts."

She smiled and, against her better judgment, finally gave in. "How can I resist such an offer? Okay, one cup of coffee, then I've got to go."

Entering the bakery, they ordered glazed and powdered jelly donuts and coffee, and then seated themselves at the small round table by the window, the first customers of the day.

"I guess you've discovered my weakness. I'm a sucker for a jelly donut," Angela said, trying to restrain herself from stuffing the whole thing into her mouth.

John bit back a smile. "I like a woman with a healthy appetite." He gazed at her lips, now covered with powdered sugar and jam, and watched her tongue flick out to lick the sugar from them, trying to ignore the tight knot forming in the pit of his stomach.

"Well, I've certainly got that. I've been eating everything that isn't nailed down, then throwing it all back up again." She covered her mouth in horror, realizing what she'd just said.

He laughed. "I don't have a weak stomach, so it's not a problem. So, have you told anyone, besides me, I mean, about the baby?"

Shaking her head, Angela lowered her voice, though she knew Mrs. Fiorelli was too far away to hear them. "No. I'm going over to my parents' house today, but I'm not sure I'm ready to break the news. I don't think they'll be too happy when they find out."

He arched a brow. "I find that hard to believe. As my

Uncle Frank would say, 'Italians and their grandchildren—*forgetaboutit*.' " He had the accent down perfectly.

Angela laughed, and then explained, "My parents sort of have this perfect-daughter image of me. I got excellent grades all through school, won a scholarship to college, and had a fabulous job at a prestigious law firm, making oodles of money. In their eyes I can do no wrong.

"Trust me, being pregnant and unmarried is totally out of character for me. My mother's already a doom-sayer. This news will put her right over the edge."

"So you're worried they'll find out you're human and have faults, just like the rest of us? Don't be. My parents and I have always had a very antagonistic relationship, sort of a love-hate thing. But if I was to come home and tell them I was going to give them a grandchild, all would be forgiven."

Angela noted the pain in his eyes. "Why don't you get along with your parents? Aren't they proud that you've become a successful attorney?"

"I don't measure up to my brother. Never have and probably never will, at least in their eyes. You're the perfect daughter in your family; Michael is the perfect son in mine."

She felt ill all of a sudden, wondering if Mia had been as adversely affected by their parents' pride in Angela's accomplishments. Not that Sam and Rosalie didn't love Mia, but Angela knew she was their shining star and always had been.

Noting the concern on Angela's face, John said, "You have a younger sibling, I take it. Don't worry. I'm sure your circumstances are nothing like mine."

She considered his words, hoped they were true, then asked the question that had been plaguing her for days, "Why are you being so nice to me?"

"I'm making up for not asking you out in high school. It was a grave oversight on my part."

Her grin matched his. "In that case, I'll have another donut. I think you still owe me."

Back at his apartment, John showered, dressed in a dark navy suit with burgundy pinstripes, and poured himself another cup of coffee—black, the way he liked it.

Carrying his mug into the hallway, he set it on the table beneath the oval mirror, where his briefcase rested and served to remind him that he had several more hours of preparation before he'd be ready to take depositions of Angela's witnesses. As astute as the lady lawyer was, he had to be ready.

Damn, but he was looking forward to seeing Angela again. He'd enjoyed spending time with her at the coffee shop, getting to know her a little bit better. She was fun, when she wasn't worrying about every little thing. She tended to worry a lot, but he guessed she had good reason. Facing a pregnancy alone had to be tough.

Straightening the Windsor knot in his burgundy-and-gray-patterned tie, he gave his appearance a final once-over, knowing he probably wouldn't pass muster with Pete, but satisfied that he looked as good as he was going to.

John was about to leave when the doorbell rang. Glancing at his watch, he cursed; it was barely eight o'clock. He needed to get to his office and wondered who in the hell could be calling at such an early hour.

Tony was home from the hospital, but was still recuperating from his surgery, so he knew it wasn't him. And his parents would have opened the dry cleaners by now, to accommodate the before-work crowd. They were sticklers about such things. In fact, the only time he could remember Franco Dry Cleaners opening late was when his father had been taken to the hospital with an appendicitis attack.

Which left John with absolutely no idea . . . unless Angela had decided to surprise him.

"Yeah, right, Franco! Dream on."

The bell rang three more times in quick succession. Someone was impatient to see him, that was for damn certain.

He hurried to open the door.

Then wished he hadn't.

"You should be ashamed of yourself, Johnny Franco!" *It's definitely not Angela.* He groaned inwardly.

"How can you go against your family this way?" Sophia Russo stood in the doorway like an avenging angel, glaring at him and nudging her mother-in-law in the arm, before stepping inside.

John was too stunned to speak, not that he'd been given the chance.

"It'sa true, Johnny, Mary isa very upset that you go against her and Dan," Grandma Flora stated, her wrinkled face pale against the black of her dress as she leaned against her cane.

Flora always wore black. She was still mourning her husband, Sal, who'd been dead for more than a decade. Sophia wore black, too; she was in a perpetual state of mourning, brought on by her husband, children, and life in general.

John held his ground, not an easy feat in the face of such formidable opponents. "I've been given no choice in the matter." He tried to explain but could see by their pinched expressions that they were having none of it. "I've been meaning to talk to Mary about my reasons for—"

Sophia's hands went up to cut him off. "My daughter is beside herself. And I won't tell you what her husband thinks about this betrayal. *Madonna mia, disgrazia!* This is a black mark against the family. We will not be able to hold up our heads in the neighborhood when this gets out. You must stop such behavior at once, or face the consequences."

Sophia had a Vito Corleone look about her, which didn't bode well.

Though he offered his aunt and grandmother seats on the sofa, they refused. Which was just as well, he supposed, since it was presently upholstered in last night's newspaper. They locked arms, preferring instead to stand in front of the door, blocking his escape.

"My partner, Tony Stefano, was supposed to try this custody case, but he had a heart attack."

Grandma tsked several times, shook her head, then crossed herself. "I'ma sorry for him, Johnny. But those nasty people wanta to takea the *bambino* away from his family. They musta find someone else to helpa them.

"*La famiglia*, Johnny. *La famiglia*. What would Grandpa Sal say if he were alive to hear such a ting? God rest his soul. The man was a saint."

John wondered why men—husbands, in particular—were always elevated to sainthood after they were dead. They could be the meanest, nastiest sons of bitches ever to walk the earth while alive, but once they were planted six feet under, all was forgiven and they joined the ranks of Saint Christopher.

"Did Mary send you over here?" The action seemed out of character for his cousin. But these were trying times, and Mary was obviously upset with him. Not that he could blame her.

Jesus! I warned Tony this was going to happen. And now it has. What's next—a horse's head in my bed?

Sophia shook her head. "Of course not. Your cousin is too upset to deal with this terrible thing. Her grandmother and I must take care of this family matter. Once you agree to drop this case, all will be well again."

John wished he could make them understand. "As much as I'd like to, Aunt Sophia, I can't. Charles Rothburg is represented by our law firm, and as the only partner available at this time I'm obligated to offer him my assistance in this matter."

"And go against Mary? Take her son away from her?" She kissed the small gold crucifix hanging from around her neck and made the sign of the cross for good measure. "What can you be thinking, Johnny? Matthew's mother is a *puttana*. A no good bum. She left her little boy."

"I suggested to the Rothburgs that they choose another attorney, but they weren't agreeable. My hands are tied. I have no choice. I'm sorry."

Stepping forward, Grandma Flora reached up to pat her grandson's cheek. "This isa very bad ting you do, Johnny. Your family loves you. We don'ta want to be mad at you, to havea bad blood between us. Please, you will tink about it some more?"

He felt his face warm. "I—"

"If you don't drop this case, Johnny Franco, I will tell your mother and father, and then I will put a curse on you."

Grandma Flora's dark eyes flashed fire. "*Bah!* You can't do that. Only I can put on the curse."

"Be quiet, old woman! Mary is my daughter, not yours. And as such, it is my right."

John couldn't believe that the two old ladies were fighting over which one of them was going to curse him.

Jesus! If this was a fucking nightmare, he sure as hell hoped he'd awaken soon.

"Ma, they've got self-sticking shelf paper now. Why do you insist on using oilcloth to line the shelves? It's such a pain." Staring at the offending material, then at the thumbtacks in her hand, Angela made a face of disgust, but her mother would not be dissuaded.

"You gotta go with the good stuff, Angie. It costs a little more, that's true, but so what? That sticky paper is no damn good. And the kitchen is where I spend most of my time. I want it to look nice. Why do you think I waited so long to get this done? I waited for the oilcloth. It had to be ordered."

"This pea green color is hideous, Ma. It reminds me of barf." And it was the same exact color and pattern that Rosalie had used at her last house.

Originality was not her mother's forte, and neither was decorating. The DeNeros' furnishings hadn't changed since Angela was a child. Dark, heavy pieces of mahogany furniture that had been handed down from Rosalie and Sam's families graced the rooms. And though the sofa and occasional chairs still bore their original green brocade fabric, they had never seen the light of day, due to the hideous autumn motif slipcovers with which Rosalie chose to cover them.

Rosalie set down her shears—for oilcloth you needed the big-ass shears, not just regular scissors—and wrapped her arms about her daughter. "I'm so happy we're together again, Angie. I've missed your insults. But you're too thin. Have you been eating enough? And those shadows under your eyes . . ." She tsked several times. "You've been working too hard. And for what? Life as we know it will end soon, and then you will have spent all that time working for nothing. It's a waste, I'm telling you. The Bible is very clear about such things."

Her mother was nothing if not consistent, Angela would give her that. Rosalie had been talking about Armageddon for as long as she could remember. So far it hadn't come to pass. God was justifiably annoyed at the world. But enough to destroy it? Angela didn't think so.

"I thought you were proud that I became a lawyer. You're always telling your friends that."

"Who said I wasn't proud? I'm very proud. Your father was saying just the other day how happy he was that you became a big-shot attorney. Coming from a cop, that's high praise. You know he has no use for them. Saw too many shysters when he walked the beat."

"Speaking of Dad, where is he? Doesn't he want to see his favorite daughter?"

"Stop!" Rosalie wagged a chastising finger at her daughter. "You know your father doesn't play favorites. He loves you and Mia just the same. We both do. Sam should be back soon. He went to the hardware store for some nails to hang the pictures."

Angela could think of someone she'd like to hang.

John had been absolutely horrible during this afternoon's depositions. He'd asked questions that she felt had no bearing on the custody issue, questioned the guidance counselor's academic training, implying the man wasn't qualified to make a judgment regarding Matthew's emotional state, and even attacked Miss Osborne's ability to evaluate her students. The pediatrician had been put through the wringer, as well, with Franco asking the poor man if he'd studied psychiatry, as well as childhood diseases.

Angela had been embarrassed, disgusted, and angry by the time the whole thing was over.

She was still seething and had decided to pay Sam and Rosalie a visit. Nothing like parents to take your mind off what was troubling you, by giving you a whole new set of annoyances to deal with. She'd been giving some consideration to telling them about the baby, but wasn't sure if this was the right time.

"So have you met any interesting men since coming to Baltimore?"

Definitely not the right time.

Angela lowered herself onto the kitchen chair and heaved a sigh. The mantra of every Italian mother since time began: *When are you going to get married?* "Don't start, Ma. I'm through with men. After what that bastard did— Please, I don't want to talk about men."

"They're not all like Bill, Angie. And someday you're going to want to get married, have children, settle down. You need a man for that."

"I've got a dog," she told her mother.

"I know you've got a dog. And an uglier one I've never laid eyes on. I'd be embarrassed to be seen with a dog like that."

Angela could hear Winston growling beneath the table. "You shouldn't say such things, Ma. You'll hurt Win's feelings. He's very sensitive about his looks." Mrs. Mattuci was right—dogs were almost as vain as humans.

"Was he abandoned? Is that why you ended up with such a homely creature? You and your sister were always dragging home strays when you were kids. Looks like nothing's changed."

"Winston is a purebred bulldog. I paid three hundred dollars for him two days after I moved here." In a weak, insane moment that she didn't regret for an instant. Win was her confidant. She could tell him all kinds of personal stuff and be guaranteed that he'd never reveal her secrets to anyone.

Eyes wide, Rosalie crossed herself, then lifted the table-cloth and peered under the table. The dog resumed growling. "Stop that, *te creatura misera,* or I'll get my wooden spoon and spank you. I'm your grandmother. Show some respect."

Angela laughed as the dog rested his head on his paws and whimpered. Win might be homely, but he was intelligent, if not a wee bit cowardly. Rosalie would grow to love him. She was a nurturing sort, incapable of withholding love from any living creature, even if she thought it was miserable.

The front door slammed just then, indicating her father's return from the hardware store. "Is that my daughter's car I see parked out in front of the house?"

Sam came barreling into the kitchen, all two hundred and fifty pounds of him, a huge grin on his still-handsome face. Fortunately Angela's father was tall and could carry the extra weight, though his belly bespoke many bottles of Sam Adams. His hair was jet black, but starting to gray at the temples.

Slapping his wife on the rear affectionately, Sam kissed his daughter's cheek. "How's things, Ang? You haven't been visiting much."

"You've been here less than a week, Dad, and I've been busy with work. I work late hours most nights. I don't have much time for socializing."

"What? We're your family. You don't socialize with family. You visit. Do you have proper locks on your apartment door? I'll be over to check them out."

"That's not necessary. My landlady is quite handy with a screwdriver. She's added a new deadbolt to the front door, and there was already a security device installed, from when Mary Gallagher lived there." She wouldn't bother to confide that Mary had had a break-in, which necessitated the security device. "And don't forget I've got a watchdog."

"That fat lump of flesh?" Sam made a face, then laughed. "Go on with you. He couldn't catch his own tail, if he had one, let alone some burglar or rapist."

Win placed his rather considerable head on her foot; Angela felt his pain, and her own.

"Did your mother tell you that Mia's quit her job and will be moving here in a few weeks, maybe sooner, if she can sublet her apartment?"

"That's great!" Angela smiled happily. Her sister was good at deflecting some of her parents' anxiety. As the youngest daughter, she'd always been fawned over and babied, which was just fine with Angela, since it gave her parents something to do besides butt into her business.

"Is she going to live with you?"

"Of course," Rosalie replied, as if it was a fait accompli, which, of course, it was.

According to the gospel of Sam and Rosalie, single women should live at home. The only reason her parents had tolerated Angela's move out of the house was because she had attended an upper-crust school like Harvard. By the time law school rolled around, she was out of their clutches.

Angela considered the freedom that living alone had afforded her to be one of the great benefits of academic life.

"Where else would your sister live? We're her parents. We've got plenty of room."

Angela would have liked Mia to live with her, but she had only one bedroom, and the apartment wasn't all that big, especially for two women with wardrobes. Not that Mia's wardrobe was anything to brag about. Her sister was somewhat of a tomboy and felt more comfortable in jeans and sneakers than in anything else.

"I see you've got it all worked out."

"You're welcome to move in here, too, Ang," Sam offered. "You know we'd love it if you did."

I'd rather have every one of my teeth extracted without Novocain.

"Thanks, Dad, but I like my apartment. It's convenient to everything, including my office. And I think I'm a little too old to be living at home, don't you?"

"Don't be silly. In Italy many bachelors in their forties—*mammoni,* they're called—still live with their families. It's the Italian way of doing things. A mother never gets tired of having her children around, even if they're grown." Rosalie patted Angela's cheek. "You'll always be my baby, Angela."

Angela decided it would be wise and a whole lot safer

to change the topic. "So how do you like being retired, Dad? Are you getting bored yet?"

Pulling a chair out from the table, Sam seated himself, shaking his head. "Not yet. But if I do, it shouldn't be too hard with my law enforcement background to find a security job. I've been keeping myself busy by watching the home shopping networks."

"Sam bought himself a lovely chenille robe and the most stunning silk lounging pajamas."

"That's nice," Angela said, wondering what she was going to tell her child about his or her grandfather. Not many kids understood that a man who dressed up in women's clothing wasn't necessarily a homosexual, or weird. Okay, maybe weird. But it was a fetish, and a relatively harmless one at that.

"What color did you order?"

"Bright blue, like sapphires. The fabric's going to be a bitch to take care of, though. I'll have to have them dry-cleaned."

"I met the mailman today," Rosalie said, her face slightly flushed. "He told me I had beautiful skin, like peaches and cream. Wasn't that nice of him to say?"

"Was he making a pass at you?" Sam's expression grew fierce, and Angela couldn't help but smile. Her parents had been married over forty years, and yet her father was still jealous of other men. She thought it was sweet.

Bill had never been jealous. Of course, now that she knew he'd been in love with another woman, she knew why.

"I always tell you how nice your skin is, don't I?" Sam pressed his wife, who nodded, but didn't seem as impressed with his compliments as the mailman's.

A big believer in Noxzema face cream, Angela's mother did have lovely skin. Unlike her own olive complexion, Rosalie was fair, with dark blond hair that bespoke an ancestry of northern Italy.

Those lovely cheeks were blossoming red at the moment. "Heavens, no! Mr. Castallano was not making a pass at me. He is just a nice man."

"Castallano, like the crime family? *Il mio dio!*" Sam swore a few choice Italian curse words beneath his breath. "Next you'll be telling me he's connected. I'll keep an eye on this mailman. Maybe he's in the federal Witness Protection Program or something."

"How should I know if he's connected? I just met the man. Just because we're living in Little Italy doesn't mean everyone's in the Mafia. Shame on you, Sam! Your parents, God rest their souls, would be very upset if they knew how you talked. Stereotypes are destructive."

"So I made a mistake? *Dio!* Always with the drama, Rosalie. What are you making, a movie here? A man can't say one thing in this house without having his balls busted." He stood. "I gotta go hang pictures."

Bending over, he kissed Angela's cheek. "Don't be a stranger. We moved here to be near you, so come visit."

"I will. I promise."

Once Rosalie was sure her husband was out of earshot, she leaned toward her daughter and whispered in conspiratorial fashion, "Mr. Castellano is a very attractive man."

"Really?" Angela was surprised her mother would notice such a thing, as devoted to Sam as she was.

Her blue eyes bright, she nodded enthusiastically. "I think he looks like Cesar Romero. You know, the dead movie actor?"

An image of dark skin, white hair, and a great smile materialized. "I'm glad you're making friends."

"There's no sin in looking, is there? I'm not dead yet. A woman can look if she wants to."

Angela was surprised by her mother's vehemence. "I'm not sure Dad would feel the same way, Ma. I think it's cute he's still jealous after all these years."

"The world is ending, Angela. I've been thinking a lot about it, and . . ."

No surprise there. "And what?"

Rosalie shook her head, but she had a peculiar look on her face that worried Angela. "Nothing. Come on. Let's go finish lining the shelves with the oilcloth."

SEVEN

*What's the difference between a lawyer
and a vulture?*
The vulture doesn't get Frequent Flyer points.

Goldman's had improved dramatically since Angela's
first glimpse of the neighborhood department store, which
was located on Eastern Avenue, just a short walk from
Little Italy and her office.

Tasteful designer clothing now decorated the storefront window according to season, thanks to Annie
Russo, who was half owner of the store. The hideous
garments that were once featured prominently—a man's
white polyester suit, à la *Saturday Night Fever*, came to
mind—had been replaced with more current fashions.

Even the mannequins were new. The previous ones
had been stolen during a series of robberies. But being
the determined woman she was, Annie had convinced
her father to replace them, which had been no easy feat.
Sid Goldman had not been in favor of anatomically correct mannequins. And he wasn't big on spending money,
either. But he'd finally given in to his only daughter's
demands.

When she'd first arrived in Baltimore, Angela hadn't
done much shopping at Goldman's, preferring instead to
order her clothing online. But since Annie had taken over
the merchandise buying, and because of her marriage to
Joe, Angela wanted to show her support by shopping at
the store.

As a working member of the community, she believed

strongly in spending her dollars where they would do the most good.

Waving enthusiastically when she spotted Angela entering the store, Annie walked toward her, smiling widely. The woman still dressed somewhat outrageously—today she wore red leather pants, a black cashmere sweater, and spiked heels—but she'd gone back to her natural dark brown hair color.

Annie had previously colored her short hair to match her moods—pink, red, lavender, you name it. Her present conservative color was a good indication that she had grown more settled since her marriage to Joe; she was definitely happier.

"Angela, how have you been?" Annie asked, hugging her. "I haven't seen you in ages. Where have you been hiding yourself?"

Angela was embarrassed to admit, even to herself, that she hadn't seen Annie since her wedding. "I know, and I'm sorry. I've been working hard, trying to get my practice going, and I haven't had a lot of extra time to shop. But rest assured, you're getting all of my business. No more online shopping for me."

Nodding approvingly, Annie said, "Good girl. Sid will be pleased to hear it. Though our Web site is up and running if you can't get into the store to shop. Tess is in charge of it."

"How is Tess? Does she still like living with your parents?" Tess Romano had been one of the teens Joe had taken under his wing when the young woman's alcoholic parents could no longer care for her.

Since becoming involved at the New Beginnings Crisis Center, which was located next door to Goldman's, and where she worked part-time handling the legal side of things while Joe tended to the counseling, Angela had met a lot of great kids. Some had been in trouble with the law, while others, like Tess, came from abusive or neglectful families. They all needed counseling, but more important, they needed love and someone to care about them.

The experience had given her new insight into what her mother and father must have gone through trying to raise two teenage girls and keep them out of trouble. She had new respect for parenting. She only hoped that she could do half as good a job as Sam and Rosalie when her baby arrived.

"Yes, she's crazy about them," Annie replied. "And my mom's in seventh heaven. Gina loves having another daughter to boss around, and you know Sid's nuts about her. Tess has Pop wrapped around her little finger. If she wants a day off from the store, he gives it to her, no questions asked. I, on the other hand, am given the third degree and made to feel guilty." She rolled her eyes. "*Oy vey!* Parents!"

Angela laughed. "Amen to that. I just came from helping my mother put oilcloth in her cupboards. Can you believe it? She's still so old-fashioned in many ways."

"Joe told me your parents had just moved here from Boston. How do you feel about that?"

"Resigned. There's nothing much I can do about it anyway, so I may as well be happy they're here. You know how it is."

"Boy, do I."

"What's going on with your cousin? Donna must be lonely since you and Tess moved out."

"Donna has her own apartment now, and a job, if you can believe that. She's working at Santini's Butcher Shop." Annie's smile filled with satisfaction. "There is a just God after all."

Angela was surprised by the news. Donna Wiseman was not a self-motivating individual; in fact, she had never worked a day in her life. "I'm glad to hear Donna's gaining some independence. Wonder how she and Lou are getting along."

"Like oil and water. And Nina Santini is royally pissed that her son hired Donna without consulting her first. She's making Donna's life miserable." Annie smiled. "Hey, what can I say? Paybacks are tough."

"*Hmmm.* Sounds like a trip to the butcher shop is in order."

"So how are things going with Mary's custody case?" Annie asked. "Do you anticipate any problems? I hope not, because losing Matt would kill Mary and Dan."

Still smarting from her recent deposition bout with John, Angela's lips thinned a fraction. "Just with opposing counsel. Do you know John Franco?"

Annie screwed up her face in disgust. "Yes, we dated way back when," she said, and Angela's brows shot up. "I was very disappointed when Joe told me he would be representing that bitch, Sharon Gallagher. The woman is nothing but trouble. How can he even think about taking their side against Mary? She's his cousin, for chrissake!"

"Don't be too hard on him, Annie. I suspect John . . . er . . . Mr. Franco had no choice in the matter. His partner just got out of the hospital, and Charles Rothburg was a client of their firm before this case was passed to him. I'd say his hands are tied."

"I can't believe you're defending him. If my mother-in-law heard you say such a thing she'd knock you off that pedestal she's placed you on." Annie's smile turned mischievous. "I might be tempted to tell her. Sophia wanted you to marry Joe, you being a lawyer, Italian, and Catholic—the triple threat, the triumvirate."

"I'm not defending John Franco." Okay, maybe she was, just a little. But the poor guy was under attack. And though she didn't want to get in the middle of a family squabble, she couldn't stand by and watch him become a pariah in his own family.

"I'm just trying to see all sides of the situation. That's

what lawyers do. We're not supposed to prejudge. At least we try not to.

"And I know by now Sophia has found out that you are the better choice for Joe. One has only to look at the two of you together to see how perfect you are for each other, and how happy."

"If you think Sophia would admit that, you're crazy. I think she's hoping Joe will come to his senses and return to the church," Annie said, peering over Angela's shoulder at the man who had just entered the store, her eyes widening in appreciation.

"John's cute, isn't he? He has a body that . . . well, as a happily married woman I must refrain from commenting further, but it's awesome."

Angela nodded, unaware that the man they discussed was walking in their direction. "He's a major hunk. But I'm trying to keep my perspective. I won't allow anything to interfere with my representation of the Gallaghers. I intend to win this case." And John was a distraction she didn't need right now.

"That's what I like to hear! I hope you kick ass, big-time. You've got the whole family behind you, and that's a formidable thing. I fear John won't be so lucky."

"Won't be so lucky about what?" he asked, sidling up next to Angela with a smile that was pure, unadulterated sexuality.

Just friends, Angela! she reminded herself. *Major distraction. Complication.*

"We meet again, Angela," he said, his deep voice sending shivers of awareness down her spine despite her resolve to ignore his finer attributes.

"I guess you two have met." A speculative gleam entered Annie's eyes as she studied Angela and John together, and Angela grew quite nervous that Annie would read more into their relationship than existed.

"Aside from our professional meetings, Angela and I seem to be in the habit of running into each other."

"Must be fate."

Suddenly uncomfortable at Annie's remark, Angela said, "Well, I'd better get back to the office. I've got a million and one things to do. But it was great seeing you again, Annie. Let's have lunch soon."

"Leave? But you haven't bought anything!" Annie protested. "And I just got in a shipment of wool coats."

"Maybe next time. I really just came in to see you. And now I'm going to run next door and say hi to Joe before I head back to the office. There are a few things I need to discuss with him." Like her pregnancy. As her employer, and friend, Joe deserved an explanation.

"What are you, the Russo *consigliere*?" John asked, a teasing twinkle in his eye.

Angela smiled. "Something like that." Turning on her heel, she walked out the door.

"Why do you think Angela took off in such a hurry?" Annie pressed. "Your presence seemed to unnerve her."

John shrugged. "Beats me. Unless she didn't like the way things went down during the depositions this morning. I was a bit rough on her witnesses. But that's my job."

"I'm pissed at you, John Franco. And I think you know why."

John did, but he didn't feel like having his ass chewed off again. Once a day was quite enough.

"I'm not going to lecture you; that's not my style. I just want you to know how disappointed I am that you're taking sides against my best friend, who happens to be my sister-in-law, who happens to be your cousin. I feel betrayed and angry, and so do a lot of other people."

Sighing, John weaved impatient fingers through his hair. "Sophia and Flora have already paid me a visit. They're putting a curse on me."

Annie's smile was filled with delight. "You are in deep shit, Franco. I almost feel sorry for you. But you brought this on yourself, so I don't."

"Yeah, well, that's a matter of interpretation. So, are you so pissed off that you won't help me pick out a couple of new suits? Pete said I should ask you for help."

"What kind of suits do you have in mind?" she asked with an obvious lack of enthusiasm.

"I guess we can start with the hair shirts and work from there."

"Angela asked me not to be hard on you, John, but I'm finding that request rather difficult. I'll help you with the suits because you're a customer, and because the explanation I would be forced to give my father if I refused would be too difficult. But don't expect me to forget that you're now the enemy."

"Angela defended me?" John arched a brow, pleased by the revelation. "Interesting."

"So you've noticed she's a babe beneath her conservative suits and goody-two-shoes demeanor, huh? You're not as dumb as you look, Franco."

"Yeah, I noticed, the same way I noticed you were a smart, sensitive woman beneath your Madonna outfits and weird hair colors."

"You always were a silver-tongued devil. Maybe you should direct your charm where it'll do you some good. You could do a lot worse than Angela DeNero. I'm sure you already have."

Annie's knowing smile ticked John off. *Damn Pete and his big mouth!* He had obviously told her about Danielle. "I'm not looking for anything permanent. I like my life just the way it is—uncomplicated." And things with Angela were definitely complicated at the moment. Real complicated.

"Yeah, that's what all men say until Cupid comes

along and slaps them silly alongside the head when they least expect it."

"Is that what happened to my cousin?"

Annie shook her head. "I'm taking full credit for Father Joe's fall from grace, thank you very much."

John's gaze flitted over Annie's extraordinary body, beautiful face, and sassy smile. The poor bastard never had a chance, he decided.

"Oh, so the prodigal son finally shows his face. You know how to break a mother's heart, don't you?"

Groaning inwardly, John plastered on a smile as he entered his parents dry cleaning establishment. He was determined to be pleasant, even if it killed him. And as he watched his mother's lips thin, he knew death was close at hand.

"Hi, Mom," he said, setting his white dress shirts down on the front counter. "Light starch, like before, please."

"Light starch?" Adele Franco's eyes widened in disbelief. "Light starch? You've wreaked havoc in the neighborhood, in our lives, and all you can say is 'light starch'? I am cursed among women!" She crossed herself, though John knew his mother hadn't stepped foot in a church in over thirty years. Not since her "sainted" brother had died from pneumonia. God had been blamed for Uncle Phil's untimely death. And now that Pete had come out of the closet, He was taking the rap for that, too.

"I take it you've heard from Aunt Sophia?" He was almost afraid to hear her reply. Sophia enjoyed making trouble, lived for it, in fact.

"Of course I've heard. Do you think Sophia Russo's going to keep quiet about something so important? Do you think she's going to miss her chance to tell me that my son is involved in the scandal of the century? I got an earful, I'll tell you that. What were you thinking? Have you lost your mind?"

John fought to keep his temper in check. He knew from experience that it was pointless, not to mention frustrating as hell to argue with his mother. She always had the last word. "Last time I looked, my mind was just where I left it. Where's Dad?"

"Out delivering cleaning orders. He'll be back soon. Why? Do you think he'll take your side in this? Because he won't." She pushed graying curls away from her face. At sixty-four, Adele Franco was starting to show her age. The unpleasant, permanent scowl she wore had etched age lines into her oval face, giving her a pinched, wrinkled appearance, somewhat like a prune, but not nearly as sweet.

There was no doubt in John's mind that Robert Franco would stand firm with his wife. It had been that way John's entire life, so why should he think it would be any different now? "I'm tired of explaining myself, Mom. You'll just have to trust that I'm doing what I have to do and leave it at that."

The front door buzzer rang just then. His mother swallowed what she was going to say and greeted the elderly white-haired gentleman who had just entered. "Hello, Mr. Fabrizi. It's nice to see you again. How's your arthritis today?"

"Hurts like hell, but I'm still breathing, so I can't complain. I got a stain on my new suit. You fix?" He placed the garment on the counter, next to John's shirts.

"Of course we'll fix it. For thirty years we've been removing stains. It'll be like new after we're done, you'll see." She proceeded to write up the ticket. "Have you met my son, Mr. Fabrizi? John is our second oldest."

The old man turned to stare at John through red-rimmed, watery eyes, then squinted. "You the doctor?"

John shook his head. "No, sir. I'm the attorney."

Mr. Fabrizi considered that for a moment before saying, "What do you call five thousand dead lawyers at the bottom of the ocean?" He paused for effect. "A good start." Pleased with himself, he chuckled, tipped his fedora to Adele, and departed.

"Ha, ha, ha." John shook his head as he watched the old geezer leave. "As if I haven't heard that one a thousand times before."

"People don't like lawyers. They think they're all crooks."

"Some are, I imagine, just like some doctors deserve to be sued for malpractice," he pointed out. "There's good and bad in every line of work."

Adele ignored the reference to the sainted medical profession. "Michael, Linda, and the kids are coming for dinner tonight. Do you want to come, too? I'm making tortellini."

He shook his head. "I've got too much work to do." At least that wasn't a total lie. "Another time, okay?"

"That's what you always say. But you never come over to visit your mother. The only time I see you is when you come in to drop off your laundry."

"You'll have a houseful with Mike's three kids. I doubt I'll be missed." Unless she was looking for a target to toss her barbs at, which was a likely possibility.

"He's bringing over slides of their last trip to Italy. Your brother goes to such wonderful places. But he should. He works hard, saving lives. A man should reap the rewards of his profession."

"Gee, sorry I have to miss that." *Not!* "Well, guess I'd better be going."

"Why do you have to rush off? We've hardly said two words to each other. How's your brother? Is he still with that man?"

"Pete's doing just great. He seems very happy with Eric, who, by the way, is a fabulous cook. I had dinner over there not long ago. You should see what they've done to their condo, Mom. It looks really nice. It would make Pete really happy if you visited."

Horrified by the suggestion, Adele shook her head. "My son is living in sin. How can you expect me to go over there and condone such an arrangement?"

"Because he's your son and he loves you."

"Peter is such a disappointment. I don't know what I did to deserve this. I gave you kids the best of everything. I tried to be a good mother. How could he choose to be a homosexual?"

"I doubt he chose to, Mom."

"It's the talk of the neighborhood. I can't hold my head up anymore. You should see the looks Nina Santini gives me when I go to the butcher shop. Like it's all my fault that my boy turned out queer."

John hated that word and tried to hold his temper in check. "If you love Pete, then you'll accept him for who and what he is. He loves you, Mom. Why can't you bend a little?"

To her credit, Adele looked conflicted. "Even if I wanted to go, your father would never agree. It is one thing to have Peter come to the house, but to go and see him living with another man . . . It breaks a mother's heart. When you have children you'll understand."

"Then I'm sorry for you, Mom, because you're going to lose your youngest son. Don't make Pete choose between you and the man he loves. You'll come out on the losing end."

"What do you know of such things, Johnny? Of course you'd take your brother's side in this. You were always sticking up for him, from when you were little boys."

"I love Pete. And I'm not going to stop loving him, or seeing him, because he's gay."

"This from a man who goes against his own blood in public?"

"That's right, Mom. But at least I was forced into taking sides against my cousin. What's your excuse for going against your own son?"

EIGHT

What do you get when you cross a lawyer with another lawyer?
Nothing. There are some things that not even nature permits.

"I'm sorry I let you talk me into this," Angela whispered to Wanda, who was standing beside her in line. They were waiting to get their name tags for the annual Maryland Bar Association dinner, and Angela was already dreading the event. "I hate these kind of functions." And now that she was pregnant she couldn't consume any alcohol to take the edge off her nervousness.

God, the idea of listening to all those speeches stone sober was enough to make her catatonic!

"They're a necessary evil, if you want to get referrals for your business," Wanda advised. "So smile, stick your chest out, and act like you're having a good time. You look gorgeous. You'll probably attract the attention of some devastatingly handsome attorney tonight. I feel it in my bones."

She had already attracted the attention of a handsome attorney, Angela thought. John had called last evening to invite her to the dinner, but she had turned down his request.

Charles Rothburg, the newly elected vice president of the Association, was going to be here tonight, and she didn't want to provide him with any ammunition that could be used against her in court. Her friendship with John could cause speculation, which is what she wanted to avoid at all costs.

John had been disappointed by her refusal to accompany him, which had bolstered her flagging spirits, for some ridiculous reason that she didn't care, or dare, to address. They had chatted over an hour on the phone, about everything and nothing, the way friends do, and she found that she enjoyed sharing things with him.

"Oh, go ply your voodoo somewhere else, Wanda. I don't feel a thing except tired. I should have never worn high heels; they're killing my feet. And I think my dress is too short." The black sleeveless knit looked attractive on her, but it was nonetheless too short, and probably too tight, not that she was showing yet.

But she would be soon, and then she'd be forced to deal with buying maternity clothes. Angela had already promised herself that nothing she purchased would be pleated or have bows attached. She refused to look like Betty Boop just because she was pregnant.

Wanda shot her a disbelieving look. "Honey, if I had legs like yours, I wouldn't be worried about the length of my skirt. Be proud you've got great legs to show off.

"I'm a firm believer in a woman displaying her best attributes to full advantage." Wanda pointed to her ample chest. "Is this not great cleavage? The Grand Tetons have nothing on my boobs. And yours aren't exactly shabby, either."

"You're just saying that so I won't be mad at you for dragging me here tonight. And why would anyone spare me a second glance while I'm standing next to you? You look like some exotic jungle creature. I love that leopard-print suit. It looks wonderful on you."

Angela sighed, thinking she'd never have the courage to wear animal prints. "I guess I'm just too conservative. I tend to drag out my same old black and go with it."

"That's because you like fading into the background. You need to be a little more flamboyant. It would do wonders for your self-esteem."

Angela's eyes widened at her friend's observation, which hit a little too close for comfort. Being center stage was not something she felt comfortable with, the exception being when she was in court and in front of a jury. Then she became Clarence Darrow and Helen Hayes all rolled into one dynamic orator.

"There's nothing wrong with my self-esteem. I don't know what gave you that impression." Did she come across as some pathetic creature, some needy, vulnerable woman? The Madame Bovary of Baltimore?

"I'm not criticizing you, Angela. I'm just saying that if it had been me who'd been dumped by my fiancé, I might feel a little less self-assured about myself. And you shouldn't. That asshole did you a big favor. You'll find Mr. Right one of these days."

Angela's face twisted in disgust. "God, Wanda, you're starting to sound like my mother! Not a good thing, I assure you. Why does everyone assume that a woman needs a man in her life? You, of all people, shouldn't be talking about lasting relationships. Didn't you tell me not long ago that you thought Kyle Stevens was getting too serious?"

At the mention of Kyle, Wanda's face radiated pure contentment. "Yes. But damn, that man is good in bed. He's got magic hands, magic lips . . . I should marry him for how he makes me feel."

"So why didn't you invite Kyle to come tonight?"

"Kyle's meeting me here later, after the boring stuff is done, and before the dancing begins. Why subject the poor guy to a mediocre meal and tedious legal talk?"

"I wonder what they'll be serving for dinner."

"Roast beef. They always serve roast beef at these things. Roast beef or chicken breasts. I have a theory that all hotel chefs once served in the military as navy cooks."

A representative of the Bar Association came up just then to show them to their table. He appeared to be in his mid-twenties; Angela figured him for a third-year law student.

The round table had been set for six and was situated smack dab in the center of the Radisson Hotel ballroom, but as yet no one else had been seated. Overhead the muted crystal chandeliers cast a soft glow, and some guy up onstage was testing the microphone, which made irritating static noises every time he tapped it. Wanda set her purse on the chair next to her to save it for Kyle.

"I just hope we don't get stuck with some stuffy old lawyer who's been around for eons and wants to pontificate on how the judicial system is going to hell in a handbasket," Angela said. "Or worse, some stud who thinks he's God's gift to women."

"Speaking of studs," Wanda's voice took on a breathless quality, "look who's walking in our direction. Now, there's a man who knows how to dress. Lord have mercy! I think my glands are tap dancing."

A bad feeling centering in the pit of her stomach, Angela shut her eyes, refusing to look. She didn't have to; she knew by the way the air had suddenly become charged whom Wanda was gushing over. But just to make certain, she lifted one eyelid, then sucked in her breath at the sight of John in a tuxedo. He flashed her a heart-stopping grin that made her toes turn downward.

"You look lovely tonight, Angela. Hope you don't mind if we sit together," he said, pulling out the chair next to her and seating himself, assuming she hadn't brought a date. She hadn't. But still, he should have at least asked if the seat was taken.

No doubt he felt sorry for her, thought she was pathetic. That was probably the reason he had invited her to the dinner in the first place. A pity date. Well, she was more glad than ever that she had turned him down.

Just because she was unmarried and pregnant— Okay, so maybe she was pathetic, but still. . . .

Angela was about to reply when Wanda, every one of her ivories flashing, butted in. "I'm Wanda Washington. Angela and I share office space. Nice to meet you, John."

"Angela didn't mention that she had a partner. What type of law do you practice?"

"Oh, we're not partners. We just share expenses and occasionally help each other out on cases. My specialty is discrimination in the workplace."

"Sounds interesting," he said.

Two attorneys Angela had never met seated themselves at their table, and she was able to ignore John momentarily and talk to the newcomers about legal issues, the weather, and other mundane matters. But she couldn't help the strange magnetic pull that compelled her to turn her attention back to the handsome man beside her.

He was really extraordinary looking. *Eat your heart out, Russell Crowe!* Those deep blue eyes could melt arctic glaciers.

Too bad things were the way they were. Though even if she hadn't been pregnant, they'd still have the custody case between them. Some things just weren't meant to be.

John and Wanda were still engrossed in conversation, and Angela sat back, listening to the deep resonance of his voice as he offered an opinion on a recent Supreme Court ruling. He had a very nice voice, strong and clear. And she had no doubt that he used it to his advantage in court.

And when whispering sweet nothings in a woman's ear. *Shut up! Shut up! Shut up!*

Wanda reached for the bottle of wine that the waiter had placed on the table and began to fill everyone's glasses. "We may as well make good use of this," she said. "We're paying through the nose for it. Can you imagine the Association having the balls to charge fifty dollars a head for this shindig? They must think we actually make a living at what we do."

Angela covered her glass when Wanda attempted to fill it. "None for me, thanks. I'm . . . I'm on a diet." She glanced pleadingly at John, who picked up the thread.

"Yeah, wine is really loaded with calories. Can't blame you for not wanting any."

"What? You love zinfandel. Come on, Angela. Let me pour you just one glass. Wine isn't that fattening, and it'll help you relax. You've been on edge all evening."

"I don't need to relax. And I don't need any wine." Why didn't Wanda just keep quiet!

"Well, I think you do. Now be a good girl and listen to Dr. Washington."

"Relax, Wanda. I don't think Angela wants any wine," John said.

"Of course she does."

Shaking her head at her friend's obtuseness, Angela took a deep breath as she felt her anxiety mounting and said, "I'm not feeling well. Please excuse me. I need to find the ladies' room," then rose from her seat.

John stood when she did, a look of deep concern on his face. "Do you need some help?"

"No! Thank you." She was grateful for his support, but mortified nonetheless, especially since this was the second time she'd felt nauseated in his presence. "I'll be fine."

John watched Angela hurry off, then turned to Wanda, who was staring after her friend in puzzlement. "Maybe you should go after her. Angela might have the flu or something."

"She was complaining the other day about not feeling well." Suspicion entered the black woman's eyes. "Maybe I should go and see what's what. Order more wine, John. Angela and I will be right back."

Wanda found Angela in the ladies' lounge, seated on a stool in front of the mirror, and looking as pale as death.

Her eyes widened in alarm. "Honey, you really are sick. I'll take you home right away."

Angela shook her head. "I was feeling so much better, but then I got nervous when you started pouring the wine, and I guess . . ."

Sitting down beside her, Wanda took Angela's cold, clammy hand in her own. "I'm confused, honey, because I don't think you have the flu. And your skinny ass tells me that you're not on any diet. So that leaves me to draw only one or two other conclusions: You have a terminal illness that you haven't told me about, or you're—"

"Pregnant. I was going to tell you, Wanda, but first I needed to get used to the idea myself."

Her friend's dark eyes filled with compassion and understanding. "That's why you didn't want the wine? Well, hell, girl, congratulations!" Wanda grabbed hold of Angela and hugged her to her chest. "How long have you been carrying this burden around with you?"

"A couple of weeks. I wasn't sure at first. I really thought I had the flu. But when the symptoms didn't go away I bought one of those home pregnancy kits, and it confirmed my suspicions."

"Have you seen a doctor?"

"I have an appointment first thing Monday morning."

"Good. You need to be taking prenatal vitamins, drinking lots of milk, and taking better care of yourself than you've been doing. What time is your appointment? I'll go with you."

"You would do that for me? Oh, Wanda, I—" Angela covered her face with both hands and started crying. She'd been dreading going to the doctor alone, which was probably why she'd waited so long to make the appointment. "Thank you. You're a good friend, and here I've been hiding secrets from you. I feel just awful."

"Do you want to go home? I can call Kyle and tell him that there's been a change of plans."

Angela wiped her cheeks with the back of her hand. "Don't you dare! I feel much better just having talked to you. I got stressed out, that's all. John makes me kind of nervous. I don't know quite what to make of him, and—"

Wanda smiled. "Well at least we know your hormones are in good working order, if he's having that kind of effect on you. You could do worse."

"The last thing I need in my life right now is a man, so don't go getting any ideas where John is concerned. We're just friends. This baby and I are going to be just fine," she patted her abdomen, "by ourselves."

"I know that, but you shouldn't try to go through this alone. My sister's had three kids. I know how hard it is. You need support at a time like this, Angela. You need to be surrounded by people who care about you. I care about you. And so does your family."

"They don't know."

Wanda seemed surprised by the admission. Angela had always spoken very highly of her parents. "Well, if you think they won't be thrilled to death, you're just plain wrong. My sister Charisse got pregnant with her first child by some sweet-talking guy who sold her a set of tires for her car and then a bill of goods about himself. She was afraid to tell my parents, but when they learned they were going to be grandparents for the first time, they were overjoyed. They weren't happy about the circumstances, but they were supportive. Just as I'm sure your parents will be when you tell them the news."

Unfortunately, Angela didn't share Wanda's optimism. Sam DeNero had a wicked temper. Not that he'd ever been abusive; he wasn't like that, didn't need to be. Her dad just flashed a look of disappointment, and Angela felt duly punished and ashamed.

"Thanks for being my friend." As much as she cherished her male acquaintances, there was nothing like having a woman, a girlfriend, to confide in.

"Oh, shut up! You're going to make me start crying, and then I'll have raccoon eyes when Kyle shows up. Speaking of which, we'd better get back. I'm starving, and at this point I could eat shoe leather."

"And that's exactly what they'll probably be serving," Angela quipped, kissing Wanda's cheek before the pair headed back to the ballroom.

"You haven't eaten much of your dinner, Angela," John said, polishing off the last of his crème brûlée. The color had returned to her cheeks, but she still looked upset, maybe even a little depressed, which worried him. "Are you sure you're feeling okay?"

"I'm fine. I'm just not very hungry."

"Would you like to dance? Wanda and Kyle seem to be having a good time out on the dance floor." John watched the tall black man swing Wanda about to the strains of "Every Breath You Take." "He's a nice guy, for a doctor."

"I take it you're not enamored of physicians."

"My older brother's a doctor, a cardiologist. I guess I've just had the whole doctor thing shoved down my throat my whole life and I've grown tired of it."

"The sibling rivalry you were telling me about."

He nodded. "And I've allowed it to ruin my relationship with Mike, and that's not fair to him. It's not his fault that he's the apple of my parents' eye. I'm the one that has to learn to deal with it."

"Maybe you should talk to him, explain how you feel."

"Maybe I will. But right now I'd rather talk to you about whether you're going to dance with me. It's not country-western, but I'm willing to give it a shot."

He liked country-western, too? The man was too perfect for words. She sighed.

"John, normally I would jump at the chance. I absolutely love dancing. But I still don't think it's wise that we socialize beyond our work environment."

He held out his hand. "Oh, come on. I promise not to seduce you out on the dance floor. However, all bets are off once I get you to myself."

His overconfidence astounded her, but her cheeks flushed with pleasure, just the same. "That's not ever going to happen, so don't hold your breath."

"Why? Are you involved with someone? I got the impression from what you said the other day that you weren't."

"That's really none of your business. But the answer is no, I'm not." And she had no intention of getting involved again, especially with him.

What she felt for John Franco was lust, pure and simple, an intense physical attraction, nothing more. She had entered into her last relationship for all the wrong reasons; she could see that now. She'd been in love with the idea of Bill, but not with Bill, the man. Oh, she had loved him, but she hadn't been *in love* with him. And she wasn't going to make the same mistake twice.

"Then don't be too sure it's not going to happen, Counselor. I'm a very persistent man. And I like getting my way."

Against her better judgment, and because she'd been wondering what it would be like to be held in his arms, Angela said, "Just one dance. But don't blame me if Charles Rothburg fires you on the spot for dancing with the opposition. I'm sure his views on the subject of fraternization are in keeping with mine."

"I'm not worried. If Rothburg doesn't like it, he knows what he can do."

"My, my, Counselor, are you this forceful and dynamic in court?"

His grin was blatantly sexual. "In court and various

other places." Leading her out on the dance floor, John wrapped his arms about Angela and drew her to his chest.

Angela's pulse quickened. She had a good enough imagination to know what he meant, and being held in his arms was heavenly. "You dance very well," she said.

"Only if I have the right partner."

"Are you flirting with me, Counselor?"

He grinned. "Damn straight. About time you noticed."

Her brow wrinkled in confusion. "But why?"

"Why what?"

"Why are you bothering? You know nothing can come of it. I'm pregnant, remember?"

He pulled her closer. "You worry too much. Has anyone ever told you that? Why not enjoy the moment and let tomorrow take care of itself."

Her laughter was caustic. "I tried that once. It didn't work out."

"Maybe you didn't try it with the right guy."

The music ended, saving her from answering. "Thanks for the dance. I guess I should think about going home."

John glanced at Wanda and Kyle, huddled at the table, deep in conversation. "I think your ride is preoccupied. Why don't you let me take you home? I promise to be on my best behavior."

She shook her head. "I don't think—"

"I'll buy us a pizza and we can pig out."

At the mention of food Angela's stomach grumbled. "Not fair. You're cheating." She grinned up at him. "Okay."

"It's a sad day in a man's life when he has to resort to bribery with pizza to get a woman to consent."

Laughing at his woebegone expression, she grabbed his hand. "Come on. Let's say farewell to the lovebirds. My appetite is back with a vengeance."

*　　*　　*

"I don't think I can wait a moment longer. Hurry and take it out."

John laughed, wishing Angela was talking about making love, not eating pizza. He hadn't been able to think of much else except making love to her, and he knew he was heading into dangerous territory. He'd offered friendship, but was wondering now if that would be enough. He had a feeling it wouldn't.

"*Mmmm.* This is wonderful." She licked sauce from the five fingers of her right hand, one at a time, and his gut tightened in response.

"You're the only woman I know that can make eating pizza look X-rated."

She blushed, but didn't stop eating. "You say the most outrageous things, John."

"But they're all true." He scooted closer to her and reached out his finger to wipe away a piece of cheese that clung to her lower lip, placing it in his mouth. "It tastes even better now than it's been on your lips."

Noting the passion flaring brightly in his eyes, Angela paused in mid-bite, hoping to make light of the moment. "John, quit teasing. You're the only man I know who would flirt with a pregnant woman."

"You don't look very pregnant, just all woman." He took the pizza out of her hands and set it on the table. "I'm going to kiss you, so don't panic."

She shook her head to refuse, but he pulled her forward anyway, his lips stopping the protest on her lips.

Like a match to dry kindling, heat sprang between them, flaring bright and intense. John's hands were suddenly everywhere, in Angela's hair, down her back, on her breasts, kneading the soft flesh through the stretchy fabric of her dress.

The thought occurred to Angela that what they were doing was wrong. But oh, God, it felt so right! And at the moment, with his lips devouring and his hands making magic, she just didn't care.

Of course, her brief lapse of sanity lasted only as long as the feel of her zipper being lowered. She pulled back, her eyes wide with shock.

"Stop, John!"

"I want you, Angela."

She wanted him, too, but she wasn't foolish enough to think that this would last, that John's need for her would be anything more than a one-night stand. If and when she ever entered into another relationship, she wanted someone who would be in it for the long haul, a lifetime.

"I thought you wanted to be friends. You have an odd way of showing friendship."

Duly chastised, he released her, plowing agitated fingers through his hair. "Damn it! I'm sorry, Angela. I didn't mean for that to happen. I just couldn't help myself."

She reached up and patted his cheek. "I've never considered myself a femme fatale before, so thanks for bolstering my ego. But I don't need to complicate my life right now, and neither do you. I need a friend more than I need a lover."

Liar! Liar! Liar!

Shut up! Shut up! Shut up!

He nodded. "I understand. It won't happen again."

His declaration made her feel sad, but she knew it was for the best. But still, she couldn't help but wonder . . . What if?

"Everything looks just fine, Angela," Dr. Adams told her.

Theresa Adams had come very highly recommended by Angela's former physician back in Boston, and so far she had not been disappointed. Dr. Adams was young, pretty, and professional, seemed to know what she was doing, and had a lovely bedside manner to soothe Angela's anxiety, which was substantial.

"You appear to be about eight weeks along, give or take. It's hard to tell at this stage of the pregnancy. We could do an ultrasound to be more precise, but at this point, I don't think it's necessary. I'll know more by next month's visit." She drew a prescription pad out of her lab coat pocket and began writing.

"Until then, I want you to take the prenatal capsules I'm going to prescribe; they contain folic acid, which is very good for the baby. I'm also giving you a prescription for nausea. If you have any problems, don't hesitate to call."

The doctor told her when to make another appointment for, and then exited the room. Angela breathed a sigh of relief. She hadn't realized up until this moment how anxious she was to hear that the baby was okay, hadn't realized, in spite of the circumstances, and the problems she would face, personally and professionally, how much she was looking forward to having this child.

She pressed her hand to her abdomen and tears of joy sprang to her eyes. A baby grew inside her, a baby who would grow up and call her Mommy, a baby who would be hers alone to cherish.

Sliding off the table, she headed toward the dressing area just as a knock sounded at the examining room door. Wanda stuck her head in. "The doctor said I could come back and keep you company."

"Come in. I'll just be a minute."

"You sound excited. Is everything all right?"

Angela pulled the curtain aside and grinned. "Dr. Adams said the baby is doing fine. We're not sure of the due date yet, though I'm fairly certain I conceived the last time Bill and I were together."

"You seem happy, more at peace, than you were a few days ago."

"I am. I guess I just needed for this to be real. And now it is."

"Well, I know of a really good pediatrician when the time comes."

"I've already thought of asking Kyle, just not yet. I still want to keep this news under wraps until I've had time to tell my family." She would deal with that hurdle first, then move on to the professional side of things.

She wasn't sure if any of her clients, many of whom were Catholics, like herself, would object to having an unwed mother representing them. Italian Catholics were not liberal-minded people when it came to such things. She didn't think anyone would buy into a second immaculate conception.

"My lips are sealed. But don't wait too much longer to tell them. From here on out, that baby is going to start growing like it's been doused with Miracle-Gro, and your body will be changing dramatically. You'll be needing to shop for maternity clothes and larger underwear soon."

"Hey, I was in a good mood. Are you trying to depress me?"

Wanda laughed at the look of consternation on Angela's face. "Let's take the rest of the day off and go shopping. We can look at maternity stuff and maybe some things for the baby, too. Then we'll have lunch. My treat.

"I'm assuming aunt status with this kid. Imagine the questions he or she will be asked when everyone finds out that the kid's aunt is black. I can't wait."

Angela smiled. "You're crazy, you know that?"

"Certifiable, honey." Wanda linked her arm through Angela's. "Come on. You can tell me all about how John "the Stud" Franco performed on the dance floor while we drive to the mall."

Angela felt heat crawl up her neck. "We only had one dance. It was hardly a performance." Except, of course, for that damn delicious kiss. Now, that was a performance.

"You lie! Your face is as red as a beet. I'd say the handsome attorney got you a little worked up."

How humiliating that it was that obvious. She never should have danced with John, never should have allowed him to take her home. The man's touch had done strange and wonderful things to her.

Get over it!

John Franco is your opponent, Angela told herself. He's also a man who could have any woman he wants, and knows it. And she'd bet any amount of money that his interest in a pregnant woman, who would soon have stretch marks across her abdomen and a crying baby at her sagging breasts, would wane faster than she could say *ciao*.

NINE

*What's the difference between a lawyer
and a gigolo?*
A gigolo screws only one person at a time.

"Tony's out back in the yard, playing with the kids."
Marie kissed John's cheek, looking tired but happier
than the last time he'd seen her. "I'm so glad you came."

Wiping his shoes on the front jute mat before entering
the Stefano's modest brick home, he replied, "Me, too."

Inhaling deeply the scents of vanilla and chocolate, his
stomach rumbled. Tony's wife loved to bake, and the Stefano home always smelled of chocolate chip cookies, or
some other wonderful confection. He had a sweet tooth,
and nobody made chocolate chip cookies better than
Marie.

"Tony's been a bit depressed lately, which is normal
after these types of procedures, the doctor assured me.
But I know seeing you will cheer him up."

John had been so busy lately preparing for the custody
case and handling other pressing client matters that he
hadn't visited Tony in almost two weeks. Though they'd
kept in contact by phone almost every day, John had been
hesitant about discussing work-related matters, feeling
that his friend needed to rest and not become too involved
in details that might upset him. Tony, of course, asked re-
peatedly about the various cases they had been working
on before his attack and was displeased that John was
not more forthcoming with information.

But work wasn't the only thing on John's mind lately.
Since he had kissed Angela, he spent most of his time

thinking about her, wanting her. No matter how hard he tried, how many times he told himself that they were just friends, that he didn't want to be involved with anyone, he couldn't get her out of his mind. He had only to shut his eyes to recall quite vividly how she felt snuggled in his arms, how soft and perfect her breasts felt beneath his hands, how her lips tasted like sweet, ripe cherries.

They had fit together a little too perfectly for comfort.

There was chemistry between them; there was no denying it. A tight knot centered in his gut every time he got within five feet of her. He wanted to pursue Angela, to take her to bed and make love to her.

But to what end?

He wasn't really sure. He knew only that he had to have her.

He was pretty sure Angela felt the same attraction, though she did her best to deny it. But there was no denying what he saw in her eyes when he had kissed her: lust, passion, excitement. Whatever you wanted to call it, it was there.

With Angela still occupying his thoughts, John entered the Stefanos' backyard to find Tony pushing his young daughter, Katy, on the swing, while four-year-old Anthony Jr., whom everyone called AJ, played nearby in the sandbox with his bright yellow Tonka truck. "I see you've got plenty to occupy you these days, Stefano."

The man turned to look over his shoulder and waved, a smile lighting his face. "Hey, Johnny! I wasn't expecting you to drop over today. I thought you were swamped with paperwork."

"I am, but I felt the need to see your ugly mug again. It's been lonely in the office without you." For all their squabbling and needling each other, the place seemed empty and rather lifeless without his partner there.

"I can't wait to get back to work," Tony admitted, sighing deeply. "I love my kids, but I'm tired of coloring within the lines and playing with Legos, although AJ has taught me to make a space station that I'm pretty proud of."

John fought the urge to smile at the mental image of Tony seated cross-legged on the floor playing LEGOs with his son. It seemed so un-Tony-like.

Brown braids flying, Katy jumped off the swing and made a beeline for John's legs, wrapping herself around him like an ivy vine and jumping up and down as only a six-year-old can do. "Uncle Johnny! Uncle Johnny! I didn't know you was coming over. Am I still your bestest girl?"

"Of course you are." John swung the little girl up in his arms, making her squeal in delight, before bussing her cheek and asking, "Have you been a good girl, Katydid?"

"Uh-huh. But I'm not no bug, Uncle Johnny."

AJ came up just then, his hair and clothing full of sand, which would not make his mother happy, John was certain. "Me, too, Unca Johnny. I been a good boy, too."

"Hey, AJ!" John ruffled the youngster's hair. "So you kids have been good, huh?" They both nodded solemnly, knowing what was coming next. John always brought treats when he visited, and today was no exception.

Reaching into his jacket pocket, he pulled out two Snickers bars, and the kids' eyes widened in delight before they started jumping up and down again. "Ask your mom first before you eat them, okay? I don't want to spoil your dinner."

" 'Kay, Uncle Johnny," they shouted in unison, grabbing the candy bars and ripping off the wrappers as they rushed toward the house. "Mommy! Mommy! Look what we got!"

"You spoil them rotten, Johnny, and they love it."

"They're great kids. I still can't believe they came from you."

Tony smiled smugly. "It's all in the genes, my friend.

And Marie gets some of the credit." He led John to the redwood chairs with the faded green cushions that rested beneath the large oak tree, whose leaves had turned deep gold. John noted the yet-to-be-carved pumpkins piled up on the rear deck.

"So how are things at the office? I know Marie told you not to discuss work with me, but I need to know. All this quiet is driving me nuts. I can't take much more of it. Have some pity on an old friend, for chrissake, and fill me in on what's been going on."

"Everything's great. I had the preliminary meeting with the Rothburgs, and they didn't seem to have any problem with my representing them, so there's nothing for you to worry about. Like I told you, I'm handling things."

"And the Langley case?"

"Settled out of court for twenty thousand. The Langleys are happy as larks."

Tony nodded in approval. "And what about your family? Has that become a problem? I feel guilty as hell about the way everything went down, John. I know you didn't want anything to do with this case."

John weighed carefully whether or not he should confide the truth, opting for a softened version of it. "Nothing I can't handle. My aunt and grandmother are upset, but some of the other family members have been supportive." Sort of. At least Uncle Frank and Joe were still talking to him.

"And how did your cousin take the news?"

"I haven't spoken to Mary yet. But I did receive an invitation to attend the grand opening of her new restaurant, so maybe she's not too upset." Wishful thinking, he was sure.

"Yeah," Tony agreed. "She can't be that mad if she wants you to come to her party."

John had been floored when he had opened the

shamrock-embossed white envelope. He was still un-decided about whether or not he should, or would, at-tend. He couldn't help but think that the request had been sent in error and was some sort of mistake.

Why would Mary invite him to the opening of Danny Boy's if she were as upset as Sophia had indicated? It didn't make any sense. Unless, of course, his aunt had blown things totally out of proportion, which wasn't out of the realm of possibility, considering Sophia's usual M.O. His aunt wasn't happy unless she was stirring things up, which was most of the time.

"It'll all work out. Nothing for you to be concerned about," he told Tony, sounding far more confident than he felt. His family wasn't perfect, but it was the only one he had.

"I hate that everyone is trying to shelter me, like I'm going to go into cardiac arrest at the least little upset. Fuck! I'm as good as new, healthy as a horse. The doc said so."

"Glad to hear it." Though John knew better. Tony had several more weeks of rest and recuperation in front of him before he could come back to work. Marie would have his hide if he suggested differently.

"So how's your love life?" Tony asked. "At least you can fill me in on that. I doubt it'll be too traumatic for me to hear, unless, of course, it's really X-rated. Mine's been rated G, of late." His friend's sigh was filled with such disappointment and frustration that John almost smiled.

"Don't feel bad. Mine's been nothing to write home about, either. Danielle's pissed at me for canceling out on her a couple of weeks ago." No loss there, he'd decided. The thrill was beginning to wane. He and Danielle had very little to talk about outside of the bedroom, despite what he had told his brother. And with Angela now in the picture, he couldn't really see himself dating Danielle again.

Tony made a face. "Consider yourself lucky, pal. That woman's a ditz." He waited for John to continue, but when nothing more was forthcoming, he shook his head in disbelief. "That's it? No other women are lined up to take her place? Man, you must be out of practice."

John became thoughtful, Tony suspicious. "Come on, cough it up. This is your old buddy, remember? You can tell me. You've met someone, haven't you? I can tell by that secretive look on your face. It's the same look you got when you were thirteen and felt up Darlene Cusimano for the first time."

John smiled at the man's perceptiveness, and the memory. His thirteen-year-old, hormone-driven body thought it had died and gone to heaven that day, until his mother had caught him and Darlene making out, among *other* things, behind the garage. It was the *other* things that had really set her off. He hadn't realized until that day how loud his mother could scream.

"It's nothing like that. And I doubt you'll be too thrilled to hear about it anyway."

Tony's brows drew together in puzzlement, then suddenly a knowing look crossed his face. "Oh, Christ! You've fallen for Angela DeNero. You've fallen for the opposition."

"I haven't fallen for anyone, Stefano, so get over yourself. I just find Angela interesting and different than the other women I've been dating, that's all."

Tony had that *"well, duh!"* look on his face. "That's probably because the other women you've been dating are all airheads. This one actually has a brain. I can see how you would find that stimulating, Franco. Not to mention that Angela's a looker. But did you have to pick opposing counsel to lust after? Rothburg will go ape-shit if he finds out."

"Rothburg saw us dancing at the Bar Association dinner, but he didn't mention anything, one way or the other."

"Probably didn't know who she was."

John shrugged. "Maybe. I don't really care. It's none of the old bastard's business."

"Who are you kidding, John? It's a fucking conflict of interest, and you know it. I think it's a really bad idea to get involved with her. Things could get sticky if your relationship progresses past dancing."

"It already has." At least as far as he was concerned. "I intend to keep seeing her."

A pained look crossed Tony's face that had nothing to do with his surgery. "You know, I haven't had this much entertainment since I got my chest cut open. At least life's never dull with you around." After a moment's reflection, he added, "Maybe I should come back to work and take over the case, so there won't be a problem."

"Nice try, Stefano, but you know that's not going to happen. You just relax and enjoy the time off. Like I said, I'm handling everything just fine. There's nothing for you to worry about. What do I need to make you believe me, a written affidavit?"

"Since taking my stress management course I don't feel as upset as I normally would over this latest bombshell you've just dropped. I must be making progress."

"Must be."

"You staying for dinner? Marie will kill you if you don't."

John grinned. "I've already sniffed out the chocolate chip cookies she made for dessert, so yeah, I'm staying."

"Do you really think Angela DeNero will go out with you? From what I've heard, she plays it pretty much by the book."

"I guess you've never seen me turn on the old Franco charm, huh? It's pretty damn potent."

Rolling his eyes, Tony grabbed his chest. "Please, all this bullshit is going to make me have a relapse."

"That's what you get for poking that big Roman nose of yours where it doesn't belong."

"I always knew you were the forbidden fruit type, Adam . . . er . . . Johnny. Just be careful you don't bite off more of that apple than you can chew."

Angela rang Mrs. Mattuci's doorbell and waited. There was an autumn nip in the air. The wind was blowing the leaves off the trees, swirling them on the ground like a blender. She snuggled deeper into her black wool coat, wishing she'd taken the time to inspect the new stock of outerwear Annie had told her about.

Of course, if she really wanted to heat up quickly all she had to do was think about the soul-searing kiss she'd shared with John. She did, and was immediately wrapped in sunshine. Sighing deeply, she thought that at least she would have that memory to warm her cold, empty bed.

Well, there was always Winston, but he didn't count.

Angela could hear Hector barking, and then a few moments later the front door opened to reveal Mrs. Mattuci's bewildered smile. "Why, Miss DeNero, what a nice surprise."

"I probably should have called first, but I was in the neighborhood, and—"

"Don't be silly. Come in." She motioned her forward. "It's chilly outside. The wind is blowing to beat the band. A regular Winnie the Pooh day, wouldn't you say? I just made a fresh pot of coffee. It'll warm you right up."

Before she could respond that she could only stay a moment, Angela was ushered into the parlor, which was garishly decorated with red velvet upholstered furniture and gold tasseled drapery. It looked a little bit like she imagined a bordello might look: tawdry but elegant. Though she had a difficult time imagining Mrs. Mattuci in the role of madam.

"Please don't go to any trouble, Mrs. Mattuci," she

called out after her hostess, who had disappeared into the kitchen. "I'll only take up a moment of your time."

The older woman reappeared with a large silver tray adorned with an ivy-patterned china coffeepot and cups. "Mr. Mattuci and I don't get that many visitors these days. My husband's been in and out of the hospital for the past six months with cancer treatments—prostate, you know—and our friends don't call as often as they used to. Which is why, I guess, I've grown so attached to Hector. He's a wonderful companion."

"I'm sorry to hear about your husband's illness, Mrs. Mattuci. I didn't know. But I do have some news regarding Hector that I'm hoping will cheer you both."

"Really? Did you already file suit? That was fast."

Angela shook her head, and the woman's elation evaporated. "I've had several conversations with the owners of Doggie Delight. After they heard of our intention to bring suit for damages, they've made a settlement offer."

Mrs. Mattuci's eyes widened. "Oh?"

"Their attorney called this morning. It seems Mr. and Mrs. Kolnicki don't want any publicity that would adversely affect their dog grooming business and are prepared to offer you a check in the amount of fifteen hundred dollars to settle the matter."

"Fifteen hundred dollars!"

"I think it's a generous offer, considering that Hector wasn't permanently damaged, except for his feelings, of course," she added quickly when the woman opened her mouth to object.

"Well, I don't know. . . . It seems like a fair amount. What do you think, Hector?" she asked the dog, who slept soundly in front of the fireplace. When he didn't respond she posed the same question to Angela.

"If we pursue this in court, there are no guarantees we will win, Mrs. Mattuci. And the amount of legal and court fees you will incur if you should lose could prove expensive. It's my recommendation that you take the money they're offering."

Angela glanced at Hector, who was totally oblivious of the drama going on around him. Just as well, she thought. His baldness was enough for him to handle at the moment.

"All right, I'll take it. With Christmas just around the corner I can put the money to good use. And I was dreading a court proceeding anyway. From what I've seen on *Judge Judy*, they seem to be very unpleasant."

"A wise decision, Mrs. Mattuci. I'll call when the documents are ready to sign and the check is issued, and then you can drop by the office and we can finish up this matter. In the meantime, I've got a little something for Hector, to get him through this difficult time." Reaching into her briefcase, Angela withdrew a pink plastic bag and handed it to the surprised woman. "I hope I bought the right size."

Eyes wide, Mrs. Mattuci examined the red-and-green-plaid wool coat with matching tam o' shanter. "Oh, my! Well, it's just beautiful." She clutched it to her chest. "Thank you so much, Miss DeNero. That was so thoughtful of you. And I know Hector is going to love it."

"I figured if Hector wore a coat and hat, he might feel more like strutting his stuff around the neighborhood again."

"Oh, I'm sure he will. He's missed our daily walks. I just couldn't subject him to the humiliation, you understand?"

The older woman's smile was full of pleasure, and Angela was glad she had made the gesture. Setting her coffee cup down, she said, "Thank you for the coffee, but I really must be going now. I need to stop at the butcher shop on my way home."

Mrs. Mattuci made a face of disgust. "Santini's has a new girl working there," she warned, "and she's not very good. Last week I ordered two pork chops, and she gave me veal. Can you imagine? The two meats taste nothing alike, not to mention that the veal set me back a pretty penny."

"I have a feeling she's still learning the ropes," Angela said, knowing it was Annie's cousin Donna about whom she was talking.

"I guess. But you'd think a body would know the difference between ground beef and sausage. I made hamburgers last night, and they tasted awful." She lowered her voice and leaned in. "Mr. Mattuci had the runs all evening." She thought a moment. "Though that could have been from the chemo, I guess."

"Um, well, thanks for the tip. I'll try to remember that when placing my order." It was actually her mother's order. Rosalie had called on her cell phone, asking Angela to pick up her meat order since she was dining at her parents' house tonight.

"Oh, don't mention it, dear. And you should know that I intend to tell everyone I know what a wonderful attorney you are. I have a friend, Josephine Locarno, who has a bunion the size of a lemon on her left foot. Said she got it from a pair of shoes she bought at Wal-Mart. I told her to go see you. I think she wants to sue."

Angela DeNero, defender of dogs, bunions, and the bizarre.

Well, it could be worse, she decided. So far she hadn't met up with any aliens.

Of course, she hadn't been to the butcher shop yet. Annie's cousin Donna was pretty far out there.

Donna Wiseman had a reputation in the neighborhood as a Jewish American Princess, which Angela considered to be very unfair. It was true, she had somewhat of a princess complex, due to the fact that her mother and father had spoiled her outrageously while she was growing up, and her father had been providing for her support for the past thirty-three years. And yes, she was a bit spoiled and self-centered.

But she was also kindhearted, intelligent, and was trying her best to change her ways. Angela liked her and admired the fact that she'd made the effort.

So when she entered the butcher shop after leaving Mrs. Mattuci's house and heard the young woman being berated by the shop's owner, Nina Santini, a most unpleasant woman by anyone's standards, Angela grew furious.

"*Stupido!* You are a stupid, stupid girl! I don't know why my son wanted to hire you. Everyone knows you don't wrap raw chicken and meat together in the same package. You want to kill someone? Get me sued? Now unwrap everything, wash it off, and rewrap it in separate packages. Mrs. Goldman is coming by later to pick it up." The older woman cursed at Donna in Italian, not bothering to see who might be listening to her tirade, and then disappeared into the back room. She would have slammed the door, but it was the swinging type that waved back and forth.

Donna stared after her, defiance dancing in her eyes, but said nothing. She didn't need to; her fury spoke volumes.

"Good afternoon, Donna." Though seething at the harsh treatment she'd just witnessed, Angela plastered on a pleasant smile, unwilling to upset the woman further. "It's nice to see you again. How's the new job going?" As if she needed confirmation that it wasn't going well.

Making a rude face, Donna stuck her tongue out in Mrs. Santini's direction, and Angela's lips twitched. The young woman might not know much about meat and poultry, but she had spunk, and in many ways reminded Angela of her sister, Mia, who also had more spirit than common sense.

"Lou's mother hates me. She criticizes everything I do, and I'm trying really hard to learn. It's only been a few weeks since I started. I don't see how Mrs. Santini can expect me to learn everything in such a short time. Even Melanie Griffith's character Tess in *Working Girl* had more time to prove herself than I'm getting."

Yeah, and she got Harrison Ford, too!

"Have you spoken to Lou about it? Maybe he can talk to his mother, explain that you're trying your hardest, and tell her to ease up a little."

"Lou has talked to her, but not because of anything I said. I don't want to come between them and start trouble. I'm grateful to him for giving me this job. I was in a bind and needed to find something quickly."

There was a persistent rumor floating about that Donna's father had mysteriously disappeared, thereby cutting off her monthly allowance and leaving her vulnerable to eviction from her apartment. Since Donna hadn't confided her troubles to Angela, she had no intention of bringing it up, especially now, when the redhead was so upset.

"I admire you for trying so hard, Donna. Don't let Mrs. Santini's criticism undermine your good efforts. I'm sure Lou appreciates what you're doing."

She shrugged. "I thought I was spoiled until I met Lou. His mother dotes on him from morning till night, cooking for him, cleaning up after him, and he laps it up like a contented tomcat.

"I've learned from experience that that kind of smothering by a parent can be destructive. I told Lou what I thought, but he just laughed at me. He thinks I'm an airhead because I didn't go to college. He's a butcher, for godsake, not CEO of Microsoft! It's that whole pot and kettle thing."

"I'm sure that's not true. If it were, he wouldn't have hired you."

"Lou's taking business management classes over at the University of Maryland and needed someone to cover for him when he couldn't be here. There weren't a lot of candidates for the job—there's not a big future in meat markets these days, what with all the large grocery chains—so he was stuck hiring me."

Donna's self-esteem, which used to be quite healthy, had taken a big hit, which worried Angela. "Maybe you would be happier working somewhere else—Goldman's, for instance. I'm sure Annie—"

Shaking her head emphatically, the young woman's cheeks flushed slightly. "Been there, done that. It didn't work out."

"Oh? I'm sorry to hear that." Angela wondered what had happened. Donna looked positively ill at the reminder. "Well, I'm sure things will work out for you here. Lou's a very nice man."

"*Hmph!* You only think that because you don't have to work with him. He's a sexist pig. And he's always hitting on all the women who come in here, even the pregnant ones, like Mary and her sister, Connie. It's disgraceful. The man's a Neanderthal."

Hey, maybe there's hope for me yet, Angela thought. If Lou hit on pregnant women, maybe other men would—
Get over it!

"I'm sorry to go on about myself, Angela. Is there something I can help you with? We're having a sale on tripe—" Donna made a face "—pickled pig's feet—" she stuck her finger down her throat "—and for the normal residents of Little Italy, lamb chops, double cut and quite good. I made some last night for dinner, and they were actually edible."

Angela couldn't help but smile. There was just something so darn likeable about Donna. "My mom asked me to come by and pick up her meat order. It'll be under the name Sam DeNero."

The woman's eyes widened. "Ooooh, like Bobby D.? I

just loved him in *Meet the Parents*, though I thought the movie was kinda dumb and beneath his talent."

According to Annie, Donna's passion was Hollywood movie stars and television. She knew everything when it came to anything concerning entertainment trivia. "No, Robert DeNiro spells his name with an *i* not an *e*.

"Too bad. Even though he's older, he's still kinda hunky. I'd like to meet him, tell him how good he was in *Godfather II*. He auditioned for the first *Godfather*, you know, but didn't make the cut. Coppola was wise to keep him for the second movie. He sure was good-looking back then." Donna finished wrapping the meat order, placing it on the counter.

"I continue to be astounded by how much you know about these kinds of things. If I ever play Trivial Pursuit again, I want you on my team," Angela said, handing Donna two twenty-dollar bills.

Donna sighed. "I guess we all have to be good at something. Maybe someday I'll figure out how to turn all of my useless knowledge into cash. Annie says if she gets on that *Millionaire* show she's going to use me as a lifeline."

"Donna!" Mrs. Santini screamed from the back room, raising the hairs on the back of Angela's neck. "Stop talking and get to work. I don't pay you to chitchat with the customers."

"Gotta go," Donna said, rolling her eyes and handing Angela her change. "The dragon lady cometh."

Angela decided that there were worse things in life than being unmarried and pregnant. And working for Mrs. Santini was at the top of the list.

TEN

*What do you get when you cross the Godfather
with a lawyer?*
An offer you can't understand.

Entering the brick building that housed Angela's law office, John's heartbeat increased to ten times its normal rate. He felt like a pimply-faced schoolboy about to ask the most popular girl in class out on a date. His stomach was tied up in knots, and dead weight had settled there. Angela had refused to go out with him before; he had no idea if she would accept, but he knew that he had to try.

He'd been too chicken to call her to let her know he was coming by her office to see her, fearing . . . knowing what she'd say. But figuring she'd be done with clients for the day, and since he was a man who liked challenges, and Angela seemed to fit the bill . . .

Discovering as he stepped into the reception area that there was no secretary to bar his movements, he smiled. The element of surprise was always best in these types of situations.

The door to Angela's office was closed. He was about to knock when he heard giggling coming from the office next door. Wanda's distinctive husky laugh was followed by Angela's high-pitched giggle. He moved in their direction, curious to know what was so funny.

John didn't approve of eavesdropping. But on the other hand, he didn't really consider what he was doing eavesdropping, because they were talking so loud that he could overhear everything that was being said.

144

"I bet his power tool is as long and thick as a tree limb."

Wanda's comment made his eyes widen in disbelief. He wondered who the poor bastard was that she was talking about. It could have been her boyfriend, Kyle, but John had the feeling that Wanda already knew exactly how long Kyle's "power tool" was.

"You can tell a man's size by how big his shoes are," she continued. "Or you can look at the distance between his wrist and elbow to take a measurement."

John glanced down at his Rockports, which happened to be a size ten, then at his arm, and he breathed a sigh of relief.

Apparently size did matter.

"You are awful, Wanda Washington. I wouldn't want to be judged by the size of my breasts. And I don't think it's fair to judge a man by the size of his penis."

The sexy woman had nothing to worry about in the breast size department, that was for damn certain! But it wasn't just her body John was attracted to. Angela had a mind like a steel trap, a sense of humor that was infectious, and—

"That's because you've never been to bed with a man who had one the size of my pinkie." He pictured Wanda wiggling her little finger to make her point. "Girl, I can tell you that it wasn't a pleasant experience. I got more jolt from my vibrator after he left.

"And don't you think *penis* is a butt-ugly word? I sure do. Of course, it kinda fits the appendage. Don't know what God was thinking when he made that wrinkled, ugly thing."

"Well, to be truthful I really don't spend as much time as you seem to thinking about such *things*." There was a teasing lilt to Angela's voice. "I guess we can refer to *it* as the magic wand from now on."

"Magic wand? Honey, I think ugly stick is far more appropriate."

Both women broke into gales of laughter again.

Shit! Is this what women talk about when they are alone? They sound like a couple of . . . men. Shit!

John knocked quickly before they could say anything else. This was definitely more than he needed to know about either one of these women. All this talk of ugly weenies was starting to grate.

"Come in," Wanda called out, and John opened the door to find Angela perched on the edge of her friend's large black desk, long legs dangling, and he couldn't help but stare. She was wearing a shocking pink suit, and she looked—God help him—hot!

Wanda's eyes widened. "Well, hello, John! Nice to see you again." She waved him forward, ignoring the choked sound Angela made. "What brings you to our neck of the woods?" Then she said loud enough so only Angela could hear, "As if I didn't know."

Cheeks reddening, Angela shot her friend an annoyed look. "Is there a problem, John?" she asked, trying to sound calm and collected, though she felt quite the opposite, slipping off the desk to her feet. She hadn't seen or talked to him since THE KISS, which was how she always thought of it. "Something you need to talk to me about?"

"Uh, it's not a problem, exactly. Do you think we can talk privately in your office?" He smiled apologetically at Wanda, who was grinning like a hyena.

Angela mouthed *"Shut up!"* to her friend, then said to the handsome attorney, "Sure. Go on in. I'll be right there."

"You don't have to act like it's such a chore when a hunk like John Franco comes calling," Wanda admonished after he had quit the room. "Now hurry up and go see what he wants. I'm dying of curiosity."

"Something probably came up about the trial date or one of the witnesses. I'm sure it's nothing more than that."

Wanda rolled her eyes. "And he couldn't pick up the phone? I don't think so. Wake up and smell the roses, toots. The man is genuinely interested in you. I'd bet money on it."

"Interested in what, though? That's the real question." Unfortunately, Angela had no answer. "I'll see you tomorrow. Have a good evening, okay?"

Shooting Angela a *have-you-lost-your-mind?* look, Wanda said, "If you think I'm leaving here before I find out what that pretty white boy wants, you've got another think coming, girl. Hey, you don't suppose he heard us talking about men's—"

"Jesus, Mary, and Joseph! I hope not!" Angela replied, eyes widening in horror, and Wanda's laughter followed her out the door.

John was standing by the window, staring down at the traffic below when she entered. He was dressed casually in jeans, a black T-shirt, and a dark herringbone jacket that emphasized his broad shoulders. "I'm sorry to take so long. Wanda and I were just finishing up with . . . things."

His grin was mischievous, which didn't bode well. "I hear good magic wands are in short supply these days."

Her face flushing much pinker than her suit, she swallowed the lump of embarrassment in her throat and wished the floor would open up and swallow her whole. "It's not polite to listen at doors, John. Didn't your mother ever tell you that?" Thank God she and Wanda hadn't been discussing him.

"It was purely accidental, I assure you." But he was still grinning, and Angela's pulse was still racing.

Damn him for having this effect on her! Why couldn't

he have been ugly, or mean, or stupid, or something other than the hunk of the world, and a nice guy, to boot?

There was no justice in the world anymore.

"Was there something you wanted to talk to me about?" She glanced at her watch. "It's getting late. I need to get home to Winston."

"Winston?" His right brow shot up. "Oh, right. Your dog. You know, I've never seen this dog of yours. You've always got him hidden away when I come over."

"That's because Winston's not keen on strangers. He's also not keen on being left home all day by himself. I need to get home and take him for a walk, or else I'm going to have a mess to clean up." She shuddered at the thought. Win's mistakes were rather substantial.

"Gotcha." John wasn't much for dogs. Had never had one, in fact. As a kid, his mother wouldn't allow it; as an adult, he didn't want the hassle of walking, feeding, and cleaning up after a dog.

"I remembered you saying the other night that you enjoyed country-western music."

"That's right. I love all music, but country-western is my favorite."

"Garth Brooks is going to be performing this Saturday night at the Center for the Performing Arts, and I was wondering if you'd like to go."

Angela's face lit with excitement. "Garth Brooks is going to be in town? I can't believe it. I tried several times to get tickets to his concerts when I lived in Boston, but they were always sold out."

Reaching into his shirt pocket, John extracted two tickets, holding them out to her. And at that moment she knew what Adam had gone through with Eve and her stupid, but tasty, apple. "I scored these this morning. I'd like you to go with me."

Gazing longingly at the tickets, she was tempted beyond all reason to say yes, but then sanity returned and she shook her head. "John, I'm flattered. But you know how I feel about socializing. I—"

The door opened just then and Wanda stuck her head in, a good indication she'd been listening just outside of it. Apparently eavesdropping was very much in vogue these days. Angela was starting to feel like the E. F. Hutton of Little Italy.

"Oh, go with him, Angela. For heaven's sake, it's just a concert! And I doubt anyone you know will see the two of you together. It's not like there won't be a zillion people milling about. You'll be two of many."

John flashed the woman a grateful smile. "Wanda's right."

"You know very well, John, that it's highly unprofessional for us to even consider going out on a date."

"I'm leaving now. Bye!" Wanda waved, shutting the door hurriedly behind her before Angela could yell at her for interfering.

Wanda was an incorrigible matchmaker. In the short time Angela had known her she had set Angela up on two disastrous blind dates. The first was with a stockbroker who had the annoying habit of referring to himself in the third person: *Tom loves hot dogs, Tom thinks you should wear your hair shorter.* Angela hated Tom. The other was an orthodontist, who kept staring at Angela's mouth all evening, but not because he wanted to kiss her. His not too subtle hints that she needed braces had really annoyed her.

When it came to matchmaking, Dolly Levi had nothing to worry about.

John moved to within inches of where she was standing. He was in her space, consuming all the oxygen, which she was sure was why she couldn't breathe. "Angela, I want to take you to the concert. Will you go?"

She gazed into the depths of his blue eyes and knew

she was in trouble. *Damn! Why did they have to be blue?* Blue eyes had always been her downfall.

Sighing in defeat, she replied, "All right, I'll go. But just this once. And only because you've already bought the tickets." Which was presumptuous as hell, but also rather sweet.

Bill never would have done anything so impetuous or risky. He would have checked his Palm PDA months before the concert and sent a memo to verify Angela's availability. Spontaneity had never been his strong suit.

"I hope you know that you're hard on a man's ego."

Angela's eyes twinkled. "Oh, I think yours is big enough not to be damaged too easily. What time shall I expect you?"

"Would I be pushing it if I asked you out for dinner first?"

There was that damn apple again. "Yes, but I'd like to go anyway."

His face suffused with pleasure. "Great! I'll pick you up at six. I know a great rib place. You'll love it." With a wink, he was gone, leaving Angela feeling breathless and full of anticipation.

Mr. Roy's House of Style, which had recently opened up in the vacant storefront next to Fiorelli's Bakery/Cafe, was crowded on Saturday mornings. Today proved no exception, except that most of the women frequenting the ultramodern, black-and-white salon were related by either blood or marriage.

"It's a disgrace, I'm telling you, Mary. Your lawyer is going out on a date tonight with your cousin. That man is trying to take away my grandson, your stepson. What kind of a man does that to his own flesh and blood? Tell me that." Sophia crossed herself, then said to the hairdresser, "Stop pulling my hair, Mr. Roy, or I'm going to slap you. You're making me bald."

Looking horrified, the man apologized before glancing at the large clock on the wall, wishing the hands would move faster and end his torture.

"Are you sure, Sophia?" Annie asked, raising her dripping wet head from the shampoo bowl and smiling apologetically at the young girl standing next to it. "That doesn't sound like Angela, though I know she felt sorry for John. I have a hunch she's just trying to be nice."

"Lunch? Did you say it'sa time for lunch?" Grandma Flora lifted the plastic hood on the hair dryer she sat beneath. "Good, because I'ma starving.

"I'ma roasting here, Mr. Roy," she called out, waving a white-embroidered handkerchief to gain his attention, then mopping her forehead with it. "Quit playing with my daughter-in-law's hair and come see ifa mine isa done. I'm older. I shoulda get better treatment, no?"

"Be quiet, old woman, and wait your turn!" Sophia admonished. "I'm almost done here."

Mr. Roy was a very nice man and tolerant of those around him, but he expected his clientele to follow his instructions to the letter, age notwithstanding. There would be no exceptions made for Grandma Flora. "Get back under the dryer, Mrs. Russo," he ordered. "You're being a naughty girl today. We don't want to damage our ends, now, do we?"

The old lady grunted at the tall man, who reminded her of Sal Mineo, which wasn't a good thing, because Flora had never liked Sal Mineo. "What do I care about ends? My scalp is burning." But she did as she was told. Mr. Roy had already tapped Connie on the head with the hairbrush for moving around too much; Grandma wasn't taking any chances.

Most of the Russo women, including Mary—until Annie had gotten hold of her—used to frequent Bertha Brucetti's beauty parlor, Curl Up and Dye. But Bertha had cataracts and was losing her sight, and Grandma Flora had made the very difficult decision not to allow the woman to burn her scalp with the curling iron anymore, friend or no friend.

When Annie suggested they try Mr. Roy's new shop, they all agreed that it was time to make the move. Especially when they found out Mr. Roy was serving cappuccino and Andrea Fiorelli's cookies to his customers.

Loyalty went only so far.

Mary's younger sister, Connie, was seated in the chair next to Sophia, waiting patiently for Mr. Roy to finish styling her mother's hair. "I like Johnny," she said. "I wish we could get this matter resolved. All this strife isn't good for the family. And I don't want it affecting the baby." Patting her large belly, Connie smiled kindly at the hairdresser as he began to style her own. "Tease it higher, Mr. Roy. Eddie likes it big."

Annette Funicello would have been pleased with Connie's do. In fact, she had Connie's do in *Beach Blanket Bingo*.

Mr. Roy looked dismayed, not to mention nauseated. "But that's so out of fashion, Mrs. Falcone. Why not let me try something new?"

"You think my daughter worries about fashion? She's got a husband to please. Keep ratting, Mr. Roy," Sophia instructed the hairdresser in a voice filled with authority.

"I wouldn't mess with Eddie, Mr. Roy," Annie remarked, smiling at the distraught man. "If you ever need a sigmoidoscopy, he might be tempted to shove that metal thing all the way up to your throat. Eddie's a proctologist. You know, a butt doctor."

"Ma, you need to quit making trouble," Mary said. "I told John to take Angela out. I'm certainly not going to fault him for having good taste. And weren't you the one who kept insisting that it was time for him to get married? I seem to recall—"

"That was before he turned out to be a traitor. Who knew he couldn't be trusted to stand with the family. I'm washing my hands of him." She wiped her hands back and forth.

Gina Goldman stepped into the salon just then, holding a small, furry dog to her chest and ignoring Mr. Roy's shocked gasp. "Is my daughter here?" she asked. "We're supposed to go shopping at the mall." She was an attractive woman, and there was no mistaking who her daughter resembled.

"Yeah, Gin— . . . er . . . Mom, I'm back here," Annie called out, waving her forward. "Lisa's putting a rinse on my hair. I won't be much longer."

Annie's mother shook her head and looked disapprovingly at her daughter. "Annie, you promised Joe you wouldn't color again. I thought you got all that crazy nonsense out of your system."

"It's not permanent. I just felt the need for a little pizzazz. Anyway, I already told Joe I was adding a wee bit of purple highlights. He doesn't care. *Oy vey!* Quit being such a *nudge.*"

"Listen to your daughter, Gina. Just because you want to look old and gray doesn't mean everybody else does." Sophia was proud that her hennaed hair was the exact same shade as Lucille Ball's had been. "Lucy always looked younger than Ethel. And you know why? Because her hair was so vibrant."

"Mrs. Goldman, you will have to take your dog outside," Mr. Roy instructed. "I don't allow animals in my salon." He stared menacingly at the canine, who yapped at him.

"Oh, lighten up, Roy." Gina patted the spoiled shih tzu. "Bubbeh isn't hurting anyone. And if you keep insulting him, he'll think you don't like him. And Bubbeh has the unfortunate habit of peeing on people whom he thinks don't like him. Just ask my husband."

At her grin, the man rolled his eyes, bit his tongue, and went back to ratting and spraying Connie's hair, wishing Annie had never recommended him to the Russo women, or her mother.

Life was too short for such aggravation.

"You and Sid want to come over to the house tomorrow afternoon for Sunday dinner, Gina? I'm making a pork roast."

"You know Sid can't eat pork, Sophia. He's Jewish. I thought he explained all that to you the first time we ate over."

"So your husband will eat the pasta, and you'll eat the pork. I'm making a nice batch of calamari. Your husband eats fish, no? Or does he think they're dirty, too? The man has some hang-up about dirty food. Did he have a bad childhood?"

The front door opened again, and all eyes turned to see who had entered.

Angela stood in the doorway, staring back at the group, like a deer who'd been caught in the headlights.

"She's got a lot of nerve showing her face here," Sophia whispered to her youngest daughter, though loud enough for everyone to hear, of course.

Mary shot her mother a lethal look before saying, "Hello, Angela. I wasn't expecting to see you again so soon."

Angela had met with Mary and Dan two days before to discuss the results of the child therapist's report, in which the psychologist had concluded that Matt was a happy, well-adjusted child who had suffered some trauma from recent events.

Angela released the breath she'd been holding. Having heard Sophia's comment, she wasn't sure how everyone else would react toward her. At least Mary was being kind, which was nothing more than she had expected from the pregnant woman. Unfortunately, Sophia's unkind behavior was also expected.

"I came in to get my hair trimmed. It's getting too long. Mr. Roy said he could fit me in, though it looks pretty busy in here."

"Everyone knows you're going out with Johnny Franco this evening," Sophia said, crossing her arms over her chest.

Annoyed by Sophia's condemnation, Angela walked farther into the room, stood before Mary's mother, and looked her straight in the eye. A collective gasp went up. Sophia paled slightly. "That's right. Do you have a problem with that, Mrs. Russo?"

Grandma Flora chuckled. "I likea thisa girl. Come over here and givea me a kiss, Angela. You and my grandson make a beautiful couple. Don't listen to my son's wife. She hasa poison in her heart, just likea I told you."

"John Franco and I are not a couple, Grandma Flora. I want to make that perfectly clear to you and everyone else. I haven't lost sight of my responsibilities to Mary and Dan, and I intend to fight hard in court to win this custody case. But John and I are associates, and we have similar interests, and I didn't see the harm in accepting his invitation to go to the Garth Brooks concert tonight."

She turned to Mary. "Do you have a problem with that, Mary? Because if you do, I'll call John and tell him I can't go. I don't want to do anything to upset you."

Mary smiled kindly. "Not at all. In fact, I've invited John to attend the grand opening of our new restaurant."

Angela's eyes widened slightly at that bit of information. Mary's mother wasn't as restrained.

"What?" Sophia blurted, bolting from her chair. "Are you crazy? You invite the enemy into your place of business? My daughter has lost her mind." She began cursing in Italian, throwing her hands up in the air, and being a drama queen, as only Sophia could be.

"I'm giving him the benefit of the doubt for the time being, Ma," Mary explained. "If things change, then my attitude will change, as well."

"You're being very generous, Mary," Angela said. "And I'm sure John appreciates that. But I want you to be aware of the fact that once we're in court before the judge, things are likely to be brought up that might cause you to become upset and angry. John will be doing his job. It'll be nothing personal. But it could be hurtful. I want you to be prepared."

Mary smiled sadly. "Well, if and when that day comes, then all bets will be off. I love Johnny, but my loyalty goes to my husband."

ELEVEN

*Why does the law society prohibit sex between
lawyers and their clients?*
To prevent clients from being billed twice for
essentially the same service.

"I've got friends in low places . . ."

Belting out the Garth Brooks song that they'd just
heard performed at the concert, John hit all the required
notes, with Angela joining in, messing up some of the
lyrics and laughing.

Her laughter was infectious, and John smiled, enjoying the sparkle in her pretty, dark eyes. Angela didn't
sing well, but then, neither did he. But they sang loud.
And what they didn't display in talent they made up for
in enthusiasm.

He'd been totally taken by surprise when he had
picked her up for their date to find that she had dressed
appropriately for the occasion, wearing tight blue jeans,
a red silk shirt, and matching cowboy hat and boots.
He'd worn his, too, and had worried the entire drive
over to her apartment that she was going to think he was
some kind of redneck dolt. But when she'd laughingly
displayed her attire, her cheeks flushed with anticipation
and excitement, then placed that red felt cowboy hat
atop her head, something good had clicked inside him,
something right.

"I think Garth Brooks put on a wonderful show tonight, don't you?" she asked, a dreamy expression on her
face. "I'm so happy I finally got to see him in person."

Turning the car off Interstate 95 and taking the Inner
Harbor exit, he nodded. "He's the best. I can't believe he

did three encores. No wonder his fans like him. Most performers wouldn't have done that."

"And did you see him kiss that woman when she rushed the stage? I couldn't believe he was so nice about it. If that had been me, I would have been scared to death that she was going to do me bodily harm."

"Well, she did mangle his lips pretty badly," he said, adding with a grin, "What I couldn't believe was turning my head to find you standing on top of your chair screaming at the top of your lungs like some teenage groupie." That image would be forever embedded in his memory, and he smiled every time he thought about Angela jumping up and down, waving her hands in the air in wild abandon.

Would she be that unrestrained in bed? he wondered.

Angela's cheeks reddened at the reminder. "I was carried away by the moment. I hope I didn't embarrass you."

"Not at all. I just thought it amusing that someone wanting to keep a low profile would purposely draw attention to herself. You continually surprise me."

"Yes, well, I have my moments."

"You're usually so prim and proper. I saw a different side of you tonight. I liked it, liked it very much."

Her smile was enigmatic. "Yes, well, you know what they say about still waters, Counselor."

He did indeed.

John's stomach took that moment to grumble, preventing any clever retort he might have made. "Are you hungry? I sure could use some refueling."

Angela nodded enthusiastically, surprising him yet again. Most of the women he knew ate like birds. It was refreshing to find one who actually liked food and wasn't afraid to admit it.

"Starving, actually, though I'm embarrassed to confess such a thing after all those ribs I ate. Do you like hamburgers? I'm a big fan of Burger King."

"No kidding? So am I. I feel the need for a Double Whopper with Cheese, strawberry shake, and large fries."

"*Mmmm*. You took the words right out of my mouth. But I want onion rings, not fries. And maybe something yummy for dessert."

John wanted to put something in Angela's mouth that had nothing to do with words, like his tongue, but refrained from saying so, not wanting to scare her off. He'd been on his best behavior tonight and didn't intend to do anything to change that.

After they had stuffed themselves to the gills with hamburgers and all the fixings, told a number of really lame jokes that they'd read on the Internet, and sang a few more Garth Brooks tunes, John drove back to Angela's apartment.

A light rain had begun to fall by the time he pulled up in front of her building and parked. Mama Sophia's was closed for the night, High Street relatively quiet, save for an occasional car passing by and the sound of raindrops pelting the windshield. The wipers made a whooshing sound as they glided back and forth to clear the glass; it seemed loud in the ensuing silence.

Angela fidgeted nervously with her purse, silently debating whether or not to invite John up to her apartment for coffee. She didn't want to give him the wrong impression, especially after what had happened the last time, but she wasn't anxious for the evening to end. She'd had a wonderful time tonight and hadn't laughed so much in ages.

She'd had little to laugh about lately, but John always seemed able to make her do so, to lighten the moment. She genuinely liked him, liked his offbeat sense of humor and easy laugh, the fact that he gorged himself on the same kind of junk food she did, the uninhibited way he blurted out a song at the drop of a hat.

He was fun; she needed fun.

And he had proved himself to be a good friend.

"Thank you for inviting me to the concert. I had a great time. And thanks for feeding me, too." At least her pregnancy gave her an excuse to eat more than she should. Eating for two was definitely the best benefit of being pregnant.

"My pleasure. I'm glad you agreed to go with me. Maybe now you realize that I'm not the ogre you originally thought."

"I never thought that." His eyebrow rose, and she smiled apologetically. "Well, maybe at first, when I saw you at the police station, taking sides against your grandmother. But now that I've gotten to know you better I don't think that at all."

"I'm encouraged."

She smiled softly, wishing she had the nerve to caress his face, to run her finger along his strong jaw and feel the stubble there. "Would you like to come up for coffee? I realize it's late, but since we don't have to work tomorrow . . ."

"Sure. Sounds good. Let me grab the umbrella out of the trunk and I'll get your door."

They entered the apartment a few minutes later and were immediately assaulted by a horrendous odor that hung in the air like thick fog.

Following her nose into the living room, Angela found a gaseous Winston reclining on the overstuffed chair she'd just purchased. He cocked one eye open when he saw her, but didn't bother getting up.

So much for Winston being a watchdog, unless, of course, he was cleverly using the skunk antiburglary method to keep intruders at bay.

Angela wondered if John had noticed the awful odor,

then saw him wrinkle his nose in disgust. Damn! she thought, feeling her cheeks starting to heat.

Damn dog! Why did he have to pick tonight to fart?

"Uh, please excuse my dog. Winston's got a bad habit of expelling gas. And I made the unfortunate mistake today of feeding him the remainder of my salad. He doesn't do well with onions. I'll just light a few candles to get rid of the smell." She immediately set out to accomplish the task, grateful when the vanilla-scented candles began to do their work.

Staring wide-eyed at the large white lump on the chair, John shook his head. "That's your dog?"

She nodded. "That's Win, such as he is. I love him dearly, but he does have some rather disgusting habits." She told him about the dog's penchant for drinking out of the toilet bowl, for messing on her landlady's doormat, and he laughed. It was a nice sound.

"I never figured you for the bulldog type. Guess I just assumed you'd have a French poodle or something."

"Poodles are for sissies. I don't know what kind of impression you have of me, John, but let me assure you that I'm no sissy. You'll find that out in court."

"You're pretty confident that you're going to win, aren't you?"

She smiled. "Of course. I wouldn't have taken on the Gallaghers' case if I didn't think I could win. Can I ask you something?"

He nodded, and she continued, "How do you really feel about representing Rothburg against your cousin? Does it bother you very much?" She thought she knew the answer already, but she wanted to hear him say it.

At first, John seemed uncertain about how he should answer, how much he should reveal. "I feel like a disloyal piece of shit, if you want to know the truth. But I couldn't let Tony down, not after everything he's done for me. Hell, I probably would have never graduated law school if it hadn't been for him."

"You don't give yourself enough credit, John. You would have never been accepted in the first place if you weren't capable and smart. Don't let others' opinions and misconceptions rob you of who you really are. The John Franco I've come to know is very nice, extremely intelligent, and quite good-looking." With that she disappeared into the kitchen, leaving John staring openmouthed after her.

Angela thought he was handsome, nice, and intelligent. There was hope. And he needed hope, because he'd come to the realization that not having Angela in his life was unacceptable. He wasn't sure as yet how much of a commitment he was willing to make—he was a failure at relationships, and a baby only complicated matters—but he knew she was as necessary to him as the air he breathed.

While he waited, John occupied himself by glancing around the apartment, wondering why everyone's home looked better than his. His apartment was larger, but not decorated nearly as nice. Maybe he should let Pete come over and fix up the place a bit. It sure as hell needed something—a woman's touch. But since he didn't have a woman, his brother's expertise would have to do. He'd give Pete a call tomorrow and ask him about it.

Angela returned, carrying a wicker tray with two ceramic mugs filled with hot coffee. "I wasn't sure how you took it."

"Black, thanks!" He took a sip, and then seated himself on the sofa next to her. "You've done a nice job with your apartment."

She explained about the borrowed furniture. "I've bought a few new pieces, like the overstuffed chair, but since I'll probably be moving soon I—"

"You're moving? Where? Are you going back to Boston?"

Was that disappointment she heard in his voice? Angela wouldn't allow herself to think so.

"No. I meant I'll probably look for a bigger place. Mrs. Foragi is always complaining about the dog. Winston really needs a yard, and so will the baby. I don't want my child growing up above a restaurant. I want a real home, with a backyard and a swing set."

"In the meantime, you could check out my building," he suggested. "My place is really large. They converted this old warehouse into lofts, so I've got lots of room to spread out. Now all I need is some furniture to fill it up and I'll be all set."

"You've mentioned family. Do they live here in town?" she asked. "I mean, besides the Russos? I believe you said that your brother was a cardiologist."

He nodded. "That's Mike. My parents live close by. And my other brother, Pete, who's head of human resources for a computer software company in D.C., has a condo at the Inner Harbor. How about you?"

"Mine just moved here from Boston. My dad's an ex-cop." A cross-dressing ex-cop, but she wouldn't get into that right now. Not that she was ashamed of her dad, but most people wouldn't understand a grown man's need to wear women's clothing. She was pretty sure a macho guy like John wouldn't. "My sister, Mia, arrives tomorrow. I can't wait to see her. We're very close."

"Is your sister an attorney, too?"

Angela laughed at the absurdity of the idea. "Mia, an attorney? Perish the thought. She's more likely to end up on the other side of the criminal justice system. She's not working at the moment." She told him about the highway construction job, and he smiled.

"I'd like to meet your sister. She sounds interesting. I like a woman with spunk."

"Mia doesn't lack spunk. What she lacks is common

sense. For some reason I haven't quite figured out, men find my sister intriguing."

What intrigued John was the sound of Angela's voice, the way she moved her hands when she talked, and how her tongue came out every so often to touch the rim of her coffee cup. His stomach clenched with every flick.

"What are you staring at?" she asked, feeling suddenly nervous.

"Your mouth. It's very enticing," he said, scooting closer.

"John . . ." His name came out on a sigh. And despite all the reasons she shouldn't allow him to go any further, Angela found herself powerless to move, mesmerized as she was by the depths of his blue eyes, the sound of his voice as he asked for her coffee cup, which he then placed on the table.

When he took her into his arms and kissed her, she didn't think to resist. His mouth on hers felt good. His lips were soft, coaxing, and when his tongue parted the seam and thrust in, she could only grasp on to his shoulders and kiss him back, giving in to the yearning to taste, to touch, to lose herself in him.

For a few moments the world rocked on its axis, time stood still, and all thought processes shut down, until all Angela could do was feel, revel in the way his lips felt pressed against hers, how his strong arms around her made her feel safe and secure.

She heard John's soft moan—or was it hers?—and was suddenly jerked back to reality, the magnitude of what they'd done crashing down on her. She pulled back and moved away from him.

"What's wrong?" he asked.

"You know what's wrong, John. We shouldn't have done that again. It was wrong."

"It felt pretty damn right to me."

"So maybe it felt right, but it's not."

"It was just a kiss, Angela."

"Was it?"

Their gazes locked, and in that moment they both knew that for them a simple kiss would never be enough. "I think it's time we ended the evening."

"What are you afraid of?"

Nothing. Everything. The feelings he'd aroused in her, feelings she never wanted to experience again. Getting involved with someone, especially an opposing counsel someone.

Like bullets pinging off concrete, her thoughts came at a rapid pace, but, of course, she admitted to none of them. "Just because I don't think it's wise for us to pursue this relationship doesn't mean I'm scared, John." But he was; she was terrified. "I think it would be best if we just remained friends." But she knew now that that was impossible. She was falling in love with John Franco, and she had to put a stop to it now.

He rose to his feet, extending a hand to help her up. "Friends, huh? That wasn't quite what I had in mind."

"I'm sorry. It's all I can offer. I just can't . . . I'm not sure . . . It's really out of the . . ."

Shut up! Shut up! Shut up!

He smiled, caressing her cheek. "You're quite a challenge, Miss DeNero. Good thing I'm a man who's always up for a challenge. I never let anything stand in the way of getting what I want. And I've decided I want you."

His honesty took her breath away, and she was speechless for a moment. Then she sucked in her breath and walked toward the door, hoping he would follow, relieved when he did.

"I had a wonderful time at the concert. Thank you. Now I think it's time we say good night."

"I don't suppose you'd be up for a good night kiss."

She shook her head. "No. Please . . . please just go." Because she wasn't sure how much longer she could resist him. She wanted him to kiss her, make love to her. Wanted it rather shamelessly. Pregnancy or no pregnancy, there was nothing whatsoever wrong with her hormones and libido, which were raging, surging, dancing the Macarena.

With a look of disappointment, John nodded, then disappeared out the door, leaving Angela to stare after him. After a moment, she shut the door, locked it, and drew a deep breath.

Men aren't trustworthy. They say pretty words, but in the end, they always leave. You should have known better than to lose control. Where's your common sense? Didn't you learn a painful lesson with Bill?

Angela patted her tummy and sighed, wondering how she had allowed herself to lose control. Wondering, why? She was always so sensible, so careful. But she'd abandoned all common sense when she'd kissed John Franco again.

And wasn't she in enough trouble as it was? Hadn't she already messed up her life by allowing Bill McElroy to take advantage of her? Hadn't she already led with her heart and not her head?

"Never again!" she said aloud, as if that would make it so.

But were her words stronger than her convictions? That still remained to be seen.

Hands on hips as narrow as any male youth's, Mia DeNero studied her older sister for several moments, then shook her head of short, brown Orphan Annie curls.

"All right, spill it, Ang. I know there's something you're not telling me. And I won't quit pressing until you confess." She resumed taking her clothes out of a black

Samsonite soft-sided suitcase and putting them in the drawers of the maple dresser that had been hers since childhood.

Arriving at Sam and Rosalie's house less than four hours ago, Mia had already deduced that Angela was keeping something from her. Her sister had always been rather intuitive unfortunately, and Angela was unsure how to respond. She opted to play dumb.

"I don't know what you're talking about," she said, reclining against the bed pillows and pretending she didn't have a care in the world. She was also thinking how wonderful it was to have her sister home. Of course, she'd forgotten how tenacious Mia could be once she got hold of something.

Mia stopped what she was doing and sat down beside her. "I may be a couple of years younger than you, and not as book smart, but I'm not stupid, Ang, and I know a liar when I see one. I've never revealed anything you've ever told me in confidence. Why won't you trust me now?"

Angela tried to make light of it. "How can I trust someone who still looks twelve years old?" With her mop of short dark hair and diminutive features, Mia appeared much younger than her thirty years. It made people expect less of her, but it also made it difficult for them to take her seriously.

And it wasn't that Angela didn't take Mia seriously. She did. Most of the time. But she didn't want to explain her stupidity once again, especially to a sibling who looked up to her.

"Quit beating around the bush. I've looked this way all my life. I know you're keeping something from me. What is it? What's happened?"

"*Sssh!* Do you want Mom and Dad to hear you?"

"They're out back raking leaves. Dad wanted to work

off his dinner. Said he felt bloated, like it was the eggplant parmesan and not all that beer he drinks that's making his gut fat."

"Shut the door, just in case they come back inside."

"This must be juicy, if we're resorting to cloak and dagger stuff." Mia did as her sister asked before sitting back down on the bed. "Okay, spill it. And don't spare me any of the gory details."

Angela sucked in her breath, then blurted, "I'm pregnant," feeling instantly better for having confided the truth to her sister. "No one knows, except Wanda, Joe, and now you. And, of course, the doctor. I want to keep it that way, for now, okay?" She wouldn't mention John. That would only stir up questions she had no answers for.

Mia's shocked gaze went from Angela's face to her tummy, then back up again. "No shit! No wonder you don't want Mom or Dad to know. Dad will go ballistic when he hears."

"Tell me something I don't already know." Angela explained the circumstances that had resulted in her pregnancy and her subsequent decision to keep the child, which made her sister smile in relief.

"I'm glad. I've always wanted to be an aunt. It's much easier than being a mother." Mia took Angela's hand and squeezed it. "You know I'm here for you, Ang. I can help out. I'll be getting a job soon, so if you need money—"

Dark eyes filling with tears, Angela hugged her sister. "Oh, Mia! I've missed you so much. Thanks for being so understanding. I'll get through this. I don't need money, just your love and friendship."

"And maybe an occasional baby-sitter?" Kissing her sister's cheek, she asked, "When are you going to tell Mom and Dad? I think you should do it today. Get it over with. I'm here now. I can run interference for you, like always."

Horrified by the suggestion, Angela shook her head. "I can't do it today. I'm not prepared. This is something I have to work up to. Plan out." *Like maybe for another ten years.* But she knew it would have to be soon. The jeans she'd worn to the concert last night had practically cut off her circulation, not to mention her breath. Soon everything in her closet would be too tight to wear.

"Dad's bark is worse than his bite," Mia offered.

"Are we talking about the same man who pulled a gun on your last boyfriend? What was his name? The guy with all the earrings who wore those horrible Hawaiian shirts."

"Jack Ratz. I think it was the name more than the body piercing that Dad took exception to."

"Actually, I think it was because Dad found Jack on top of Mia, and he didn't have his pants on at the time."

Mia blushed. "We didn't do anything."

"Only because Dad got up in the middle of the night to get a glass of milk and interrupted you in mid-lust."

"I need my own place. My love life is shit when I live at home."

"Yeah, well, there's something to be said for using protection, and Dad makes a better condom than most."

Mia started to laugh; then Angela followed suit.

"So what are you going to do now that you've arrived? Any employment plans in the works?"

Angela's sister shook her head. "I'll buy a newspaper tomorrow and see what's available. I've decided not to get back into construction. It ruined my nails, not to mention that I was getting hit on by some pretty gross men. It was that whole saggy-jeans-butt-crack thing."

"Grosser than Jack? I find that hard to believe."

"Hello? Bill McElroy had glasses. Not to mention he smelled peculiar all the time, like dog piss."

"There's nothing wrong with a man wearing glasses. And Bill happened to use a lime-scented aftershave."

"Well I hope your taste in men has improved. Are you dating anyone, or is that out of the question now?"

"I went out last night, as a matter of fact. Saw the Garth Brooks concert."

"Does this mystery man have a brother? I hope so, because I'm desperate. I can't remember the last time I had sex, but I'm pretty sure condoms hadn't been invented yet."

Angela smiled. "As a matter of fact, he does. Two of them. But one's married, and I've never met the other one. And probably never will. I'm not going to see John Franco socially again."

"Why not? Does he smell as bad as Bill?"

"John smells wonderful. But he's opposing counsel in a difficult custody case and it would only complicate matters to keep seeing him." Especially when her attraction to him was so powerful. "Not to mention that it isn't seemly for a pregnant woman to be dating. People will think I'm easy. It could ruin my reputation."

Mia rolled her eyes. "You worry too much about your precious reputation. You always have. I don't see anything wrong with your dating. You're pregnant, not married to someone else, and certainly not dead. And wouldn't it be nice for your child to have a father? A real one. Not just a sperm donor."

"There are plenty of single mothers who are successfully raising their children alone. Look at Rosie O'Donnell. I don't need a man to make a family. I can be both a mother and father. And you'll be around, not to mention Mom and Dad."

"You're just rationalizing all of this to suit your purpose. And you're a heck of a lot more attractive than Rosie, even though she's got more money. In reality, you're worried that your stupid career is going to go down the toilet, or that you'll end up being hurt again by some big bad male. Isn't that the truth?"

"Bill did a number on me, used me. I'm not going to be taken advantage of again. And yes, I am worried about my reputation. I've got good cause, don't you think?"

"Eventually you won't be able to hide your pregnancy."

"I know. Why do you think I'm so worried? Pretty soon everyone will know and my career will go down the toilet."

"If anyone dares say anything bad about you or my niece or nephew I will personally knock their lights out. Never fear, Mia is here."

Angela wrapped her arms about her sister and smiled. "And I thank God for that."

TWELVE

What's the difference between pigs and lawyers?
You can learn to respect a pig.

Angela had concluded long ago that Judge Dexter Baldridge had come by his name quite honestly. He was balder than the proverbial eagle—not a single strand of hair topped his shiny pate; and his long, ridgelike nose, as he peered down over wire-rimmed spectacles, would have made an excellent ski run, save for that one unfortunate wiry hair growing out of the end of it, which would, she decided, have looked much better had it been on his head.

All this conjecture was moot, however, because Judge Baldridge was going to decide the fate of Matthew Gallagher in Mary and Dan's upcoming custody hearing, and Angela needed to concentrate on what the man was saying, not on how he looked. She and John were presently in the judge's chambers, discussing their clients' legal positions.

"Let me get this straight." The judge addressed his comment to John. "Your client, Sharon Gallagher Rothburg, wants custody of a son that she previously relinquished to her ex-husband? Is that correct?"

"Yes, Your Honor. Mrs. Rothburg was given legal custody of Matthew after her divorce from Daniel Gallagher. So in essence she legally retains custody of the boy, even though the child is presently residing with his father."

Judge Baldridge smoothed a palm over his head. "Then I don't see the problem—"

"Judge Baldridge," Angela interrupted, "there are extenuating circumstances in this case, and I'd like a chance to explain them."

"Aren't there always?" he asked, though not unkindly. "Proceed with your explanation, Miss DeNero."

"My client, Daniel Gallagher, is protesting the original custody decision, and is petitioning the court for legal and physical custody of his son."

"On what grounds?" He shuffled officiously through the papers on his desk, frowning when he was unable to find what he was looking for.

"We intend to show that Mrs. Rothburg is an unfit mother, Your Honor. That she abandoned her son to Mr. Gallagher's care in order to run off with a man ten years her junior, who happened to be her aerobics instructor. We further intend to show the court that the Gallaghers have demonstrated their willingness and ability to raise Matthew and provide him with a caring, loving home, where he is thriving under their guardianship. To disrupt him further would be detrimental to his emotional well-being."

"Have the parties involved sat down and tried to work out a satisfactory agreement on their own? I prefer these types of custody cases be resolved without dragging the court into it."

John nodded. "No, Your Honor. Miss DeNero and I attempted to get the parties to enter into a reasonable discussion a few weeks back, but the Rothburgs were not amenable to the meeting."

"Which is why, Your Honor," Angela interrupted, "the Gallaghers are asking the court for relief in this matter. We would like our request for custody heard."

Judge Baldridge steepled bony fingers under his chin, looking none too pleased by the whole turn of events. "A child's natural mother is generally the best person to care for that child, Miss DeNero. Though maternal preference isn't strictly considered under Maryland law, it does hold a lot of weight with me. It will take a preponderance of evidence to convince me otherwise. Are you prepared to present that evidence?"

"Yes, Your Honor. I intend to convince the court that Matthew Gallagher will be irreparably harmed if he is allowed to return to the care of his mother, a woman who abandoned him with no explanation, who never saw fit to contact him once she'd left, and who has confused and frightened a child she purports to love.

"Mary Gallagher might not be Matthew's birth mother, but she has given him, and continues to provide, the love, guidance, and attention he requires during this difficult time." She glanced out of the corner of her eye at the tall man standing next to her, daring John to deny it, relieved when he didn't.

In fact, John hadn't raised any objections, which surprised Angela. She had expected him to protest vigorously the unflattering portrait she had painted of Sharon Rothburg, and wondered if this was some type of strategy to throw her off base, or if he agreed with her depiction of the woman and couldn't in good conscience bring himself to object. She hoped it was the latter, though she knew John was too good a lawyer to compromise his case with sentiment.

This was the first time she had seen John since they'd both taken leave of their senses and locked lips for that memorable kiss. He had called her office and home several times, but she hadn't wanted to talk to him, letting the answering machine pick up the calls. He'd even stopped by her apartment on two different occasions, but a peek out the peephole told her not to answer the doorbell.

Admittedly, she'd taken the chicken's way out by

avoiding him. But she had made her feelings perfectly clear to him on several occasions and couldn't help that he wouldn't take no for an answer.

Damn stubborn man! She sighed.

"Will you be ready to proceed with this case in three weeks? I'd like to hear it before the Thanksgiving holiday, if possible."

"Yes, Your Honor," they said in unison, then turned to look at each other. John smiled. Angela didn't.

Once she had gathered up her notes and briefcase, Angela made a beeline for the door, but she wasn't fast enough to make good her escape, and John caught up to her.

"Angela," he called out, grasping her elbow. "Wait up! What's your hurry?"

"I'm going to be late for a meeting. I have a new client coming in." It wasn't quite a lie. Mrs. Mattuci was coming in to sign legal documents and retrieve her settlement check from the owners of Doggie Delight, and she was a relatively new client.

"I know you've been avoiding me, Angela. And I know why. It was only a kiss, for godsake! You don't have to treat me like I've got the plague. I want to see you again. I'll apologize for kissing you again, if you want me to. Though you didn't seem to mind at the time."

Her cheeks flushed at the truth of his words. "That's not possible, John. You know that, and so do I. It's essential that we avoid the appearance of impropriety. I've already explained this to you, ad nauseum."

"What's improper about two colleagues meeting for lunch or dinner? Or having a conversation over cocktails? As long as we don't engage in any ex parte communication regarding the custody case, we—"

She shook her head. "I'm sorry. I've got to go."

"You can run, Angela, but you can't hide. I'm not giving up."

"Good-bye, John. I'll see you in court."

"Does that mean you're not going to the grand opening of Danny Boy's?"

Stopping in her tracks, she turned. "Of course I'm going. Mary and Dan are my clients. How would it look if I didn't—" She gasped when she caught his satisfied grin.

"You're going? I can't believe you'd want to put yourself through what is surely going to be an agonizing experience. You're not exactly popular with the Russos right now. Sophia is unhappy that Mary invited you and is sure to make your visit very unpleasant."

"If it means seeing you again, then it'll be worth it."

Why is it that when you don't want a man in your life, that's when they always appear?

If that was Murphy's Law, then she'd like to smack that stupid Murphy bastard upside the head.

Angela looked about to make sure they were alone. "Look, John, if this is purely about sex, then you should know that I'm not interested in pursuing that kind of a relationship with you."

Liar! Liar! Liar!

Shut up! Shut up! Shut up!

The hurt in his eyes gave her pause. "It's not just about sex, Angela. I genuinely like you, like being with you. I want to keep seeing you."

She heaved a sigh full of what-ifs, maybes, and regret. "I like you, too, but there's a lot going on in my life right now, you know that."

He took a moment to consider her words. "You're using the baby as an excuse, Angela. To be perfectly honest, I'm not sure what I want out of our relationship, or what I can offer you. I only know that I want to have one."

"But for how long, John? How long will it be before the novelty of dating a pregnant woman wears off? How long before you decide to leave? I can't go through that again. I'm sorry."

"It doesn't have to be like that, Angela. We'll take it one day at a time and see what happens. I know what it's like to be hurt. My ex-wife did a number on me, but I'm willing to try again, with you, if you'll let me."

But in the end Angela couldn't bring herself to agree, though she was tempted. Her heart was a fragile thing, and she feared getting hurt again. She knew this time she would not recover.

John had been honest with her about his feelings. She couldn't repay that honesty by telling him lies and half-truths. She was basically a straightforward person. Okay, most of the time. Sometimes little white lies were necessary to protect the innocent, and not telling the whole truth and nothing but the truth was needed for survival.

"I can't. My relationship with my fiancé ended badly. I'm not looking to enter into another relationship right now, with you or anyone else. It's too soon. I'm not ready."

"Not even a friendly one? No strings attached?"

She searched his face, and found his intentions honorable. Maybe it was hers that weren't. "I think we both know that's not possible. We proved that the other night."

"I can't stop thinking about you."

The admission made her heart beat faster. She hadn't been able to stop thinking about him, either. But she wasn't about to admit that, as it would serve no purpose and only fuel the flames of his tenacity.

"You're a nice man, John. I don't always agree with your motives for doing things, but I know deep down that you do only what you think is best. I'm truly flattered by your interest, but—"

"But I should shut up and leave you alone."

Before she could respond, Wanda came rushing up, a distraught look on her face. "I'm sorry to interrupt," she said, "but this is an emergency. I hope you don't mind, John, I need to talk to Angela right away."

"Not at all. Angela and I are finished . . . for now." He stared meaningfully at her, then turned and walked away. Angela released the breath she didn't know she was holding.

"That looked heavy."

"It was. So what's wrong? Did something happen with the Beccacio case?"

Wanda shook her head. "No, thank goodness! We won. It's about Kyle."

"Come on. Let's talk while we walk. We can get a cup of coffee downstairs. I presume we're talking about your handsome doctor."

"That's just it. I'm not sure Kyle's mine anymore. My sister Charisse took her kid to see him this morning and she said he was really cozy with his office nurse. I think I blew it with him. I think he might be interested in someone else."

Wanda wasn't the type to wear her feelings out for everyone to see, so the fear and uncertainty in her eyes gave Angela pause. "That's just her opinion, Wanda," she tried to reassure her. "Maybe Charisse read things wrong, saw more than there was to see. She doesn't know Kyle that well, after all."

"Kyle wants to get married and settle down, have a passel of kids. He's told me that more than once."

"But he hasn't asked you to marry him, right?"

"Well, no. But I got the impression that if I gave him the least bit of encouragement, he would. And that's just not who I am right now. What would I do with a baby?"

Angela winced at the comment, and Wanda placed a hand on her arm. "Oh, sorry. I forgot. Sometimes my mouth doesn't catch up with my brain."

"It doesn't matter. Don't worry about it."

They stopped at the trendy coffee shop on the bottom floor of the court building and went inside, sitting down at a table near the window. The aroma of coffee was heady, and Angela inhaled deeply. Since confirming her pregnancy she had cut down on her caffeine intake, and it was killing her.

"If you're not ready to get married and have a family, then you shouldn't worry about what Kyle wants. You have to do what's best for Wanda."

The black woman sipped her coffee thoughtfully, then said, "I think I'm in love with him."

"Oh." Angela noted the conflicted look on her friend's face and felt bad for her. She knew exactly what it was to feel conflicted, knew it in spades.

What would have happened if I had met John Franco under different circumstances?

Her feelings for him had changed. They may have started out as antagonists, then moved toward friendship, but after the other night, she knew they could be so much more, if she allowed it to happen.

But she couldn't.

Not with a baby on the way. And not while they were on opposite sides of the same case.

"Well, that does put a wrinkle in things, doesn't it?"

"Yeah, quite a large one. Because even though I love Kyle, I still don't want to get married and have kids. I've worked hard to establish my law practice, Angela. I don't want to give it all up for some man, who may or may not be in it for the long haul. I'm sure you of all people can understand that."

"I think you're getting way ahead of yourself, sweetie. First of all, Kyle hasn't asked you to marry him. And secondly, even if he does eventually, that doesn't mean you two can't come to some sort of compromise regarding your professions. You're a lawyer, Wanda. You negotiate every day. And if you truly love Kyle, then you should try and work things out with him. He seems to be a reasonable man. But like I said, I think we're putting the cart before the horse."

Wanda sighed. "I guess you're right."

"Are you seeing him tonight?"

"No, he's on call at the hospital."

"Good." Angela smiled in satisfaction. "That means you can go out with me. I can use some cheering up, too. We'll pick up Mia, head over to Mama Sophia's for dinner, and then go upstairs to my apartment for a good old-fashioned gab session. How does that sound?"

"I'll bring the margarita mix," Wanda said, then added as an afterthought, "and chocolate milk for the mommy-to-be."

"Throw in some of Mary's chocolate cannoli to go with it, and you've got yourself a friend for life."

"Girl, you're too easy."

"I think that's already been proven, unfortunately."

"Thanks for coming with me tonight, John," Pete told his brother as they drove to their parents' house for dinner. "I don't think I could have faced Mom and Dad by myself, not with everything that's happened to me today. You know how confrontational these family dinners can be."

Pulling the car into the driveway of the familiar two-story yellow house with the olive green shutters, John set the brake, and turned to look at his brother. In truth, John wanted to be anywhere but at his parents' house for dinner. Robert and Adele Franco were not Ozzie and Harriet, that was for damn certain. But he sensed Peter was upset about something, and John wanted to lend whatever support he could.

"Is something the matter? When I spoke to you on the phone earlier today I sensed you were upset. Did Mom make another remark about Eric? I told you to ignore her. She's not—"

Pete shook his head. "No, I'm not upset about anything Mom said. Not this time. It's much worse than that. Mom's comments I can handle." Pete brushed agitated fingers through his hair and took a deep breath.

"I got fired today, John. Morgan Trent called me into his office and said my services were no longer required."

"What?" John's eyes widened in disbelief. "I don't fucking believe it." Pete had worked for the computer software company for almost eight years, had even won Employee of the Year back in 1996. He'd always been conscientious and hardworking when it came to his job at Trent Enterprises, and now he was getting fired? That didn't make any sense at all.

"What reason did Trent give for firing you? Did something happen to upset him?"

"Yeah, I guess you could say that." Pete's frown deepened. "I took Eric into the office the other day to show him where I worked. It was Saturday, so I figured it would be safe, that there wouldn't be many people around. I don't usually flaunt my relationships in public. Unfortunately we ran into Trent. The next thing I know I'm being canned. I know there's a connection. What I don't know is if I can prove it."

"Haven't you missed work over the years because of those migraines you get? Could that have been the reason you got fired?" John had a gut feeling that it wasn't, but he had to be sure.

"I know it's because I'm gay. Trent has suspected it for some time, has hinted around about it. But, of course, he never came right out and asked me. When I showed up with Eric in tow, and he saw how happy we were together, he added two plus two, came up with homos, and gave me the boot.

"Of course, he's claiming unsatisfactory work performance, time lost on the job, that sort of thing."

"How much work have you missed in the last eight years?"

Pete shrugged. "I don't really know. I've probably averaged a day or two per month, sometimes more, sometimes less. I've gone to work with the headaches, but oftentimes have had to leave. The pain is just too severe, and I become nauseated. The light bothers my eyes, and staring at a computer screen all day doesn't help."

The porch light came on, and Robert Franco stuck his head out the door. "You coming in or not?" he demanded in a voice filled with impatience.

Rolling down the window, John waved, noting how small his father looked framed in the doorway. He used to think his father was a giant, a man to be reckoned with. Sadly, that wasn't the case anymore. Robert Franco had shrunk in stature right before his eyes, and it wasn't just his height that John was thinking about.

"Be right in," he replied.

"Well, hurry up. Your mother's getting anxious to put the food on the table. We can't wait all night to eat. I've got to go to bed soon."

John glanced at his wristwatch. It was barely six o'clock, hardly bedtime by anyone's standards.

"Tell me more," John urged.

"There's really nothing more to tell. I think I'm being discriminated against. It happens all the time, but no one ever admits to it, or is taken to task for it."

"Unfortunately you don't have much of a case based on sexual persuasion discrimination. Your employer is within his rights to fire you, downsize, or whatever else he wants to call it. And he really doesn't have to give a good reason. If you had been a federal employee, then that would have been a different matter. There are federal guidelines against such things."

John could see Pete's face pale, even in the dim light of the car's interior. "Then I'm screwed. We just rented that condo, spent a small fortune on furniture and redecorating. . . ."

"Not necessarily. I know a woman, a lawyer, who specializes in these types of cases. Let me talk to her, see what I can do. She may be able to help."

"That would be great!" Pete said, adding, "But who's going to help us with Mom? She's standing at the door, waving a dinner napkin in our direction."

Turning to follow his brother's gaze, John shook his head. "You owe me, little brother. And I know a great way you can pay me back for making me come here tonight."

"I'm not double dating. I've already told you how I feel about pretending with women, and—"

John laughed. "I want you to decorate my apartment, ace. I intend to start entertaining soon, and I need to spruce it up a bit."

Peter's smile was filled with relief and curiosity. "Anyone I know?"

"Not yet. But you will. And soon."

"So this mystery woman is crazy about you, huh?"

"Not exactly." John's smile melted. "But I'm working on it."

"Your father and I have talked it over, Johnny, and we've decided that you should drop this custody case against your cousin," Adele stated while dishing out the rigatoni. The white apron she wore around her waist was splattered red with the efforts of her cooking.

"It's causing too much grief. I'm not able to hold my head up in the community. People are talking, and business at the dry cleaners has fallen off. And it's all your doing. You need to make it right." She wiped her hands on the apron, as if the matter were already settled, and took her seat.

John's eyes narrowed slightly as he looked down the long length of mahogany table at his father, waiting for the agreement he knew would be forthcoming.

"How does it look, Johnny?" Robert Franco said. "Your mother is Mary's aunt. You're her cousin. It looks bad that you would turn on your own family. We need peace in the family, not dissension."

Though he knew it would do little good to explain, John made the attempt, yet again. "I'm not turning on anyone, Dad. I'm merely representing a client of our law firm in a custody case. I don't think Mary has as big an objection to my handling this matter as everyone else does. In a few weeks the hearing will be over and things will get back to normal."

Adele's lips thinned. "Well, her mother certainly objects. I ran into Sophia this afternoon at Santini's. She was raging at me about how you were a traitor to your blood, that you had no loyalty to the family. And Nina Santini agreed with every word she said. I was so embarrassed. And what was I supposed to say? I could only agree. She's right. My son is a traitor, though it shames me to say it." She crossed herself, then resumed eating her pasta.

"Well, being a traitor sure as hell beats being gay, doesn't it?" Pete's wounded gaze bore into his mother, who was too stunned by her son's outburst to answer.

"Watch your mouth, Pete," his father warned. "We don't use that kind of perverted language in this house. This is a respectable Catholic family."

John appreciated his brother's attempt to defend him, but knew it would only make matters worse. His father wore his religion like a shield, bringing it out only when it suited him.

"Now I have two sons who are a disgrace to this family," Robert stated, his face reddening. "We raised you boys right. What did we do wrong? Tell me that."

"Not a damn thing!" Pete said with uncharacteristic fervor. "I think John and I turned out pretty good, if you want to know the truth. We didn't do drugs, didn't end up in jail. Your eldest son is a doctor, the second one a lawyer, all three of us went to college. You've got a great deal to be proud of as parents. But are you?" he scoffed, shaking his head.

"Have you ever stopped to consider that we succeeded without any support or help from you? Oh, sure, you were supportive of Michael when he wanted to go to medical school. But even then you made it clear that you couldn't afford to help pay for it, and that he would have to find the money on his own. You wanted the glory but not the pain. Well, it just doesn't work that way."

Pete pushed himself away from the table. "I've had my fill for tonight. Thanks anyway."

John watched his brother walk away, heard the front door slam, and then gazed at his parents' shocked faces. Pete usually kept his thoughts and feelings close to his chest, but not tonight. Tonight he had let them have it with both barrels, and John was glad. It was time his brother stood up to them, made his feelings known. John had no illusions that they would change because of it; he knew better than that. But if speaking his mind made Pete feel better, then he was all for it.

"Pete, come back here," his father ordered.

"Pete's upset. Leave him be."

"I don't understand any of this." Adele's eyes filled with tears. "First Pete brings disgrace to our family by admitting he's queer, and now you take sides against your family. I'm losing all of my children."

"Only because you choose to, Mom. If you and Dad would open your minds and hearts, you would see how different things could be. And don't forget you still have your precious Michael, the only child in the family who can do no wrong."

"Michael respects his parents. He's a good son," his mother pointed out.

"I'm supposed to accept that my son sleeps with a man?" his father asked. "That he does perverted things?" Robert downed his wine in one gulp, refilling his glass from the Chianti bottle. "You think people don't talk? There's been plenty of talk about the both of you, about Peter sleeping with a man, and you with that woman attorney. The one who's related to Bobby D."

Outraged at the idea that Angela had been brought into his family squabble, John slapped the table with both hands, making the glasses shake, along with his mother. "That's a lie! Who's been spreading rumors about me and Angela DeNero?"

Wide-eyed, Adele leaned back in her chair. "People talk in Little Italy. That's the way it's always been here, Johnny."

"So, it's not true, then?" His father appeared relieved. "Though it doesn't matter if it's true or not. What matters is what people believe."

"Then you had better set them straight, Dad, or I'll take matters into my own hands, and you won't like the outcome."

Leaning across the table toward John, who sat opposite him, his father replied, "What kind of son threatens his father?"

"One who's fed up with family, bloodlines, and bullshit. I'm ashamed to be a Franco, ashamed to be related to some members of the Russo family. But most of all, I'm ashamed of the way my parents treat their own children. If anyone has disgraced this family, it's both of you."

THIRTEEN

How can a pregnant woman tell that she's carrying a future lawyer?
She has an uncontrollable craving for bologna.

Angela entered her parents' home full of trepidation. After talking things over with Mia and Wanda during their girls' night out fest the previous evening, where she'd gorged herself on chocolate cannoli and chocolate milk, thanks to Wanda's generosity and her sudden craving for all things chocolate, she had decided to tell her parents about the baby.

She wasn't sure exactly what she was going to say, how she would handle the disappointment that was sure to be on their faces, but she knew it was something she had to do, now, before any more time elapsed.

At nearly three months along, her tummy was starting to pooch, and before too long her pregnancy would be obvious on its own. Her parents had always been honest with her; she didn't want them to find out about the baby through local gossip.

"Anybody home?" she called out, shutting the front door behind her and hanging her coat on the oak hall tree that had once stood in her grandmother's foyer. The house smelled of onions and garlic, and she knew her mom was preparing spaghetti sauce for dinner; she simmered her sauce all day.

Rosalie rushed out of the kitchen with a huge smile on her face, wiping her hands on a dish towel as she approached. "Angie! I wasn't expecting you to drop by today. Don't you have to work?" She studied her daughter more closely. "You don't look so good. Is something wrong?"

There had to be something to the phenomenon known as mother's intuition. It was as if they had some type of extrasensory perception and could read minds. Angela wondered if she would suddenly become imbued with it, now that she was going to be a mother.

"Where're Dad and Mia?" she asked, avoiding the questioning look in her mother's eyes. Rosalie would have her answers soon enough, but Angela doubted she'd like them.

"Mia just left for her new job," her mother explained. "They called at eight o'clock this morning and told her to come in. Can you imagine the nerve, calling at the last minute like that? What's this world coming to?"

"What's she doing? Mia didn't mention a thing to me about a job when I saw her last night."

"Telemarketing. Your sister's going to be one of those horrible people who call you up on the phone and harass you at all hours of the day and night." Rosalie crossed herself, looking skyward. "Another burden to bear. Give me strength, dear Lord."

Angela was disappointed that her sister wasn't around to provide moral support, but she knew telling her parents about the baby was something she needed to do on her own. "I hope Mia doesn't solicit me. I hate getting those annoying phone calls. You can always tell when it's one of those salespeople, because there's a lull before they start talking, so I hang up."

"I'm going to try that. They're driving me nuts. I got a call the other day about diaper service. Can you imagine? At my age? I told them I had no babies, that I needed diapers like I needed a hole in the head. But they said it didn't matter, that I could save them for my grand-children. I told them I had no grandchildren. They didn't care."

She had no grandchildren . . . yet. Angela's face paled.

Sam came into the living room just then, wearing a loose-fitting black jersey jumper over a frilly white blouse, and looking like a hairy Martha Stewart.

No matter how many times she'd seen her father dressed like this, it always took her brain a moment to register that this was dear old Dad and not some over-the-hill lounge singer.

"Hi! Just thought I'd drop by and share some news with you," Angela said.

"Good news, I hope. Bad news gives me indigestion." He tapped his chest with a fist and belched loudly, which earned him a frown from his wife. "Or maybe that's your mother's cooking," he said with a wink, before taking a seat in his battered old wing chair and reaching for the newspaper. "What is it? You got a new fella? I hope he's better than the last one. That Bill was a real putz."

"Yeah, well, that's sort of what I wanted to talk to you guys about."

Rosalie exchanged a concerned look with her husband, then plopped herself down on the sofa. "My hair is a mess." She moved her hand over the dark blond curls. "I haven't had time to comb it yet. We weren't expecting anyone so early."

Angela smiled. "You don't have to primp for me, Mom. I already know you're beautiful." Blinking back tears that suddenly rushed to the forefront, Angela sucked in her breath, saw the worry on their faces, and plunged ahead before she lost complete control of her emotions.

"I have some news, and I'm not quite sure how you're going to take it."

"You're not sick, are you? You don't have cancer?" Her mother's face filled with fear and anguish, and she clutched her throat. "Dear God! Spare me."

Angela felt terrible for alarming her. "No, Mom, it's

nothing like that," she was quick to reassure her. "But I do have a medical condition."

"I knew it. You never come to visit this early in the morning. You're always at work by nine. Something bad has happened. It's serious, isn't it?"

Turning to look at her husband, Rosalie said, "Sam, our daughter is dying." She crossed herself again.

Evoking help from the Almighty was standard operating procedure for Italians. Being Catholic, whether you practiced the religion or not, gave you an automatic inside track to the Big Guy upstairs, or so it was thought. Angela hadn't seen any evidence of it as yet.

"What's wrong, Angie?" her father probed, flashing his wife a disgusted look. "Just tell us what's the matter. It will be easier that way. Your mother always imagines the worst."

"I'm pregnant. I'm going to have a baby."

Her parents' mouths fell open in unison, and the room turned deathly silent. Only the ticking of the cuckoo clock on the wall could be heard clicking off the seconds.

Sam bolted to his feet, his face a mask of outrage. "What bastard did this to you? I'll kill him with my bare hands. On second thought, where's my gun? Rosalie, where's my gun?"

Angela stared wide-eyed as her father grabbed the skirt of his jumper, exposing his knobby knees, and ran around the room like a chicken with his head cut off, shouting for his gun. She felt as if she were in some type of bad B-movie and couldn't have responded if her life depended on it.

Her mother moved to her side and took hold of her cold, clammy hand, as if her husband's behavior was nothing out of the ordinary. Scary thought. "Who's the father, Angela?" she asked, softly but firmly. "You must tell us so we can make him pay for what he's done."

She heaved a sigh. "There'll be no contacting the father. He's left the country, and good riddance. It's Bill McElroy's child, if you must know. But I have no intention of allowing him to have anything further to do with it or me."

"The bastard's done enough already, if you ask me," her father said. "When did this happen?"

"That's not important. What's important is that I'm going to have a baby, and I'm going to need all the love and support you can give me. I know you're disappointed, that you expected more from me, but—"

"Don't be stupid, Angela!" her mother interrupted, putting comforting arms around her distraught daughter. "You have never disappointed us, and you never will. We've always been very proud of you, and we still are. These things happen in the best of families. Your father and I will always be here for you." Rosalie turned to her husband once more. "Won't we, Sam?"

He nodded vigorously. "Of course! So you're pregnant. So what? You didn't disown me when you found out I dressed up in women's clothes. Why should you think I'd behave any differently toward you? We're family. Families stick together during good times and bad. Blood is thicker than water. You think there's no truth to that expression? Ha! It's the blood that counts."

"Thank you," she whispered haltingly, before bursting into tears and covering her face with her hands. "That was a really nice thing for you to say, Dad. I'm sorry for acting like such a baby," she blubbered.

"What am I, an ogre? Of course we'll be here for you, Angie. We love you. And to tell you the truth, I'm looking forward to being a grandfather. If you have a boy, I can teach him to fish and play baseball. I doubt that sissy McElroy would even know how to teach a child those things. He'll be better off with his grandfather."

Yeah, and you can teach him what kind of panty hose has the best support. Oh, God!

All three sat on the couch, Angela sandwiched between her parents. "You guys are the best. I didn't think you'd take the news this well."

"What are you talking about?" Rosalie admonished. "I've been waiting years to get my hands on a grandchild. I'm just sorry things"—translation: getting married— "didn't work out for you and Bill. He was a nice man, but I could tell right off that he wasn't right for you. He was too fussy, too caught up with himself. He wore monogrammed shirts." She screwed up her face in obvious distaste, as if she had just accused the man of having congenital herpes.

The need for revenge was written all over Sam De-Nero's face. "He seemed a little light in the heels to me," he said.

"Bill was as straight as an arrow, Dad. I guess that was part of the problem. He was so structured, so determined to have his own way about everything. Even if he hadn't had an affair, it wouldn't have worked out be—"

"The no-good bastard dumped you for another woman?" Rosalie's shock turned to anger, and her cheeks flushed bright red. "Why, that no good son of a bitch! I wish your father could beat the crap out of him. It's no more than he deserves.

"Imagine him leaving our lovely girl for a bimbo, Sam," she said to her husband, who in turn replied, "Good riddance! Angie is well rid of the no-good bastard."

"I agree, Dad, but it's not going to be a piece of cake raising this child by myself. I still have to earn a living."

"We'll help out as much as we can, you know that, Angela," her mother said, patting her hand. "You won't need to hire strangers to take care of the *bambino*."

Angela filled with gratitude and relief. Her parents

might be a few slices short of a loaf, but they were good people, and she loved them. "Mia's already offered to baby-sit."

"Your sister knows?" Rosalie was clearly put out by this discovery. "How does she know before we do?"

Angela realized her tactical error. Sisters, being lower on the family food chain, could not usurp a mother's right to know first. She wasn't sure if that edict had been handed down on Mount Sinai, but that didn't matter, because her mother thought it so and claimed executive maternal privilege.

"Mia guessed her first day back. Don't be angry that I didn't tell you first. I just needed to wait for the right moment."

If there was such a thing.

Maybe she should suggest to those women who wrote *The Rules* that they add a chapter called "When and How to Tell Your Parents You've Been Knocked Up." Or maybe that had been covered and she'd just missed it.

"Mia's going to baby-sit?" Her father threw back his head and laughed. "Who's going to baby-sit her, that's what I want to know? Your sister's still as irresponsible as ever. I don't think that girl will ever grow up. She's got strange ideas, that one."

"You're being too hard on her, Dad. You expect Mia to be like me, and she isn't. We're nothing alike. Mia's a doer; she's fearless. Adventure is more her style. And now that she has a job—"

"What kind of a job has she got? Calling people up at all hours and annoying them? I hate those damn telemarketers. They shouldn't be allowed to harass taxpaying people. There should be a law."

"Well, at least it's a job. Mia's trying. And she's not working on a highway crew, which drove you crazy, if you recall," Angela pointed out.

"*Hmph!* Small consolation. Still, she's not walking the streets. It could be worse."

"Why don't you come for dinner tomorrow, Angie?" her mother suggested. "We'll have a party to celebrate the baby."

"Thanks, Mom, but I can't. I've been invited to the Gallaghers' restaurant opening. It would be awkward for me to say no, seeing as how I'm their lawyer and all."

"So you'll come on Sunday. We'll do it then."

Smiling, Angela nodded, hugging both her parents and feeling better than she had in days. Of course, that euphoria would end tomorrow night if John Franco kept his promise to be there.

Did she say *promise*? *Threat* was more like it.

Angela was not looking forward to putting herself through the wringer again. The man had a way of jumbling her emotions, turning her inside out, and making her feel things she had no right to feel.

"What's wrong, Angela?" her mother asked. "You look like you've got a bad case of heartburn."

"Yeah, Mom, I do. And I don't think it'll be going away any time soon."

"Angela! I'm so glad you could come to our grand opening tonight." Mary threw welcoming arms about Angela's waist and hugged her to her breast. "Dan will be so pleased. He was hoping you'd be here. You've been working so hard on our case, and . . . well, we just want you to have a good time tonight and forget about everything else."

Smiling warmly at the thoughtful woman, Angela replied, "That's kind of you." She looked about, but didn't spot Mary's husband. "Where's Dan? Since this restaurant was his brainchild I thought for sure he'd be manning the door."

"He's in the kitchen, supervising the new chef, if you can believe that. I think if Dan had his way, he would have cooked everything himself. He loves to cook as much as I do. We're always fighting over the stove."

Mary studied Angela for a moment, cocking her head from side to side. "You look different. Have you done something new with your hair?"

Angela knew a moment of apprehension. Leave it to another pregnant woman to divine the truth. "No, not really. I had it trimmed by Mr. Roy, that's all." There was an old wives' tale that pregnant women glowed from within. Was she starting to look like an incandescent lightbulb? Angela prayed that wasn't the case. She didn't want to sport a neon sign that read, *"Look at me; I'm pregnant!"*

Rock music blared suddenly in the background, and Mary had to raise her voice to be heard above the din. "Dan hired a local band for the opening. They're not too bad, just loud. I'll probably have a headache before this night is over."

Angela scanned the crowded restaurant, where hordes of people gathered in groups, eating, laughing, and having a wonderful time. "Looks like you've got a good crowd tonight. You must have invited the whole neighborhood."

"Most are family and friends, with a few neighbors thrown in for good measure." Angela spied Mary's mother on the other side of the large dining room, waving frantically at her daughter to gain her attention.

"*Uh-oh*. I've got to go, Angela. Duty calls. But I'll be back. Order whatever you want from the bar, and be sure to try the crab cakes. Everything's on the house tonight."

"Thanks, I will."

Angela recognized many familiar faces as she moved farther into the room. Mrs. Foragi was feeding Benny Buffano from her plate, looking adoringly at the geriatric undertaker. Must be love, Angela concluded. Donatella didn't usually share her food.

Grandma Flora held court at one of the dining tables. Dan's son, Matthew, was seated next to her, hanging on to the old woman's every word, while Mary's uncle Alfredo was out on the dance floor with Dan's mom, Lenore.

The two had become an item after Mary and Dan's wedding, and there was speculation that they would be getting married soon. Angela thought they made a nice-looking couple, though she worried that Alfredo's obsession with John Gotti—the old man believed he was connected to the imprisoned crime boss—would prove troublesome.

Retrieving a soda from the bartender, Angela made her way over to the buffet table, where a massive array of hors d'oeuvres and hot dishes were on display. She selected a fried scallop and bit into it, savoring the moist, delicate flavor.

"I see you've found the food."

Recognizing John's voice instantly, Angela felt the little hairs on the back of her neck stand up at attention. She turned to find him standing right behind her. He was smiling, looking far tastier than the scallop she'd just shoved into her mouth.

"I'm hungry. Did you just get here?" she asked, trying to chew around her words.

"I crept in under the cover of darkness," he quipped. "Just in case Sophia has organized a lynch mob."

"You don't look bruised or battered, so I'm taking it that your aunt hasn't spotted you yet."

"I've been avoiding her as much as possible. My aunt loves the spotlight, and I don't want to ruin Mary and Dan's opening night with a scene."

"Just their lives," she found herself saying, then wished she hadn't. The wounded look on his face made her feel small, stupid, and just plain awful. "I'm sorry. That was uncalled for."

He shrugged. "It doesn't matter."

"Yes, it does. It was a horrible thing for me to say. I'm not usually so thoughtless. Please forgive me. I—"

"Johnny, good to see you," John's uncle said, coming to stand next to his nephew and wrapping his arm about his shoulders, cutting off the rest of Angela's apology.

"I just want you to know," he said, lowering his voice, "that not everyone in the family is against you. My wife likes to cause trouble, that's all. You know how your aunt is. But me and Joe, we have our own minds made up, no matter what the women say."

Apparently they'd said a lot, Angela thought, judging by the furious stares being directed their way by various members of the Russo family and their friends. Sophia looked as if she'd just choked on a tainted piece of meat.

"I appreciate your support, Uncle Frank. Hopefully this will all be over soon."

Frank smiled warmly at Angela. "You've got some tough competition, huh? Angela is a smart woman. I think she could beat the pants off you, Johnny. In fact, I'm hoping she does." He winked, and Angela smiled.

"My thoughts exactly, Mr. Russo." Though she wasn't entirely certain she was still talking exclusively about the case.

"Hey, I thought you were on my side, Uncle Frank."

"Only from the standpoint of family. As far as the hearing goes, I have to be on the side of my daughter and son-in-law, you know that, which is why we're so happy to have Angela representing us."

"Thanks for your vote of confidence, Mr. Russo. I'll certainly do my best," she said just as Sophia came up to grab her husband's arm. The woman didn't bother to acknowledge Angela or her nephew.

"Come, Frank. We have to help Mary in the kitchen."

"Hello, Aunt Sophia," John said politely, which Angela thought was very brave, considering he was bearding the lioness in her den, so to speak.

"Frank, you will tell your nephew not to speak to me. He is dead to me now. I don't talk to traitors who turn on their own family."

Anger coursed through Angela, and she felt her face heat with guilt. *Had I sounded as callous and unfeeling?* "Mrs. Russo, that was uncalled for. John is only doing his job. He really had no choice in the matter."

Sophia turned on Angela. "You should talk, young woman. I told my daughter to get rid of you and hire someone else. But would she listen to her mother? Now you are sleeping with the enemy, and—"

"I most certainly am not! Where on earth did you get that idea?"

"Angela, leave it be," John cautioned, grasping her elbow. Frank looked on in disgust, shaking his head at his wife's blunt comments.

"You must excuse my wife, Angela. Sophia has a big mouth and doesn't know when to keep it shut. She listens to gossip all day long. She's like one of those tabloid journalists—all mouth, no brains."

Gasping in outrage, Sophia directed a few choice Italian epithets at her husband. "You will be sorry you said that, Frank," she said before storming off.

"What's going on?" Joe asked as he approached, looking troubled. "I could hear Mom shouting clear across the restaurant."

"Your mother's upset," Frank explained. "She'll get over it." Though he didn't sound at all convinced.

"Yeah? Well, she's upsetting everyone else. She's got Annie all worked up over John coming here tonight. Sorry, John," he said to his cousin before smiling at Angela.

Frank shook his head. "I'll go calm Sophia down.

Why don't you and Angela go and get some dinner, Johnny? She must be hungry, and we don't want her to think that we Russos have no manners, just because my wife is a little crazy."

John looked as if he was going to make a nasty comment regarding Sophia's mental health, or lack of it, and Angela, fearing the worst, latched on to his arm. "I am rather hungry. Would you like to go to the buffet table?" she asked.

"John," Joe said as they made to leave, "you've got friends. Don't forget that. This too shall pass."

John squeezed his cousin's shoulder. "Thanks! It seems weird being an outcast among my own family."

"Feelings are running high right now, but cooler heads will prevail. You'll see." Joe kissed Angela's cheek. "Take good care of John. He needs a friend right now," he whispered.

Seated at one of the tables, admiring the publike atmosphere of Danny Boy's, Angela was consuming a generous portion of roast beef, mashed potatoes, and thick milk gravy. "I'm sorry you had to go through that, John. Your aunt can be very unreasonable. I knew she was domineering and opinionated, but I had no idea she could be so vindictive."

John set down his beer and grew thoughtful. "Sophia's not a bad woman. She's like a terrier when it comes to her family, protective and scraping for a fight. Once she gets hold of something, she isn't likely to let go.

"My aunt has always liked having things her own way, even when we were kids. Of the three Russo children, Connie is the only one she was able to manipulate into doing what she wanted, which was marrying a doctor. Mary and Joe rebelled and followed their hearts, despite her strenuous objections. But, of course, it took them a while before they were able to figure out exactly what it was they wanted."

"I did try to warn you that tonight could be a tad unpleasant," she reminded him.

"So you did. But I'm my own man, and I won't be intimidated by Sophia, my parents, or any other family member who doesn't agree with what I'm doing.

"As I told you before, I didn't want this custody case, Angela, but now that it's mine, I must do all that I can to serve my clients to the best of my abilities, and that means trying to win."

She admired him for that, but still worried that the cost would be too dear. "But what if winning means losing everything else? Will you be able to live with that?"

He shrugged. "I don't know. I don't want to lose my family. I love them, despite their narrow-mindedness and many faults. But I don't see that I have a choice. I'm playing the hand I was dealt."

"I'm sorry you've been forced to choose sides. How is Tony, by the way? Is he doing better?"

John nodded. "Tony's doing great. I spoke to him this morning, as a matter of fact. He's taking his family to Disney World for a couple of weeks."

"Good for him. I'm glad he's not trying to come back to work too soon."

"Oh, he's been trying, never doubt that. But Marie isn't letting him get away with anything."

She smiled. "Well, then, good for Marie."

He reached out and covered her hand. "I've missed talking to you, Angela. When are you going to put me out of my misery and let me see you again?"

"You're seeing me right now. And it's only been a few days since we last saw each other in Judge Baldridge's chambers. Hardly long enough to miss me." She extricated her hand and placed it in her lap, safely out of the way of his captivating touch. She missed him, too, but she had to remain strong.

"Afraid people will think the rumors are true?"

"What rumors?"

"That we're sleeping together."

Angela gasped. "I thought your aunt was just saying that to hurt me. Who would make up such a lie?"

"Well, it wouldn't surprise me to find out that my aunt's the one who started the rumor. Sophia's a great one to speculate and twist things to her satisfaction. And don't forget—you thwarted her by allowing Joe to marry someone else."

"There's never been anything except friendship between Joe and me. Not that your aunt didn't try her damnedest to throw us together. I've never seen a more single-minded woman."

"There's always Grandma, but I don't think she has the heart to hurt anyone."

"Absolutely not! I refuse to believe that sweet old woman had anything to do with the nasty rumor. She's much too caring to do such a thing."

John smiled fondly in remembrance. "When we were kids, me and Pete, and sometimes Michael, but not as often, would go to my grandmother's house to take refuge when we got upset with our parents. Grandma would sit us down at the big table in her kitchen and feed us warm Italian bread and big bowls of coffee that had been diluted with lots of milk and sugar. We always felt better afterward."

"If an adult did that now, they'd probably be accused of child abuse for giving caffeine to a child."

"Things were different back then, better, in many ways. There was certainly a lot less violence among children than there is now."

"Some of the things I've seen and dealt with at the Crisis Center would break your heart. Why do parents bring children into the world if they don't really want them?" She patted her tummy, knowing she wanted the child growing within more than anything. John didn't miss the gesture, and smiled.

"I don't know. I sometimes wonder why my parents had children. They're not exactly cut out for the job. I often think they should have quit after Michael. They would have been much happier that way."

Angela's heart twisted at the raw pain she saw reflected in his eyes. "I'm sure your parents love you, John. They might not know how to express it, that's all."

He gulped down the remainder of his beer, trying to hide his emotions. "I'm a grown man. It doesn't matter any longer. I've learned to let most of their criticisms roll off my back."

"Of course it matters. I don't care how old we get or what we become, we never outgrow the need for our parents' love and approval. I'm sorry if you haven't been able to get that from yours."

"Some people have only so much warmth to give. I'm not sure I have what it takes to be a good father. I wouldn't want to be cold and detached, to find fault with my children, like my father did. Though I do know I'd like to have kids someday."

"Don't underestimate yourself. Your father's failings are not your own. I'm sure you'd make a wonderful father. You're kind, caring, and—" She blushed, worried she'd said too much.

"Yeah, well, I guess I'll never know, thanks to my ex-wife."

Angela's brow wrinkled in confusion. "What do you mean? Didn't she want to have children? Is that why you never had any?"

"We were going to have a child, for a while."

"I'm sorry. What happened?"

"Grace had an abortion after finding out that she was pregnant. Didn't bother telling me until after the fact."

Gasping, Angela looked on, horrified by the discovery. "But why? Why would she do that?"

"She was in love with her career more than she ever loved me. The baby would have gotten in her way."

She covered his hand with her own. "I'm so sorry, John."

"It's one of the reasons I'm so proud of you, Angela. You had every reason to get rid of your baby, and you didn't. You chose not to take the easy way out."

"I hope I've done the right thing. I don't know anything about being a mother. And it's doubtful I'll ever marry, so I feel guilty about depriving my baby of a father."

"I take it you haven't told the baby's father that you're pregnant. You should, you know. If it were mine, I'd want to know."

"Bill made it perfectly clear that he didn't want children. If he told me once, he told me that a hundred times. Besides, he would have made an awful father. He has no patience and is too persnickety about everything."

"So why were you with him? The guy sounds like a loser."

"I guess I thought it was time I got married, and when Bill proposed, it just seemed like the sensible thing to do. Knowing how poor my judgment was where Bill was concerned is another reason I don't want to get married."

"Oh, you'll marry someday, Angela. You've got too much love and goodness inside you not to share it with someone."

His words touched her heart like a warm caress, and her eyes filled with tears. "Thank you."

"Well, hell, I wouldn't have paid you a compliment if I'd known it was going to make you cry."

"I'm not crying." She sniffed. "Not really. Besides, crying jags are just a part of pregnancy, like going to the bathroom every hour on the hour, or eating horrible combinations of food, like bananas and orange marmalade." He looked horrified, and she nodded matter-of-factly. "It's true. No sane person would eat such a thing, but when you're pregnant all bets are off."

John listened intently as she went on to describe all the other symptoms of pregnancy, and he couldn't help the huge grin that spread across his face. "You're adorable, do you know that?"

She blushed. "All pregnant women are adorable, silly. It's how we get away with being so fat for so long. It's like that Klingon cloaking device you see on *Star Trek*. It's all a deception, hiding what's really beneath."

John threw back his head and laughed, knowing at that moment that he was never going to let this woman out of his life.

FOURTEEN

*What's the difference between a mosquito
and a lawyer?*
One is a bloodsucking parasite;
the other is an insect.

"I'm warning you, Rosalie. I don't want to see that mailman inside this house again. If I do, there'll be hell to pay. *Capisce?*"

"This is my home as much as yours, Sam DeNero, and I'll invite whomever I want to come here. It's a free country. You're not my jailer."

"That's right! I'm your husband. Maybe you should try harder to remember that. *Dio mio!* What's wrong with you?"

Her parents' loud argument reached Angela as soon as she stepped foot in the doorway of their home the following day. She rushed into the kitchen to find them squaring off on opposite sides of the cloth-covered kitchen table. Mia was standing near the sink, her hands raised in supplication, as if she had tried to intervene but had had no luck.

"What on earth is going on?" Angela dropped her purse on the table and removed her coat, tossing it over the back of a chair. "You're new in this neighborhood, remember? I'm sure everyone for miles around can hear you arguing. Some impression you're making with your neighbors."

"Who cares?" her father said, turning to face her. "My wife is having an affair. You think I care what the neighbors think?"

Rosalie gasped, paling at her husband's accusation.

"How dare you say such a horrible thing in front of your daughters? Have you no respect?" Her eyes filled with tears. "I am not having an affair, though I probably should be."

Sam looked as if he was about to burst a blood vessel; the veins in his neck were protruding quite alarmingly, and his face was turning a reddish-blue color.

"Why don't we all calm down and try to get this misunderstanding straightened out," Mia offered, stepping forward, and Angela nodded in agreement.

"Mia's right. You two are behaving worse than children. I can't believe you would say such awful things, Dad. I think you should apologize to Mom."

"Ask her. Ask your mother who I found sitting at my kitchen table this morning. Since when does the mail get delivered on Sunday? Never. That's when."

It was very difficult to take a man wearing a silver-sequined T-shirt that claimed BIG MAMA LOVES YOU and black Capri pants seriously, but Angela was doing her best to do just that. "I'm sure there's a reasonable explanation for the mailman's visit. Isn't that right, Mom?" *Please let there be a reasonable explanation.*

Was that guilt she saw on Rosalie's face? Angela remembered how her mother had gone on and on about how attracted she was to the mailman, how handsome he was. Her mother's cheeks filled with color, but she nodded nonetheless, and Angela released the breath she was holding.

"He forgot to deliver my *Good Housekeeping*, so he brought it by this morning on his way to church. I thanked Paul . . . er . . . Mr. Castallano by giving him a cup of coffee. Is that so terrible? The way your father's behaving, you'd think a crime had been committed."

Mia and Angela exchanged worried glances; then Mia asked, "Where was Dad? Wasn't he at home?"

"Of course he was here. He was in the bathroom, shaving his legs. You know how long it takes him to primp, and he wanted to look especially nice for Angela's celebration party, which he's ruined, I might add." She crossed her arms over her chest, glaring defiantly at her husband.

Sam threw his hands in the air. "You and Mia talk some sense into your mother, Angela. I'm going outside to rake the lawn. *Dio!* I don't need this aggravation at my age. I'm supposed to be enjoying my retirement, not reliving scenes from *The Postman Always Rings Twice.*"

"Are you going outside dressed like that, Dad?" Angela's voice filled with alarm. She wasn't sure the conservative Italian neighborhood was ready for Sam DeNero in sequins. She sure as heck wasn't.

He shook his head. "I have overalls I can put on over this." He departed, slamming the back door that led to the attached garage.

Rosalie seated herself at the table, folding her hands on top of the blue oilcloth. "Your father is a very unreasonable man. Do I say anything when he wants to borrow my makeup? Do I mind when he puts runs in all of my stockings? No. And I can't even entertain a friend in my kitchen?" She grunted. "I refuse to be held prisoner in my own home by a jealous husband."

"Mom, you had a pretty good inkling of what Dad's reaction would be to the mailman after the first time you mentioned that Mr. Castallano had paid you a compliment."

"When was this?" Mia wanted to know, pulling out a chair and reaching into the gold ceramic bowl that held an assortment of fruit, nibbling a few red grapes.

"It happened before you moved here." Angela explained their father's previous episode of jealousy, which she had thought cute at the time. Not anymore. The man was obviously enraged. Not an unusual occurrence for Sam. He hadn't earned the nickname Mad Dog while on the Boston police force for nothing.

"Hey, Mom, you been holding out on me?"

At Mia's question, Rosalie's cheeks filled with color again. "I see Paul Castallano every day. He's my mailman. What's wrong with that?"

"Have you invited him in before?" Angela asked, dreading the answer. Her mother seemed infatuated with the guy, and Angela wondered if he really looked like Cesar Romero. She rather doubted it.

"A few times. We just talk. Sometimes I make him lunch. But only if your father isn't at home."

"Do you think that's a good idea, considering how jealous Dad is?"

"I'm entitled to have friends, Angie. Bad enough we don't go out anymore. I can't remember the last time your father took me out to dinner or a movie, or complimented my hair and skin, the way Mr. Castallano does. Paul says I have beautiful skin."

"Perhaps this mailman is a lothario and is trying to get into your pants, Mom," Mia said pointedly. "There're a lot of men who prey on older women."

"So what if he is? Maybe I'll take him up on it, if he offers. The world is ending, girls. We need to enjoy life to the fullest."

Mia's mouth fell open. Angela just sighed.

"But you love Dad," she protested, wondering if she had stumbled into a segment of *Candid Camera* and everything that had transpired would turn out to be a joke. Angela looked up at the overhead fixture, hoping to find a miniature camera. No such luck. "Why would you even think about doing such a thing?"

"The spark is gone. You think it's easy sleeping with a man who has a better wardrobe than I do? I feel dowdy next to Sam. And he never compliments me or lets me borrow his clothes. He's very stingy. My mother, God rest her soul, warned me that cops were cheap. I should have listened."

This surely had to be one of the strangest conversations that Angela had ever had with her mother, or anyone else, for that matter. And as an attorney, she'd had some doozies. "Perhaps you and Dad should go for counseling. Maybe it's time he tried to overcome his cross-dressing fetish."

Rosalie shook her head. "The man's been this way all of our married life. At first it bothered me, but then he explained that he loved me, and that his dressing up didn't mean anything bad. I was young then. We were in love, and life was good. But now, with the end of the world coming, I feel like I'm missing out on something, that maybe there's more I should be seeking. I'm not getting any younger, you know."

"Mom, adultery is a sin," Mia said. "I'm pretty liberal, but even I draw the line at that."

"I'm not planning to sleep with Paul right now, though I admit that I'm very attracted to him. I've always been a sucker for a man in uniform."

Mia rolled her eyes, and Angela bit back a smile. "Uh, I think it might be better if you don't invite Mr. Castallano inside the house anymore, Mom. The neighbors could get the wrong idea. You know, like the one your husband has already formed."

Her mother looked wounded. "I was hoping you girls would understand and be more supportive."

"We do understand. Mia and I have both been attracted to men who weren't necessarily good for us. But we're single, and you're not. If you want to pursue a relationship with Mr. Castallano, then you're going to have to leave Dad. Are you willing to do that?"

Instead of the abject horror Angela expected her mother to project at the question, which was meant to shock her to her senses, she calmly shook her head instead. "I'm not sure."

"You're not sure! Mom, listen to what you're saying." Mia had actually paled, which was unusual for a woman who allowed most things to roll off her back. "You're willing to leave Dad for a man you hardly know? That's crazy. I'm supposed to be the nutcase in the family. You're the stable one, remember?"

"Sometimes a woman needs more than just being a wife and mother. Sometimes she needs romance in her life. I want to feel cherished and loved. I want Sam to treat me like Mr. Castallano does, as if I'm some type of adored object that he worships and can't live without."

"Hey, does this Mr. Castallano have a brother?" Angela shot her sister a scathing look, and Mia added, "Just kidding."

"When you've been in a relationship for as long as you and Dad have it's hard to sustain the giddy, euphoric feeling of falling in love. But you have other things to be thankful for: stability, a man who loves you, even if he doesn't say the words often enough, two daughters who adore you. And don't forget you will soon have a grandchild to occupy your time. You should be counting your blessings."

"I understand what you're saying up here, Angela." Rosalie pointed to her head. "But here, in my heart," she pounded her breast, "it's different. I want things to be different."

Angela took her mother's hand. "Then you need to talk to Dad, explain all of this to him, make him understand how you feel. There's a lot at stake here, Mom. You don't want to make a mistake that you'll regret for the rest of your life."

"Sam won't listen. He never listens to anything I have to say, not really. He thinks I'm just a foolish old woman that he needs to protect from life."

"I'll talk to him for you," Mia offered, and Angela's mouth fell open.

Was her sister on a suicide mission, or just plain insane?

"I appreciate the gesture, dear, but your father thinks you're as nutty as I am. Angela is the only one he'll listen to. If anyone talks to your father, it has to be your sister."

Angela made a choking sound, her eyes growing round as saucers. "Are you serious? You want me to tell Dad that if he doesn't change his ways, you're going to have an affair with the mailman? Do you want to see me killed?"

"Stop with the drama, Angela! You're starting to sound like your mother." Rosalie smiled, patting her daughter's cheek. "You can do this for me, can't you? Make Sam understand that I have needs that aren't being fulfilled."

Needs? Jesus! Did her mother really expect her to talk to her father about sex, about love and adoration?

"Uh, that's kind of a touchy subject for a man," she said.

"It's time Sam faced his responsibilities. I've given your father the best years of my life, now I want some in return. Will you talk to him, Angela, tell him of my feelings? I know it's asking a lot, but I don't think we have any other choice."

Cursing the fates that had brought her here today, Angela thought for a moment, cursed again, then nodded. "All right," she said in a small voice barely above a whisper. "I'll talk to him."

But she would rather walk barefoot over flaming hot coals, have her facial hair waxed, cut her toenails with a dull knife . . .

Bottom line, she didn't want to do it.

No way! No how! Oh, God!

First thing Monday morning Mia came waltzing into Angela's law office, carrying a box of Krispy Kremes and two cardboard containers of coffee. She set both down on the desk, plopping onto the chair, while waiting for her sister to finish her phone call.

"That's correct, Mrs. Carpelli. I don't expect your husband to contest the divorce. Okay. We'll talk soon."

As soon as Angela hung up the phone, she reached for a donut. "Thanks! These look delish. But why are you here? Not that I'm not happy to see you, but shouldn't you be at work, making those hideous phone calls that drive people insane?"

Mia bit into a chocolate glazed donut, then noting the yearning she saw on her sister's face, handed the remainder over to Angela, who smiled gratefully and shoved it into her mouth. "I quit," Mia said, licking her fingers. "It was boring making all those calls. Most of the people hung up on me, and those who didn't cursed me up one side and down the other. I can take only so much abuse for minimum wage."

"*Mmmm.* These are so good. I was starving." Angela sipped her coffee, then asked, "So what are you going to do now? I bet most of the stores are hiring for the holidays."

Mia grinned an impish grin and reached into her purse, pulling out a magazine and tossing it on top of the desk. It was *Soldier of Fortune.* Angela cringed, thinking, Here we go again. "Please tell me you're not going to join a militia group. I don't think Mom and Dad could take the stress. I know I couldn't."

Her sister opened the magazine, pointing to an ad for a school specializing in bodyguard training. "I've decided to enroll in the Serve and Protect Bodyguard Training School program. The classes are being held in Towson, which isn't very far from here, and it says I can learn to become a bodyguard in just a few short weeks. Isn't that cool?"

Angela could see by her sister's determined expression

that she was very excited about this new venture. Angela, on the other hand, was skeptical, not to mention worried that her sister could get hurt, but she tried to remain supportive. "Are you sure this is something you want to do? Isn't being a bodyguard dangerous, Mia?"

"I guess, maybe a little. But that's where the adventure comes in. Mostly I'll be protecting business executives and people like that, but occasionally I could land some noted crime figures. Wouldn't that be cool?"

Angela's eyes widened. "Crime figures. My God, Mia! Do you know what you'll be letting yourself in for? Those kinds of people don't fool around. They kill first and ask questions later."

Mia shook her head. "You're such a worrywart, Angela, always the big sister. Trust me, I'll be fine."

"I am your big sister and I have reason to worry. Some of your decisions over the years have been questionable, you've got to admit that."

"I do. But I'm all grown up and need to figure things out for myself, live life on my own terms. And I feel that I have to do this. You of all people should understand that, Angela. You've made choices, done things that others— Mom and Dad—might not have approved of, had they known."

Angela sighed, knowing the truth of her sister's words. "I was young and foolish then, Mia. And I wasn't in any danger of getting killed. When did you come up with this idea anyway?"

"I've been trying to decide what it is I want to do with my life. I'm just not cut out for the mundane. I enjoy being outdoors, and I'm very athletic. And even though I'm small, I'm strong from lifting weights."

Unlike Angela, Mia had muscles, despite her petite stature. She was very dedicated to her daily workouts and weight training.

"I hope you'll support me with Mom and Dad, especially when Dad finds out about the shooting program. They're going to teach me to shoot a gun. Isn't that cool? And once Dad calms down I can probably get him to teach me a few things. He always wanted me to join the police force."

"As a secretary," Angela reminded her. Sam was going to shit bricks when he heard Mia's latest idea.

"This will be the closest thing to police work. And I won't have to wear a uniform. I can just hang out in my jeans and Nikes, like I always do."

Angela sighed. "You should have been born a boy."

"Is that a derogatory statement about my lack of breasts?"

"I hope this all works out the way you've planned, Mia, because I'm apprehensive about you carrying a gun and dealing with the criminal element. But I'll try to convince Mom and Dad that your being a bodyguard is a good thing. Now, if we're finished, I really have a lot of work to do."

Mia grinned. "Thanks, Ang, you're the best! Actually, the real reason I came here this morning was to find out if you're really going to talk to Dad, like Mom wants you to. I've thought it over and I've decided that it might be too risky. He's got a short temper, and . . . well, I'm worried about what might happen."

"Too bad you didn't voice those fears yesterday, instead of volunteering to do the deed yourself."

"I was overcome by the moment and lost my head. But now that I've had time to think, I'm not sure you should do it. It might not be good for the baby, you know, to get upset and everything."

Angela should be mad at Mia for butting into their parents' marital woes and sticking Angela with the unpleasant task of talking to their father. But she wasn't.

Mia's heart was in the right place. She was like an eager puppy who needed a leash, or maybe a spanking for messing where she shouldn't. Her sister tended to make a mess of a lot of things. Angela guessed her father was right: Mia hadn't grown up yet.

"Thanks, I think. But don't worry. I know I'll be able to talk to Dad in a rational manner. I'm a lawyer. I'm used to handling people in difficult situations." *Ha! Ha! Ha!*

"Dad is not people. He's not normal. He's like Hannibal Lecter. He chews people up, then spits them out. I love him, but he's not exactly the calm and collected type. Hello? He wears a bra."

"I can handle him."

"Okay, but don't say I didn't warn you." The future bodyguard picked up the donut box and put it under her arm.

"Hey, where are you going with those? I thought you bought them for me."

Mia grinned. "I just wanted to sweeten you up while I told you about the bodyguard thing. No sense in wasting good donuts for no reason. See you later."

Angela watched her sister stroll out the door, then glanced down to find that Mia had forgotten her magazine. Rereading the ad for the bodyguard training, she winced.

She had her doubts that Mia would be able to pass the vigorous, demanding training courses they listed. Not to mention the firing of a handgun. The woman was near-sighted and never wore her glasses. Not to mention clumsy. She was likely to fall and shoot someone, quite possibly herself.

Why did Angela have this awful feeling in the pit of her stomach that this whole bodyguard idea was somehow going to turn out disastrously?

Because she knew her sister, that's why.

*   *   *

A couple of hours later, Angela wandered next door to Wanda's office to see if she was ready to go to lunch. The donuts hadn't quite quenched her appetite, and they had plans to eat at The Cheesecake Factory at the Inner Harbor, where she intended to devour about three pieces of their delicious cheesecake.

She was hungry all the time lately. It was as if she had a bottomless pit for a stomach that she couldn't quite manage to fill. Angela knew she was going to start resembling a two-ton elephant if she didn't stop pigging out.

Entering her coworker's office, she pulled up short at the sight of John seated in front of Wanda's desk. Her heart started flip-flopping in her chest—a clear indication that she was more than thrilled to see him, although she had no intention of admitting that to herself, or anyone else. It was a lot harder making convictions than actually sticking to them, she'd discovered.

Wanda smiled and waved her in. "Come on in, Angela. I'm sure John won't mind if you listen in on our conversation. And you may become involved in this anyway, so you might as well hear what's going on."

"Sounds intriguing." Curious, she ventured forward, returning John's smile as she took the seat next to him. "What's up? You two look like coconspirators."

"You could say that," he replied, his expression grave. "I've come to ask Wanda's opinion about a possible discrimination case. It involves my brother."

"Oh?" Angela's eyes widened. "I hope it's nothing too serious."

"Peter's been fired and believes he's being discriminated against because he's gay." John explained the particulars, while Angela listened raptly and Wanda took copious notes.

"This isn't my area of expertise, but it sounds like he might have grounds for a judgment," Angela said. "What do you think, Wanda? You're the expert in these matters."

"As I was just telling John, I'm not certain anything can be done about the homosexuality aspect of his brother's case. The law is pretty clear on that.

"But I think we might have a shot if we use the migraine headaches as a defense. John has indicated that his brother is still being treated for the condition. This defense has been successfully argued in various states, and I think it pertains here. If nothing else, we may be able to get Peter a settlement of some sort, so he'll have the resources and time to find himself another job."

"What sort of work did your brother perform for Trent Enterprises?" Angela asked John.

"As ironic as it sounds, Peter was head of human resources at Trent, so he's fairly familiar with the rules and regulations governing employment. I think he'll make a credible witness, if it comes to that."

"I've got a pretty heavy workload right now, John," Wanda began, purposely sounding as if she might not be willing to take on his brother's case.

"But Wanda!" Angela protested, taking the bait. "You're the best person to represent Peter Franco, and you know it."

"That's true," the attorney said confidently. "But I won't be able to do it alone. I'll need help with the grunt work, gathering the facts, that sort of thing. With any luck this will never go to trial, but just in case . . . are you willing to help?"

John and Angela exchanged startled looks; then John replied, "I am, of course. I'd do just about anything to help my brother. What about you, Angela?" he asked. "Do you have the time?"

Angela knew she should say no. Putting herself in close proximity to John was only going to complicate matters more than they already were. But John looked so distraught about his younger brother's present circumstances that she just didn't have the heart to refuse.

And she wasn't entirely certain that what she was planning to do was ethical, considering the circumstances of the other case they were working on. Well, she would cross that bridge when she came to it, she decided.

"Yes, I'll help. Aside from the Gallagher hearing, my caseload isn't too heavy right now."

Wanda grinned in satisfaction, and Angela didn't like the mischievous gleam that suddenly entered her friend's eye. "Excellent. Let me think about the best way to proceed, and then I'll let you know how you guys can help.

"Angela, why don't you walk John to the elevator while I make a phone call."

Angela was tempted to stick her tongue out at Wanda. Her matchmaking was quite obvious and embarrassing. "Of course."

"You look very pretty today," John remarked as soon as they stepped into the hallway. "Red is a good color for you. You should wear it more often."

Why was it men always liked red?

It was the bull–red flag scenario thing, Angela decided. *Machismo disgusto.*

"Thank you." She had on a loose-fitting red wool jersey dress with a cowl neck. It wasn't one of her nicer outfits, but it was definitely comfortable. And comfort was at the top of her list these days. She had recently succumbed to buying larger bras and underpants. Her days of shopping at Victoria's Secret had come to a screeching halt, at least for a while.

"You're welcome. And thank you for agreeing to help with my brother's case. I really appreciate it. I've always been protective of Peter. I can't stand to see anyone take advantage of him."

"Then that makes you a nice guy and a good brother."

He grinned. "Hey, we're making progress. You think I have some redeeming qualities."

"I've always thought you had good qualities, John, you know that. Of course, after the custody hearing I may feel differently."

"This is one hearing that I'm not looking forward to," he replied, his expression suddenly glum.

"Ditto. But I'm going to do my best to win."

"When you go to court, Counselor, don't wear red." The elevator door opened, and he stepped inside. "It'll be too distracting. And I won't be able to concentrate on the case."

Angela watched the doors shut with regret. "Why is life so damn difficult?" she muttered.

It's not. Just yours, Angela.

FIFTEEN

*What would happen if you locked a cannibal
in a room full of lawyers?*
He would starve to death.

Angela had asked her father to meet her at Mama Sophia's for dinner that evening. She had picked a night when she knew her mother and sister would be at the movies, and a public place to have their discussion where he would be less likely to go ballistic.

They were just finishing up their main course of pasta marinara with shrimp, and were waiting for the dessert they had ordered, when Angela decided to broach the subject of her father's relationship with her mother.

She took a deep breath. "Dad, there's something we need to discuss."

Worry flashed across his face, and he reached out to pat her hand. "If you need money for the baby, Ang, all you have to do is ask. This is my grandkid we're talking about. I'm happy to help in any way I can, you know that."

Angela was touched by his words—his very loud words. She looked about to make sure no one had overheard his comment about the baby. "It's not about the baby, Dad," she said softly, "but thanks for offering. I wanted to talk to you about Mom. I sense that she's not happy, and—"

He rolled his eyes, as if he'd heard this all before. "Your mother is never happy. She lives to be unhappy. Why do you think Rosalie wants the end of the world to come? Do you think happy people look forward to death and destruction?"

Good point. "But there are probably underlying reasons for her unhappiness, don't you think? I know she loves you, but this business with the mailman isn't like Mom. I think she's trying to make you jealous, so you'll pay some attention to her. That could be the reason for the Armageddon talk, too."

The fork he was about to put in his mouth clattered noisily to the tiled tabletop. "What? Is she crazy? I see the woman every day. I pay attention."

"I think you see right through her, Dad. I don't think you stop to see that Mom is a very attractive woman who would like you to make a fuss over her every once in a while, take her out for a nice dinner at some romantic restaurant, and pay her some compliments."

He grew thoughtful for a moment. "She told you this?"

"I think she might have mentioned that she would like it if you were more attentive." No way was she going into that "needs" thing.

"And this is why she's inviting the mailman into our home, so he'll pay attention to her?"

"I think they're just friends. And it's okay for a woman to have male friends who aren't her husband. I'm sure when you were working on the police force you had a lot of female acquaintances."

He nodded, understanding finally starting to dawn.

So he needed to be knocked over the head a bit. So what? At least he was starting to get it. She hoped.

"My partner was female. Remember Linda Simone?"

The waitress brought two servings of cheesecake just then, so Angela was prevented from answering until the coffee was poured and she departed. "Yes, I do. And I'm sure you guys were good friends, right?"

"We worked together. The friendship grew over the years. I resisted having her for a partner at first and made her life kinda rough for a while." He looked embarrassed by his chauvinistic attitude. "But she proved herself more times than I care to think about. Linda was okay. I kinda miss her. She knew a lot of good jokes, mostly dirty ones, of course."

Taking a bite of cheesecake—her latest craving, with Hostess Twinkies running a close second—Angela sighed in pure, unadulterated pleasure.

Who needed sex when you had cheesecake that was this creamy and delicious?

"I don't think Mom's relationship with the mailman is any different than yours was with Linda. They're friends, that's all."

He nodded. "I see your point."

Thank you, Lord!

"You know, Dad, it can't be easy for Mom . . . ah . . . with your particular fetish for wearing women's clothing." Feeling guilty at the hurt look that suddenly crossed his face, she added quickly, "I'm not judging you or anything. I'm just saying that most women wouldn't have been as understanding as Mom's been all these years."

"Rosalie's a good egg."

"I think Mom would like to be thought of as more than Humpty Dumpty, Dad. I think she wants you to treat her like a lover."

His face bright red, he reached for his coffee and gulped it down. "These are personal matters, Angie, not to be discussed with children."

"So is separation and divorce."

"This is what your mother threatens?" His red face turned white, and he looked genuinely shocked by the possibility that his wife might actually leave him.

Well, good. Maybe it was just what he needed to jolt him out of his complacency. Make him think twice about taking his wife for granted.

Men were nothing if not dense.

"Mom's not threatening anything. I'm merely saying

that in my business I see a lot of marital problems. One partner is unhappy, they don't communicate, pretty soon the resentment builds and . . . well, you know what can happen. You broke up enough family disturbances when you were on the force."

Sam heaved a sigh. "I need to try harder, I guess."

"Exactly. It wouldn't take much. Flowers, dinner, a few compliments, maybe a romantic evening where you wore something other than a negligee."

Mortification choked him. "She told you about that?"

Angela nodded, trying hard not to embarrass him further. "Don't worry. You're covered under attorney-client privilege. And even if you're not, I love you. I would never betray a confidence."

It took him a moment to finish his dessert and absorb everything she had said. "Thanks for having the guts to talk to me about this, Ang," he finally said. "You've had a lot on your plate lately, a lot of difficult things to deal with, and I know this wasn't easy for you. Me being your old man, and all."

Her eyes filled with tears. "I love you, Dad."

He winked. "Same goes."

Angela was thinking about the conversation with her dad as she climbed the steps to her apartment. Lost in thought, she didn't see the man sitting at the top of the stairs until she had fallen over him.

"Oooh!" she shouted, landing across John's lap, mortified to have been so careless. She looked up into bright blue eyes, her face hot with embarrassment, and found him smiling at her.

The smile that had launched a thousand . . . Never mind!

John cradled her to him. "Careful. I didn't mean to startle you."

"Well, you did. Why are you here? Is there a problem with Peter's case that I should know about?" She was so happy to see him she couldn't keep the annoyance out of her voice, if that made any sense. It did to her.

Rising to his feet, he pulled her up with him. "No, my being here has nothing to do with Peter, or business, for that matter. It's personal."

Personal? She swallowed.

Reaching down to where he had left his packages, John handed her a couple of pink cardboard bakery boxes that had been tied up with string. Though Angela had just scarfed down a large slice of cheesecake, and four Twinkies before dinner—sort of an appetizer, she had told herself—she felt the stirrings of hunger in her belly and the sudden urge to oink.

"Cannoli and donuts. I wasn't sure which you liked better, so I decided to get both."

The gesture touched her more than if he had gifted her with a diamond tiara. It was obvious John had put some thought into his gift. Of course, that meant he knew she was a foodaholic, but still. . . . "Thank you! That was so thoughtful." Her hand was shaking slightly as she unlocked the door, trying not to feel pleasure at the sweet gesture and failing miserably.

John was such a warm, caring person. It was a side he didn't show that often to too many people outside his close circle of friends and family, but she had seen through his brusque, macho demeanor early on. She tried not to think of him in those terms, tried not to think of him at all. But lately that had become impossible.

Because she loved him.

She loved him with all her heart and soul. And there wasn't a thing she could do about it. She'd tried to deny it, tried to keep her distance, tried to keep her heart from becoming involved. But that had been impossible.

Her heart had always ruled over her head, and this time was no different.

Winston came rushing forward just then, jumping at

her legs and licking her hand as she bent over to pet him, so she didn't have time to ponder the disturbing thought. "I'm happy to see you, too, baby.

"I've got to take Win out or he'll mess on Mrs. Foragi's doormat," she explained to John, who was staring contemptuously at the dog and shaking his head.

"Baby? That's the fattest, ugliest baby I've ever seen."

"Don't listen, Win." She covered the dog's ears. "John's just jealous that you're better-looking than he is."

Winston barked in what could only be construed as agreement, making John laugh. "I'll do it. You look too tired to climb those stairs again."

She smiled gratefully. "All right. I'll make some coffee to go along with all the goodies you brought."

He took the leash she handed him, gave her a thoughtful look that sent her pulse skittering, and bounded down the steps with Winston close on his heels.

Why had he come? And why was he bringing her gifts?

Beware of men bearing cannoli, she thought, but she was happy he had come.

The coffee was ready by the time he returned, and they sat down on the sofa. John was sitting so close she could smell the muskiness of his aftershave; the enticing scent was doing dangerous things to the butterflies now presently beating themselves to death in her belly.

"So, are you going to tell me why you're here?"

He reached out to touch her hair, and she felt her face warm and her toes tingle. "I had to see you, Angela. I know that sounds crazy, but a strange feeling came over me today. I just had to touch you, hear your voice."

Did she say tingle? *She meant three hundred volts of electricity had just turned her toes into twinkle lights.*

"John," she whispered, her heart beating fast at the declaration she found startling and altogether too thrilling. The guy really knew how to pull the rug out from under an unsuspecting female. "I don't think—"

"Don't think. Just feel. I want you. You're the best thing that's happened to me in years."

She caressed his cheek. "I feel the same way, John, but that's not going to change things. All the obstacles in our way are still there."

He took her hand and caressed it. "I have feelings for you, Angela. I'm not sure I've sorted them all out yet, but I know I can't stand not being with you, talking to you. I want to make love to you, be inside you and feel your heat surround me. This doesn't have anything to do with the custody case, my family, or the child you're carrying. It has to do with us. You and me."

She pulled her hand back, unsure of what to say. He hadn't mentioned love. Would just being with him, having him in her life be enough? Or would she yearn for more than he was willing to give?

His hand moved to her thigh, and he leaned in. "I want to make love to you. Will you let me?"

Angela had never felt so giddy. In fact, she was excited as hell. If hell was exciting. She wasn't really sure that was a good analogy. But she was definitely hot. And from everything she had learned in catechism, hell was hot, too.

He drew her into his arms and kissed her, thrusting his tongue deep inside while unbuttoning the jacket of her suit and removing it, then sliding his hands inside her blouse and bra and over the warm curves of her breasts. "You've got such beautiful breasts. So full and soft and perfect."

"They're not usually this large," she blurted, twinkle-light toes flashing furiously and turning into large neon signs.

Shut up! Shut up! Shut up!

"Mmmm. I think they're just right."

"I'm . . . I've gained some weight. I've been eating a lot of cheesecake and Twinkies lately, and—"

Shut the fuck up, Angela!

"I don't care if you weigh as much as the fat lady in the circus. I want to see you naked. I want to get you under me, and I want to get inside of you. Will you let me make love to you, Angela?"

His voice was like warm chocolate as it slid over her, sexy and coaxing. His clever fingers were doing torturous things to her nipples, turning them hard as pebbles and making them throb with longing. Her panties felt uncomfortably damp, and she wasn't sure how much longer she'd be able to hold out.

Angela wasn't sure that she wanted to hold out.

Actually, she was pretty sure that she didn't.

"Yes," she finally whispered.

Removing her bra, he eased her back on the sofa, brushing the hair from her face with gentle strokes, then kissed her cheeks, eyelids, and nipples. "You won't regret this. I promise you."

She covered his lips with her fingertips. "Don't make promises you can't keep, John. We'll take this relationship one day at a time and see what develops. That way, if things don't work out, neither one of us will be disappointed."

He took her face between his hands and smiled into her eyes. "You worry about the damnedest things at the damnedest times, Angela. I guess that's why I'm so crazy about you." He kissed her then, a slow languorous kiss that made her forget all her apprehensions and the reasons she shouldn't get involved.

His searching tongue darted into her mouth, as his hand moved up her thigh to pull down her nylons. The feel of his hand on her bare skin sent her thermostat into high gear. Heat flowed through every pore, and she began to yank at his shirt, pulling it up from his waistband, as he in turn removed her skirt.

"Take your clothes off," she ordered brazenly, in a hoarse voice that hardly sounded like her own.

He grinned. "With pleasure." Straddling her, he unbuttoned his shirt, and she could see the dark chest hairs matted there, the muscular pectorals, the tanned skin that invited her touch, and her heartbeat accelerated. "You're beautiful," she whispered, and he laughed, his eyes twinkling.

"Men aren't beautiful, sweets. But thanks!" His shirt off, John unbuckled his pants, but didn't remove them. He wanted Angela to relax, to enjoy the experience without worrying about pleasing him. He wanted to give her the best sex of her life; he wanted to wipe away thoughts of any man who had come before him.

Moving alongside her, he pulled her to him and began to explore, insinuating his finger beneath the elastic band of her panties, as he planted kisses on her neck, arms, and breasts. "God, you're so beautiful, Angela. You have no idea what touching you does to me. Feeling your heat beneath my fingers, tasting your sweet nipples . . ."

Her face flamed in embarrassment and pleasure. No man, including Bill, had ever said such things to her. "I think I'm getting the picture."

John had just begun to ease down her panties when a knock sounded at the door. Winston rushed from the bedroom, barking at the top of his lungs.

"Shit!"

"You can say that again." Angela moaned in frustration. He did.

"Don't answer it."

Winston kept barking. "If I don't, the dog is never going to shut up. Why don't you wait for me in the bedroom? I'll just grab my robe and get the door. I'll get rid of whoever it is."

Not having any other choice, John nodded, plowing frustrated fingers through his hair. "Don't be long. I don't think I can wait."

"I won't." She smiled apologetically, shouted at Winston to be quiet, put on her robe, and ran to the door.

She opened it to find her father. "Dad! What are you doing here?" She inwardly cursed his poor timing.

"I was driving around, thinking about everything we talked about over dinner. I didn't feel like going home yet. Your mother and sister won't be home for another hour, so I thought I'd drop by for a visit."

"Ah, gee, that's really nice of you. I—I was just finishing up some paperwork." She belted her robe tightly around her, then glanced toward the couch. John's loafers were sticking out from beneath it, and she prayed her father didn't notice. "As much as I'd like to visit with you, Dad, I've got a ton of work to do before morning. I hope you understand."

Sam nodded, bending down to pat the dog, when he spied the bakery boxes on the table. "I see you went to Fiorelli's. Did you get cannoli?"

She hurried into the kitchen and grabbed the box off the table. "Yes. Here." She shoved it at him. "Take them. I'm trying to watch my weight. You'll be doing me a favor."

His eyes lit. "If you're sure. I love cannoli."

She smiled, trying not to seem too impatient, wondering what John was doing in the bedroom, all by himself. "Enjoy them." She glanced at her wristwatch. "I bet Mom and Mia are going to be home any moment. Maybe you can share these with them."

"Good idea, Ang." He kissed her cheek. "By the way," he indicated John's shoes with a lift of his chin, "you shouldn't wear those mannish shoes, even if you're pregnant. They're not stylish at all. I think they make a woman's legs look heavy."

Angela's face turned bright pink. "Thanks for the tip. I just bought them and they're really not all that comfortable. I was planning to ditch them."

He moved to the door and opened it. "Bye, Ang. See you soon."

Angela bolted the door and ran for the bedroom, but John was just emerging. Unfortunately he was fully dressed.

Disappointment swept through her. "You're dressed. But I thought—"

"As much as it pains me to say it, I think we'd better save this for another time. I didn't realize it's so late, and you need your rest. I'll call you tomorrow. We'll set a date and do something fun, okay?"

She wrapped her arms about his waist and looked up. "All right. I'm sorry about what happened."

He kissed her tenderly. "Don't be. Your dad sounds like a nice guy. Maybe I'll get to meet him soon."

Oh, boy! Should she tell him about her father? No, Angela decided. The poor guy had had enough shocks to his system for one night. "I'm sure you will."

"Sleep tight. I'll see you soon."

She leaned against the door. Sleep tight! That was a good one. If only Dad had waited a few more minutes—

Timing was everything.

Yours sucks, Angela. Remember?

Right.

SIXTEEN

What do you call an honest lawyer?
An impossibility.

"Mom, why are you crying? I thought things were starting to get better between you and Dad."

Angela checked her wristwatch—John would be arriving at any moment—holding the phone away from her ear when her mother began screaming invectives again, all having to do with her husband's insensitivity.

"I thought you talked to your father, Angela, told him how unhappy I am, that I have needs that cannot be ignored."

Jesus! Not the needs thing again! Please. Anything but that.

"I did. We had a very nice chat, and he told me that he understood perfectly. In fact, Dad told me just yesterday that he had bought you a present—a surprise that you are just going to love. I think he's making an effort, don't you?"

"The Federal Express man just left. You know what the present is that your father bought me?"

Uh-oh. A loaded question. Angela hoped her cheerfulness came through the receiver. "No. What? I can't wait to hear. It must be something wonderful."

"A box of frozen steaks from Omaha, that's what."

Or not.

"Your father bought me a box of steaks for the freezer. Isn't that romantic? I want to scream. Then I want to punch him in his fat stomach."

Angela's gaze rose heavenward. *Why me?* "Where's Dad now? Does he know you're upset?"

"Of course not! How could I tell him? He was like a little kid, looking out the window, excited for the delivery truck to come. The way he acted I thought the crown jewels were on their way. I can't tell him how much I hate those steaks. It would hurt his feelings.

"And you know the worst of it? They're not even filet mignons, but rib steaks. How cheap can the man be? A good porterhouse I could have lived with, but a rib? *Pleeeze!*"

"Maybe they'll be delicious. Maybe he's planning some kind of romantic dinner with them. You know—wine, candlelight, the whole bit."

Rosalie sniffed loudly, and then quieted as she thought over the suggestion. "Do you really think so? I hadn't thought of that."

No doubt, neither had Dad, but Angela would make certain he did.

"Be happy that he's trying to make an effort. Rome wasn't built in a day. It's a first step."

"If you say so, Angie. You seem to know more about this relationship business than I do. Why is that? I'm older, and I'm your mother. And I read romance novels. I know things are supposed to be different between a man and a woman. You don't see any of those romance heroes bringing home boxes of steak."

"Mom, that's fiction. Relationships are portrayed the way we'd like them to be, not the way things really are." *Too bad about that.* "Maybe I know a bit more about this relationship business because it's a little newer for me, and things have changed drastically from when you were dating Dad."

Rosalie considered the comment, then moved on to another subject. "Are you going out with that lawyer tonight, the one you told me about? I hope you know what you're doing, Angela. I'm worried you might fall for him and get hurt. Men are not like women. They have no sensitivity, no feelings."

"Yes, as a matter of fact I'm going out with John Franco tonight. We're going to see a football game." And she couldn't wait to see him again, to finish what they'd started the other night.

The last two days had been heavenly. They'd met for lunch, shared confidences, and gotten to know each other better. In fact, they had so much in common it was scary. It was as if God had found this perfect man and plopped him down in Angela's lap.

"Go forth and be happy, my child. And try not to screw things up this time."

But, of course, she had. She patted the slight bulge in her abdomen and sighed for what would never be.

"See? What did I tell you? The man sounds like your father. Football! Ha! What kind of man takes a woman to see a football game while on a date? What do his parents do? Is he low class? He sounds low class."

Angela heaved a sigh of pure frustration. "No, Mom, he's not low class. John's very nice. You'll probably meet him soon."

Just as soon as I can figure out how to tell him about Sam's wardrobe choices: John, this is my father. Oh, you think he looks like an ugly Barbra Streisand? Well, I've been meaning to talk to you about that.

"I hope you're using protection, Angela. Just because you can't get pregnant doesn't mean you can't get AIDS."

"Mom! Stop! I am not having this conversation. And just so you know, not that it's any of your business, I might add, I have not been to bed with John Franco."

Yet.

But that was going to change tonight, if she had anything to say about it. John's kisses and caresses had devastated her defenses. She wanted him as much as he wanted her. Maybe more.

"Life is short. Don't waste yours like I did," her mother advised, ruining a perfectly good reverie.

The doorbell rang, and Winston began barking furiously.

"I gotta go, Mom. John's here. I love you. Be nice to Dad. All of this will work out, you'll see."

"The man is as dumb as dirt sometimes, but I'll try. Have fun, Angie. I'll talk to you tomorrow. And wear your coat. It's cold out."

Angela rushed to the door, hoping the black slacks she wore didn't make her butt look like the back end of a Volkswagen Beetle. She pulled down the hem of her red sweater—she'd been wearing red an awful lot because John liked it so much—and went to answer the door.

"I may be geographically challenged, John, but I know this is not the way to my apartment. If I had to guess, I'd say we were heading to Fell's Point."

He smiled. "Bingo. We're not going to your apartment; we're going to mine."

Eyes wide, Angela felt her heart pounding. When a man brought a woman to his apartment, that usually meant one thing. But would John respect her afterward, still want her? Either way, consummation was imminent.

"We are? You're going to allow me into the inner sanctum? What's the occasion?" After he had told her about his loft, she had asked to see it, but each time John had always made up an excuse why she couldn't.

Angela said, "I didn't think we'd be celebrating, since the Patriots beat us so badly." Thirty-four to seven, it was too painful to even think about.

"Don't remind me. I finally score tickets to a home game, and the Ravens lose. What kind of luck is that?"

"If you think you can kidnap me and keep me a prisoner in your apartment just so you can win the custody case, think again, Franco. My mother knows I'm with you. And my dad's an ex-cop. They'll hunt you down."

Smiling, he tweaked her nose. "However tempting that idea may be, sweets, I'm actually taking you over to my place to get your opinion on the interior decoration. My brother picked out all the colors and furniture, and I wrote the checks. I like it, but I want to get a woman's opinion."

So he wasn't after a passionate night of sweaty, heart-stopping, loin-throbbing sex. How disappointing.

"Any woman's opinion will do?"

"I want your opinion, Angela. You know you're the only woman in my life right now."

But for how long?

John had never mentioned making their relationship permanent.

And she knew their relationship was doomed before it ever got off the ground. Why would any man accept a woman who was carrying another man's child?

"You want my opinion on your decor? And here I thought I was finally going to get ravished." She heaved a deep sigh. "Real life is certainly nothing like a romance novel."

John's smile was purely erotic, belying that fact and sending shivers down her spine. "Oh, you are, sweets. Never doubt it. I've just been waiting for Pete to put the finishing touches on the place. I didn't want to invite you over when the apartment looked like a dump. It's rather nice now, suitable for double occupancy . . . and ravishment."

He pulled up in front of a tall brick building that had once been a grain warehouse. FINLAYSON'S GRAINERY was stenciled in faded white letters near the top. "This is great. You must have a fabulous view of the water."

"Yeah, I lucked into this place several years back. I handled the sale of the building, forgoing my fee, with the stipulation that I got first pick of the apartments once it was renovated."

They took the elevator up to the sixth floor at the top of the building and entered John's apartment.

Angela was impressed and surprised by how spacious the rooms were. "It's huge. I could fit two of my apartment in here." She took off her coat and dropped it on a nearby chair; John did the same.

"I use some of the space as an office, so it does double duty," he explained. "I like having plenty of room to spread out, in case I get the urge to shoot hoops." With childlike enthusiasm, he pointed to the basketball hoop mounted on the far wall. "Would you like a tour?"

Nodding eagerly, Angela followed John from room to room; each had been done in shades of green and navy blue. Comfy leather couches and chairs were scattered about the place, accented by brass-and-glass tables and lamps. Plants were set at various locations in the rooms, providing warmth and additional color. Exquisite oriental rugs graced the dark oak flooring in the living and dining rooms, and there were floor-to-ceiling bookcases that formed the law library in his office.

The entire effect was manly, yet homey enough for a woman to appreciate. She could definitely picture herself living here, which was a very dangerous thing to do.

"The bathroom's in there, in case you need to use it, and this is the master bedroom."

He pushed open the wide double doors, and Angela's eyes widened yet again. A king-size bed rested on a platform, with three carpeted stairs leading up to it. Over the bed hung a black wrought-iron chandelier with tiny candle fixtures. Behind the bed, a wall of windows revealed a beautiful star-studded sky and the water beyond.

"Wow! Your brother did a fabulous job of decorating. I may ask him to do mine. He's very talented."

"Now that Pete's out of a job he may welcome the opportunity to make a few bucks on the side. And he does have the talent for it, I think.

"But enough about the decor. You're far more beautiful to look at," he said, turning her in his arms and kissing her passionately and hungrily. She melted into him like sweet, warm honey. "I've been wanting to do that all night," he confessed, his hands moving to cup her buttocks and bring her closer.

"I've been wanting you to do that all night." She began to toy with the buttons on his shirt. "Your kisses make me forget that we're on opposite sides of a complicated legal issue; they make me forget just about everything."

"Good." He deepened the kiss, thrusting his tongue inside, moving his hands beneath her sweater to caress her breasts. "You've got on too many clothes. Shall we go into the master bath and try out the new whirlpool tub? It's big enough for both of us."

Her heart was in her throat as she gazed up at him. Yes! she wanted to shout. Let's get naked. But she knew that before she could agree she had to reassure him about something.

"I have something I want to say before we ... *um* ... get naked, because once you see me naked you'll no doubt lose all ability to concentrate."

Grinning, he replied, "No doubt," then sat down in one of the big overstuffed chairs and pulled her down on his lap, a teasing grin on his face. "I know you don't have three breasts. I've already peeked."

She smiled. "I wanted you to know that I don't expect anything from you, John, even after we take our relationship to the next level. I'm entering into this with my eyes wide open, and I don't want you to feel obligated in any way because of the baby. I—"

"Angela, will you just shut up and kiss me? You talk too damn much."

She smiled impishly. "Okay."

John was crazy in love with this woman. If he hadn't been certain before, he was damn certain now. She was honest, sweet, and sexy as hell. "I admit that this baby is a strange complication, but not enough of one to scare me off. Are you still happy about having it?" He patted her abdomen reverently.

She nodded. "Yes. Even though I know it's going to be difficult raising a child alone, I know I'll be able to manage."

She looked so small and fragile that every protective instinct John possessed rose to the forefront. He wrapped his arms about Angela tightly, drawing her close to his chest. "If you're happy, then I'm happy. Now, if you're as astute as I think you are, then you've probably noticed that there's something hard and compelling beneath you."

Angela nodded enthusiastically.

"Good, because I promised you a night of ravishment, and that's exactly what you're going to get." He smiled, kissing the top of her head.

"I want to be with you, John, make love with you."

"I admit, Angela, that I've never made love to a pregnant woman before, but I'm always up for new experiences, so to speak."

"Yes, I can feel that you are." She felt his arousal beneath her and kissed him full on the mouth; she was more madly in love with him now than she had been just moments ago.

Scooting off his lap, she held out her hand. "I think I'm ready for that bath now," she announced brazenly.

"If you're sure. I don't want to pressure you or make you feel that you have to do this."

Has he changed his mind? Is he backing off?

She hesitated a moment, trying to get a handle on his feelings, then went for broke. "I don't feel the least bit pressured, but if you'd rather not—" Before she could finish, he scooped her up in his arms.

"Hot damn, woman! I've waited for you long enough. Let's not waste another minute talking this to death. I'm so hard I could drill holes in the floor."

She giggled, and all the tension she'd been feeling just seemed to disappear. In fact, she was smiling and laughing the entire time they were stripping out of their clothes, and when John accidentally put too much bubble bath oil in the tub, and when the whirlpool turned those bubbles into a nightmarish mess.

"I love this," she said, leaning back against his hard chest and blowing bubbles from her hand. The warm water felt soothing and sensuous, as did being cocooned in John's strong arms. "I feel so utterly relaxed. But I think you might have put a few too many drops of bath oil in. We're likely to drown in all these bubbles. I feel like I'm in the middle of the *Lawrence Welk Show*." The fragrant bubbles covered her completely.

"I've never taken a bubble bath before, so how was I supposed to know how much to put in. Pete left the bottle as one of his decorative items."

Angela grinned. "I think I'm going to like this brother of yours."

"You'll have a chance to meet him. We're going over to his place tomorrow to do a more formal interview, ask him some of Wanda's questions. That is, if you're game."

"I'm looking forward to it." She held up a washcloth and arched a brow. "Care to scrub my back?"

John groaned, then reached for the soap. "I prefer to use my hands, thanks. I like to be thorough, you understand."

A lump rose to her throat as his soap-slicked hands roamed over her aching breasts, his fingers paying particular attention to her nipples, which were now hard and standing stiff at attention.

"You were right, your breasts have gotten a bit larger, I think. I don't recall them feeling quite this bouncy before."

Laughing, she slapped his hand. "Stop that, or you're going to embarrass me. Bouncy, indeed."

"Well, in that case, I'll just tend to matters a bit lower." Sliding his hands down to the juncture of her thighs, he gently pushed her legs apart. With soapy fingers, he caressed her, teasing the taut bud of her femininity, all the while kissing the back of her neck, her ears, until she moaned in mindless pleasure.

"You're making me crazy," she admitted with a groan. "And two can play this game, you know."

Turning around, she straddled his lap, reaching for his member and caressing it with soft silken strokes until his eyes glazed over. She kissed his chest, his chin, and finally found his lips, which were partially covered with soap. "You don't taste very good at the moment." She spit out some soap bubbles.

"Let's get outta here and into bed. I've had about all the bathing I can take for one night."

"Really?" she quipped. "And I was just getting to the good part, too."

Grinning the sexiest of grins, he helped her out of the tub after they had rinsed off. "You mean my 'power tool'?"

Face flaming, Angela ignored John's laughter and reached for the large bath sheet, wrapping herself in it and heading straight for the huge playground of a bed. "Now, this is what I call a bed. There's even room for Winston. I'll have to bring him the next time I come to visit."

"I wouldn't want that innocent dog watching the depraved things I'm planning to do to you." He wiggled his brows like a dime-store novel villain. "He might bite me."

Reclining against the mound of bed pillows, she quirked her finger and smiled enticingly. "So might I."

With a growl, John dived onto the bed and tackled her

playfully, pulling her to him and kissing her until she couldn't breathe. "I've waited so long to do this, Angela. You're the most beautiful woman I've ever met." With gentle reverence, he kissed her abdomen. "And you're going to have the most beautiful baby in the world."

She choked with emotion, her eyes filling with tears. "That's so sweet, John. Thank you."

"Yeah?" He kissed her chin. "Well, I can be a pretty sweet guy when I put my mind to it. But right now I don't want to be sweet. I want to ravish your body and make you cry out. I want to wipe away the touch of every other man you've known, so you'll only remember mine."

Pulling her nipple into his mouth, John swirled his tongue around the tip, then sucked, and Angela thought she would die from ecstasy. She felt a stirring deep inside her belly, then groaned aloud as the delicious sensation traveled all the way down to her toes. When he moved his mouth lower, she tensed.

Pausing, John looked up. "Relax. You're going to enjoy this. I promise."

"I've . . . I've never done this . . . this particular thing before."

He looked surprised at first, and then utterly delighted. "Then just lay back and enjoy the ride, sweets."

When his mouth caressed her most intimate part Angela had to grip the sheets to prevent herself from flying up to the ceiling; and when his tongue searched out the pulsing bud and he began to flick it lightly, she knew she was a goner.

Every feminist notion she had ever harbored suddenly flew out the window; she was ready to declare herself John's sex slave for life. "Oh, god! That feels sooo good." She clutched his shoulders, unable to stop from moving up to meet him. "Don't stop! Don't ever stop!"

Angela could barely draw a breath, she was panting so hard. When he ripped open the condom package with his teeth, spread her legs and began to enter her, she was more than ready, more than willing to have this man inside her, now and forever.

John slid into her slowly, allowing her body to adjust. She was tight, very tight, and felt so damn good. He pushed harder, feeling her legs wrap around him as she bucked impatiently. "Jesus, Angela! This'll all be over in a second if you don't slow down."

"I can't slow down. I feel out of control, like I've been possessed by demons."

With a devilish smile, John clutched her butt and drove in, increasing his pace until they were rocking so hard she thought the bed would collapse. "Oh, my! Oh . . . my . . . god!" Angela cried out, her breathing matching his short, rapid strokes. "So good. So good."

"Reach for it, sweets. Come on. Stay with me." She was close. He could see it in her eyes, which were glazed over in passion and wonderment.

"I—I—" She screamed as he took her over the edge into a free fall that Angela never imagined possible. She felt the earth move, the sky come tumbling down. She was having a Carole King moment.

"My god!" she said when she could finally talk again, totally in awe of the experience. "That was fantastic. You should get a medal or something."

Brushing sweat-dampened hair away from her face, he smiled down at her. "I take it you haven't had too many orgasms."

"Well, on a scale of one to ten, if what we just did was a ten, I may have had a one."

Rolling off, he wrapped his arms about her and pulled her to him, feeling more replete and content than he ever had before. And he'd had a lot of *before*s. He guessed love had something to do with that. "You sure do know how to make a man feel good."

"Did you ... you know, have an orgasm? Was it okay?"

He was grinning like a cat with a full bowl of cream, looking totally content with the world. "Wonderful. If I still smoked, I'd light up. As soon as I rest, we'll do it again and try to improve our score."

Her eyes widened. "Really?" She grinned. "I'm game. I've never felt so good in my life."

John's heart expanded, and he felt a rush of love that was humbling. Angela was still naive in the ways of love-making, and he wanted to be the one to teach her everything, to explore all the hidden facets of her desire. "Oh, Angela." He wanted to tell her he loved her, tell her how crazy he was about her. But he couldn't. Not yet. He had to sort things out first.

Was he ready to be a father, to raise another man's child as his own? And was he ready for another permanent relationship? He thought so, but he had to be sure.

Angela was slowly erasing all his preconceived notions about love, marriage, and happily ever after. He now thought it entirely possible that such things did, in fact, exist.

SEVENTEEN

What do lawyers use for birth control?
Their personalities.

Pete opened the door to his condo the following day to find his brother and the woman he knew to be Angela DeNero grinning at each other like a couple of lovesick fools. They were so absorbed in each other they were unmindful of the fact that the bell had been answered.

He'd never seen his brother look so smitten, and he was pleased that John had finally found a woman whose brains were bigger than her breasts.

"If you're selling something, I'm not interested," he quipped to gain their attention; they turned to face him, and Angela's face was bright red.

John caught his brother's amused grin and smiled. "Hey, Pete! This is Angela DeNero. She's working on your discrimination case with Wanda and me. You're lucky, because she's a crackerjack lawyer."

"Nice to meet you. *Hmmm.*" Pete took a moment to study Angela, then said, "Angela DeNero. Sounds familiar. In fact, you look kinda familiar. Have we met before?" He stared at her a moment longer, shrugging when she shook her head. "You must have one of those faces, I guess. Though I rarely forget a face."

Angela smiled. "Guess so. I've been told that before."

John's brother ushered them into the living room, and Angela took a seat on the sofa next to John, observing Peter Franco beneath her lashes. She searched her brain, wondering if she'd ever had occasion to meet the man, possibly at Harvard, but she was positive she hadn't.

"So what do you need to know?" Peter asked, leaning back in his recliner. On the surface he looked calm, but she could tell by the way he was twisting his hands he was anything but. "My life is an open book. And soon everyone in town will be reading it. I should make the best-seller list in no time."

"Not necessarily," Angela said, hoping to ease his mind regarding unwanted publicity. If this case hit the newspapers, every detail of Peter's personal encounters would be exposed. She was well aware of how the media twisted everything and tried to sensationalize. It was one of the reasons she'd always tried to lead a circumspect life, keep her personal life private.

"Wanda's hopeful that we may be able to settle this lawsuit out of court."

"Wanda wants to use the Americans with Disabilities Act as your defense, Pete, specifically your migraine head-aches," John said, relieved that his brother's medical condition had been thoroughly documented over the years, thereby providing a foundation upon which to base his claim.

"Wanda thinks we'll have a better chance of getting Trent to the bargaining table if we do. It's an argument that's already been successfully argued in the courts, and the ruling went in the plaintiff's favor."

Peter looked totally confused. "But I'm not disabled. I don't understand how having headaches can be a defense. I was fired because I was gay. I believe that without a doubt."

"There are many types of disabilities, Peter," Angela explained. "If you cannot perform your job because of debilitating headaches, then the court looks upon that as a disability. You have a condition that is not always successfully treatable, one that interferes with the day-to-day routine of your work.

"It will be much easier for Wanda to make that argument in court than to try to convince a judge or jury that your employer discriminated against you because of your sexual persuasion."

Pete digested the information, then shook his head. "I'm embarrassed to say that I'm not very familiar with the Americans with Disabilities Act, though I guess I should be because of my position in Human Resources. I've just never had occasion to use it."

"That's why you have lawyers, Peter," Angela said.

Grinning at his brother, Pete said, "Looks like you've met your match, bro. I think Angela's a keeper."

John watched in amusement as Angela blushed all the way down to the tips of her toes.

"Has John introduced you to our parents yet?"

John's smile suddenly disappeared, and he shot his brother an annoyed look. "I've told Angela a bit about Mom and Dad, but she hasn't met them yet. I'd like to leave it that way for now."

"Don't want to scare off the pretty lady, huh?" Pete winked at Angela. "Just kidding." His voice lowered. "Sort of."

The fact that John had family problems endeared him to her all the more. She'd come to the conclusion that all families were dysfunctional, in one way or another. And it was comforting to know that she wasn't alone, that they shared yet another thing in common.

Angela and John entered Santini's Butcher Shop later that afternoon, to find Mrs. Santini behind the refrigerated meat case and Sophia Russo in front of it. The two women were arguing, which was nothing new—they had a long history of disliking each other—but they stopped as soon as they realized they were no longer alone.

"Hello, Mrs. Russo, Mrs. Santini," Angela said, pasting on a polite smile as she walked up to the meat counter with John, but wishing she could turn tail and run.

Why oh why had she insisted on making John a steak dinner tonight? If they'd just gone out for pizza, as he had suggested, they wouldn't have had to face two of the nastiest women in Baltimore. But Angela had wanted to show off her cooking skills, and now she would no doubt pay the price for that decision.

"*Madonna mia, disgrazia!* I cannot believe my eyes." Sophia crossed herself when she spotted her nephew and Angela together. "This is not right. You two should not be so friendly."

John bussed his aunt on the cheek, and her frown deepened. "Hello, Aunt Sophia," he said with a smile. "You're looking well these days."

"No thanks to you, you fresh boy," Mrs. Santini informed him. "Your aunt is right. You two should not be keeping company. It's the talk of the neighborhood. Usually I don't listen to gossip"—Angela felt like rolling her eyes at the bald-faced lie Nina Santini had just told—"but I see what people are saying about you two is right."

Eyes darkening, John asked, "And what is that?"

"That you are a couple," Sophia replied, shaking her head in disgust. "That you can't keep your hands off each other, that—"

"I get the gist of it, Aunt Sophia," John said, cutting her off. "Well, it's true." He reached for Angela's hand, despite his aunt's shocked gasp. "Angela and I are a couple, and we don't care who knows it."

Angela wondered why John was so blatantly flaunting their relationship. They'd had a few dates, great sex, but were they really a couple? Didn't being a couple constitute a commitment, an implied exclusivity? They'd never discussed anything like that.

"You don't care? You don't care?" Sophia kept repeating like an out-of-control parrot.

Eyes wide, Nina tsked several times. "The young have no shame. Look how my son sniffs after that Donna Wiseman's skirts. Disgraceful. In my day a son would never go against his mother's wishes. I tell Lou that the woman is a fortune hunter, but does he listen? My son will be well-off one day when he inherits the butcher shop, and she knows it."

Sophia threw her hands up in the air. "Like my Joe. Do you see what happened to him? He's no longer a priest. He gave up the church for a woman. Now we are being punished."

"Annie's a lovely woman, Mrs. Russo," Angela stated, unwilling to let John's aunt malign her friend. "You should be thrilled to have her for a daughter-in-law. You don't know how lucky you are."

"Well, after seeing how you turned out, Angela DeNero, I guess that's so. To think that I actually encouraged my Joe to keep company with you." She slapped herself on the forehead. "What was I thinking?"

Turning away from his aunt and her unwanted opinions before he said something he would regret, John attempted to get his anger under control. Facing the meat counter, he said, "We'd like two filet mignons, please, Mrs. Santini. And make them large. I'm hungry."

"I don't understand how you can ignore the trouble you are causing Mary and Dan, Angela," Sophia continued, as if John had never spoken. "They are counting on you to win custody of little Matthew. He is my grandson. I love him as if he were my own flesh and blood. I can't bear to think that . . ."

Angela's voice softened at the anxiety and anguish she saw on the older woman's face. *So Sophia had a heart? Who would have ever guessed?* "I'm going to do my best, Mrs. Russo, truly. My relationship with John has nothing to do with my professional behavior in the court-room. We don't discuss the custody case. Our personal and professional lives are kept totally separate." The case had been put on the back burner while Judge Baldridge attended to some health problems. She and John were hopeful the matter would be resolved in the next week or two.

Sophia didn't look convinced. "My daughter likes you, Angela. Believes in you. And she loves her cousin, so Mary doesn't mind that you two are seeing each other. But I'm old-fashioned. I don't like that my nephew has gone against his family and is causing trouble for my daughter. But I can see that you are very smart, and that you are probably the better lawyer and will beat my nephew when the time comes."

Angela's mouth dropped open, and John finally laughed, once he got over his surprise. "Hey, thanks. I'm happy for the vote of confidence."

"Everyone says that Angela will beat you, John," Nina said, wrapping up the steaks and handing them to John. "We are all very happy about that. No one wants that nasty woman and her rich husband to get their hands on Matthew. He's a good kid. He needs to be with his father."

"Angela is an excellent attorney, and the best choice to represent Mary and Dan in this matter. I've said that many times."

Angela smiled up at him. "Thank you."

Before either Sophia or Nina could respond, the bell over the front door tinkled and in strolled Adele Franco.

John groaned aloud. "I'm in hell," he whispered. "This makes my life complete now."

Angela was confused by his words until the pinched-face woman opened her mouth to speak. Then she felt very sorry for him.

"Well, if it isn't the big-shot attorney, who doesn't

have time for his mother." She turned her attention to Angela, who was standing next to him. "And I suppose you are the reason my son doesn't come around. At least this one likes women; my other son likes men."

John bit back a curse. "Angela, meet my mother, Adele. Mom, this is Angela DeNero, a friend of mine."

Adele made a face of disgust, and then said, "A mother is cursed to have sons. My sons bring me nothing but pain and shame, except Michael. He loves his mother."

John opened his mouth to respond, but his aunt never gave him the chance. Sophia was flashing her sister-in-law an angry look, which surprised him.

It was no secret that Sophia had never cared much for Frank's sister, whom she considered a whiner and cry-baby. Of course, she didn't like Nina Santini much, either, whom she claimed had overcharged her once for lamb chops. But no one, most of all John, had expected her to defend the nephew she had just finished maligning.

"You should think before you speak, Adele. John and Pete are fine young men. And John is a good lawyer. A mother shouldn't play favorites with her children, which is what you've been doing all your life. God gave you three sons. You should love them all the same."

John's mother gasped and appeared genuinely hurt by the remark. "I most certainly do not play favorites. I love all of my children. It's just that Michael was so much easier to deal with. He never gave me any trouble. John knows I love him, don't you?"

John remained conspicuously quiet.

"All my children give me trouble," Sophia stated matter-of-factly. "That is a mother's burden to bear." She crossed herself. "We are put on this earth to give wisdom and guidance, are we not?"

"That is so true, Sophia," Nina agreed. "But do they listen? We might as well talk to the wall."

Both women looked smug, as if they'd just been awarded Mother of the Year medals.

John and Angela exchanged commiserating looks, before Angela said, "It's lovely to meet you, Mrs. Franco. I'm sorry we have to rush off." She glanced up at John. "I guess we'd better be going, right?"

He took the hint and nodded. "Right!" He paid for the steaks, kissed his mother and aunt on the cheek, grabbed hold of Angela's hand, and in the space of two heartbeats hauled her out of the butcher shop, leaving the three women inside staring after them with mouths agape.

When they were safely outside and out of earshot they turned to look at each other and burst out laughing.

"The only thing that would have made that whole episode more interesting would have been if my mother had been there, talking about Armageddon and her infatuation with the mailman," Angela told John, watching his eyes widen.

"Your mother is infatuated with the mailman? Never mind. I don't want to know. This is the woman I'm meeting tomorrow night, correct?"

Angela grinned. "You're going to love my family. They are every bit as weird as yours. You'll feel right at home."

"Your mother and father couldn't possibly be as strange as mine. God broke the mold when he made Adele and Robert."

"*Um.* I wouldn't be too sure of that," Angela told John with an amused smile. "But you'll find that out for yourself soon enough."

"John, there's something I probably should have told you before we got here," Angela said as she opened the front door of the DeNeros' home. The howling November wind had chapped their cheeks and noses red.

She pushed hard, leaning her weight against the door to slam it shut once they were tucked safely inside. "But—"

But she'd never found the right moment, or the courage, if she were truthful with herself, fearing what John's reaction would be, and now it was too late to warn him about anything. John's face was pale, his gasp audible, and his eyes had grown round as saucers.

Shit! Shit! Shit!

Standing in front of the brick fireplace, with his back to them, was Sam DeNero. Angela's father was tossing logs onto the fire, looking very manly, except for the fact that he was wearing tight stretchy pants with black and white stripes that looked like something a deranged zebra on *Wild Kingdom* might wear. The black T-shirt, she saw when he turned, had sparkly things all over the front that spelled A WOMAN'S WORK IS NEVER DONE. On his feet he wore very chic sling-back heels. They were adorable, and Angela was tempted to ask him where he'd bought them.

Catching sight of his daughter and her friend, Sam grinned. "Angie, I've been waiting for you!" He nodded to John, sizing him up, and apparently liking what he saw, smiled warmly at him, like they were long-lost buddies.

"Dad, this is my friend John Franco."

Sam reached out his beefy hand to shake John's. "You're another lawyer, I hear. Hope you don't mind the apparel. Angela told us to just be ourselves tonight, so I'm wearing one of my most comfortable outfits."

When she'd told her parents to be themselves, Angela had meant that it wasn't necessary for them to put on airs, that John was a very down-to-earth kind of guy. She had no idea that her father would appear as Joan Collins, before the face-lift.

"Pleased to meet you, Mr. DeNero," John finally said after he found his voice and got over the shock that Angela's father was wearing high heels, not to mention rhinestone earrings in the shape of zebras that matched his ensemble.

"You've got a good handshake, son. You can always tell the mettle of a man by his handshake. Don't let these clothes fool you. I'm as macho as they come. Ex-cop, you know. I'll go get your mother," he told Angela with a wink that almost dislodged his fake right eyelash.

With mouth agape and lower jaw hanging almost to his chest, John watched Angela's father walk out of the room, heard him shout, "Rosalie, get your butt out here. Angie's come with her fella," and wondered if someone was playing a joke on him.

Reaching for his hand, Angela squeezed, trying to offer what comfort she could. Seeing a man dressed as a woman for the first time was rather shocking, not to mention disconcerting. She hoped John wasn't too appalled.

She remembered the first time she'd seen her father similarly attired. She had walked into the house one day after school—she'd been in junior high at the time—and found her dad lounging in his favorite recliner, wearing her mother's red velvet robe with matching slippers.

When she'd asked him why he was dressed that way, he'd explained, rather lamely, she thought, that his clothes were in the dryer and he was waiting for them to get finished. But she had seen the carefully applied mascara, eye shadow, and lipstick he wore, and knew immediately that something wasn't right.

Angela had kept the secret of that day for almost four years, trying to protect her mother and sister, and it wasn't until she was in high school that she'd learned her mother had known all along about her father's penchant for dressing up in women's clothing, and that her sister had been keeping the very same secret.

"I'm sorry I didn't give you more warning, John, but I wasn't quite sure how to explain something like a cross-dressing fetish. My dad's normal, other than that." Well, sort of. As normal as a father who dressed in women's clothes could be.

At his distracted nod, she smiled ruefully. "I told you they were weird. Guess you know now that I wasn't exaggerating."

"Is the mailman coming tonight, too?"

He looked horrified at the prospect, and she swallowed her smile. "No, just my sister. Mia's not too strange, though she is taking a course in bodyguard training." And succeeding at it, apparently, which was nothing short of amazing. But then, Mia constantly amazed Angela with her derring-do and eccentric behavior. She was most definitely her father's daughter.

John's eyes widened. "She must be a lot bigger than you."

"No, actually—"

Just then the front door slammed shut, and Mia came bounding into the house, dressed in navy sweats, and carrying what looked to be a gun.

Oh, hell! Would this nightmare never end?

"Drop your pants or I'll be forced to shoot!" she commanded John, assuming a squat shooting stance. She flashed a teasing smile, and Angela wanted to strangle her.

Spinning toward the direction of the voice, John caught sight of the gun and nearly fell over onto the couch. "Jesus Christ! Who the hell is that mad midget, Angela?"

"Hey, watch it, buddy!" Mia shouted in mock outrage.

"Mia, put down that gun, for heavensake! You're scaring my guest. I'm going to tell Dad that you're playing around with a firearm. You know what'll happen then."

Her sister made a face and then dropped the gun into her shoulder bag. "You always were a tattletale, Angela. And it's not even loaded, so don't go getting all hysterical."

She grinned impishly at John. "Hi, I'm Mia, Angela's younger and much smarter sister. She's told me a *lot* about you." Her eyebrows rose meaningfully.

Angela's face crimsoned. "Shut up, Mia! You're embarrassing yourself."

"Embarrassing you, is more like it. Don't worry, John. She hasn't told me any of the nasty stuff yet." Her grin widened.

"I'll just go and change. I need to take a shower. I've been learning karate-type stuff all day. Makes a body sweat." She sniffed her right armpit. "*Oooh*. Gross. See ya." She spun out of the room like a tornado, leaving John and Angela standing in her dust.

Shaking his head in bemusement, John laughed aloud, pulling Angela into his chest and kissing her breathless. "Okay, you win. Your family is weirder than mine. Do you think it's hereditary?"

Horrified at the prospect, her face paled. "God, I hope not!" She patted her softly rounded abdomen. "Don't get me wrong, I love them. It's just . . . well, I don't want the baby to . . ." *Wear sequined diapers?*

He kissed her nose. "Your baby is going to be as perfect as you are, sweets. No doubt about it."

If John didn't stop being so nice, she was going to cry. After all those frogs she'd kissed, she had finally met a prince, and the timing couldn't be worse, especially since she was starting to look like a bulging peasant, instead of a princess. The new blue velour maternity pants outfit she wore didn't do much to enhance her image.

"I bet you say that to all the pregnant women you come across."

"Come to think of it, there are an awful lot of pregnant women in Little Italy these days. Mary's sister, Connie, for one, then there's Mary, and now you. I think there must be something in the water."

Too many condoms flushed down the toilet, she thought, smiling to herself. "Italian women are very fertile. We make good breeders." *Breeders! My God! She'd* gone from Gloria Steinem to Mrs. Brady in the space of a few short weeks.

He smiled and chucked her chin. "I'll try to remember that."

"Angela!" Rosalie came bursting into the room with a huge grin, delighted to see her oldest daughter. "I was busy in the kitchen frying the calamari," she explained, wiping her hands on the apron tied around her waist. "I didn't mean to be rude to your guest." She smiled warmly at John. It was the kind of smile that said the wedding invitations had been addressed, posted, and were ready to mail.

Angela performed the introductions; then Rosalie said, "I hope you don't mind how my husband is dressed, John. He's really very harmless. Sam just enjoys dressing up, like Halloween, only for grown-ups."

"Not a problem for me, Mrs. DeNero. No need to explain. Your husband is just eccentric. Nothing wrong with that. Makes life more interesting, in my opinion."

Angela's heart warmed at the generosity of his statement. Even if he didn't believe a word he'd said, it was kind of him to say it. But then, as she had already discovered, John was a very kind man.

Her mother breathed a huge sigh of relief. "Shall we sit down? Your father went to the basement to fetch the olives for the antipasto. I wanted the large green ones, not the black, because today is so special. It's not often our Angie brings a man home to meet the family."

"Mom!"

Angela looked mortified, and John swallowed his smile. "You have a very nice home, Mrs. DeNero," he said, trying to think of pleasantries that didn't involve Mr. De-Nero's fashion sense or Angela's previous boyfriends.

"Thank you. But I don't know how long we'll be able to live here."

Rolling her eyes, Angela braced for the worst. "Mom, don't get started. Please."

"I think John should be warned."

"Is there something wrong with the house, Mrs. De-Nero?" He looked genuinely concerned, until Angela's mother shook her head, opened her mouth, and blurted, "The end of the world is coming! Save yourself, before it's too late."

As carefully as he could, John cradled Angela to his chest and carried her up the flight of stairs leading to her apartment. She had fallen asleep on the short ride home from her parents', and he was doing his best not to wake her.

When he reached the landing, the door next to Angela's opened and Donatella Foragi stuck her head out. She looked even more grim than usual, which was pretty damn grim.

"If you've given that girl one of those date-rape drugs, I'm gonna call the cops on you, Johnny Franco. You'd better be treating Angela decently. I know how you operate. You've got a bad reputation, always have."

John didn't feel like having this conversation at the moment. He especially didn't like seeing Mrs. Foragi in her nightclothes. It would probably give him nightmares for weeks to come. "I didn't give her anything, Mrs. Foragi. We were at her parents' having dinner, and Angela fell asleep in the car on the way home."

Suspicious by nature, Donatella drew closer to make sure Angela was breathing normally. She grunted, apparently having decided to accept his story. "Wait a minute. I'll get the spare key to her apartment and let you in. You'll wake her if you go through her purse searching around for them."

"Thanks. I'll try to control myself and not molest Angela until you get back."

Disgust pinched her lips. "Always with the smart mouth, Johnny. I can remember when you were a kid and you and your brothers used to throw snowballs at me. You coulda put my eye out. You were a bunch of juvenile delinquents, except your older brother. Michael was the only sensible one of the three Franco boys."

"For your information, Mrs. Foragi, Michael was the one who tossed that particular snowball. He had a great arm, played baseball, you know." Her eyes widened at that disclosure. "So how come you never told on us?"

"Because one of you managed to hit Benny Buffano's wife smack-dab in the middle of her back with one of your snowballs and she fell facedown to the ground. Keeled over like a beached whale." The memory made Donatella smile. "It's a day I shall always remember with fondness."

When John frowned, she added, "Don't worry. She wasn't hurt. Her fat stomach and big boobs kept her from hitting the ground too hard. But even if she had died, you boys would have been doing the world and me a favor. That woman is a menace to society."

"You've still got it bad for the undertaker, huh?" He grinned at the older woman's outraged expression.

"What kind of question is that to ask a respectable widow? Shame on you, Johnny Franco! Your mother should wash your mouth out with soap." She disappeared into her apartment, returning a moment later with the key to unlock Angela's door.

Winston barked as soon as she opened it. "That damn bulldog! I think he's starting to like me. He hasn't taken a dump on my doormat in almost two weeks." She patted the dog's head, got her hand licked for the effort, then said, "Well, good night. Tell Angela I said hello, and that it's not nice pretending to be asleep."

The door closed behind her, and John looked down, to find Angela wide-awake and smiling up at him. "Busted!"

He set her down gently. "Damn! And here I was hoping to have my way with you before you awakened. You've ruined all my nefarious plans."

"Wouldn't you rather have me an eager participant?"

"*Hmmm.* Since you put it that way." He drew her into his arms and closed his mouth over hers, but the kiss was short-lived because Winston began whining to be let out.

John sighed in frustration. "Damn that dog! I'll go let him out and be right back. Get naked. I've been thinking about making love to you all evening."

"I bet you weren't thinking about it when my father showed you some of his nicer outfits that he bought from the Home Shopping Network."

"Give me a break, okay? I'm still trying to figure out how to deal with all this. And I did compliment him on the black-beaded dress."

Angela sighed happily as she watched John walk out the door. He'd made a real effort tonight with her family, complimenting her mom's cooking, asking Sam about his work on the police force, and he'd even scored points with Mia by telling her that he thought women made great bodyguards.

They, of course, adored him.

And she, of course, would hear all about it tomorrow.

True to his word, John was back with dog in tow in less than five minutes. Angela was waiting for him in bed, naked beneath the sheets.

"What did you do, sprint?" she asked, eyes twinkling.

"I just threatened your dog with a violent death if he didn't do his *thing* in record time."

"I see. Well, I've been waiting anxiously for you. I want you to strip for me." His mouth fell open. "Do it nice and slow, okay? I want the *Full Monty* treatment. In fact, maybe I should put on some music. What was that Donna Summer song they played in the film?" She started humming "Hot Stuff."

Winston jumped on the bed, staring at John intently, and John actually blushed.

"Can we get rid of the dog first? I don't like him watching me while I undress. It's weird."

"Hey, he's a DeNero. What can I say? Weird is what we do best. We're thinking of applying for a patent."

John pulled the long-sleeved navy polo over his head, and Angela's heart rate increased at the sight of his muscular chest. He had just the right amount of hair, and it dipped into a V below his belt. "Oh, my! I can't wait to see what other large attributes you possess."

Winston barked in agreement.

"Pervert!" John frowned at the dog, unbuttoning his belt and slacks. "You know, sweets, paybacks are going to be tough."

Stretching her arms above her head, she allowed the sheet to fall to her waist, baring her naked breasts, and watched his eyes darken in passion. "I'm counting on that. *Oooh.* I see we're not wearing any underwear tonight." She licked her lips. "Aren't we the naughty boy?"

John crossed to the bed, yanked Winston off, and hauled him to the door. "Sorry, boy, but there's only room in this bed for one stud tonight." He slammed it shut.

Angela tossed her head and laughed. "Come over here, *stud.* I'm waiting for you." She threw back the sheet and invited him into her bed. John didn't need a second invitation.

"You're so beautiful, so perfect," he said, showering kisses over her face and neck. "And you excite the hell outta me, woman. I'll never get my fill of you."

If only that were true, Angela thought.

And then he kissed her, passionately, thoroughly, and oh so tenderly, that she thought it might be true, for something was delivered in that kiss that had never been communicated before.

They pleased each other with their mouths and hands, and when they finally came together, they exploded in such a burst of heated passion that it left them totally spent for minutes afterward.

"Jesus!" John whispered, clearly in awe of what had just happened. "It's never been like that for me before."

His confession made her deliriously happy. "For me, either."

He kissed the top of her head, her nose, then made a path to her lips. "We're very special together. You know that, don't you?"

Smiling softly, she caressed his cheek. "I suspected as much."

Tell me! Tell me you love me and want to be with me always, as I want to be with you.

But he didn't.

He just kissed her again, until all thoughts fled from her head.

EIGHTEEN

*What is the difference between a lawyer
and a sperm cell?*
At least the sperm has a 1 in 600 million chance
of becoming a human being.

"What the hell's the matter with you, bro? I haven't seen you looking this miserable since you failed to get into law school on your first try."

At Pete's question, John heaved a sigh, then reached for his beer and took a swallow. He didn't normally drink during a workday, but he'd come over to his brother's condo to pick up Pete's medical records for Wanda, and suddenly felt the need to sort everything out over a Bud.

John's encounter with Angela the previous night had left him stunned. Their coming together was so beautiful, so unworldly, like nothing he'd ever experienced before. There were a million clichés he could use to describe what had happened. But basically, she had just knocked his socks off. And he hadn't been wearing any!

His safe little world now tilted on its axis, and it was all because of Angela.

"I'm in love."

Plopping down next to him on the sofa, Pete couldn't contain his grin. "I knew it! Angela DeNero, right? At least you picked a good one this time. So why are you so glum? She's a great lady. You guys make a terrific couple."

"There are complications." He tunneled fingers through his thick hair. "Angela's pregnant."

Pete made a noise of disgust. "Dammit, John, you stupid son of a bitch! I'd think at your age you'd be wise enough to use a condom. And I'm sure I don't have to detail all the reasons why."

"Give me a little credit, Pete. It's not my kid. I wish it were. I'm just unsure about what to do. Angela's wonderful. I love her like crazy. But I'm just not sure I'm ready to get married or willing to raise another man's child. I don't want to make another mistake, especially when there's a kid involved. And I don't want to do anything that would hurt Angela."

"If you're talking about marriage and babies, bro, then you're ready. It's time you took the plunge again. Why let that bitchy ex-wife of yours ruin your life? It's no fun growing old and senile by your lonesome. And think how happy you'll make Mom."

Pete was right about Grace. He'd hung on to his bitterness and resentment for too long. And what good had that done him? He had a chance to start over with Angela. He'd be a fool not to take it.

The subject of his mother, however, was a whole different story. "Can you imagine Mom as a mother-in-law? God! She's not even that good as a mother. She'd make Angela's life hell, not to mention mine." Okay, to be fair, Adele was nice to Linda, but only because she loved Michael so much and wouldn't do anything to hurt him. She didn't have that problem with her other two sons.

"You're really dumb, you know that? Mom would love to get her hands on another grandchild. She's not going to be that picky about the circumstances. And you don't even have to tell her whose baby it is. From what I could tell, Angela's not that far along. You can pass it off as yours, and no one will be the wiser."

"That would be dishonest. Angela would never go along with that, and neither would I."

His brother shrugged. "Just a thought. And speaking of honesty, I've got something to show you, and I hope you won't be too upset or think any less of Angela after you've seen it."

"Angela?" John's brows furrowed. "What are you talking about?"

"Remember when we first met, and I told Angela that she looked familiar and I wondered if we'd met?"

"Yeah. So what?"

"So I've been racking my brain about where it was that I could have seen her before. I finally came up with the answer this morning while brushing my teeth." Pete pulled open the drawer beneath the coffee table and reached in, pulling out a photo album.

"Remember when I lived in Boston and took those photography classes? I did it mostly to meet men, but that's another story."

John tried to keep his face impassive and remain non-judgmental, but these little revelations of Pete's always knocked him for a loop. "So? I still don't understand—"

Pete pointed to one of the photographs. "Look at this photo, John. It's Angela. Angela DeNero."

John took the photograph out of the album and stared at it. The woman in the picture did resemble a younger version of Angela. The dark hair was longer, and the woman certainly had as good a body as Angela. But it couldn't be her. The woman he knew was reserved and circumspect. She would never have posed nude in front of a bunch of photography students; he was positive of that.

"That's not Angela. It couldn't be."

"It was a long time ago, John, when she was still in law school at Harvard. There was this guy in class, Randy . . ." Pete thought a few moments, then shook his head. "Can't remember his last name, but he was always bragging about how beautiful his girlfriend was, said she would have made a great model. Anyway, he took these pictures to prove his point and developed the film as part of a photography project. Got an A on it, too. Of course, with a subject as pretty as Angela, who wouldn't?"

"So how did you get your hands on the photo?"

"Randy was proud of his work; he handed a few prints out to the guys in class."

"And you think this woman is Angela? My Angela?"

Pete nodded. "I figure if you're seriously thinking about marrying Angela, then you should know about the skeletons hanging in her closet. I'm deducing from that astonished look on your face that she hasn't told you about Randy."

"It's not her, I'm telling you, Pete, which is why she hasn't told me. Besides, Angela and I haven't told each other everything yet."

Angela was a strong woman, strong enough to handle whatever she encountered. It was one of the things he loved best about her. She didn't whine, didn't complain, she just took what life threw at her and dealt with it. Her decision to keep the baby was admirable. She could have taken the easy way out, but didn't. He was glad.

"Well, if it is true, and it does turn out to be her," Pete said, "then I hope you won't let it interfere with your relationship."

"If I didn't let another man's baby interfere, I doubt I'd get upset over something that happened so long ago. But I'm still saying it's not her."

"Great! Then you won't mind taking a bet on the outcome of who's in that photo. Because I'm so sure it's Angela, I'm willing to bet a hundred bucks to prove I'm right."

"And you'll abide by whatever Angela says?"

Pete nodded. "Angela strikes me as an honest individual. If it's not her and she says so, then I owe you a hundred bucks." He held out his hand to shake on the wager. "Deal?"

John grinned confidently and shook his brother's hand. "Deal. This is going to be the easiest hundred bucks I've ever made." He took the photo, stuck it in his coat pocket, and headed out the door, smiling confidently to himself.

At the sound of the office door opening, Angela looked up from her paperwork, to find John entering her office. He was wearing a rather mischievous smile, and she wondered what had put it there.

"Hi! I didn't think we were meeting for lunch until one." She glanced at her watch: twelve-fifteen. "I thought you had to stop by your brother's house first to pick up those records Wanda needed."

"I've already been there." He shut the door behind him. "Am I interrupting? I saw Wanda outside in the hall, and she said you weren't with clients."

"Just finishing some paperwork. So how's everything with Pete? Is he doing okay?"

John stepped closer to the desk, then perched on the edge of it. She could smell the musky scent of his cologne from where she was seated, and it was doing strange, fluttery things to her insides.

"Pete's fine. In fact, he's the reason I'm here a bit early."

She arched a brow and leaned back in her chair, making it squeak. "Is there a problem I don't know about?"

"My brother thinks he remembers where he knows you from."

"Really? Because I'm positive that I've never met him before."

"You haven't."

Her brows drew together in confusion. "Then how—?"

"Pete used to take classes at a photography studio in Boston."

"So? I still don't understand. What's that got to do with me?"

Relieved when she didn't make the connection, he asked, "Are you acquainted with some guy named Randy? He was in Pete's photography class."

Randy Newsome. Oh, God! How could I have forgotten?

Angela's ears started ringing; she swallowed with a great deal of difficulty, praying her face hadn't turned as red as it felt. "Yes. I used to date a man named Randy Newsome when I was in law school."

John reached into his pocket to retrieve a photograph, and Angela held her breath, though she was sure she knew who the subject was. *Damn you, Randy!* And damn her own stupidity.

Why me, God? So I haven't been to church lately. Why do you have to keep punishing me for my past transgressions?

Or maybe it was the present ones He was pissed about. Whatever!

Mouth hanging open wide enough to catch flies, John stared in disbelief at the photograph once again. "This is you?"

She took it from him, horrified to see herself in a totally nude state. At least she looked good—that was some consolation. "Yes, it's me. Randy and I had an intimate relationship. He was taking a photography course and asked me to pose for him. I didn't see the harm in it at the time. Of course, I had no idea that he was going to develop the film and share the photos with the world."

"He didn't. Just with my brother and a few other guys in his photography class."

Angela's hands went to her flaming cheeks. *John's brother had seen her naked? John's brother had seen her naked!* "I'll never be able to face Pete again. I'm so embarrassed."

John stared at her so intently Angela could barely look him in the eye. Modeling nude for the man she'd been involved with had seemed harmless enough at the time, but now with her pregnancy, and the fact that she and John had been intimate, she worried that he may have formed the opinion she had loose morals, was some type of promiscuous woman, which couldn't be further from the truth.

She'd only ever been with three men in her life: Randy Newsome, during law school; Bill McElroy, after graduation; and now John.

"Hot damn, woman! You are full of surprises."

Bracing herself for the inevitable, Angela rose to her feet and gripped the edge of the desk until her knuckles whitened. Raising her face to his, she looked John straight in the eye and said, "I'll understand if you don't want to see me anymore." She choked on the words as she said them. "I mean, I come with a lot of baggage, my parents are definitely weird, and I'm pregnant, so—"

She never got to finish, because John did something totally unexpected. He threw back his head and laughed, great big laughs that made his chest heave and his shoulders shake. It was almost insulting.

Had he lost his mind?

Was she losing hers?

"I don't see what's so funny. I don't appreciate your mocking me, or making light of what I've done. And I especially don't like being laughed at."

He finally recovered enough to say, "Sweetheart, I'm not laughing at you. I'm laughing at myself. I've had a lot of preconceived notions where you're concerned, and you've managed to flush every single one of them down the toilet, and rightly so.

"My brother is going to have the last laugh with all of this because I bet Pete a hundred dollars that it wasn't you in the photograph."

Her eyes widened. "You did? Are you very disappointed that it's me?"

He took the photo and looked at it again, pretending to consider the question. Finally, he replied, "Hell, no! How can any man be disappointed when the woman he loves looks like this?" He put the photo back in his pocket. "And now I've got plenty of ammunition to keep you in check, sweets," he teased. "We wouldn't want the world to discover what the prim and proper Miss DeNero is really like, now would we?"

Though Angela heard every word John said, she hadn't gotten beyond the phrase *the woman he loves*. She moved out from behind the desk to where he was now standing. "You said 'loves.'" Her heart started beating really fast, and she felt light-headed and giddy. "You did say 'loves,' didn't you?" In situations like this—not that she'd ever been in one before—it never hurt to clarify.

"Hell, yes, I said 'loves.' I love you like crazy, Angela." He opened his arms wide and grinned.

Angela rushed into them, wrapping her arms about his waist. "Are you sure? Because . . . well, I love you, too. Only I don't know how you can love me after everything you know about me, and—"

"Will you shut up and kiss me? You had me at 'I love you, too.'"

The kiss went on for what seemed like forever, then Angela pulled back and looked up. "I'm afraid I'm going to open my eyes and realize this has all been a dream."

He flicked the tip of her nose with his forefinger. "I can think of a way to make it very real for you, sweets." With quick hands that would have made any football receiver proud, he moved under her loose-fitting top, unhooked her bra, and began to caress her breasts.

Angela gasped. "John! Stop! We can't. What if someone comes?"

"I'm counting on that, sweets." He grinned wickedly, and then moved to lock the door, dragging Angela with him. "Have you ever done it on a desk before?"

She looked over her shoulder at the desk, which was covered with papers and assorted items, and felt a shiver of excitement course through her. Then sensibility reared its head. "No. But I think the sofa would be a lot more comfortable, don't you?"

Scooping her up in his arms, he carried her to the leather sofa that stood against the wall. "You're the best thing that's ever happened to me, Angela. I love you."

Later that night, as Angela lay in bed, snuggled up next to Winston—John had a previous engagement with a buddy from college—she recalled his words and replayed them over and over again in her head.

"I love you. I love you. I love you."

John loved her. But he hadn't asked her to marry him. Even after the best sex he'd ever had—his proclamation, not hers, and it hadn't been coerced, either—he hadn't uttered a marriage proposal, made any long-term commitments.

And she wasn't sure he ever would. It was one thing to be in love, have great sex, and enjoy intimate dinners with someone you could talk with easily. But it was quite another to marry someone who was carrying another man's child, to get up in the middle of the night to a screaming baby's demands, to be permanently saddled with a wife and child and take on the additional monetary burden that comes with raising a family when you were just starting to get your career off the ground.

Angela knew all the reasons why John hadn't and probably wouldn't propose. But dammit! She wanted him to. She wanted to be with him, forever and ever. She wanted him to be a father to her child, to have lots of other babies with him, to grow old together, sitting side by side in matching porch rockers, and reflect back on their wonderful life together.

She wanted all of it.

NINETEEN

Why did God make snakes just before lawyers?
To practice.

Angela's palms were sweating. Judge Baldridge had just called the custody hearing to order, and she was trying to concentrate on the instructions he was issuing, and not on the snide remarks certain Russo family members who had gathered in support of Mary and Dan were making.

Sophia Russo had been giving Charles and Sharon Rothburg the evil eye from the moment she'd entered the courtroom. Her unflattering comments about the Rothburgs' lack of parentage—a polite way of saying she'd been calling them *"bastardos"*—had no doubt been heard by the couple, even though they sat on the opposite side of the large room.

As usual, Sophia hadn't bothered to keep her voice down while invoking the wrath of God, and numerous dead Russo relatives. Angela half expected to see one of the Rothburgs drop dead as ordered, before the hearing was through.

John looked mouthwateringly handsome in his dark gray suit and red silk tie, and as nervous as she felt. For the most part, he had avoided making eye contact with his family, focusing instead on his clients, who were seated next to him at the table, as Mary and Dan were seated next to her.

He looked pained, and Angela's heart went out to him. She knew that facing his family in court wasn't easy for him, especially Mary, whom he adored. And it was going to get a whole lot tougher before the day was through, she feared.

"Are we ready to proceed, Miss DeNero? Mr. Franco?" Judge Baldridge asked, and they both nodded. "Good. Then I would like to begin with Mrs. Rothburg's testimony. I want to hear her explanation regarding the defendant's claim that she abandoned their child."

Her face an unflattering beet-red color, Sharon rose from her seat as confidently as she could, flashing her husband a tremulous smile as she was sworn in, then took a seat on the witness stand. She was impeccably dressed in a winter-white wool suit that had been accented with a navy-and-red print scarf.

"You understand, Mrs. Rothburg, that I will need to ask you some questions to ascertain certain facts pertinent to this proceeding?"

"Yes, Your Honor. I'll do my best to answer your questions as honestly as I can. I love my son and want him back. A child belongs with his mother."

Her response served to annoy him, and he drummed his fingers as he spoke. "That's what we're here to determine, Mrs. Rothburg. Please refrain from offering more testimony than you're asked, is that clear?"

She nodded. "Yes, sir."

"Now, please tell me what prompted you to leave your son—a child remanded to your custody, one Matthew Gallagher—in the care of your former husband, Daniel Gallagher—and disappear without letting anyone know of your whereabouts."

"I believe I had some sort of mental breakdown, Your Honor. My job as a lobbyist was very demanding, and the divorce from Dan had taken its toll. It all became too much for me to handle, and I felt the need to escape."

"*Putanna!* A crazy woman shouldn't be allowed to

have a child," Grandma Flora shouted before her son clamped a hand over her mouth and smiled apologetically at the judge.

"I must insist that there be no further outbursts. If there are, I will clear this courtroom. Do I make myself clear? Good," Judge Baldridge stated, not waiting for an answer. "Please continue, Mrs. Rothburg."

Sharon went on to explain about how she had suffered a nervous breakdown from all the stress she'd been under, and that she had foolishly decided that a change of scenery was the only thing that would help to clear her mind.

At the conclusion of her statement, Angela stood to be recognized by the court. She felt confident in the bright-red two-piece suit and matching heels that she had worn in the hope of throwing John off his stride. The skirt was short, showing her legs off to their best advantage, and she knew by the ardent gleam in his eye that he had noticed.

"Do you wish to say something, Miss DeNero?"

"Yes, Your Honor."

Judge Baldridge addressed the room. "A hearing is different than a court trial in that the attorneys present are allowed a bit of latitude in presenting their cases. I am going to allow Miss DeNero to make her statement, though I caution her to be brief."

"Thank you. I don't believe Mrs. Rothburg is being entirely truthful with the court, Your Honor. She failed to mention the substantiated fact that she ran off with her aerobics instructor, a Mr. Robert F. Collins. She also failed to mention that she never once contacted her son, either by phone or letter, during the many months she was gone.

"And the divorce from Mr. Gallagher happened four years prior to her so-called 'breakdown.' Surely she wasn't in shock after such a long period of time, especially since she was the one who had instigated the divorce proceedings to begin with."

"Objection, Your Honor!" John stated, rising to his feet. "Miss DeNero is not qualified to offer opinions regarding Mrs. Rothburg's mental state."

Brows raised, the judge overruled the objection, then turned to look at Dan's ex-wife. "Do you have an explanation for this, Mrs. Rothburg? I think Miss DeNero has raised a valid point."

Sharon burst into tears, and the judge graciously handed her a tissue. "No, Your Honor. It must have been due to my mental breakdown. That's the only explanation I can give. It was quite out of character for me to behave in such a fashion. I've always taken excellent care of my son. I think even my ex-husband will attest to that fact."

"Over my dead body," Mary whispered to Angela, who hoped no one had overheard her. She had enough to deal with without upsetting the judge, who was a stickler about courtroom decorum.

"Did you seek medical attention for your alleged mental condition?" the judge continued.

"No. I didn't realize at the time how dangerous it was. It was only after I met and married Charles that he made me see how serious my mental state had actually become. At his urging, I visited a doctor."

"Do something, Franco!" Charles, whose face had reddened in embarrassment, was clearly agitated by the judge's line of questioning. "My wife is making a fool of herself. It's obvious Baldrige doesn't believe a word she's saying. I barely believe her myself. She's an awful witness."

John stared at the man in disbelief. "You know I can't prevent Judge Baldrige from asking Sharon probative questions. To object at this point would put your wife in an even poorer light; it might look as if she has something to hide." Which was probably closer to the truth than not.

"I demand you do something."

With a sigh of disgust, John rose to his feet once again; he could feel every Russo and Gallagher eye upon his back and heard his aunt mutter "traitor" in Italian, making his heart twist a bit. He'd tried to ignore his family's harsh attitude and remain oblivious of the nasty looks and unkind comments, but it was getting increasingly difficult. He hadn't expected it was going to be so damn hard to be thought of as a pariah, but it was.

"Your Honor, I believe Mrs. Rothburg has already explained her reasons for leaving as she did. I can produce documentation that she was treated for nervous exhaustion upon her return to—"

"I don't see the relevance, Your Honor," Angela blurted. "Mrs. Rothburg clearly wasn't too exhausted or nervous to run off with her aerobics instructor, a man ten years her junior, I might add. I would think a woman would have to possess a certain amount of good health and stamina for that."

John flashed Angela a disappointed look that said her attack was unjustified. "Your Honor, Miss DeNero is clearly out of line with her comments."

"I quite agree, Mr. Franco."

The judge's brow wrinkled in consternation as he turned his attention on Angela, who felt like cringing under his sharp-eyed scrutiny. "Miss DeNero, what you think isn't at issue here. I need facts. And you will have the opportunity to present them. But for now, I'm asking you to please be seated so I can continue questioning Mrs. Rothburg."

"Yes, Your Honor."

"Who does he think he is?" Sophia said loudly to her husband. "Mr. Big Shot? Why should he be allowed to tell Angela what to do? Her question was very good. She's very smart. She would have made Joseph a good wife. I always said so." She punctuated her comment with a grunt.

Annie, seated on the other side of her mother-in-law, stiffened but remained silent.

Angela had overheard Sophia's thoughtless remark and turned to glare at Mary's mother, wondering how anyone could be so insensitive, then placed a finger across her lips to hush her. Sophia sat back, but her lips were still moving, though thankfully nothing audible came out.

The judge continued to question Sharon Rothburg, asking her pointed questions about her relationship with the aerobics instructor, who, she finally admitted, had been married at the time of their alliance. He then turned the discussion to her son.

"Do you love Matthew, Mrs. Rothburg?"

Sharon nodded emphatically. "Yes, I do, more than anything in this world. If I could take back what I've done, I would. I never meant to hurt Matthew. I've always wanted what's best for him."

"Do you think Daniel and Mary Gallagher have provided a good home for him in your absence? Does your child seem well-adjusted and happy?"

She hesitated a moment, gazed at her husband, whose frown had deepened, then said, "Yes. Matthew told me he was happy living with Dan and his wife."

"That being the case, you don't feel that it would be detrimental to your son's well-being to be uprooted again, especially in light of the fact that he's doing so well in school, and seems to have adjusted to his new environment?"

She opened her mouth to reply, but John shot to his feet before she could answer. "I don't think Mrs. Rothburg is qualified to answer that question, Judge. She's not a child psychologist."

"No, but she is this child's mother and, as such, should be able to know whether or not her son is better off remaining where he is," he replied. "I'm asking for an opinion, Mr. Franco, not a medical evaluation."

Angela couldn't help the triumphant smile that crossed her lips as she made eye contact with John, who was looking downright dangerous. His gaze bore into her like bolts of blue lightning, and she felt the heat of his anger before turning away.

"But I'm his mother, Your Honor!" Sharon protested, dabbing her eyes. "A child belongs with his mother."

"That is the prevailing notion. But I intend to determine what is in the best interest of Matthew, not his mother or father. You may step down now, Mrs. Rothburg."

The judge made some notes, checked his wristwatch, and then addressed the courtroom. "We'll continue this hearing after lunch recess. At such time, Mrs. Rothburg will resume testimony and Miss DeNero and Mr. Franco will have the opportunity to ask their questions.

"Court is adjourned." Judge Baldridge banged his gavel, rose, and walked out.

Well, that was about as much fun as stepping in a large pile of horse shit, John decided, exiting the courtroom and hoping to avoid a confrontation with family members. To his relief, he found that most had already departed.

Angela had been a formidable opponent. She was doing an excellent job of presenting Dan and Mary's position, and he couldn't honestly say that he felt anything but glad about that. He wanted Mary and Dan to have the best possible representation, and Angela, it seemed, though it wounded his ego a bit to admit it, was the best.

He wanted to congratulate her on a job well done, but she was still talking with his cousin and her husband about the afternoon session, and there was no way he was getting into the middle of that conversation.

Dan had been staring hatefully at him throughout the morning's proceedings, and John knew that if looks could kill, he'd be a dead man by now. Not that he blamed Mary's husband for being upset with him.

If someone tried to take away his child, a child he had nurtured and loved, as Dan loved Matt— Well, there'd be hell to pay, that was for damn certain.

Which made this whole custody hearing business such an ordeal. There would be no winners in this, none at all.

As much as he disliked Charles and Sharon Rothburg, he knew Sharon loved her son. She had used poor judgment, been selfish, and probably self-serving, but he sensed that deep down where it counted she really, truly loved Matthew.

If only he could find a way to resolve this matter amicably, where both parties could share joint custody and visitation. He decided to speak to the Rothburgs again and feel them out about it, see if they would be agreeable to discussing the possibility further and avoiding what was already becoming a nasty situation.

"I'm very disappointed in how things are going with the custody hearing, John. I thought this case would be a slam dunk. Instead, it's been going from bad to worse. I'm starting to worry that we're going to lose. You seem to have lost your edge in the courtroom."

They were in recess during the second day of hearings, and Rothburg had good reason to be concerned. Angela continued to kick butt in the courtroom—his butt. Her handling of witnesses had been textbook perfect, and she'd offered reasonable and plausible arguments for why Matthew should remain with his father, supporting those arguments with expert testimony and character witnesses.

She'd made mincemeat out of Sharon on cross-examination, getting the flustered woman to admit that she'd had an affair while married to Dan. That announcement had stunned the courtroom, taking everyone, including her ex-husband and John, by surprise.

Charles hadn't fared much better when it came his turn to take the witness stand. In fact, he had come off looking arrogant, resentful, and the mean-spirited son of a bitch that he was. Not exactly Daddy Dearest, but close.

John had done his best to turn things around, but he could tell Judge Baldridge hadn't bought a single word of the testimony.

"I think we need to come up with something drastic, Franco. I'm not going to lose that kid. Do you hear me? Sharon will make my life a living hell if we do. And how would it look, me being vice president of the Bar Association and a successful attorney here in town? It would ruin my reputation. I'm not going to allow that to happen."

John couldn't believe what he was hearing. Rothburg's wife had brought this entire fiasco upon herself, and now everyone else was supposed to shoulder the blame?

"Be reasonable, Charles. Lawyers and clients lose cases like this every day of the week. Your reputation won't suffer because of it.

"Perhaps you and Sharon should reconsider my earlier suggestion of settling for joint custody. I'm certain the Gallaghers would be amenable, once the advantages are explained to them. And you and Sharon will be assured of time with Matthew, which is your primary concern, is it not?"

The older man's eyes turned glacial, and his lips slashed into a thin line. "Are you telling me that you're throwing in the towel already? Because I don't have to tell you how much power I wield in this city, Franco. I can throw a lot of business your way, and I can also make things tough for you and your partner."

Rothburg would do it, too. John didn't give a shit about himself. He was a survivor, had always landed on his feet, and would do so again if it became necessary. But he was quite aware of his responsibility to Tony and his wife and kids. Stefano would be the one to suffer—not just financially, but emotionally and perhaps medically, too.

John couldn't allow that to happen, even if he had to eat crow. Tony had always been there for him, had been a friend when he needed one. He wouldn't repay him by tossing him to a bastard like Rothburg. He would not be the cause of his ruination.

Unclenching his fists, John plastered on a confident smile. "I'm not throwing in the towel. I was merely weighing all the options. I know it's been hard on your wife. And it's going to get worse before it gets better."

"There's only one option. We want to win, and win big. I'm not settling for joint custody. My wife wants her son back, and we want you to make that happen. Do you understand?"

John chose his words carefully. He didn't want to give false hope. "I still think we can win this case. Sharon is the boy's mother. And though Baldridge claims otherwise, I know that fact will weigh heavily with him."

Pushing himself to his feet, and looking somewhat mollified by John's reassurances, Rothburg shot his cuffs. "Good. Then let's see some results, or I'll be forced to take matters into my own hands, and I promise you, you won't like my methods. I intend to win, no matter what I have to do to achieve that end."

John didn't like to be threatened. Rothburg wasn't above reaching into his bag of dirty tricks if the situation warranted. He had a reputation for dealing from the bottom of the deck, paying off witnesses, making evidence disappear. He should have been stripped of his license to practice law long ago. Instead he was made vice president of the Bar Association. It was obvious he had friends in high places, or low, if you counted the devil, who had probably bought the bastard's black soul long ago.

If John had felt disgust toward the older attorney before, he now felt hatred mingling with utter contempt. The man was the lowliest of creatures. To think that the arrogant bastard actually had the nerve, the unmitigated gall, to come into his office and threaten his and Tony's livelihood.

"It's not a secret that you and Miss DeNero are an item, Franco. I hope you've been able to keep your professional objectivity. It would be a shame to have you both brought up on ethics charges."

Furious, John clenched his fists, a hairsbreadth away from pummeling the attorney. If Rothburg even looked sideways at Angela, or treated her in any way that wasn't totally professional and aboveboard, he would regret it.

At this point, he didn't need much of an excuse to teach the old bastard a lesson. In fact, he relished the idea.

Angela was bummed.

Oh, she knew she should be happy. She had a million reasons to be happy: John loved her, they made fabulous, earth-shattering love every night, her baby was healthy, and things were going extremely well with the custody hearing.

In fact, the formal proceedings had ended earlier today, and Judge Baldridge was close to making his decision. She anticipated a ruling by the end of the week, if not sooner, and she was eager to put this whole miserable episode behind her.

Wanda had observed the proceedings this morning and predicted victory for Mary and Dan. Even John agreed the Gallaghers would probably win custody, believing his chances of getting a favorable ruling were dwindling every time Sharon Rothburg opened her mouth.

Angela thought John had put up a good fight, and she was very proud of his performance, and of him, for sticking it out as long as he had, what with all the pressure he'd had to endure. The Rothburgs just hadn't given him enough to work with. They did not present themselves well in court, especially Charles, who came across as arrogant and nasty each time he opened his mouth, in and out of the courtroom.

And she knew that Matthew's recent interview with the judge was likely to carry a lot of weight. Dan's son had previously confided to Angela that he wanted to remain with his father and Mary. He would miss them and his extended family too much if he was forced to move in with his mother and new stepfather, a man he didn't care for.

But regardless of how great some aspects of her life were going, there were others that were going nowhere, and Angela was still bummed.

So, she had decided that since she was already feeling pretty lousy about life in general, why not invite her mother to go shopping at the mall for baby things. A little "end of the world" talk might be just the right pick-me-up she needed to make her forget her problems.

Misery loved company, and no one could exude more misery pound for pound than Rosalie DeNero.

"Look at this beautiful crib blanket, Angela. I'm going to buy it." They were standing in the baby department at Macy's, where Rosalie had already purchased enough baby clothes to cover an entire infant army.

"Mom, you shouldn't. You've already spent way too much money. Besides, it's pink. I might have a boy."

"So what? Boys can't have pink? Look at your father."

Angela's brows raised, as if to say, "Exactly."

Rosalie got the message. "You're right." She put the pink blanket back and reached for a white one. "This can be for a boy or girl."

After they had charged almost three hundred dollars' worth of baby stuff on her mother's Visa card, they headed over to the lingerie department, where Angela was determined to find something that would knock John's socks off. Again. He was coming over tonight, and she wanted to look especially pretty and sexy.

"*Oooh*, isn't this lovely?" she said, holding up a very low-cut black satin gown that she knew would be perfect. She smiled to herself, wondering how long it would take for John to tear if off her. About ten seconds, she decided, which was about as long as any garment stayed on her body once they began to make love.

She was beginning to feel like wallpaper because John was always ordering her to "strip it off." She also came unglued during sex, so that fit, too.

"Your father isn't wearing his negligees to bed anymore," her mother stated, adding with a knowing expression, "You should buy that. John would like it."

Angela was mortified that her mother felt free to comment on her sex life. "Mom! You shouldn't make such personal remarks. You don't even know if John and I are sleeping together."

"What? Am I blind? Of course you're sleeping together. Why wouldn't you be sleeping together? Unless one of you is sick in the head."

Quick, change the subject! "So Dad's getting better about things, I take it."

Her ploy worked. Rosalie frowned. "I wouldn't say better, but he's now wearing silky pajamas to bed instead of the nightgowns, and he bought me a matching pair. The only trouble is that now when we try to get close to each other, we slide in opposite directions."

Angela laughed at the image. "So get naked."

Cheeks filling with color, Rosalie grinned. "Who says I don't? You think you're the only one who—"

"So I take it you're not seeing the mailman these days?" Angela interrupted, unwilling to get into a discussion of her parents' bedroom behavior. She already had way more information than she wanted.

"Paul is a nice man, but I'm not attracted to him anymore. At first I thought he looked like Cesar Romero; he had such a nice smile. But something happened. Maybe he got dentures, because now when I look at him, he smiles like Jerry Stiller; it ruined everything."

"You used to think Dad looked like Paul Newman, remember?" Angela had never seen the resemblance and suspected that the old adage "Love is blind" was particularly true in this instance.

Her mother nodded, smiled, then said, "But now I think he looks more like Joanne Woodward."

They looked at each other, and then burst out laughing. Angela suddenly realized how much she enjoyed being with her mother and decided to confide in her as they headed for the mall's coffee shop. "Mom, I'm not sure about my relationship with John."

"He loves you." Rosalie said it so matter-of-factly it made Angela stop in her tracks.

"Yes, I know. But how did you—?"

"What? Am I blind? I'm a mother. I know these things. I just don't like to interfere, especially after I heard how awful that Sophia Russo's been to her children. I get an earful every time I go to Santini's to buy meat."

"Mrs. Santini's no better than Mrs. Russo, Mom. She's trying to tell her son, Lou, how to live his life and who he should date. The man is almost forty and can make up his own mind. Besides, I think Donna Wiseman is a lovely person."

"Lovely, yes, but I've met brighter bulbs. I'm not sure that girl is all there. She doesn't know anything about working in a butcher shop. And who ever heard of wearing designer suits to work?"

"But she's trying, and you've got to give her credit for that."

Suspicion lit Rosalie's eyes. "Don't be so quick to change the subject. I wasn't born yesterday, you know. What's wrong between you and John? I like him. He would make you a good husband, Angela. He seems like a good egg."

A tear slid down Angela's cheek, and she wiped it away with the back of her hand, feeling foolish for giving in to her tears. She'd been doing that a lot lately. "I know, Ma," she wailed, "but he's never going to ask me. I'm pregnant."

"So you're pregnant. So what? It saves him the trouble. Now he can relax because he doesn't have to worry about getting you with child. He's a busy man. He'll look on this as a bonus. You'll see."

Angela often had trouble following her mother's convoluted reasoning; today was no exception. "Uh, I think we should order. The waitress keeps staring at us."

"So what? Let her stare." She turned toward the woman in question and shot her a dirty look. "I'm having an important discussion with my daughter." To Angela she said, "We don't have many important discussions these days, and I'm savoring this one." Reaching out, she patted Angela's hand.

"I'm very excited about this baby, and so is your father. Whatever happens happens. I'm not going to worry about the end of the world coming anymore, and you shouldn't worry about what's going to happen with you and John. We have no control. It's in God's hands; everything is. Your father finally made me realize that."

"Wow, you and Dad are really connecting again! I'm so happy for you."

"Like a plug and socket. Trust me. The man is impressed and impressive." Rosalie winked.

Angela had no intention of touching that comment with a ten-foot pole, and tucked into her salad.

TWENTY

*Why is doing business with a lawyer like having
sex while using a condom?*
**Because you enjoy a wonderful feeling of safety
and security while you know you're being
screwed!**

"Good luck, John!" Angela said a few moments before they were to enter the courtroom. "I don't want you to win, but I don't want you to lose, either."

"I'd kiss you senseless if we weren't standing in front of God and all the relatives. Somehow I don't think Aunt Sophia would approve."

Angela wanted to laugh, but didn't, owing to the fact that they weren't alone. "Guess you're not looking to die young, huh?" She smiled softly at him, trying to communicate her love without saying the words.

"If you keep looking at me like that, sweets, then all bets are off, because I'm going to drag you into an empty courtroom and have my way with you."

"Promises, promises," she whispered.

The doors to the courtroom opened, and the bailiff announced that Judge Baldridge was about to present his decision. Angela and John exchanged one last look, then found their clients and entered the courtroom.

Judge Baldridge's facial expression didn't offer any hint as to how he was going to rule this morning, but Angela had her fingers crossed under the table that the ruling would go in Mary and Dan's favor.

"Try to relax," she told Mary, who was chewing her nails fast and furiously. "You're making me nervous. And biting your nails is not going to help."

Dan reached out and took his wife's hand. "We want

you to know, Angela, that no matter what happens, we think you did an incredible job. We couldn't have asked for better representation. Thank you."

Mary nodded, but she was too nervous to speak.

On the opposite side of the courtroom John Franco barely spared a glance at his clients; he certainly didn't offer them any advice or commiseration. After the way Rothburg had threatened him, besmirched Angela's name, the man was lucky he wasn't dead. He felt sorry for Sharon, but he figured she had made her bed when she married the bastard.

"As you know," the judge began, and everyone quieted, "deciding a child-custody issue is never easy. And this case, in particular, has been most difficult, owing to the peculiar circumstances, which is why it has taken me longer than usual to come to a decision.

"I wanted to be sure that the decision I made was fair to all the parties concerned, but my main objective was to do what was best for the child in question, Matthew Gallagher."

Sharon Rothburg grabbed her husband's hand and squeezed it. Mary Gallagher did the same.

"It is, therefore, the decision of this court that legal and physical custody of Matthew Gallagher shall be awarded to his natural father, Daniel Gallagher, and his stepmother, Mary Gallagher. If visitation is allowed, it shall be at the discretion of the Gallaghers."

A cheer went up from the gallery.

"Thank you, God!" Sophia shouted, kissing her cross.

"God blessa America!" Overcome with joy, Grandma Flora actually hugged her daughter-in-law, who seemed quite startled.

Sharon jumped up. "You can't do that! Matthew is my son."

"I'm afraid I already have, Mrs. Rothburg. I'm sorry.

Court is adjourned." The judge banged the gavel to indicate the end of the proceedings.

Charles Rothburg glared lethally at John, while wrapping his arm about his wife. "You bastard! I warned you about this. You deliberately tried to lose this case, so your girlfriend would win. A first-year law student could have done a better job than you did."

John's face flushed, but somehow he managed to keep his anger in check, mostly because he felt sorry for Sharon. "I don't appreciate your comments, nor do I appreciate being called a bastard, Rothburg. The case was thin at best. I did everything in my power to win, but Sharon's abandonment of her son was just too difficult to overcome. And Angela DeNero is an excellent attorney. She beat us fair and square."

"You're both going to pay, Franco. On that you have my word."

"Charles! That's enough. I want to go home now. I'm not feeling well," Sharon told her husband, dabbing her tears with a tissue.

"Shut the hell up, Sharon!"

"Now wait just a goddamn minute, Rothburg. Angela had nothing to do with your losing, other than the fact that she presented a better argument. You leave her out of your sick need for revenge."

"You've left me no choice. I have to take matters into my own hands."

Tingles of apprehension tripped down John's spine. "Matters? What the hell are you talking about?"

"You'll find out soon enough. Now get the hell out of my way. I'm a busy man."

John felt uneasy as he watched the couple walk away, but he eased into a smile when Angela approached. "Congratulations, Counselor." He held out his hand to shake hers. "You did a wonderful job representing Dan and Mary. I'm glad they had you on their side."

"My victory isn't as sweet, knowing it was you that I defeated."

"You know, I just realized something. The case is over. I don't have to behave myself anymore." That said, he drew her into his arms and gave her a long, lingering kiss.

"Well, at least you waited until the courtroom was cleared," she said, smiling up at him.

"Let's go home, Angela. I need to make love to you."

She looped her arm through his and grinned. "To the victor go the spoils."

Since Friday's courtroom victory, Angela felt like she was walking on cloud nine. Her bad mood of days ago had disappeared. The chat she'd had with her mother had left her feeling optimistic about the future, and making love with John until the wee hours of this morning hadn't hurt one bit, either. It had had a calming effect, better than any antidepressant drug she could have taken.

"Love conquers all" had become her new mantra.

Things would work out with John, she told herself, over and over again, ad nauseum, needing to believe it, wanting to believe her mother's predictions about happily ever after, and Mia's assurances that men like John didn't come down the pike very often and were worth waiting for.

For once she agreed with her sister. John was a very special man. She would bide her time and wait for him to make a commitment. She was sure he would. It was only a matter of time and patience. Unfortunately she'd never been a very patient woman, but . . .

He loved her. She loved him. Love conquers all.

It made perfectly good sense to Angela.

Glancing at the kitchen clock on the wall, she smiled in anticipation. John was due to arrive for dinner in about thirty minutes. She had taken the day off work to prepare a special gourmet feast for him.

Sex was all well and good—very good, actually—but she'd decided to tempt him with something a little more practical than boudoir cheesecake, knowing how much he enjoyed eating home-cooked food. She was no Mario Batali, her new favorite cooking-show chef—but then, she was no slouch in the kitchen, either. When push came to shove, she could grill, steam, and roast with the best of them; she just didn't do it very often.

The standing rib roast she'd prepared was roasting to perfection in the oven and smelled divine. To accompany it, she would serve spinach salad with hot bacon dressing, and garlic mashed potatoes.

And for dessert—aside from herself, that is—a yummy chocolate cake with chocolate chip frosting. It was her mom's special recipe, and one of her favorite desserts. The cake was a confectionary masterpiece, if she said so herself. She had taken several inconspicuous bites, just to be certain it would pass muster, then covered up the gaps with extra frosting.

Hey, she was entitled! Everything was going to work out just fine, she was positive.

When the phone rang ten minutes later she grew somewhat apprehensive. John wasn't coming! Something had come up at work and he was canceling out on her. All her hard work, her plans for a seductive evening to bring him to his knees—literally! she was holding out for the official proposal position—was all for naught.

The phone kept ringing. Winston kept barking, drawing her out of her maudlin thoughts, and she hurried to answer it.

"Hey, girl. It's me."

Wanda's voice filled Angela with relief. John wasn't canceling after all.

"Have you seen today's paper?" she asked, the worry in her voice unmistakable. "If not, I think you should, and right away."

"Why? What's going on?" As if she really wanted to know. "I've been busy cooking all day and haven't bothered to pick it up off my front mat." She hadn't bothered to answer the three previous phone calls either, figuring they were from her mother, who'd be calling to quiz her about John.

"You're on the front page, Angela. And you're not wearing much more than a smile."

All the air left her lungs in a whoosh, and Angela gasped, leaning against the countertop, praying she wouldn't faint. Dropping the phone, she ran to the door and opened it to find that day's edition of the *Baltimore Sun*.

She picked it up, staring in horror at the photograph Randy had taken of her. Thank God the newspaper had placed one of those black bar thingies across her boobs so you couldn't see them clearly. But her face was unmistakable.

What were her parents going to think when they saw it?

Oh, God! She couldn't go there now. She just couldn't.

The photo was the one Peter had given John—the very one John had had in his possession, the one he had threatened her with: *"And now I've got plenty of ammunition to keep you in check, sweets."* At the time she thought he was kidding.

Joke's on you, Angela!

"Goddamn you, John Franco! How could you do such a horrible thing? And to someone you professed to love?" Love. Ha! Bill professed to love her, too, and look how that ended up. All men were the same. Lying, cheating, conniving—

Would she never learn her lesson?

With a wounded cry, she dropped the paper as if it were contaminated and slammed the door shut. Inside the kitchen, she picked up the dangling wall phone, to find Wanda still waiting. Her hand was shaking badly when she lifted the receiver to her ear.

"My God! I'm ruined. Why would he do such a thing?"

"Who?" There was confusion in her friend's voice. "What are you talking about?"

"John, of course. He had that photo in his possession. I saw it myself."

She explained about posing nude for Randy, to which Wanda replied with unconcealed admiration.

"You go, girl! I never thought you had it in you."

"Yeah, well, look where it's gotten me. How many clients want to be represented by Miss Nude USA, tell me that?"

"I predict that you'll get a lot of male clients."

Angela cursed beneath her breath. "I don't know why I bother talking to you, Wanda Washington. This is not a joking matter."

"I know it's not, honey, but you need to calm down and think this whole thing through rationally. I doubt very much that John had anything to do with that photograph appearing in the newspaper. He's too honest, and he loves you a great deal. Any fool can see that."

But Angela was adamant. "This was John's doing. I know it. He lost the custody case. This is his way of telling me that it's over. He couldn't come right out and say it, so he did this instead. He had his fun, and now he wants out."

"Angela, listen to yourself. You're distraught. You sound ridiculous. If you want to know who I think is responsible for this entire ugly episode, it's—"

The doorbell rang.

"John's here." Her stomach hurt just thinking about it. "I have to go."

Angela slammed down the phone before Wanda could finish. She'd apologize to her friend tomorrow, if she hadn't done away with herself before then.

Or murdered John.

The latter seemed far more appealing at the moment.

The preselected murder victim was extremely nervous, but not because of anything Angela was contemplating doing to him.

John had come to propose marriage, and he was scared.

He patted his jacket pocket for what seemed like the hundredth time since purchasing the diamond engagement ring that morning and shoving it into his pocket.

He was going to ask Angela to marry him. He'd thought about it long and hard, and had finally come to the decision that he couldn't live his life without her. They belonged together, were perfect for each other. He wouldn't risk losing her to another man, he'd decided.

He loved her, wanted to be with her, always. And he wanted her child, too. Watching Angela's body ripen with pregnancy made him realize how much he was looking forward to her having this baby . . . their baby. He would raise it as his own and love it unconditionally.

They would be a family.

The kind of family that did things together, like go on picnics, push the stroller in the park, attend Little League games and dance recitals.

Having no experience with fatherhood, except for looking out for his younger brother, John didn't know what kind of a father he would make, but he thought he could do a good job, better than his own father, certainly!

He already knew that he wouldn't be the kind of parent who criticized constantly, or gave preferential treatment to one child over another. He would always be there for his kids, no matter what kind of life choices or mistakes they might make. And he knew they would make them; all kids did. Hell, even grown men made mistakes; he was proof of that.

And Angela would be there to help him through it all. Together with the baby they would make a happy, loving family.

Speaking of Angela, why wasn't she opening the door? She'd told him to be here on time, not to show up even a minute after six. Well, here he was, so where was she?

John banged the door again.

"Go away, you unfeeling, underhanded bastard! I never want to see you again!"

His mouth unhinged. Angela was obviously distraught about something, or mad at someone. She'd been crying. He could hear it in her voice. He wondered with whom she'd been fighting. A well of protectiveness surged within him. If anyone had hurt Angela . . .

Had Rothburg paid her a visit? He would kill the bastard if that was the case!

"Angela, it's John. Open the door. What's wrong? Has something happened? Is it Rothburg?"

"As if you didn't know. Quit pretending and leave. I thought you were different, but you're like all the rest of the deceitful bastards I've known. You just hide it better."

At the realization that she was talking about him, John paled. Angela was totally irrational; none of what she was saying made any sense.

Is this what pregnancy does to a woman?

Scary thought.

"I don't know what you're talking about. Now open the damn door so we can talk this out."

"Liar! Did you think I wouldn't see this morning's paper? Did you read it?"

"No, I—" John glanced down, finally noticing the newspaper beneath his feet, and stepped off of it. His face whitened, and he let loose some very ugly curses.

"Jesus!" It was the naked photo of Angela—the one Randy Newsome had taken. But how? John had put it in his bedroom dresser drawer.

Angela thinks I did this. She thinks I went to the newspaper with this photograph.

The thought hurt him, as no other had, but then he tried to look at it rationally, from her point of view. Though there was nothing rational about her reaction, about her thinking he had done such a thing. "Son of a bitch!"

Her hormones were out of whack, that could be the only answer, and that would make everything ten times worse when it came to being rational.

He banged on the door again. "Angela, I just this minute saw the paper, and I swear to you that I had nothing to do with it. I love you. Why would I want to publicly humiliate you? I want you to be my wife. Does that sound like the kind of thing a man who's come to propose marriage would do? I have the ring to prove that I'm telling you the truth. I'd hoped to give it to you under more romantic circumstances, but—"

The door opened, and Angela stood there, face streaked with tears, eyes rimmed red, and looking lost and alone. His heart ached at the sight of her. "I didn't do it," he whispered, praying she would believe him.

"I don't believe you, about any of it, the newspaper or the marriage proposal. Go away and leave me alone. I never want to see you again."

Her words pricked his heart like a knife, and his hand went to his chest as he felt physical pain. "Angela—"

"If you'd wanted to marry me, John Franco, you would have asked long before now. We've been sleeping together for weeks. I was honest about the baby, and I know the baby is the reason you'll never marry me. Now go away. I've nothing more to say to you."

She slammed the door so hard he was forced to take a step back. "Dammit, Angela! I love you."

Silence.

"I want to marry you."

Silence.

"I have a good idea who's behind this, and I'm going over there right now and kill Rothburg with my bare hands."

He thought he heard her gasp, but couldn't be sure.

"I'll be back. You're not getting rid of me this easily."

Winston barked once, twice, then nothing.

Like a man possessed, John headed over to the Rothburgs' residence, determined to get the truth out of the old bastard.

He pressed hard on the accelerator, needing to confront Rothburg as quickly as possible and confirm his suspicions. What he would do to the bastard once he got there was anyone's guess. But he was feeling murderous at the moment. The same way Angela must have felt when she saw that photo in the newspaper.

Betrayed. Abandoned. Hurt beyond belief.

And she blamed him for all of it.

Why had he waited so long to propose?

Angela was right. He'd had ample opportunity and he'd waited. But he'd wanted to be sure. Marriage and fatherhood were big steps. And he had so much baggage from his own childhood that he needed to be certain he would make a good husband and father.

Shit! Why hadn't he just thrown caution to the wind and followed his heart in the first place? Now Angela thought he was the Antichrist and would probably never talk to him again, let alone marry him.

And it was all Charles Rothburg's fault.

The minute John mentioned Charles Rothburg's name something clicked in Angela's overwrought mind.

Wanda had warned her about Rothburg's underhanded tactics. Was this one of them? And the woman had been about to reveal who she thought was responsible for the photo in the newspaper.

"Oh, God!"

Well, it wouldn't be the first time she'd screwed up her life. In fact, she seemed to have a real knack for it.

Dialing Wanda's number, Angela waited anxiously for her friend to answer. When she did, Angela blurted, "It's me. A few minutes ago you were going to tell me who you thought was responsible for the newspaper incident. I want you to tell me now."

"Hello to you, too. And I didn't mention Charles Rothburg's name because you slammed the phone down on me."

Bile rose thickly to her throat, and waves of nausea swamped Angela. Wanda had just seconded John's suspicions. "What makes you think it was Rothburg?"

"He has a reputation for underhandedness and dishonesty, Angela. I told you a long time ago that you needed to be careful. The man has a thing about winning. If he thinks he's going to lose a case, he uses every underhanded method at his disposal to make sure things go his way. And they're not always legal. He's just never been caught. He's smooth as snot on a doorknob, as my granny Washington was fond of saying. And I suspect that this was his way of paying you back for beating him in court."

"Your theory makes perfectly good sense."

"Of course it does. I'd bet money he's behind it. Now don't you feel better knowing it wasn't John, as you originally suspected?" Silence, then, "Angela, are you still there?"

"I told John that I never wanted to see him again."

"What?" Wanda's voice rose two octaves with incredulity. "Are you insane?"

"Sort of. He came to propose. Said he had the ring and everything, and I called him a liar to his face." She went on to relate the entire conversation, feeling more depressed by the minute.

"Girl, you are going to have to do some serious groveling when all this is said and done. I hope you know that."

"Only if it turns out to be Rothburg. That's not been proven yet."

"You are one of the smartest women I know, Angela DeNero, so how come you're being so stupid about this? In your heart you know that John did not do this terrible thing. And when that realization reaches your brain, you are going to feel like the lowliest piece of dog doody on the planet. And I'm going to take great delight in telling you I told you so."

"I pretty much feel that way now." She glanced at Winston, who refused to look at her. He had obviously sided with John. Men!

"I'm free for dinner," Wanda said. "Want me to come over and console you? I'm a big fan of chocolate cake. And I've got something important to tell you."

"Something good, I hope, because I sure could use some good news at this point. I've had about all the bad I can stomach for one day." *Make that one lifetime.*

John walked into his office the following morning and was surprised to find Tony seated behind his desk. His partner looked up at him and smiled, looking tanned, relaxed, and the picture of health.

What John had to tell him would probably cause him to have a relapse.

"Hey, Stefano! Why didn't you tell me you were coming in this morning? Glad to have you back, buddy. You're looking fit. I've missed you."

"I wanted it to be a surprise. So how's everything going with the custody case? Are you pounding nails in

Angela DeNero's coffin yet?" Tony grinned. "Or just pounding Angela DeNero?"

John wasn't amused. "Not funny, Stefano. There's a lot that's happened that you don't know about. I'm in love with Angela. I want to marry her. And we lost the case."

"Christ!" His friend nearly fell off his chair. "I knew you were interested in her, but I never thought you were thinking about marriage."

"Yeah, well, shit happens. I guess you may as well know the whole of it, because you'll hear it soon enough. As of last night Charles Rothburg is no longer our client. I told him to shove his head and his retainer up his ass. I'm just sorry that I didn't follow through with my plan to beat the living crap out of him."

"I take it that this has something to do with the revealing photo I saw in yesterday's *Sun*?"

"You saw that, did you?"

"Like I'd miss it. Tell me about Rothburg."

"The slick bastard admitted to me that a few weeks back he'd hired a private investigator to dig up dirt on Angela. It was his insurance policy, as he called it.

"Apparently the guy went to Boston, found out some things about her past, and managed to get his hands on either the negative or a print of the photo Angela's old boyfriend had taken."

Tony whistled, leaning back in his chair, his fingers laced over his chest. John found it odd that his friend didn't seem all that upset by the news, which in itself was very uncharacteristic of the hotheaded, hardheaded Italian.

"You can probably smooth things over with Rothburg. Maybe he'll continue to have you represent him as long as I'm not involved. But I'm done with him and others like him. I'm sorry, Tony. I know this might place you in a bad financial situation, and I'll do what I can to help out. Just don't ask me to compromise my principles again. I won't do it."

"Wish I could have been there to see Angela make mincemeat out of you."

"Yeah, it was a regular bloodbath. But nothing more than I expected. The Rothburgs were their own worst enemy."

Tony surprised John by saying, "Rothburg can go straight to hell, for all I care. Based on what the bastard did, and what I know of his tactics, I think you made the right decision. I'll stand behind it, and you, one hundred percent."

John studied his friend's face carefully. "Are you sure you're the real Tony Stefano, and not some alien replica, like on *The X-Files*?"

Tony threw back his head and laughed. "I think you're going to find out that I've changed quite a bit, John. I'm not going to let things get to me like I used to. And I'm not going to compromise my principles for the almighty dollar, either. I'm through with all that.

"From here on out, we take on only the cases we truly believe in. And I think we should lessen our workload, enjoy life more, don't you?"

Nodding, John replied, "I've got an idea on how we can do just that."

"I thought you might. When are you going over to see Angela?"

"Right now. It's been a long, agonizing night for me. I've had a lot of time to think things through. Don't know what I'll do if she won't listen to reason. Life's not worth living without her.

"Christ! What if she won't listen? I'm scared, Tony. For the first time in a very long time I'm really scared of losing the one thing I've waited my whole life for. Angela's more important to me than anything."

"Angela's a woman. She's not supposed to be reasonable. But I figure you'll turn on the old Franco charm that you're always bragging about and convince her you're right. Quit worrying. It's going to work out."

John was touched by his friend's words. But, of course, he wasn't about to let him know it. "Hell, Stefano! You're starting to sound like a woman. Are you sure Dr. Mike didn't replace your heart with Mother Teresa's, instead of just fixing the one you had?"

"When you come close to dying you've got a lot of time to figure things out. I'm happy as hell to be alive, to be able to hug my kids and put them to bed at night, to make love to Marie.

"You and me, we tend to take things for granted, trying to make a success of our careers, paying more attention to material matters than the ones that count. Now that you're in love I guess you've figured all of that out for yourself, am I right?"

"Damn straight. Now I've just got to convince Angela of it."

TWENTY-ONE

What do lawyers and sperm have in common?
Only one in two million ever does anything
worthwhile.

By the time the knock sounded at the door, Angela had already eaten her way through two quarts of pralines and cream ice cream and was about to indulge in a third.

She hadn't slept a wink all night, hadn't gone into work this morning, hadn't showered or dressed, and all the remnants of the beautiful dinner she had prepared the previous day, sans the chocolate cake, which she and Wanda had devoured at midnight, were still sitting on the table.

She and her kitchen looked like tragic victims of war.

Dragging herself to the door, she pulled the edges of her ratty terry-cloth robe together, wondering who could possibly be calling at such an ungodly hour.

Her mouth fell open in surprise. The last person she had expected to see on her doorstep was John, looking like the best thing God had ever created, with the possible exception of chocolate.

"John! I'm—" She brushed her fingers through her hair self-consciously, feeling her cheeks warm at the disastrous way she looked. "I wasn't feeling well. I just got up. Why are you here?"

Thank God you're here!

"May I come in this time?" He didn't wait for a reply, just pushed his way into the apartment and shut the door behind him before she could say no. "We need to talk."

Rushing up to greet him, Winston brushed against his leg, and John bent over to scratch his ear. The sight brought tears to Angela's eyes. But then, what didn't? After yesterday's episode she had cried a million tears; she didn't think she had any left, but she was wrong. She felt a full-blown gusher coming on.

"I'll make coffee."

"No, that's not necessary." He glanced into the kitchen, his eyes widening imperceptibly. "Looks like the dinner was going to be good. Sorry I missed it."

She fidgeted with the tie of her bathrobe, wondering how she could make amends. She knew in her heart she'd been wrong. Why oh why had she jumped to conclusions? She was usually so rational, thought everything out. Of course, at the time it all seemed to make sense.

It was time to grovel. "John, I'm sorry. I never should have jumped to the conclusions I did. I feel so stupid. I know you can never forgive me for the awful things I accused you of, but for what it's worth, I'm miserable about the way I behaved. And I'm truly sorry."

"Good. I hope you've suffered like I have. Last night was hell for me. Especially when I couldn't bring myself to beat the shit out of Rothburg."

Her mouth fell open; then she snapped it shut. "You went over there? Are you crazy?"

"Didn't I tell you I would?"

"Yes, but I didn't think you were serious. You could lose your license for beating up a client, especially one as old and well connected as Rothburg."

"That's why I didn't do it. Age notwithstanding, I couldn't bring myself to drop to the old bastard's level. But I wanted to, make no mistake about that. When he smirked in that arrogant way of his and told me that he'd hired a private investigator to find a way to discredit you, I almost lost it. If his wife hadn't shown up at that moment, I may have strangled him with my bare hands.

Instead, I told him that I would no longer represent him. Period."

Angela gasped. "You told him to take a hike? This is all too much to take in. I'm still trying to understand why Rothburg would do such a terrible thing." She shook her head. "Never mind. Wanda explained to me how he operates.

"If I thought I could have him disbarred, I would, but I know I would never be able to connect him to what was in the newspaper. He's too smart. And I don't want to dredge up any more unfavorable publicity."

John caressed her cheek. "Yeah, I guess you've had enough."

"My parents are still in shock. I thought my father was going to combust right over the phone. I won't even get into my mother's reaction. Mia said she had to be sedated." And she'd have to deal with their disappointment and barrage of questions soon enough. But not today.

John pulled her into his arms. "I love you, Angela. I hope you know that. I'm sorry you had to go through all of this. But nothing you've said or done changes the fact that I want to marry you." He reached into his jacket pocket and extracted a small black box, opening it. "Will you marry me, Angela DeNero?"

Hands flying up to her cheeks, Angela stared openmouthed at the diamond ring he proffered, then began to cry again, stammering, "But . . . but why would you . . . you want to . . . to marry me, after all the horrible things I said, the way I behaved? I don't deserve you."

Lifting her chin, he smiled tenderly. "Because I'm so crazy in love with you that my life wouldn't be worth anything without you in it. And I know that pregnant women sometimes behave irrationally, and that you weren't thinking too clearly when you said all those things. In my heart I know you love me."

"I do. I love you with all my heart and soul, John. And what you just said is true. I was irrational, hormonal, hysterical, whatever you want to call it. And I'm ashamed of myself because of it."

"I forgive you. Now, will you marry me?"

"But what about the baby? Are you sure you want to take on another man's child?"

He placed his hands tenderly on her slightly distended abdomen. "This will be my baby, and no other man's child. Understood? From here on out, we are to think of this child as ours. We'll be a family, the three of us. And later on, we'll have more kids, if you want. I'm all in favor of a big family."

"Uh, let's get through this first one and see how we feel. Poopy diapers can sometimes alter your perspective."

"Then, you'll marry me?"

Angela looked down at the dog, who was gazing up at John as if he were a god. "What do you think, Win? Do you want to live with John? He's got a really big bed you can sleep on."

The bulldog began yapping and turning in circles, making both John and Angela laugh.

"Looks like we have his blessing, sweets." John took the ring and placed it on the ring finger of her left hand. "Say yes."

"Yes!" She threw her arms about his neck and kissed him. "I love you, John. Thank you for forgiving me. I'm not sure I'll ever be able to forgive myself for almost throwing away the best thing that's ever happened to me."

"You've made me the happiest man in the world, Angela. There's only one more thing that would make me happier."

She blushed. "I've got to take a shower first."

To her surprise, he led her to the sofa instead of the bedroom. "*Tsk, tsk*, Miss DeNero," he said, pulling her down next to him on the sofa. "Your mind is in the gutter this morning."

"Oh, well . . . I just thought . . ."

"We'll get to that in a minute. First, I want to discuss our future. I've been thinking about something for a while now, and I'm hoping and praying that you'll think it's a good idea, too."

"What is it? You sound so serious. Should I be nervous?"

"Tony and I had a long discussion this morning. He's back at work, and—"

"That's wonderful! You must be ecstatic."

He nodded absently. "Tony's in favor of cutting down on our workload, and so am I. From here on out we're only taking on cases that we feel really strongly about, that we can commit ourselves to. We want to make our law firm one of Baltimore's finest, and we want you to join us, Angela."

She couldn't believe her ears. "What?"

"I know you've got your own practice, and I'm sure in time it'll grow and be quite profitable. We hope the same thing for ours. But if you join forces with us as a full partner, we can achieve the same goals together as Stefano, Franco, and Franco. What do you say?"

Stefano, Franco, and Franco. It had a nice ring to it, almost as nice as the one she had on her finger. Gazing at the sparkling multifaceted stone, she smiled happily. "I'd say that this offer couldn't have come at a better time, both offers, in fact.

"First of all, before I forget, Wanda told me last night that Trent Enterprises is willing to talk out-of-court settlement with Peter."

John looked relieved. "That's great."

"She also told me that she's marrying Kyle. Wanda is planning to move out of the building we're presently located in so she can be closer to his medical office. I wouldn't have been able to afford the space by myself, and I wasn't looking forward to finding another lawyer with whom I could share expenses."

Wanda's bombshell had been another reason Angela had cried herself silly last night. In one fell swoop she had lost not only the man she adored, but her office mate, as well. But she was happy for Wanda, who seemed to be overjoyed with her decision to marry. She and Kyle had worked out a compromise regarding children: They would wait two years, and then discuss it again.

"Is that a yes?" John asked.

"That's the only word I seem to be able to say this morning. Yes! Yes! Yes! I love you, John. And I will do everything in my power to make you a good partner, both in marriage and in work."

"I hope you're not one of those women who are superstitious about making love before the wedding. Because I don't think I'm going to be able to wait."

"Actually, you happen to be in luck, because I'm not at all superstitious. In fact, I've heard that in some ancient tribes 'power tools' are prized and considered to be quite lucky. It's said that in Turkey—or was it Italy? I really can't remember—a man's—"

He pulled her into his arms and kissed her, thoroughly, and when she could no longer string two coherent words together asked, "You were saying?"

"I forget. Kiss me again."

"With pleasure. But first we're going to get naked."

"*Oooh,* a free demonstration of the Franco power tool! Does it come with a warranty?"

"A lifetime warranty, sweets. A lifetime."

TWENTY-TWO

How many lawyer jokes are there?
Only three. The rest are true stories.

The sign on the front door of Mama Sophia's said CLOSED FOR PRIVATE PARTY when John and Angela entered the noisy restaurant two evenings later.

Angela was to be feted as the guest of honor tonight, but she had her misgivings about dragging John through another family get-together; the last one had been rather disastrous. "Are you sure you're all right with this? I told you I didn't mind coming by myself."

"And make me look like a sore loser?" John kissed her cheek. "I'm happy you won the custody suit, Angela. And the fact that Dan and Mary are going to allow Sharon visitation is a small victory for me, as well. Besides, now that you'll be joining Stefano and Franco, your sterling reputation will only enhance ours."

"Stefano, Franco, and Franco," she reminded him, kissing him back, but on the lips. "Don't look now, but your aunt is making her way over here, and she's smiling, of all things."

Sophia placed a hand on either side of Angela's face and gave her a kiss. "*Grazie,* Angela! You have kept our family together. I will be in your debt forever."

Or until Angela did something to piss the woman off. The leopard did not change its spots that easily.

The older woman then turned to John and patted his cheek affectionately, much to his surprise. "All is forgiven, Johnny. Mary told me that you and Angela are going to be married. I am very happy for both of you. If you like, I can arrange for the Paisans to play at the wedding. They're pretty good, and they come cheap. Just ask my daughter."

"Uh, thanks. We'll give it some thought. Where's Uncle Frank?"

As soon as he asked the question, Dean Martin's voice filled the air with "That's Amore." "You see where your uncle is? He is making the disc jockey play my favorite song. I must go and dance with him. Frank can be so romantic sometimes."

His aunt floated away, and John looked at a grinning Angela, saying, "Who was that woman? She looked like my aunt, but she was too nice to be Sophia Russo."

"Yes, well, even a viper has its quiet moments."

"There you two are!" Mary exclaimed, rushing forward to gush over her two favorite lawyers. "Dan and I can't tell you how grateful we are for everything you've done for us, Angela. I know we've told you before, but if there's anything we can do for you, just ask."

"You can cater their wedding reception," Dan suggested, stepping up and shaking John's hand. "I hear congratulations are in order. When's the wedding?"

"We haven't set a date yet," John replied, relieved that Dan had decided to forgive him.

Dan's smile was full of apology. "I'm sorry the family gave you such a rough time during the hearing, John, but it was a difficult period for all of us, especially Mary. We were worried about the baby. I guess you can understand that." He glanced at Angela meaningfully and smiled.

"I understand totally. I'm just glad it's all over with and that you and Mary have custody of Matt. And it was generous of you, considering everything, to allow Sharon visitation."

"I'll say it was generous," Mary concurred, still looking a mite put out by her husband's decision. "That husband of Sharon's is scum. I'm thinking of asking Uncle Alfredo to get involved."

"Why?" Dan asked. "Does Rothburg need a new car?"

Mary slapped her husband playfully on the arm, and everyone laughed. Alfredo Graziano was a much better car salesman than he was an alleged Mafia don.

Annie and Joe came up just then. Annie wrapped her arms about John and gave him a hug, while Joe did the same to Angela. "We're so happy for you," Annie said. "Why don't you come by the store next week. I'll give you a good discount on maternity clothes."

Angela's face turned bright red, and she wished that the floor would open up and swallow her whole. "How did you—?" She looked up at John, who shrugged as if to say, "Don't blame me."

"You can't expect to keep a big secret like that here in Little Italy. Oy! My father heard it first at Santini's, came back from lunch, and then told me, and about fifteen of his customers. Plus, you've been wearing very loose-fitting clothes lately. I just listened to the gossip and put two and two together."

"Well, after what was published in the paper I doubt my reputation can be ruined any more than it has been already." Angela sighed, and John squeezed her waist.

"What? Are you kidding?" Annie was wide-eyed at the conclusion Angela had drawn. Of course, Annie was the type of woman who didn't give a fig about reputation or what other people thought. If she had, she would have never married an ex-priest.

"You've got a great body. Be proud of it. A woman should flaunt what she's got. Just because your old boyfriend was a jerk doesn't mean you have anything to be ashamed of, Angela."

"That's right," Joe said, nodding in agreement. "You've done nothing wrong."

"Thank you, both," Angela said, grateful she had such good friends.

"Joe's probably wishing he was still a priest," John quipped. "He would have gotten an earful these past few weeks."

"Joe's got other things to occupy his time these days," Annie told him with a wink. "Come along, Joseph. Sid must be hiding out; we need to go rescue Gina from the Goldman girls. They've got her cornered, and she looks about ready to faint."

"That's your mother's natural look," Joe reminded her.

"Where are your parents and sister?" Mary asked Angela. "Your mom told me they were coming tonight."

"Oh, they'll be here soon. My dad probably had to shave his legs and find a girdle."

Dan's eyes widened. "What?"

Angela shook her head. "I'll tell you about it later. Or you may find out for yourself when Dad arrives." Sam had bought a black sequined gown for the occasion, and had asked Angela's permission to wear it, which she gave.

Her parents, she'd decided, weren't any nuttier than the other eccentric inhabitants of Little Italy. If Mary's uncle could pretend a connection to John Gotti, and Donatella Foragi could make love with a married undertaker in the back of a hearse, then her father could damn well come to a party dressed like a woman.

When John and Angela were alone once more, she turned to him and said, "I think I'm going to like being part of this family."

"That's because you haven't spent much time with my parents yet."

She shook her head disapprovingly. "Now, stop it, John! You said your mother and father were delighted when you told them about our engagement. I'm looking forward to meeting your father. I'm sure he's much nicer than you've let on.

"You're much too hard on them. They're only human, after all, with all the flaws and faults we all possess."

He wrapped his arms about her. "I love you. You're pretty smart. You know that, don't you? I am going to make a real effort to make amends with my family, all of them. I want our child raised in an atmosphere of love and happiness."

"All that earnestness is turning me on. Kiss me like you mean it."

Pulling Angela into his arms, John covered her mouth with his own and began to devour her, little bits at a time.

A short distance away, Grandma Flora was talking to Donatella Foragi, nudging her friend in the arm.

"You see why Angela's with child," Flora stated, looking pleased by the whole turn of events. "My grandson is very virile. They are going to have many, many children. And I think they will name one after me."

Overhearing the old woman's comment, John and Angela broke apart, and smiled happily at each other.

"Grandma Flora always says, *'La famiglia é tutto'*—the family is everything," John said. "I'm beginning to think she's right."

Read on for a sneak peek at

MAD ABOUT MIA

The next delicious romance by

Millie Criswell

Coming in March 2003

ONE

Childhood is what you spend the rest of your life overcoming.
Hope Floats

"Broke, busted, disgusted, parents can't be trusted
And Mia wants to go to the sea . . ."

Holding the firm banana that she'd brought for her
lunch like a microphone, Mia DeNero belted out "Creeque
Alley" at the top of her lungs, accompanying the Mamas
and the Papas, whose '60s song blared from the boom
box in the corner, while changing the lyrics slightly to
suit her miserable state.

Actually her state wasn't really all that miserable, just
disappointing. The kind of disappointment that gives
you that funny little sick ache in the pit of your stomach
every time you think you might fail.

She'd finally opened her protective services business,
The Guardian Angel—Mia was quite pleased with the
name—despite major protests from her parents, and had
set up business in an old, smelly vacant storefront on
Eastern Avenue; the place used to be a fish and chips
restaurant and still reeked of old grease and vinegar. But
the rent was cheap, and right now, she needed cheap.

"Greasin' on American Express card . . ."

Ha! Wasn't that the truth? Soon her credit cards would
be maxed, and then she'd be in major deep doo-doo. And
she was determined not to borrow a cent from her parents, or from Angela, though her big sister had offered to
help numerous times. But Mia was too proud to accept a
handout, and determined to make it on her own.

Failure was not an option.

Been there, done that!

Surely there had to be someone who wanted to hire her. She had placed an ad in the local newspaper, the *Baltimore Sun,* more than two weeks ago, and had even passed out flyers to all the local businesses in her area, hoping someone might need her services or could recommend a friend who did.

Of course, Little Italy wasn't exactly the crime capital of the world, and there might not be too many people in need of protection. But she needed only one.

Plopping down in the rickety old swivel chair she had bought at Carboni's Used Furniture, Mia propped her feet up on the equally battered gray metal desk and peeled her banana. No longer in the mood for singing, she took a bite out of her "microphone" and chewed.

Glancing around the small office, she grimaced at the badly dented filing cabinet, the ugly metal chair that fronted her desk, and the hideous, bent-out-of-shape venetian blinds covering the front window that she'd tried to clean before moving in and had ended up ruining in the process.

All in all, it was not a place to inspire prospective clients, unless, of course, they were Jack the Ripper. Though her diploma hanging on the wall behind her desk did certify that she had passed a bodyguard training course at the Serve and Protect Bodyguard School in Towson, Maryland. It was signed by Mike Hammersmith, her instructor, the man she'd nearly killed at the shooting range one day.

Mia was a bit nearsighted, which made shooting a gun at any distance a bit problematic. But she wasn't about to let that little detail deter her.

Munching on her so-called lunch, which her mother would have found abhorrent—Rosalie DeNero was of the opinion that everyone should consume at least ten thousand calories per day—Mia focused all of her attention on the front door, willing someone to appear.

At this point she didn't much care if it was a client. Sitting in her tiny office day after day, waiting for the phone to ring, or a living entity to visit, was not only lonely, it was damn boring, depressing, and totally disheartening.

Did she mention boring?

So when the front door opened, Mia was so startled that she shifted in her chair a little too quickly, trying to move her feet off the desk at the same time, hoping to present the best appearance to whomever it was that was calling. But she ended up pushing back on the old chair too hard, causing it to topple over backward.

Which was how Niccolò Caruso found her.

Nick leaned over the desk to make sure the woman who'd suddenly disappeared from sight was okay. One minute she was eating a banana and the next . . . boom! Gone.

"Are you all right?" He pushed his glasses back up his nose and extended a hand, biting back a smile. Mia DeNero, with her Orphan Annie curly locks, was fifteen shades of red, but seemed otherwise unhurt.

"Yes, thanks. I was just daydreaming, and you caught me off guard. Let me assure you that I am not usually so clumsy," she said, trying to right her chair and brush off her jeans at the same time. "How can I help you?"

Nick gazed at the pint-sized woman before him and wondered the same thing. His idea to hire Mia DeNero as a bodyguard might have been a little too presumptuous.

Presumptuous, hell! It was downright insane!

"I'm in need of protection, Miss DeNero. I found one of your flyers, and it was like an answer to my prayer." Nick hoped he sounded nerdy enough. He was certainly making himself sick.

Folding her hands atop the desk, Mia DeNero tried her damnedest to look professional and totally together. Unfortunately there was a blob of banana clinging to the end of her pert little nose. Leaning toward her, he proffered his handkerchief. "Allow me. It seems you're still wearing your lunch."

"Oh, Jesus!" She shook her head, swiping her nose with the back of her hand, and then wiping the blob on her jeans.

Eyes wide, Nick could only stare.

"I'm sure you think I'm a complete moron, but let me assure you that I'm a trained professional and very good in my field."

Taking a seat, he arched a disbelieving brow and crossed muscular arms over his chest. "Really? And how many clients have you protected this past year, Miss DeNero? Can you provide references?"

She shook her head, her cheeks filling with color. "Well, no. You're my first one, actually. I've just opened up for business, you see. But that means you're in luck, because I can give you our special introductory rate." She hoped he was impressed. He didn't look very impressed. Maybe she should throw in a free pizza or something.

He rubbed his chin. "I see."

Yanking a yellow legal pad across the desk, Mia picked up her pen. "Perhaps we should start with your name, and the reason you need a bodyguard."

"My name is Niccolò Caruso. Perhaps you've heard of me, read one of my books? I'm an author."

An author! Now that was impressive. Mia should have guessed from the thick-framed glasses and ugly tweed jacket he wore. Tweed! She wrinkled her nose. Even the name was horrific, conjuring up old Sherlock Holmes movies.

"Afraid not. I don't have much time to read." A flaw she intended to correct. Someday. Maybe. Mia had made procrastination into an art form. "What kind of books do you write?"

"Mostly nonfiction. I've dabbled in true crime from

time to time. I'm presently working on an exposé of the Mafia."

Mia's eyes widened. "Really? Aren't you afraid?"

"Well, yes, actually I am, which is why I've come to you. I've had threats made on my life."

She gasped. "They're trying to silence you."

"That's right. But I won't be deterred. I intend to finish my book, and the consequences be damned. That's why I'm here, Miss DeNero. I'm hoping you'll be able to help me."

Mia's heart was beating so fast she felt like a hummingbird on speed. The Mafia was big-time stuff. If she could pull this off— Okay, the odds were slim, but her motto had always been "no pain, no gain." "Of course, I'll help you. I can offer you twenty-four-hour protection; that's twenty-four/seven, until you finish your book. Do you live here in Baltimore?"

"Well, actually I was hoping that we could come to some sort of an arrangement whereby I could move in with you."

Her jaw unhinged, allowing her mouth to form a cavern of disbelief. "Move in with me?" *Was the man insane?* "But that's not the way it's done. Normally the way it works is that I move onto your premises, and—"

He shook his head emphatically. "Out of the question. My elderly aunt would be quite distressed if you were to move in. I don't date much, and having another female in the house would raise all sorts of questions. I don't want to alarm my aunt, you understand. And I'm quite willing to pay whatever you deem necessary, if you'll agree to let me stay with you."

"We could get adjoining hotel rooms?"

"I can't write in such an environment, I'm afraid. I require total silence when I'm working. I don't like distractions of any kind." And the impish woman before him was going to be a major distraction, that was for damn certain.

"My apartment is small, Mr. Caruso. I live above Mama Sophia's Restaurant, here in Little Italy. It's not as quiet as you might like. And my landlady is a bit of a harridan." Major understatement. Donatella Foragi was a two-hundred-plus-pound walking, talking nightmare. She made the Bates Motel look welcoming by comparison.

"I'm prepared to give you three thousand dollars per month, to cover the cost of your services, and for the inconvenience of allowing me to live with you. I don't mind admitting that I'm scared of these hoodlums, Miss DeNero."

"Three thous—" She tried to catch her breath. Three thousand dollars a month would solve all of her problems, and then some. The guy must be loaded. The most she would have charged him would have been a thousand, but she had no intention of letting him know that.

"Well, that certainly seems fair. Do we need to go by your house to get your things?"

Are you insane, Mia? Are you really going to allow a total stranger you've just met to move in with you? A man you know nothing about? Caruso could be a serial rapist or killer.

Although on further reflection she thought he looked more like a serial geek. He certainly had clothing issues, not that she should talk, but jeans were preferable to—

Was that corduroy he was wearing? My god! The man was a regular Howdy Doody. All he needed was a plaid shirt.

"Is there something the matter, Miss DeNero? You look distracted."

"How do I know you are who you say you are? Do you have identification? I need to be careful in my position, Mr. Caruso. I'm sure you understand."

"And I'd fault you if you weren't." Nick pulled out his

wallet and showed Mia his ID. His wallet was bulging with hundred-dollar bills, which did not go unnoticed by the young woman, whose pupils were dilating rapidly.

"You'll have to sleep on the couch. I have only one bedroom." Too bad he wasn't her type. She hadn't had sex in so long she'd probably forgotten how to do it. Not that she would do *it* with him. Mia preferred the macho, virile type, not a Milquetoast. Though Mr. Caruso seemed kind, if not dull as dirt.

"That's not a problem."

Surprise, surprise! He probably doesn't get urges like normal men, she thought. After all, he still lived with his elderly aunt. What kind of man does that? Of course to be fair, the woman could be sick, which would make him a dutiful nephew. On the other hand—

"Miss DeNero?"

Smiling warmly, she stuck out her hand to seal their agreement. When he grasped hers in what felt like a pretty strong grip she felt a tiny shock of electricity race up her arm, which astounded her.

"I'm certain our arrangement will work out quite nicely for both of us, Mr. Caruso. You're in good hands."

His thumb moved over the back of hers, and Mia swallowed. "I can see that. I think I'm going to like having my very own guardian angel."

"Oh, I'm sure you will. I can be very accommodating."

His smile was almost wicked. "I'm counting on that, Miss DeNero."

"I can't believe you are going to allow a stranger you know nothing about to move in with you! Have you lost your mind? Wait till Mom hears. She's going to come unglued."

Like that was something new. Rosalie DeNero gave new meaning to the term *hysteria*. Until recently, she had believed that Armageddon was descending. Now she just worried incessantly about every little thing.

Do you have enough toilet paper, Mia?

Are you bundling up when you go outside?

Did you remember to pay your electric bill?

Whoops! Well, two out of three wasn't bad.

Mia's gaze fell on her older sister seated behind the impressive mahogany desk. Angela was a lawyer and partner in the firm Stefano, Franco, and Franco. She was married to John Franco, one of the partners. Her sister was an alarmist who saw evil lurking behind every bush. She was also the only woman on the face of the planet who looked good pregnant.

"I checked him out," Mia replied, but Angela's expression remained skeptical.

"How, if you don't mind my asking?"

She shrugged, trying to sound confident. "The usual methods—visual profile, driver's license . . . Did I tell you Caruso's a published author? The notoriety from this case alone could put my business on the map."

Rising to her feet, Angela tugged on the hem of her green jersey maternity blouse, then rounded the desk to take a seat in the chair next to Mia. "Did you actually run his plates, check with the department of motor vehicles to see if his driver's license is real? It could be a fake, you know."

"Oh, for heavensake, Angela! Quit trying to tell me how to do my job. I've been trained, in case you've forgotten." Mia ignored the way her sister rolled her eyes.

"I know you're a hotshot lawyer, and smarter than me, but give me some credit for knowing what I'm doing."

"I take it that means no."

"Niccolò Caruso is an author. If you saw the way he was dressed, Angie, you'd know he poses no threat. Did I mention he wears corduroy pants?" Her sister's eyes widened, and she smiled smugly, adding, "He lives with his elderly aunt. He's not a sexual deviate"—*I should be so lucky*—"or a serial killer. My instincts tell me Niccolò Caruso is exactly who and what he says he is.

Geek. Nerd. Major nerd.

"And I need this job. I've gone through most of my savings. And you know very well, having had Mrs. Foragi for a landlady, that she isn't going to wait much longer for the rent money that's overdue."

"I can lend you the—"

"No!" Mia shook her head emphatically, her curls bouncing every which way, like an out-of-control Slinky toy. "I'm going to do this on my own. I have to prove to myself that I can. And I have to prove to Dad and everyone else who's ever doubted me that I'm not the scatterbrain, impulsive woman they think I am."

Her expression softening, Angela reached for her sister's hand. "Now, Mia, you know that's not what everyone thinks. We love you. Dad loves you. He doesn't think those things about you."

Mia smirked. "Oh, really? That's news to me. Dad thinks I'm a flake, a complete moron, and just because I've had some rather unorthodox jobs over the years." Okay, so maybe driving a bulldozer on a highway construction crew wasn't the greatest job she'd ever taken. But she'd stuck it out, had proved, if only to herself, that she could compete with men at their own level. Not an easy feat, when your on-the-job nickname was Munchkin.

"I'm trying to be supportive, Mia, but I'm worried that you've bitten off more than you can chew. The Mafia is nothing to fool around with. These guys play for keeps. Be realistic. You don't pose much of an obstacle. If they want to get to this Caruso, they're going to find a way.

"Didn't you see *The Godfather*? Don't you remember how they took Sonny out in broad daylight and riddled him with bullets?"

"Of course I remember. James Caan was so cute. But they're not going to get Caruso. Not if I have anything to say about it. I have a gun, don't forget."

"How could I? As I recall, I had to represent you in court when Mr. Hammersmith tried to have you thrown out of the bodyguard program. Not that I could blame him. You did almost kill the man."

"That wasn't my fault. How was I supposed to know that I needed glasses for distance?"

"Have you had your prescription filled yet?"

Mia squirmed restlessly in her seat. "I'm going to get glasses." Someday. Maybe. Probably never. She'd never before considered herself vain, but every glass frame she'd tried on at the optometrist's office had made her look like a bullfrog in the throes of death; she couldn't bring herself to fill the prescription.

"Just be careful, okay? I don't want to read about your demise in the newspaper. Who would run interference for me with Mom and Dad if you disappeared?" Angela shuddered at the thought.

"Now that you're married you don't need my help anymore. Mom thinks the sun rises and sets on John. And Dad's been making a valiant effort to tone down his ensembles when you visit."

Angela laughed. "Quite a sacrifice, I must say."

Sam DeNero was a cross-dressing ex-cop, retired from the Boston Police Department. His sense of fashion was a bit different from most men—he liked wearing women's clothing, which he bought off the Home Shopping Network. Sam had a real weakness for sequins and rhinestones. On his best day he was a Bob Mackey nightmare.

"Dad shouldn't criticize me when he's got his own problems."

"Dad doesn't think he's got a problem."

"Well, I know I don't. From here on out all of my

problems are solved, thanks to Niccolò Caruso and his generous retainer."

Angela looked as if she had more to say, but she merely smiled and said, "I hope you're right."

Mia flashed her sister a confident grin. "I know I am."

Staring at the heavyset older man seated across the table from him at O'Grady's Irish Pub, Nick knew Burt Mulrooney was as close to a best friend as he was ever going to have.

They'd worked together at the FBI and had been part of the Organized Crime Investigation Unit for the past nine years. Burt had been his mentor, and the father figure he'd never had. The older man hated to shave, always sported at least three days' growth of beard, now gray, and his belly confirmed his love for Guinness. He was a good guy and a damn good agent.

"I bet Higgins ain't too pleased about this undercover op of yours, boy. You'd better not screw up or he'll have your ass for dinner."

Nick popped a handful of peanuts into his mouth, then sipped his ice-cold beer. "Special Agent in Charge Higgins is the one who authorized this plan. My ass is covered, old man, so quit worrying. It's not good for your blood pressure." Burt had gained a considerable amount of weight since his divorce over a year ago, and Nick was concerned that his friend was going to have a heart attack one of these days.

"How can I quit worrying? You're using an innocent civilian, Caruso, and if anything should happen to that girl—"

"Relax. You're starting to sound like an old woman. Nothing's going to happen. Mia DeNero is thrilled to death to have a client to protect. She promises to be accommodating." Nick flashed a grin. "I'm moving in with her this evening."

"Jesus!" The older man's mouth hung open; then he shook his head. "Not smart, boy. Not smart, at all."

"It's perfect, Burt. She lives right above Mama Sophia's Restaurant, eats there quite often, as a matter of fact. I'll be able to keep a close eye on the suspect, who frequents the establishment. Granted, it's not a perfect arrangement, but it's the best one I could come up with. Plus, Miss DeNero's sister married into the Russo family recently, which gives me another in."

Burt scoffed. "Can't believe those assholes at the Bureau think Alfredo Graziano knows anything about anything. He's strictly small potatoes, despite his claim to the contrary. He'd probably shit his pants if he ever got close to John Gotti, or any other *Mafioso*."

"That's probably true, but he might be able to lead us to those who are involved. Money laundering is a very lucrative business, and our friend Alfredo has been flashing around big bucks lately. Legitimate car dealers don't make that kind of money. Besides, Graziano has only himself to blame for raising everyone's suspicions. The man should learn to keep his bragging to a minimum."

Reaching for the peanuts, Burt swallowed a handful, then nodded. "How'd you get the woman to agree to let you move in with her? I realize you're God's gift and all, but even that's going beyond decent."

"Money. I made her an offer she couldn't pass up. Told her my elderly aunt wouldn't approve of her moving into my place."

"You don't have an elderly aunt."

"Miss DeNero doesn't know that."

"Is this woman stupid? She sounds stupid."

Nick shook his head. "Not at all, just naive, which is why I chose her. She's new to the bodyguard business and green as that ugly shirt you're wearing."

Burt ignored the insult. He and Nick exchanged them

on a regular basis, so he was used to his friend's teasing comments. "I suppose she's a looker."

"Not really. Just cute as a button."

"I'm surprised you noticed, Caruso. You don't usually give women the time of day."

"Because I'm not looking to get involved with anyone, Burt, certainly not with Miss DeNero. She's merely a means to an end."

"Yeah, that's what I said about wives one through three. Only the end stank." Burt motioned for the waitress to bring them another round.

"You can't blame Gloria for bailing on you, Burt. You're overweight, you drink too much, and you dress like shit. Plus, your hours suck, and you never took her out anywhere. A woman will only stand for so much football and poker parties."

The older man shook his head. "Gloria was too young. As much as I hate to admit it, I never should have let Muriel go. She was the best of the lot."

Muriel was Burt's first wife. A homebody through and through, she'd been content to wait on her husband hand and foot. She had adored Burt, and he'd never appreciated what he had until she was gone. Burt had tried to replace Muriel over the years with an assortment of bimbos, but none had measured up. "So maybe you and your ex should think about a reunion? Absence makes the heart grow fonder, dontcha know?"

Burt looked at Nick as if he'd lost his mind. "Are you nuts? The woman hates my guts. I cheated on her. Remember Vivian, wife number two? Besides, I heard she remarried, some pharmaceutical salesman."

"You haven't spoken to Muriel in over ten years. She may be widowed or divorced for all you know."

Burt thought a moment, then finally shook his head, a resigned look on his face. "Nah. It's best to let sleeping dogs lie, too much muddy water under the bridge. And who are you to be giving me advice? They call you the heartbreaker at the field office, or have you forgotten the trail of disappointed females you've left in your wake."

"I'm always up front with the women I date. They're never under any illusions that our relationship is ever going beyond friendship and sex. That's just the way it is."

"You don't know much about women, Caruso. No matter how many times they tell you they understand, that it's fine with them, it's not. They're always thinking they can change your mind, turn you to the dark side."

"You been watching *Star Wars* again?"

"Best damn movie ever made. And don't change the subject. I'm on to you."

Nick shrugged. "I'm happy living the life I lead. If they can't deal with it, too bad."

"I think you're full of bullshit. So you had a rotten childhood, so what? Lots of people have. That doesn't mean you should push people away—women, in particular."

"Let it go, old man. I'm not interested in hearing your opinions and psychological babble again."

"Someday you'll be sorry for being such a callous bastard, Caruso."

"Maybe. But until that day, I'm quite content to remain exactly as I am."